The Pilgrim's Revenge

Scott Mariani is the #1 Sunday Times bestselling author of the Ben Hope thriller series. He grew up in the ancient historic town of St Andrews in Scotland, where his misspent youth hanging around castle ruins and old graveyards gave rise to his passion for all things medieval. He later read medieval literature as part of his studies at Oxford, has trained in longsword fighting and been known to shoot the occasional arrow, though not very accurately.

Scott lives in the wilds of west Wales with his partner and their menagerie of animals.

Also by Scott Mariani

The Ben Hope series

The Alchemist's Secret
The Mozart Conspiracy
The Doomsday Prophecy
The Heretic's Treasure
The Shadow Project
The Lost Relic
The Sacred Sword
The Armada Legacy
The Nemesis Program
The Forgotten Holocaust
The Martyr's Curse
The Cassandra Sanction
Star of Africa
The Devil's Kingdom
The Babylon Idol
The Bach Manuscript

The Moscow Cipher
The Rebel's Revenge
Valley of Death
House of War
The Pretender's Gold
The Demon Club
The Pandemic Plot
The Crusader's Cross
The Silver Serpent
Graveyard of Empires
The White Knight
The Tudor Deception
The Golden Library
The Templar Secret

The Pilgrim's Revenge

SCOTT MARIANI

HODDER &
STOUGHTON

First published in Great Britain in 2025 by Hodder & Stoughton Limited
An Hachette UK company

This paperback edition published in 2025

The authorised representative in the EEA is Hachette Ireland, 8 Castlecourt Centre,
Dublin, D15 XTP3, Ireland (email: info@hbgi.ie)

1

Copyright © Scott Mariani 2025

The right of Scott Mariani to be identified as the Author of the Work has been asserted
by him in accordance with the Copyright, Designs and Patents Act 1988.

All rights reserved. No part of this publication may be reproduced, stored in a
retrieval system, or transmitted, in any form or by any means without the prior
written permission of the publisher, nor be otherwise circulated in any form of
binding or cover other than that in which it is published and without a similar
condition being imposed on the subsequent purchaser.

All characters in this publication are fictitious and any resemblance to real persons,
living or dead, is purely coincidental.

A CIP catalogue record for this title is available from the British Library

Paperback ISBN 978 1 399 73674 9
ebook ISBN 978 1 399 73675 6

Typeset in Perpetua Std by Manipal Technologies Limited

Printed and bound in Great Britain by Clays Ltd, Elcograf S.p.A.

Hodder & Stoughton policy is to use papers that are natural, renewable
and recyclable products and made from wood grown in sustainable forests.
The logging and manufacturing processes are expected to conform to the
environmental regulations of the country of origin.

Hodder & Stoughton Limited
Carmelite House
50 Victoria Embankment
London EC4Y 0DZ

www.hodder.co.uk

Europe, 1190

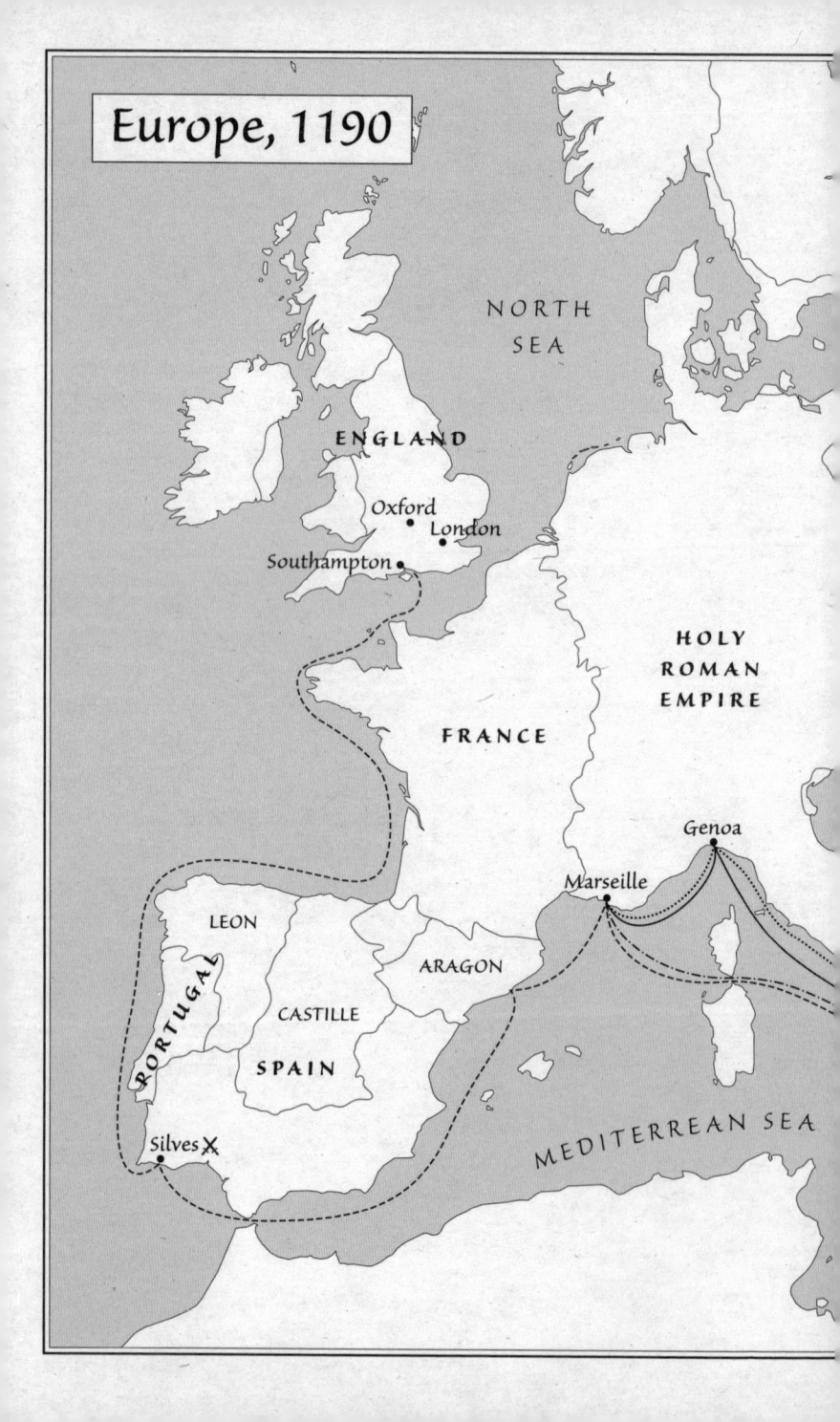

NORTH SEA

ENGLAND
- Oxford
- London
- Southampton

HOLY ROMAN EMPIRE

FRANCE

Genoa
Marseille

LEON
PORTUGAL
CASTILLE
ARAGON
SPAIN

Silves ✗

MEDITERREAN SEA

Key
Will's route
Richard's fleet
Richard
Philippe of France
LITHUANIA
RUSSIA
NGDOM
OF
OLAND
KINGDOM
OF
HUNGARY
BLACK SEA
SERVIA
BYZANTINE EMPIRE
CALABRIA
Bagnara
Messina
ICILY
CYPRUS
Nicosia
Limasol
Acre
Jerusalem
HOLY LAND

Chapter 1

It was a fine morning soon before Easter in the year of our Lord 1190, and the early spring sunshine shone down upon the quiet rural community of Foxwood.

The somewhat disorderly and rambling arrangement of thatched wattle-and-daub dwellings on their narrow little streets, the tiny church, the smithy, the old watermill and sundry other buildings, barns, pens and stables, and of course the grand house belonging to the lord of the manor, stood nestled in a pleasant green valley on the southerly banks of the River Windrush. Home to three hundred and eighty-seven souls at the last count, the village and surrounding farmland occupied some thousand or so acres at the heart of the county of Oxfordshire, though for the majority of the villagers who spent their days working the land, crafting their wares and minding their livestock, the great city of Oxford was so remote as to belong to a different world – to say nothing of faraway London.

Life continued here in much the same fashion as it had for countless generations, largely untouched by whatever went on beyond the boundaries of the manor estate. The neighbouring hamlet of Clanfield lay an hour's leisurely ride to the south, while the slightly larger town of Wexby stood some way further west. Midway between there and the village, the other side of the half-forested mound of Foxwood Hill and across the river, was the ancient greystone Benedictine monastery and convent of Wexby Abbey, housing some two dozen nuns and a few monks who pursued their unobtrusive, contemplative existence under the auspices of the formidable but kindly Mother Matilda.

And it was towards Wexby Abbey that a solitary cart could be seen travelling at this moment, pulled by an old grey mare and plodding its unhurried way westwards along the narrow road. The tall grass verges that rolled by on either side were bursting into colour with the first springtime wildflowers, bluebells and primroses and cow parsley; a family of swans gently glided along the course of the meandering river that sparkled in the sunshine. The dirt road was often impassably muddy during the wintertime, but the coming warmer months would soon bake the ruts as hard as fired clay.

The swaying, creaking cart was laden with fresh firewood, split logs of oak, beech and ash and bundles of cut sticks for kindling, along with other supplies that its lone driver was transporting for delivery to the abbey. He was a young man, christened William though everybody called him Will, and simply dressed in the loose-fitting attire of a countryman.

The village of Foxwood and its surrounds were the only home young Will had ever known, and never in the course of his score of years had he ventured more than a few miles in any given direction. He was as familiar with every individual villager as with every inch of the village itself, and for him it was a place synonymous with peace, harmony and a kind of inner contentment that buoyed his spirit, especially at this happy time of his life. He loved Foxwood's traditions and unchanging routines, the clutter and industry of its narrow streets, its smells of woodsmoke and hay and freshly baked bread in the mornings, the sounds: the crying of babies; the squeal of hogs being butchered; the clatter of cartwheels; the ringing of the church bell; the metallic *clang-clang* of the smithy; the barking of dogs and the honking of geese; the grind and splash of the miller's waterwheel; and the thwack of the flail come threshing time. All of it was dear to his heart: the good, the gritty and the plain disreputable, like the bloody bare-knuckle brawls that now and then broke out in the alley behind the alehouse, and the things that were known to go on in the upstairs room of *that* abode at the end of Main Street.

Though he firmly considered himself one of the people of Foxwood, Will had been born and always lived outside of it, on a small humble homestead half a mile from its outskirts and on the edge of the forest. His life also differed markedly from those of many of his fellow villagers in that, unlike the peasant labourers who tended to the lord's fields and were for all practical purposes his property, he was neither a serf nor a cottager and served no direct master other than God Almighty Himself – except perhaps the king, who seemed to him such an obscure and nebulous figure that he might as well not have existed in real life. No; Will was instead that rarest of things among the common people of the world he inhabited, a free man: free to marry as he pleased, to make whatever use he wished of his modest landholding, and to pursue his own living unshackled to the demands of the manor that dominated the existence of the majority of its population.

He knew only too well how blessed he was by good fortune, even though in his own way he worked just as hard as any of those who were tied to their duty of labouring in their lord's fields. It was by no means a life of comfort but a privileged one nonetheless, come down to him from his father who had earned these advantages for his family by his own blood and sweat. Will's mother had died when her only child was still just a small boy, and he had been raised by his father until he, too, passed away when Will was around fifteen years of age. The inheritance left to his son consisted of a half virgate of pasture and woods — some fourteen acres that included a stretch along the river, on which Will kept a small rowing boat for going fishing.

It was now eighteen months since Will had married Beatrice, the lovely, lively golden-haired miller's daughter with whom he'd been besotted and had admired from afar since they were both little more than children, never daring to speak to her until the day he'd discovered, to his amazement and joy, that she had also had a fond eye for him. The home the young couple shared was a simple timber-framed house furnished with a trestle table, a wooden bench, a straw bed in one corner and a rudimentary kitchen area in another, equipped with a few iron pots, a little pottery ware and wooden spoons used for cooking and eating. In the adjoining byre lived their four pigs, a dozen chickens, two goats and a sour-tempered cat called Gyb, who kept the vermin down and came and went as he pleased. Next door was a larger outbuilding that served as a stable for the grey mare and Will's pair of plough oxen, the laziest and most intractable brutes he'd ever come across. He worked hard to produce enough wheat, barley, oats and rye for the household and as a cash crop, along with peas, beans, onions and cabbages. But truth be told, Will wasn't much of a farmer and there was much else he would rather have been doing.

From the top of the grassy knoll by the house could be seen the dwellings and barns of Foxwood village and its ancient stone church; while in the other direction, on a clear day, you could make out the stately residence of the lord of the manor, Robert de Bray. Sir Robert was seldom ever seen locally, which was perhaps partly why he was generally regarded with affection by the people of the manor, either the free or the unfree, as a decent and accommodating master — indeed the best kind of all, being little involved in their lives and allowing them almost complete autonomy in the running of their community.

A community of which young Will was a dutiful and law-abiding member. He readily submitted his various tax payments to the royal authorities who periodically came to collect them, along with the token yearly rent of one penny due to the village bailiff for the liberty to otherwise tend to his own affairs, plus the additional scutage tax the manor required in return for being excused military service. The regular supplies of cut and split firewood logs and fresh meat were the extra tithe that he paid to Wexby Abbey in return for the seven acres of the Church's woodland and pasture licensed for his use. That was where he often exercised the skill that had earned him the name of 'Will the bowman', harvesting rabbits and woodpigeons and other small game thanks to his prowess with the longbow. Needless to say, the many deer that roamed Sir Robert's own woods were strictly out of bounds to any commoner not a sworn forester of the king, as many a poacher had learned at the cost of his right hand for a first offence, blinding for those determined or desperate enough to attempt a second. But those were the laws, however harsh; and like most people, Will accepted their necessity.

On his journey towards Wexby Abbey, Will crossed the new wooden bridge over the Windrush and felt his usual satisfaction at the rumble of his cartwheels over the solid timbers. When an overladen wagon had collapsed the original rotten bridge supports under its weight during the last winter, causing its load to be scattered into the river, Will had been among the men of Foxwood who had cut and carried the replacement timber pieces and laboured for three days in the cold to rebuild it. It pleased him to think that the fruit of their efforts would outlast his own lifetime.

A little further along the road he spied a raggedy figure making its shambling way along the verge and saw with pity in his heart that it was a wandering beggar, a most pathetic and starving one at that. Halting the old grey mare Will called to the man, then from the sack in his cart he pulled out one of the dead rabbits intended for the abbey and tossed it down to him. The beggar thanked him with a toothless smile and tears in his eyes, clutching the carcass to his chest. 'Bless you, young sir.'

'Take care of yourself,' Will told him, and drove on as the road gently climbed the hill up towards Wexby Abbey. Presently he was steering the mare through the ivied archway into its main courtyard, where he jumped down and tugged the bell-pull outside the smaller entrance designated for tradesmen and the like. After a short wait he was met there by Sister Edith, one of the nuns, not much older than himself and always smiling and cheery.

'Good morning, Sister Edith,' he said with a warm smile of his own. 'I have brought you firewood and some fresh game for the kitchen.'

'How pleasant to see you again, Will. Isn't it a beautiful day, so early in the spring?'

'As radiant as could be wished for,' he agreed. 'And I hope I see you in good health, Sister?'

'By God's grace I am well, thank you for asking. And busy helping with our preparations for Easter. How is Beatrice?'

Will's smile widened as the mention of his wife's name brought her face vividly into his mind, though in truth she was never far from his thoughts. 'She's doing fine. Counting the days.' As was he, because during the coming summer season, in three months' time, the couple were to be blessed with the birth of their first child.

'I am sure it will be a boy,' Sister Edith said. 'And that he will be born with his mother's beautiful golden hair and blue eyes. Not to mention his father's courage and handsome looks,' she added coyly, and not for the first time Will wondered if the young nun might be innocently flirting with him. As to his handsome looks, Will had never seen his own reflection in anything other than still water or polished metal and so could have no particularly well-informed opinion of himself in that regard; but from the reaction his presence seemed to inspire in some women, and the way many men either looked twice at him or avoided making eye contact altogether, he was aware that his physical size gave him a certain bearing that might be considered attractive or imposing, depending on the beholder. He was taller than most men, and had inherited his father's broad-shouldered build and long, powerful arms, made more muscular by plying his wood axe and saw – and though (as far as he could count them) he had seen only twenty birthdays, there was nothing boyish about his demeanour.

'For my part,' he replied with a chuckle, 'it makes no difference to me whether Beatrice and I are to receive a son or a daughter. Either would give us as much joy. And how happy she'll be to become a mother.'

'With the Lord's blessing all will go well for her, when the time comes,' said Sister Edith. 'I will say an extra prayer for her every morning and every night, that mother and child be safe and healthy.'

'That's very kind of you, Sister.' Reaching again into the back of the cart Will brought out the sack containing the seven remaining rabbit carcasses, five brace of woodpigeon and pheasant and the fresh pike he'd fished from the river early that morning. 'I know it's not much,' he said, laying the sack at Sister Edith's feet. 'I had been hoping for a March hare. I spotted as big and fat a one as you have ever seen running about the top of Foxwood Hill only yesterday, but when I went back to hunt for him, he had made himself scarce.'

'Do not trouble yourself,' Sister Edith said, peering into the sack. 'The Mother Superior will be delighted with these, and just in time for the ending of the Lenten fast now that Easter is almost upon us. It will be so good to taste butter, cheese and meat again, after six weeks! Thank you, Will.'

'And here,' he said, handing her a bulging linen bag, 'are some more candles for the refectory. A few are made from beeswax, the rest tallow. I'm sorry there couldn't be more, but Beatrice tires easily these days.' Candle-making was another small industry carried out at the homestead. Naturally, the wax ones were superior, brighter and cleaner burning. Beatrice took great pride in her bees and was completely fearless when it came to collecting their produce. Will, on the other hand, was secretly terrified of the buzzing, crawling, swarming insects and was extremely reluctant to venture anywhere near the hives. So much for his great courage, he thought to himself.

'What finely shaped candles,' Sister Edith said, holding one up to admire it. 'They give far better illumination than those we get from the chandlery in Wexby, and hardly any smell at all. Please tell Beatrice that she works too hard, slaving over a hot melting pot hour after hour in her condition. She needs to rest and conserve her energy.'

'You try telling her so,' Will laughed. 'One might as well ask the Windrush to stop flowing. Now here,' he said, 'let me help you carry these heavy things to the kitchen and pantry. I have wrapped the carcasses as carefully as I could to stop any blood leaking out, though even so you wouldn't want to get any on your habit.'

But Sister Edith's willowy frame belied the strength she'd gained from a lifetime of hard work, and with a gracious refusal she hefted the sack and the linen bag, one over each shoulder. 'I hope to see you again soon, Will,' were her parting words as she turned to go back inside. 'May God's peace go with you. And don't forget to give Beatrice my love.'

Moments after the nun had disappeared through the stone doorway with a final smile, Will was joined by the surly presence of old Godfrey. He was a dour, hunchbacked, one-eyed man of indeterminate age who had seemed very ancient to Will for as long as he could remember. These many years past he had been employed to tend to the abbey grounds, dig the graves in the churchyard and perform general labours. 'Come along now, young feller,' he grumbled, 'you'll have to give me a hand unloading all this lot. My poor old back ain't doing so well today.'

The abbey's wood and grain stores were housed in the great thatched tithe barn at the rear of the main buildings, by the ruined and moss-covered archway marking the spot where St Aethelwine's Priory had stood in ancient times. Will held on to the mare's bridle as she obligingly backed the cart up to the open doors of the barn. He rewarded her with a rub on the neck and a nose bag filled with oats and barley to munch on while he and Godfrey did the rest.

The two men spent the next while carrying armfuls of logs down from the cart and stacking them on the woodpile, in such a way that the older ones that had already been seasoning under cover would be at the front, ready for use. In so doing they disturbed a nest of rats, which scattered in all directions as Godfrey shouted 'Shoo! Shoo! Hell rip and roast 'ee fucking little buggers!' in a rising screech of indignation while he flapped his arms and leaped about the barn trying to stamp on the darting rodents, a spectacle so absurd that Will had to suppress his laughter. It was just as well Mother Matilda was far out of earshot, or else she would likely have had Godfrey clapped in the stocks for his language, and the monks pelt him with rotten eggs.

Once the logs were taken care of, they piled the bound sheaves of dry kindling sticks in a heap nearby. 'That's the last of them,' Will said, dusting his hands. 'Thank you for your help, Godfrey.' The older man grunted something unintelligible and stumped away to attend to his other chores.

His duty to the abbey done until next time, Will climbed back aboard his cart and set off for home. The sun was warm on his head and his heart was light. At her usual plodding pace the grey mare clip-clopped away from the abbey, over the hill and back across the wooden bridge. Presently they took the right fork in the road that would bring them through the woods, and from there to the well-trodden track up to the homestead. The oak, beech and rowan buds were bursting back into leaf after their long winter sleep and the birds were singing brightly in the treetops.

As Will was passing Foxwood Hill, a faraway movement on the hillside caught his sharp eye, and reining the mare to a halt he muttered to himself, 'God's bones. There he is again.'

Sure enough, the big old hare he'd spied in the very same spot the previous day was back. His burrow must be somewhere nearby. As Will watched, the animal, little more than a tawny speck against the green at this distance, darted a way through the long spring grass then sat on its haunches and stayed perfectly still with one long ear cocked, seeming to be watching him from afar.

Will was all for abstaining from meat during these weeks of Lent, but he insisted on Beatrice getting the nourishment she and the unborn infant needed. Having given all his catch of the last three days to the abbey and the wandering beggar, he had left himself with nothing to take home for tonight's supper and there was little in the larder except a few eggs, some hard cheese and stale bread. The hare would provide a welcome meal.

'Don't you move, now,' Will said to his prey. He reached under the seat of his cart and lifted out his bow, along with a single arrow: his hunter's experience told him that, hit or miss, one shot would be all he'd get at his quarry. The bow was one that Will had fashioned himself from a perfect piece of yew, in the way that his father had showed him many years ago. Likewise, he made his own arrows, all but the sharp triangular iron heads that he obtained from the smithy in Foxwood.

Moving very slowly so as not to frighten the hare away, he climbed down from the cart, braced his bow stave against his right ankle and behind his left knee. Then with his left arm he applied enough backward pressure to bend the stave far enough to slip the string up onto its notch. It was a procedure he had performed so many times that it was second nature to him. With the bow ready for use he fitted the nock of the arrow to the hemp cord. It was a powerful weapon, tailored exactly to the length and power of his draw. Will lacked a scale to measure the weight of pulling back the bowstring to its full extent, but he estimated it as not much under his own. The energy it delivered to the arrow gave the weapon a maximum range of some three hundred yards, twice the distance from which the hare, still perfectly immobile, sat watching him.

Will took a breath, fixed eyes on his quarry, raised the bow, pulled it all the way to full draw in one smooth, powerful movement and took aim. Still the hare didn't move a muscle. It almost seemed to be taunting him. *You'll never get me from that far, my foolish friend.*

But Will knew better than the hare, and had proved time and time again that he could easily hit a target half that size at this range. Then, just as he was on the verge of releasing his shot to prove the creature wrong, the hare bounded quick as a flash into the long grass, disappearing from sight.

'Damn and blast,' Will said, lowering his bow and letting the tension off the arrow. It seemed as though the wily old beast would live to be hunted another day, either by himself or by one of the foxes that ranged through the woods and meadows. It was in the nature of things, and Will couldn't allow himself to be disappointed as he unstrung his bow and climbed back aboard the cart. 'Come, let's go home,' he said to the mare, and she plodded on.

It was as Will was clearing the brow of the last rise before reaching the homestead that he caught the acrid smell of burning, and felt a sudden chill of apprehension go through him. And then he looked up over the trees and saw the thick, dark smoke rising into the sky.

Chapter 2

A confusion of possibilities all flew through Will's mind. Beatrice had been taken ill, fainted or collapsed and somehow set fire to the house; or else a spark from the chimney had ignited the thatch; or a dozen other things that occurred to him all at once, all of them equally alarming. But the reality was far worse. From the direction of the homestead, he faintly made out the high-pitched whinny of a horse, the sound of a man's voice raised in a shout. And Beatrice's scream.

Will's hands began to shake as he urged the mare to go faster. 'Come on, move yourself!' Her ears turned back towards him at the sound of his voice, but nothing short of a lashing with a bullwhip could have broken her out of her sedate pace and he knew that he'd be quicker on foot. He leaped down from the cart, grabbing his bow and arrow quiver, and ran for all he was worth the rest of the way up the track with the mare towing the empty cart behind him. His heart was pounding violently and his legs felt watery-weak with terror.

So bewildered that he could barely think or even see straight, Will reached the break in the trees where the track forked off into his own property. There were fresh overlapping hoof prints in the dirt, confirming what his ears were already telling him. More than one horseman had come through here, and very recently. As he ran on, he could hear more clearly the neighing and snorting and pounding hooves of several horses and the loud voices of their riders. Behind those sounds were the sharp crackle of flames, the screech of panic-stricken chickens and the lowing of the oxen in the barn. Above all were Beatrice's piercing cries of distress.

And then, as he rounded the great old oak stump that marked the entrance to his yard, the sight in front of him filled him with chilling horror. The thatch of his and Beatrice's home was blazing out of control, pouring black smoke. The yard was a scene of confusion and fury as the four horsemen who had attacked the homestead wheeled their mounts in all directions. The riders astride their tall, powerful horses were soldiers – as was instantly apparent to Will from their chain mail, iron helmets and shields. But they were soldiers unlike any Will had ever seen before. The fifty or so men-at-arms who served Sir Robert de Bray were an occasional sight in Foxwood, and everybody recognised the noble coat of arms displayed on their shields, a simple white stripe on a background of crimson and blue. The motif that Will could see on these men's shields and surcoats was a black eagle, menacing with spread wings, a cruel hooked beak and three long tail feathers pointing downward like spikes.

Whoever they were, they had clearly come here with the intention of causing death and destruction. Three of them had drawn swords and the fourth was still clutching the flaming brand with which he had fired the thatch. Will looked for Beatrice but she was nowhere to be seen, and he could no longer hear her screams.

Will kept running, shouting at the top of his voice, but either the riders couldn't hear him over the chaos, or their attention was too taken up with wreaking devastation on the homestead. As he sprinted wildly across the yard towards them, he saw one of the soldiers jump down from the saddle and disappear into the byre adjoining the burning house. The man reappeared an instant later, clutching a wildly struggling Beatrice by the arm. In her other hand she grasped Will's wood axe, which she had taken from the chopping block to defend herself with. Now she swung the axe at the soldier who was dragging her from the byre; but with only one free hand it was too heavy for her to wield, and her wild swing missed him by a foot, the momentum of the iron axe head unbalancing her. The soldier easily knocked the shaft from her grip and roughly grabbed her other arm in his gauntleted fist. Her golden hair was tousled and covered her face. Her frantic cries were half drowned out by their crude shouts and laughter as a second soldier jumped from his horse to join his comrade in dragging her out into the yard. It was obvious what these men intended to do to her, even though she was visibly with child.

By now Will had almost reached the nearest of the horsemen on his side of the yard. Up close, the rider was an intimidating figure looming far above him in the saddle with the blade of his drawn arming sword glinting in the sunlight. Before Will reached him the horseman saw his approach and wheeled his mount around to face him, dust flying from its hooves. With an angry shout the rider spurred the horse towards Will, swinging his sword down at him. Will ducked, and the double-edged blade hissed through the air above him.

It had been a blow meant to separate his head from his shoulders, and it had only narrowly missed its mark.

The horse thundered past, shaking the ground. The rider reined it brutally around and charged at Will again.

Nothing like this had ever happened or even been heard of in Will's experience. He had never been in a real fight, except a minor scuffle once when he was a lad, settled quickly with a couple of punches. This was deadly serious combat, and he was unprepared for it. But the terrible shocking sight of Beatrice in the soldiers' clutches and the sound of her screams was enough to dispel his confusion and fear, filling him with rage and determination to do anything he could to drive these raiders away and make this stop. And the obvious realisation suddenly occurred to him, for the first time, that he was holding the very means of doing that in his hands. His bow was still unstrung, no more than a long wooden shaft with its hemp cord loosely attached at the bottom end. But practice had made him very adept at readying the weapon in moments; as the horseman bore down on him with the sword raised high, he bent the stave against his foot and looped the string into place.

The rider was almost on him. Will snatched an arrow from his quiver, nocked it to the string and simultaneously raised his bow and pulled it to full draw. He had never before pointed any weapon in anger at another human being, but there was little time to reflect on that fact, or even to take aim, as his enemy closed in. Will stood his ground until the last moment, released his arrow and saw it fly and hit the rider full in the chest.

The soldier flinched violently at the arrow strike. A normal opponent would have been a dead man, his heart split in two by the power of the longbow at such close range. But instead of piercing deep into his flesh the iron point glanced off his heavy chain mail and the broken pieces of the arrow shaft spun away through the air. Then Will had to leap out of the way of the charging horse, and he threw himself to the ground to avoid being trampled down by its hooves.

Half blinded by dust, he was rolling and springing back up to his feet as the rider thundered by him. Will glanced around and saw that Beatrice had torn free from her two captors and was running away from them. There were three of them chasing her now: big, strong warriors and much faster than she was, and almost immediately one of them had caught her again. But Beatrice was a fighter too, and the same courage she showed when surrounded by a swarm of bees she showed again now in the face of attack. Before the soldier could stop her, she had torn the long heavy dagger from its scabbard on his belt and was turning it determinedly on him. Will nocked another arrow and trained his aim on the soldier, aiming at the weak spot in his armour below the base of his helmet. Will was on the verge of loosing his shot when he saw that her assailants' still-mounted comrade had wheeled his horse around once again and was coming in for a third attack, his determination redoubled to kill this peasant who had dared to stand up to him.

Will turned the bow towards the charging rider, drew and released his arrow all in one hurried movement. The instant the bowstring twanged loose from his fingers he knew that he had jerked the shot; and sure enough the arrow went wide of its target.

But not so wide as to miss entirely. The hissing shaft with its deadly iron tip passed through the open front of the soldier's helmet, glanced off the nose bar that protected the middle of his face and ripped a furrow across his left cheek. Blood flew in the sunshine and Will heard the man's roar of pain. It was not enough to stop the horse, however, and nor did the arrow strike prevent the swing of the sword blade that came flashing towards him in such a rapid arc that Will was unable to react in time to avoid it.

It was only the wound he had inflicted on the soldier that saved Will now from an instantaneous and bloody death. The pain and shock of the gaping injury to his face caused the man to momentarily slacken his grip on his sword hilt, and the fumbled blow caught Will across the top of the head with the flat of the blade. The slightest deviation of its angle, bringing it into contact edge-on, and it would have cleaved through flesh and bone to take the crown of Will's skull cleanly off. Instead, it was like being hit by the end of a wooden plank – only ten times harder with the rigidity of steel and the unstoppable weight and momentum of the horse behind it.

Will's vision exploded into stars, and he was thrown backwards off his feet. He barely felt himself hit the ground; but then by some miracle he managed to scramble back upright, though the stunning force of the blow had left everything spinning. Blood was pouring into his eyes. He could no longer see where Beatrice was or hear her cries. A dark tide seemed to be rising up to swallow him, no matter how hard he tried to resist it. He tried to call out her name. He staggered, blinked, wiped the blood from his eyes, but more kept coursing down his brow and blinding him again. He felt his knees buckle under him. The sounds around him had become a dull, confusing swirl. Then the rising tide of darkness took him, and it was as though the world had been plunged into the blackest, most starless night. Will vaguely felt himself pitching forwards, and after that he knew nothing more.

*

By the time consciousness returned at last, the first thing he saw in his dazed confusion was that the sun was sinking over the trees to the west. Several hours must have gone by. He stirred and groaned as the terrible pain burst through his head, followed by acute dizziness when he tried to prop himself up on one elbow in an effort to struggle to his feet.

He managed to get up on his knees and knelt there for a few moments waiting for the pain to dissipate, which it did only very slightly, becoming a tortured ache that pulsed with his heartbeat. At first, he couldn't understand why he could see so little, until he realised that the sun had dried the blood that covered his face, crusting over his eyelids. He wiped it away and looked dully at the brownish stains on his hands. The strike of the sword blade had split the skin of his scalp just below the hairline. As it began to dawn on him now, there must have been so much blood that the soldiers had thought he was dead.

Then as the full memory came flooding back he forced himself upright with a croaking shout of 'Beatrice!' The dizziness nearly caused him to fall back down but he stood there swaying, blinking at the scene around him. The house was by now just a smoking ruin, burnt almost completely to the ground, thatch gone, just a few blackened timbers among the ashes. The byre had partly been destroyed with it. Nothing remained of the livestock except for the crudely butchered carcasses of the oxen. No sign either of his old mare, having either wandered off or been taken by the marauders along with the cart in which to carry away their spoils.

None of that mattered to Will. A cry burst out of him as he saw Beatrice's inert body a distance away among the devastation of the yard. She was lying on her back with her face turned towards him, partly obscured by her hair.

He ran over to her, his pain completely forgotten, and fell to his knees beside her. 'Beatrice! My Beatrice!' He reached out with a trembling bloodied hand and gently brushed her hair away from her face. And with a shock that nearly stopped his pounding heart his eyes met her own, those beautiful blue eyes, once so lustrous and full of happiness, now staring at him lifeless and unseeing. The rose of her cheeks had turned to chalk and her lips were pale.

'No. No! NOOOOO!' Will raised his face to the sky and let out a howling inhuman scream of grief.

The sun slowly went down behind the trees and the shadows of dusk lengthened over the ruined homestead as he knelt there beside his wife's body. For a long time, he clutched her; sobbing, gently rocking, the tears washing the encrusted blood from his cheeks. Then when he had no more tears left in him, he lovingly closed her eyes and folded her limp arms across her chest, clutched her cold hand and sat watching over her. At first there was the total refusal to believe this had happened; the fervent conviction that she must be only in some trance from which she would suddenly awaken at any moment, smiling at the sight of his face gazing down on hers.

How long have I been sleeping?

Not long, my love, he would have replied with a tender kiss.

But as that hope faded, came the sense of utter helplessness, of being trapped in a present reality that was unendurable and yet from which there was no possible release. And then, at last, when all other emotions had been spent, a curtain of absolute numbness came down to blot out his senses and his ability to think, as if he too had fallen into the realm of the dead. He would gladly have joined her there. Joined both of them: not only his beloved wife but the child they had made together, now never to be born.

Time seemed to have come to a standstill, with only the coming of darkness and the rising of the moon to mark its passing. The temperature dropped. The night creatures would soon be out: Will could hear the eerie cry of a vixen not far off, and an owl hooted among the trees. If none of the villagers of Foxwood had seen the smoke earlier and come running to offer assistance, it was unlikely they would do so now. No, nobody was coming. No locals, no law in the form of village bailiff or sheriff's men. Will knew that it was up to him, and him alone, to do what was necessary.

Beatrice had loved the home they'd shared together, and had often told him she would never leave it. But the time to leave had come. He could not bury her here, for fear that God would refuse her entry into Heaven unless she was interred properly, on holy ground. He must deliver her body into the Lord's hands, the only way he could.

Will had no blanket to drape over her. He gathered her up in his arms and got to his feet, still swaying from the dizziness that threatened to unbalance him as he began his long journey down the track and towards the road. Full darkness fell, only the soft moon's glow to light his way as he trudged on and on with her body clasped to his chest, her head nuzzled against his shoulder and her hair brushing his face, in just the same way they had often lain together when she was alive. This would be the last time they would ever be close to one another. One of her arms flopped loose and dangled limply. With an effort he replaced it over her chest so that he could pretend to himself, at least for a while, that she was only sleeping.

Will followed the same winding road he had travelled earlier, making for the haven of Wexby Abbey. He murmured into her ear as he went, telling her that she would soon be in God's hands and in a safe place where nobody could ever harm her.

The words brought back his tears, and they dripped from his face onto hers. All the strength seemed to have been sapped from him, so that by the time he had reached the bridge he was staggering from dizziness and blinking the sweat out of his eyes. His arms were burning, and his legs would hardly support his own weight, still less both of them. Still, he forced himself to go on, step by tortured step until, deep into the dark night, he had wound his way up the long, steep hill and could see the walls and towers of the abbey silhouetted against the sky ahead.

Twice his failing strength almost made him collapse before they got there. But he wouldn't give up, and he gritted his teeth against the agony and the exhaustion and the harrowing grief that made him want to drop to his knees and scream his rage at God for allowing her to be taken from him. Now at last he stood swaying on his feet in front of the arched abbey gates, closed at night for safety. He could barely muster the power to whisper any longer, but from somewhere inside him came a strong voice that shouted, 'Help us, for the love of Christ help us!' Then he could take no more, and he sank to the ground with Beatrice still in his arms. He closed his eyes and waited for whomever, whatever, might come and take him.

It could not have been long, though it seemed like hours, before the iron deadbolt of the abbey gate drew back and the door inched open with a creak. 'Lord love us, it's Master William,' said the voice of old Godfrey in the dim glow of lantern light that appeared in the darkness. Then another voice, that of Sister Edith, gasped at the sight of them and murmured a prayer.

'Quickly, Godfrey, we must bring her inside.'

Chapter 3

The events that followed seemed hazy and fragmented to Will as he drifted back and forth between conscious moments that felt like being trapped in some waking nightmare, and the alternating periods of merciful oblivion where he was aware of nothing at all. There were snatched glimpses of flickering torchlight against stone walls and the silent dark-robed and hooded figures of monks as he was carried through the arches and cloistered passages of the abbey to a chamber where he was laid on a wooden trestle with a straw mat under him, covered with a blanket and told to lie still. He made no protest in any case, as every movement or attempt to sit up brought only pain and nausea. Then he was alone again for a time, in darkness except for a sputtering tallow candle. He lay gazing at its tiny flame and wondered if it was one of Beatrice's candles, and he thought that once it was gone, all that remained of her would be gone, too.

He wept, and now and then slipped back into unconsciousness, and at other times floated in a half-awakened state where he was haunted by the visions of that awful day, a day that had changed everything forever. The sounds of hooves and fire and harsh voices filled his head. He saw Beatrice's face smiling at him. Then when he went to touch her, her eyes became sightless holes and her cheeks were hollow like a skull. He jerked awake with a cry and the pain in his head made him gasp.

'There now,' said a soft voice from the darkness. 'Be calm.'

He weakly raised his head off the straw and whispered, 'Beatrice? Is that you?'

'Shh. You must not speak or exert yourself,' said the voice. A small hand pressed against his chest, firmly but gently urging him to lie back. By the glow of the candle he saw that it was Sister Edith. She sat quietly on a stool by his trestle, with a table nearby on which rested a bowl and jug, and in her hands was the linen cloth she was using to apply some kind of herb salve or ointment to his wound. As she carefully dabbed, she went on talking to him in a tender, reassuring tone, and he closed his eyes and did as he was bid. He found her presence to be of comfort to him, and presently his body relaxed, the pain eased a little and he became peaceful.

Time passed. He became dimly aware of other presences having entered the chamber. Sister Edith had been joined by another two nuns, one of whom Will faintly recognised as the abbess, Mother Matilda. She spoke in a low voice that was kindly but authoritative, and although his mind was confused and he kept drifting off, he was able to catch snatches of their hushed conversation.

'Tomorrow she shall be laid to rest in a corner of the churchyard, her salvation assured. It's the least we can do. William has been so good to us, and she was such a dear sweet creature, the poor, poor girl.'

'But what is to be done about the animals who did this?' Sister Edith's voice, whispered and urgent and audibly close to tears. She was speaking quite out of turn to her mother superior, but was too grief-stricken to care. 'Such evil surely cannot be allowed to go unchecked.'

'It is not given to us to decide who is to be judged, child. That authority sits only with our Lord in Heaven. You must find it in your heart to forgive those who trespass against us and our fellow man, as God in Christ forgave us.'

'In my heart—' Sister Edith began, then restrained her outburst before she said too much, if she had not done so already.

'However, I do agree that we are duty bound to see to it that the necessary steps are taken to bring the perpetrators to justice,' Mother Matilda went on, benevolently ignoring the young nun's display of passion. 'I will send word to Sir de Bray. He will know what to do.'

A third voice, unfamiliar to Will, said, 'But begging your pardon, Ma'am, our Lord de Bray is away tending to his estates in Normandy and may not return to England for months.'

'Then we will have no choice but to wait,' Mother Matilda replied patiently. 'In the meantime, we can only pray that God sees fit to prevent any more suffering. Now I will leave you to tend to our patient. Come, Sister Millicent.'

Will heard the creak of the door, the departing footsteps and the fall of the latch as the door closed again behind them, leaving the chamber in silence. He peered through the yellow halo of candlelight. 'Sister Edith? Are you still there?'

'Yes, William. I thought you were asleep.'

'Where is Beatrice?'

'She is safe now. As are you. Nobody can touch you here, inside the house of the Lord.'

'I don't care about myself,' Will tried to protest, but she silenced him with a warm finger pressed to his lips.

'Quiet. Lie still. The bleeding is stemmed for now, but you may easily disturb the dressing with all this fretful shifting about. Let the poultice do its work and the wound will not become poisoned. The aching in your head will pass, in time. You have suffered a terrible bad blow. Let me see, now.' She took the candle from the table and held it closer to his face, examining him and seeming not pleased with what she was seeing. 'The blacks of your eyes are still different sizes, one too large and the other shrunk as small as the head of a pin. I have seen it before, when Brother Jocelyn took a fall from horseback and struck his head upon a rock. He was never the same afterwards. But with God's grace you will recover. He was old and sickly, you are young and full of health. The dizziness ought to diminish in a day or two. Does the light bother you?'

The glow of the candle near his eyes seemed to sear right through to the back of his head. He nodded. 'It hurts.'

She took the candle away and set it back on the table. 'Close your eyes. Sleep is the best healer. Dawn is still hours away.'

'I prefer to talk.'

'As you wish,' she said, returning to her stool to sit demurely with her hands resting in her lap. He could see the outline of her long, flowing habit and her face half lit in the candle glow. 'I am here to listen.'

'Thank you for your care of me,' he murmured. 'And your wisdom.'

'Oh,' she chuckled sadly. 'I'm not wise. Not like Mother Matilda.'

There was a question he desperately needed to be answered, but he found it hard to summon the right words. 'Is . . . is she going to be at peace now?'

'You did the right thing in bringing her here, William. Our dear Beatrice's spirit will find its way into the arms of the Lord, where it belongs.'

Tears came back into his eyes, tears of relief but born also of other emotions. He fell silent for a long moment, then said in a strangled voice, 'I could have stopped it, Sister. I had my bow with me. I could have shot them all. But I hesitated too long. It's *my* fault that this happened. I was weak and stupid, and I can never forgive myself. It should have been me who died, not her.'

'You must not blame yourself, William. You did all you could to protect her. God knows that. And so does Beatrice.'

More tears streamed down his face. He felt ashamed for crying like a child, in front of a woman. But he couldn't help himself. 'She was the strong one,' he said. 'She would not let the soldiers violate her, and she fought them like a mother deer protecting her fawn from a pack of wolves. They killed her for it.' He shook his head, utterly disconsolate. 'And now I have lost everything. Everything I have ever loved or could ever love. My life is over.'

Sister Edith wiped away her own tears and reached out to clasp his hand. 'No,' she said. 'You haven't lost everything. It only feels that way, as real as it may seem to you at this terrible moment. But you will come to feel differently.'

'How would *you* know that?' he replied, with a sudden surge of resentment. 'What gives you the right to tell me so?'

Her eyes gleamed in the soft light, and she squeezed his hand more tightly. 'Do not be so quick to anger. Why do you think I am here myself? I was not always a sister of the convent, you know.'

Her words stunned him for a moment. 'You—?'

'Yes, I lost everything too. God knows it was not in the same terrible fashion as what has befallen you and Beatrice, but nonetheless, at the time it felt as though my life, too, had ended. And were it not for my faith,' she added, 'perhaps it might indeed have been over, in a real sense. But now I am here, and the Lord has given me a new purpose. Every day brings me greater strength and joy in His service.'

Will was silent, unable to find a reply.

'Dear Will,' Sister Edith went on in a different tone, 'you must know that they would have killed her anyway. You could not have prevented it, and so Beatrice sacrificed her life to shield her virtue. We should all wish for such an honourable passing.'

'Perhaps one day I can accept that,' he whispered hoarsely. 'But at this moment all I can feel is rage. I want to find those men. I want to destroy them, to take from them what they took from Beatrice.'

She shook her head. 'It is not for us to make that judgement.'

'That's what Mother Matilda said. But I also heard what you said, about not being able to forgive evil men for their sins. I know that is how you feel, deep down in your heart.'

'I was wrong to speak that way. And you ought to be more mindful of your words, lest Mother Matilda hear you utter such blasphemy under God's roof. Now, William Bowman,' she said with a look of the most sisterly affection that belied her firm tone, 'there has been quite enough talk for one night. You have been placed in my charge, and as your temporary physician I am *ordering* you to lie quiet and get some rest. Is that understood?'

Chapter 4

He did rest, though only for a few hours. A golden shaft of dawn light was shining through the small window as he awoke to find himself alone in the chamber. It was the abbey bells that had roused him from sleep, summoning the monks and nuns to Lauds, the first sacred office of the day when all would gather to make their devotions in the church before recommencing their daily duties of labour, reading and worship.

Will raised himself tentatively up from his thin bed of straw matting, and found that both the physical discomfort of his wound and the dizziness had eased greatly from yesterday, thanks no doubt to Sister Edith's medicine. Only the agony of his grief had worsened, a raw emptiness that made him wish he didn't have to face the day. But face it he must, and would. Because during the hours of the night his resolve had only hardened, and there was no longer any doubt in his mind what he must do.

He got down from the wooden trestle on which his bed lay. Kneeling on the hard, cold stone floor of the chamber, bathed in the rays of the rising sun, he bowed his head and squeezed his eyes shut and said a quiet prayer of his own, one that Mother Matilda would not have approved of. Where the words came from he didn't know, but they seemed to tumble out of him.

Lord, I come to you in my anguish, with a heart seeking justice and a prayer that the wicked face the consequences of their actions. The pain I feel is overwhelming and my human nature cries out for retribution. Let your anger be kindled against them, that they be struck down with swift and unyielding power.

He paused in his prayer, eyes still tightly closed and head still bowed, reflecting on jumbled and half-remembered phrases from the Bible he had never learned to read but whose verses he had so often heard repeated in church. Somehow, though, they weren't enough to express what was in his heart.

I know I should step back, O God, and leave room for your Divine wrath to repay these wrongdoers for their cruel and evil deeds. But the wicked walk freely, their actions causing harm and devastation, and I cannot wait for your mighty hand to move in my favour. I pray for your forgiveness, and for the strength and resolve to do what I must do. Amen.

He sat up and opened his eyes, blinking in the strong light. That last part had sounded rushed and clumsy to his ears, but he knew no other way to express it. Nor had he any idea whether the Almighty would listen favourably to his prayer, or instead condemn him for the sinful intentions he had confessed to. But if he was to burn in hellfire for his words, then so be it; nothing could deter him from his course.

Upon the stool on which Sister Edith had sat he found his tunic and breeches, clean and dry and neatly folded, along with his belt and the sheath with the hunting knife that had been his father's and his father's before him. Will washed his face and hands in the water from the jug that had been left for him, slipped the clothes on over his linen undergarments and buckled the belt around his waist. Then finding the door of the chamber unlocked, he ventured outside and found himself in a small, cloistered quadrangle deep within the abbey. The place was deserted, with everyone attending Lauds.

He wandered tentatively through the passageways, still reeling a little from his head injury, quite lost at first but then finding his bearings as he spotted the old mossy archway of St Aethelwine's Priory, and beside it the familiar shape of the tithe barn. From there he made his way around to the churchyard, filled with gravestones. Some were new, others more time-worn and weathered than the abbey itself. The lawns were neatly scythed and the paths were lined with the gravel that came up by the cartload from the quarry in Clanfield, driven by Will's cousin Hob. Crows circled and cawed among the high towers. Coming from inside the church he could hear the sound of the solemn Lauds service taking place. Closer by was another sound, the rhythmic clang and scrape of Godfrey's shovel as he dug the fresh grave in the corner of the churchyard.

Will stood and stared, finding it difficult to believe that he was watching his Beatrice's grave being dug. The tears burned his eyes for a moment; then he blinked them away, gathered himself and walked over to where Godfrey was hunched over his shovel, grunting with the effort and muttering to himself as usual, the long hem of his tunic stained with dirt. He was already up to his knees in the hole he'd made. As Will came within a few steps of him Godfrey suddenly turned, startled, his one eye opening wide. He made a sour grimace and clutched a big, earthy hand to his chest.

'Christ in Heaven, lad, you gave me a fright, sneaking up on me blind side like that. I thought you were a spirit.'

'Perhaps I am,' Will replied.

'What the devil are you thinking of, leaving your sick bed to go off a-wandering about the place alone? If Mother Matilda sees you—'

'Let me do that,' Will interrupted him, holding out his hand for the shovel. Godfrey hesitated, then handed it to him and stepped out of the hole. Will jumped down and began to dig wildly, slamming the blade into the clay and flinging up great shovelfuls to add to the mound that Godfrey had already piled up. He felt possessed with an energy that seemed to be coming from somewhere else. He suddenly imagined that he was digging the grave not of his dead wife and unborn child, but of their murderers.

Godfrey was not the most sensitive of men, but even he looked uncomfortable at the sight. 'You shouldn't be here doing this, lad.'

'She was my wife,' Will replied, without looking up from his work. 'I mean to be here until she is laid to rest, before I go on my way.'

'Back 'ome to Foxwood, I expect?'

'I no longer have a home there.'

'Where to, then?' Godfrey asked, narrowing his eye.

Will paused his digging, planted the shovel in the ground and rested on the handle. His head had started throbbing again and his vision was less than perfectly clear. He didn't care. 'Those soldiers. I need to know who they were. Where they came from, and where they could have gone.'

Godfrey gave a grunt. 'And why would you want to know that, lad?'

'Because I want to find the four men who murdered my wife and child,' Will replied. 'And when I have found them, I'm going to kill them.'

If old Godfrey were shocked to hear such talk on holy ground, he made no show of it. 'Else they'll kill you,' he said. 'You're just a lad, big and strong though you may be, and there's only one of you. You have had but a taste of what such men are capable of. They make their living by the sword and are used to the bloody butcher's yard of war and conquest. What do you know of such things, a young feller like you?'

'I don't fear death,' Will said, casting a defiant eye at the gravestones around him.

'Then you're a braver man than I,' Godfrey answered with a dark laugh. 'Can't say that I blame you for wanting to do what is right. I'd come with you, too, if it wasn't for all my ailments. Believe it or not, I was a fighting man once meself. Travelled all over and seen a battle or two in my day, that's for sure. Seen an' done all manner of things, and a lot of them weren't too pretty neither, may the Lord forgive me for my sins.' He rolled his eye heavenward and crossed himself.

'You know much more than I do about the world,' Will said. 'I have been nowhere, lived my whole life within a few miles of where I was born.' He described to Godfrey the black eagle motif emblazoned on the marauders' shields and surcoats. 'If you had ever seen it, you might remember whose coat of arms it was.'

Godfrey considered for a few moments, then shook his head. 'They wouldn't be from around here, and that's for sure. Passing through on their way to the seaports down south, no doubt.'

'For what reason would they be headed to the coast?'

'Why, for the king's campaign, lad,' Godfrey explained, not impatiently. 'They are most likely *crucesignati*. Which is your Latin for them that have taken the cross, so to speak, and answered the call to go off and fight against them bloody infidels in the Holy Land, as payback for what the buggers done to Jerusalem and the One True Cross. Not that some of them filthy devils of ours is any better than them godless Saracens, mind. Looting and pillaging all the way along their journey, taking the good lives with the bad.' He spat in the dirt, turning first to direct it well away from the grave. 'Fucking scum. Lord forgive me for saying it.'

'Then,' Will said, 'that means I have to catch up with them before they reach the south coast. Is it very far?'

'Oh, quite a way, some days' ride. But you'd best get going without delay. That is,' Godfrey added, 'if you can abide the travelling. You ain't looking so healthy, lad. And I would give the whole matter some thought, if I were you. This ain't going to be no easy task. Many's the man who would shy from it, knowing he most likely ain't coming back.'

'I can make it,' Will replied. 'And I mean to be on my way as soon as I can. Today. But I must ask your help, Godfrey. There are things I need for my journey.'

*

Beatrice was laid to rest that afternoon, her burial attended by Mother Matilda, Sister Edith and a small gathering of other residents of the abbey. It was a solemn moment and there were many tears, including those that trickled down the abbess' portly cheeks as she spoke the appropriate words in Latin over the grave. Sister Edith hung her head and did all she could to restrain her sobs, while Will stood in grim silence and made not a sound.

The last funeral he had been to was that of his father, buried in the cemetery in Foxwood. Never would he have thought he would attend that of another of his family so soon, if ever.

The ceremonial words that Mother Matilda spoke had no meaning for him, but he understood that they were an important part of sending Beatrice off to the heavenly haven where she would spend eternity. Perhaps one day, he thought, he might join her there, unless God had other plans for him.

Soon after the burial was over, the abbey bells began to ring again to signal Nones, mid-afternoon prayers. Sister Edith gave Will a teary smile as she hurried off with the other nuns, clutching at the skirts of her habit to keep the hem from trailing in the dirt. He supposed that he would never see her again, though he would always remember her friendship.

'Mother Matilda,' he said to the abbess, 'I can never thank you enough for what you have done for Beatrice and me. I'm forever in your debt. But now I must take my leave.'

'All we have done is what any good Christian would do,' she replied. 'As to your leaving us, do you not think you should remain with us for a few days at least, until your strength returns? You are far from recovered, I see. But I sense that your mind is made up, and once that happens you cannot easily be dissuaded. I shall look forward to seeing you again soon.'

He shook his head and ignored the jolt of pain that shot behind his eyes from the movement. 'I am going far away and will not likely be coming back, Reverend Mother. There is nothing for me here now. All I leave behind is my little patch of land, and I would like to give it over to Wexby Abbey. Will you accept it from me? I ask for nothing in return.'

The abbess looked at him fondly. 'Rest assured it will be well tended to, and will be there for you should you ever decide to come back from your travels. As to the future, dear William, only God knows what lies in store for any of us. But whatever direction you choose to take, you have my blessing and my love. Take care of yourself, my child.'

Later that same afternoon Godfrey drove Will back to the ruins of the homestead in the abbey's horse-drawn wagon. It was hard seeing the place again, and even harder to think he might be doing so for the last time. So much had changed in the course of a single day.

Will's purpose in returning here had been only to retrieve his bow and arrow quiver. He found them among the debris, either undiscovered or ignored by the raiders. They had left nothing else behind, save for a few chicken feathers strewn about and the entrails and bones of the slaughtered oxen, now covered in flies and beginning to stink in the warm sun. There were not even enough scraps left to use as provisions to see Will on his way. The outbuilding where he had his workshop was still standing, and he was able to retrieve his bag of arrowheads and a selection of unmade shafts and goose feathers. But with the rest of his and Beatrice's meagre possessions now buried under the burnt-out wreckage of their home, he would be journeying virtually empty-handed – or so he thought, until to his surprise, Godfrey reached under the seat of the wagon and produced a large, finely made leather satchel that was bulging from its packed contents.

'Sister Edith asked me to give you this. Told me to wish you Godspeed and good luck.'

Will undid the brass-buckled fastenings and found to his amazement that the good nun had packed provisions and other necessaries for his travels. There was a warm woollen blanket carefully rolled up, inside which were a leather flask for water, a small wooden box containing flint and tinder, a copper cooking pot, some strips of dried meat and several apples and a draw-string pouch holding a modest handful of silver pennies, more money than Will would habitually spend in months. 'The nuns had a bit of a whip-round for that,' Godfrey told him.

'Bless them,' Will said, deeply moved. 'These things will serve me well on the road.'

'Still, four legs is better than two,' Godfrey said doubtfully. 'I'd gladly let you have this here horse and wagon, if they was mine to give.'

'I know that,' Will replied. 'And I thank you all for your kindness. Farewell, Godfrey.'

Will stood and watched as the wagon rattled away down the track and disappeared around the bend. Then he took a deep breath, slung his quiver and the leather satchel over his shoulder, gripped the unstrung stave of his bow like a walking staff, and took the first step of the greatest, longest and most dangerous journey of his life.

Chapter 5

Setting off at a good pace, Will descended the track back down to the road and followed it the way he would have for Wexby Abbey, before turning onto a narrower lane that he travelled less often but which he knew would take him in the direction of Clanfield. Walking briskly, he expected he could reach it in little more time than his old mare would have taken to carry him there. It was now late afternoon; he hoped to cover a good distance before nightfall.

As dusk approached, his road gradually veered away westwards towards where the sun was dipping behind the hills. Will turned off it and instead followed the course of the river, keeping the sunset on his right in order to maintain his southerly bearing. Thirsty from his long walk, he ventured down the reedy riverbank to the water's edge to fill the leather water flask that Sister Edith had given him. He was fortunate to have such friends, and with every step he felt more bereft of their kindness and support.

Presently the river merged into Little Clanfield Brook, where two mills sat by the water's edge spaced a quarter mile apart, their great wooden wheels slowly creaking around with the gentle current and paddles slapping the surface. To the south of the second mill he came to a broad, uncultivated meadow where rabbits darted to and fro in the failing light. He had eaten almost nothing all day, and though the hunger was sharp enough to pierce even his deep unhappiness, he knew he must preserve his supply of dried meat for when fresh game might be hard to find. Pausing in his stride he strung his bow and drew an arrow from his quiver.

Moments later, the largest of the rabbits that had lacked the good sense to run back to their burrow was lying pierced through by his hunting broadhead shaft. Will waded the sixty paces through the long grass to retrieve his catch. He plucked out the arrow and looped the rabbit onto his belt with one hind leg threaded through a slit in the other, first squeezing out the creature's bladder to prevent its contents dribbling down his breeches as he carried it. Then he unstrung the bow and continued on his way.

Darkness fell, promising a starless, moonless night with the threat of rain. Will was loath to stop and make camp, wanting to cover as much distance as possible. He had made reasonable progress that day, a dozen miles or more, but a man on foot had little hope of keeping pace with horse riders unless he travelled without a rest, and he was anxious to keep going. Soon, though, the moonless night grew so dark that he was stumbling over ruts and risked spraining an ankle, while the lack of a single visible star in the inky sky made it all but impossible for him to orientate himself towards the south. In the end he reluctantly settled for the night in a copse of oak and beech trees.

The warmth of the day had dwindled sharply and a chilly wind was blowing from the east, a reminder of the winter not long since past. He used Sister Edith's flint and tinder to make his blaze of dry twigs, then cut a pair of forked greenwood branches to use as a cooking stand and a long skewer to rest across them and roast the skinned, cleaned rabbit over the fire. *Lent be damned*, he thought.

While he waited for his meal to cook, he turned his attention to his arrows. All that day, as he had been walking, he had been troubled by the memory of how that first shot he had fired at the soldier had failed to penetrate his chain mail. Sure enough, as he now sat examining the heads of his arrows by the light of the flames it dawned on him that the iron rings of his opponent's hauberk were too closely interlinked to be easily pierced by the broad, sharp swallow-tailed triangular points that he favoured for hunting his usual quarry of rabbits, hares and the like. That explained why the arrow had simply shattered on impact, causing his enemy no more than a momentary anxiety. Even more dismally ineffective against such armour would be the twin-pronged, crescent-shaped heads, called 'forkers', that were used for hunting birds.

'That won't do,' Will muttered to himself. He rummaged through the bag of loose arrowheads that he had retrieved from his workshop and to his satisfaction, among the selection that the Foxwood smithy had fashioned for him in his forge were a good number of bodkin heads with their longer needle-pointed taper. Will had previously found these to be over-penetrative for hunting small game and had discarded them with the intention of asking the smithy to melt them back down to reconvert into broadheads. He was glad now that he'd kept them, because there was little doubt that the power of his longbow could send these lancing through anything short of solid iron.

Godfrey might have been right in pointing out Will's inexperience in serious combat, but already an important lesson had been learned for the apprentice warrior: that failure to match his ammunition to his target was a deadly weakness that could all too easily prove fatal to him, next time he came face to face with his enemy.

As the rabbit sizzled and turned golden brown over the fire, working by the flickering light of the flames Will used the spine edge of his knife blade to gently tap off and remove the broadheads from all sixteen of his remaining arrows. One by one he then carefully replaced them with the long-needle bodkins. By the time he was done, not only did he feel much better equipped to deal with whatever he might encounter at the end of his quest, but his meal was cooked.

The spit-roasted rabbit was succulent and tender but in his black mood he took no pleasure in it and ate purely for sustenance, barely even tasting the meat as it went down. Then as his fire died, he wrapped himself up in Sister Edith's warm blanket and fell into a fitful sleep. Twice he was awoken by the yammering of wolves, the second time so close by that he readied his bow and kept it to hand with an arrow fitted for the remainder of the night.

Come the first silvery-grey light of dawn, waking damp and cold from a light overnight rainfall and troubled by his dreams that only brought his grief back tenfold, he packed up his things and moved on again. Sometimes his way took him along roads used by other traffic, sometimes along empty country lanes and over wooden footbridges that spanned the meandering rivers; or else his course led him across fields and meadows, over green hills and through shady wooded valleys where the wild boar had made tracks and paths among the bracken and brambles.

Late in the morning he arrived at the village of Radcot, a place he had once visited as a boy with his father. The village sat on the Thames River, which his father had told him had once marked the border between the ancient kingdoms of Wessex and Mercia. His father had known all those kinds of things. In modern times the river separated Will's home county of Oxfordshire from neighbouring Berkshire, into which he now must pass on his way southwards. By so doing, he was about to venture further away from Foxwood than he had ever done in his life.

As he neared the river, he found a scene of bustling activity where the local people, assisted by craftsmen and stonemasons, were laying the foundations for a great new stone bridge. Wooden towers had been erected over the water to drive the piles deep into the muddy riverbed, after which huge cut stones suspended by nets of rope were now being carefully lowered into position. Everywhere, masons were chipping and chiselling, carpenters were building, wagons were arriving with fresh loads of quarried stone, workers of all kinds milling around each with their job to do. Will would normally have stopped and talked to people as was his natural inclination, and most likely would have volunteered to linger a while and lend his strength to some of the more laborious tasks. But he was in too great a hurry and his heart was too heavy to enter into conversation, so he kept walking on by. A little way further down the riverbank he came to a wooden pontoon bridge that the workers had built, and slipped across without anyone seeing.

The sun had been shining brightly for some hours, but early in the afternoon more murky clouds rolled in to blot out its rays, and it wasn't long before the rain was lashing down to soak Will through and turn the road into mud. The further he walked, the slower the going seemed to become and the more frustrated he became by his rate of travel.

'You'll never catch up with them at this pace,' he told himself. 'That's if you're even going in the right direction.' Refusing to let his doubts overwhelm him he pressed on anyway. The soldiers with their black eagle coat of arms were constantly in his mind's eye as he revisualised the attack on the homestead, over and over. He could see their faces behind their helmets, hear their harsh laughter and the crackle of the flames and the agitated snorting and whinnying of their horses.

Who were they, he kept wondering: men-at-arms like those who served Sir Robert de Bray at Foxwood manor? Did their lord know his vassals were conducting marauding attacks against defenceless country dwellers as they made their way south? Or had he been there himself, as commander of the raiding party?

Late afternoon had come round once again by the time the rain finally subsided. By now his weariness was beginning to get the better of him, and he plodded along a waterlogged road bordered by dense forest in the knowledge that it was leading him off his southerly course, but lacking the energy to leave it and venture through the dark woods. Now that he was in unknown country, he had little idea of where he was and could only depend on the road leading him to the next town or village where he might be able to ask the locals for better directions. Dusk was already beginning to close in on the second day of his journey and so far he had nothing to show for it except weary feet and a steadily sinking heart.

He was rounding a sharp bend in the road, part obscured by low-hanging tree branches and deep shadows, when he heard the sound of a voice up ahead – the first living soul he had encountered since the crowd of workers at Radcot Bridge that morning. As he came further around the bend, peering ahead through the dwindling light he saw that the voice belonged to an old peasant man leading a donkey by a rope halter. The animal was heavily laden with bundles of firewood sticks and the old man was cursing violently at it as he tried in vain to urge it to move faster. It appeared that the donkey had made up its mind to the contrary and planted itself in the middle of the road, refusing to go another step. The harder its owner yanked and tugged at its lead rope, the more stubbornly it resisted.

'Excuse me, sir,' Will said politely, approaching them. 'Can you tell me where this road is leading?'

The old man stopped tugging the rope and turned to peer guardedly at the tall stranger walking up to him in the dusky light. 'Why, don't you even know where you are a-going?' He pointed back down the road in the direction he had come. 'That is the way to Faringdon, in the Vale of the White Horse.'

Will had heard of the market town, but it was so far outside his familiar domains that the name sounded quite foreign to him. 'Is it far from here?' he asked, and the old man snorted derisively.

'You are quite lost, aren't you, stranger? Then you'll be glad to know that the town is not two miles distant. And I would aim to get within the safety of its walls sooner than later if I was you. There's talk of dangerous folk at large in these parts. Keep your wits sharp and whatever you do, do not stray from the road.'

'These dangerous folk you speak of, would they be soldiers?' Will asked, feeling a surge of anticipation. 'I seek a troop of men on horseback, travelling south. They wear a lord's livery marked with a black eagle.'

The old man shook his head. 'Can't say as I have seen any soldiers around here lately, black eagle or no. Brigands, I'm a-meaning. Them Colvin brothers, and other outlaw gangs that make easy prey of travellers and pilgrims passing through.

One was robbed only last week in these very woods' – pointing a bony finger at the darkness of the forest – 'and the bloody villains took his purse with near a hundred pennies in it and sliced the poor devil's ear off for his trouble, I hear tell. But I see you are well armed,' he added, eyeing Will's bow stave and the arrow quiver on his shoulder. 'And you are a hefty enough fellow to look after yourself, I reckon.'

'I shall be careful,' Will said, disappointed and yet strangely relieved at the news about the black eagle soldiers. He desperately wanted to find them, but the thought of facing up to them in his present weary and demoralised state was deeply unsettling.

'And where might you be heading, alone and lost in a strange county, young traveller?' the old man asked him.

'Unless I first catch up with the men I seek, my destination is the seaports on the south coast,' Will replied. 'Though I do not know which one.'

'I will not ask you what business you have with these men,' the oldster said. 'But you have a fair long road ahead of you and you should hasten on your way, as I must do myself if I am to have any chance of getting home tonight. Come on, you ugly brute,' he said to the donkey, jerking impatiently at its halter rope.

Will was grateful for the old man's information, but he hated to see such a placid and good-natured animal so roughly treated. He stepped past the old man and delicately stroked the donkey's neck, running his fingers over its bristly, erect mane and whispering soft reassuring words in its ear.

'What are you saying to my beast?' the old man demanded suspiciously.

'Telling him not to be afraid,' Will replied. 'He dislikes being handled that way. Act gently towards him and reward his loyal service to you, and he will be more agreeable to follow wherever you lead him.'

Sure enough, the donkey allowed himself to be led off without resistance as the old man went on his way, muttering to himself about these fucking youngsters who thought they knew better than their elders, and what was the world a-coming to in this day and age. Will watched them disappear into the darkness, then turned back towards Faringdon and continued walking. 'Very well,' he said to himself. 'We've managed to come a good way south. That's something, at least.'

But as it turned out, Will wouldn't reach the town that night. He had scarcely walked fifty paces before the rain began again, pelting down more heavily than ever and rapidly soaking through his tunic and running in rivulets through his hair and down his face. Soon afterwards he saw the warm, welcoming light glowing from the windows of a roadside inn, and decided to take shelter there. 'Only for a short while,' he told himself. He had his little money pouch containing the pennies the nuns had given him, and he thought God would forgive him for permitting himself just a small cup of ale to fortify him on his journey.

Will couldn't have known it then, but his decision to stop at the inn would soon turn out to be the most important he had made since leaving Foxwood.

Chapter 6

The entrance to the inn was low and framed with ivy, and candle lanterns flickering on each side of the studded oak door seemed to beckon him inside. Will hesitated, feeling a momentary doubt as he heard the sound of lively conversation and hearty laughter coming from within. He didn't know if he felt up to the company of his fellow men just yet.

As he stood wavering undecidedly, he glanced around the stable yard that stood to the side of the inn. Horses peered curiously out from their stalls and a pair of smaller ponies were tethered under a lean-to shelter, heads lowered and munching from a trough. A rickety wooden cart stood unhitched nearby, glistening from the rain. Streams of water spattered from the eaves of the thatched roofs and ran in rivers over the ground. The inn ostler, a young lad of about fifteen who had been tending to the horses, appeared from behind the stables and ran across the yard to take refuge from the downpour.

If Will were to stay out here any longer, he would be soaked through to the skin. Making his decision he pushed through the inn door, having to duck his head for the low lintel. The warmth enveloped him as he stepped inside. The interior of the inn was one large room, with a wide inglenook fireplace at one end. A haze of fire and candle smoke drifted among the thick oak ceiling beams. A few faces turned to look at him as he entered, and the burr of conversation faltered momentarily. Some men were sitting on bare bench seats at trestle tables, more of them over by the fireplace, others perched on stools at the long bar where the innkeeper and a stout younger woman with flaxen hair were serving ale in wooden tankards to their eager customers, who were clearly not observing Lent as assiduously as they might. Most of the drinkers appeared to know each other well, judging by the level of familiar chatter in the place; Will guessed that the inn must double as a tavern for local clientele as well as passing travellers. Another customer aside from Will obviously belonged to the second grouping: an elderly man in a loose brown hooded robe sitting alone in an alcove seat. He seemed detached from the rest of the company as he concentrated on his bowl of pottage stew, spooning it down as though it were his first meal in days.

Will had seldom frequented taverns in his younger days, and never once since his marriage. Feeling somewhat awkward and even less sure about bringing a weapon into the place, he unslung his satchel and quiver, set them down on the sawdust floor and propped his bow stave in a corner by the entrance. A couple of the drinkers sitting hunched over their tankards at the far end of the bar had interrupted their conversation to stare at him in a not entirely friendly manner. One was thick and large, his hair and beard long, greasy and black; while his companion was weaselly and scrawny, with a squinty eye and a look about him as though he were not quite right in his head. Will thought neither of them had a very agreeable air, and he didn't return their gaze as he approached the other end of the bar. The innkeeper, a much more friendly fellow with a balding head and thick, droopy whiskers, bade him good evening.

'What can I do for you, friend? A hot meal and a room on this dreary wet night? My son will take care of your mount. We've plenty of stabling and good clean hay and straw.'

Will replied that he was travelling on foot and not planning on stopping long. 'But I would welcome a tankard of good ale, perhaps some warm stew and a chance to dry myself a while by your fire.' He laid a coin from his pouch on the counter.

'Elspeth,' the innkeeper told the flaxen-haired serving wench, 'a pot of ale for the gentleman.' To Will he said, 'I don't believe we've had the pleasure of welcoming you to this establishment before, young stranger. And what would be your name?'

Will settled on a stool by the bar and gratefully accepted his ale from the smiling maid. The brew was tepid and bitter but refreshing enough, and he drank down a long swallow before he replied, 'My name is Will. I'm not from around here. Travelling south.'

'I have family down Swindon way,' the innkeeper said, by way of small talk.

Will hadn't intended to strike up a conversation with anyone, but now he thought perhaps he might learn something more of use here. 'I don't know if my journey will take me near Swindon,' he said, 'or how far I must travel. I follow the trail of a group of riders.'

'Riders, eh?' the innkeeper replied, raising an eyebrow. 'And you being on foot? Pardon me for enquiring.'

'Men at arms,' Will said, 'bearing on their shields the mark of a black eagle. They were at Foxwood two days ago, and if they are headed south as I suppose, they might have passed through this area today or yesterday.'

The innkeeper looked thoughtful and scratched his chin. 'A black eagle,' he repeated. He looked about to shake his head and say nobody of that description had been seen locally, when one of the men seated at a nearby trestle table, his ears having pricked up at their conversation, said knowingly, 'Soldiers riding south? Aye, there's a good deal of that going on these days. They'd be journeying to one of the ports on the coast is my guess. Joining the rest of the army there, to set sail aboard the king's fleet.'

'You know of them?' Will asked, setting down his tankard and turning round.

The man gave a shrug. 'Of a black eagle? Not to speak of. But they are coming from all over. What stone do you live under, not to have heard of it?'

'There's no need for rude talk,' the innkeeper warned the man, pointing a finger. To Will he said, 'Sounds to me as though these soldiers of yours have been causing trouble. Not that it is any of my business.'

Will only nodded, not wanting to say too much. But by now the discussion had been overheard by some of the other men sitting over by the fireplace and seemed to be drawing the interest of one of them in particular, who got up from his seat and came over. He was a middle-aged man with a strong look about him and the lean and weathered features from a lifetime of hard work in the fields.

'Percy Naldrett is my name,' he told Will. 'I have a cousin, John Babcock, over in Thatcham and have just returned from there. That is my cart outside. He told me that a band of soldiers have been raiding and pillaging from villagers, burning homes and carrying off livestock. Only yesterday morning John's sister's husband was killed trying to prevent them from firing his barns.'

'He was killed?' Will said.

Percy Naldrett gave a grim nod. 'Arabel is John's sister's name. She watched it happen. Her husband was called Adam Foreman. Took his head clean off his shoulders they did, with a single sword stroke. And not a thing the bailiff will do about it, most likely, them being in service to a noble.'

'These were soldiers in armour, mounted on horses?' Will asked. A chill was rising through him, despite the warmth inside the room.

Percy Naldrett nodded again. 'Arabel said they wore the same sign that you speak of, marked on their shields and on their person. A black bird, with a curved beak and a long tail.'

'The tail forked, like this?' Will used his fingers to show. His hand was shaking. There could be no doubt that these had to be the same men. The black eagle soldiers were cutting a swathe of destruction everywhere they went. 'And you say this happened only yesterday.' He tried to think where Thatcham was, to get an idea of the soldiers' route and how far ahead of him they were. He asked Percy Naldrett, 'Who are they, do you know?'

'I can't say if what I heard is true,' the man replied. 'But folks reckoned they hailed from up north. Their lord's estate is in Derbyshire, according to some. They are on their way south to join King Richard for his journey to Outremer.'

Will had never heard of such a place. 'Where is that?'

The innkeeper, who had been leaning on the bar listening with great interest, said, 'Why, the Holy Land, of course. Where our Lord Jesus came down from Heaven and died for our sins. The king is sailing off to take back Jerusalem from them wicked heathen Saracens that stole it from us three years back, along with the One True Cross. A dark day that was.'

This brought a scornful grunt from one of the men sitting along the bar from Will, portly and grey-haired, with a foaming pot of ale and a cold leg of chicken on a platter in front of him. 'Ay, marching off to war in all their finery, flying their fancy flags and banners,' he muttered sourly. 'And who's to pay for it all, I ask you? Us, that's who, thanks to King Richard's bloody Saladin tithe. A tenth part of all our hard-earned pay he wants to rack from us in taxes, on top of what we give him already? Why, that's like asking for . . .' he hunted around for the appropriate simile, and as it came to him he held up his greasy hands in indignation. 'Like asking for one of your ten fingers to be cut off. It's a fucking disgrace, I tell 'ee. How's a poor man supposed to care for his children, with a parcel of thieving rogues taking the food out of their mouths?' He emphasised his point by picking up his chicken leg and tearing off a large chunk with his teeth. 'Eight hundred sides of cured bacon I hear tell the king collected from one county alone to feed the army on the way to Jerusalem, worth more than fifty-eight pounds and eighteen shillings. Along with a hundredweight of cheese and ten thousand horseshoes. Ten thousand!'

'Since when can you eat a horseshoe?' piped up someone else.

'You ain't had my wife's cooking,' came the reply from another corner, and there was a good deal of laughter.

'Now, Hubert Brickenden, if I was you I'd be more careful what I said about the king in here,' scolded the innkeeper, shooting the portly man a stern look.

The shifty-looking pair at the end of the bar, who had been giving Will unfriendly looks and since returned to their own private conversation, were staying out of the discussion. But another man sitting between them and Hubert Brickenden chimed in, 'I hear tell there's been riots over the tax. Folks who won't pay rounded up and clapped in irons, put out of their homes, flogged in the streets.'

'But someone must put an end to that devil Saladin's capers before he invades England,' said another man at the nearby trestle table. 'Mark my words, he will, if we give him half a chance.'

'Ballocks,' snapped Hubert Brickenden, and he snatched up his tankard and gulped down his ale so vehemently that it ran down his chin.

'He's right,' argued one of the men with whom Percy Naldrett had been sitting by the fireside. 'I say you don't like paying for the army, you could always go off an' join 'em. Wouldn't have to pay the tax, then.'

'And what's more, we'd be rid of the old sodomite once and for all, I reckon,' laughed the man sitting next to him.

'A bunch of damned fools, the lot of you,' rasped Hubert Brickenden, and turned his back on them in disgust.

'I'm not saying they shouldn't ride off to protect the Holy Land,' Percy Naldrett said angrily. 'But they ain't got no call raiding farms and villages in their own country, have they? What's my cousin's sister going to do for a husband now?'

The debate that Will had unwittingly sparked off was now being loudly argued all around the inn. Apart from the shifty-looking pair at the bar, the only other person disengaged from it was the elderly man in the brown robe sitting finishing his meal alone. But Will was barely listening to them either, as thoughts churned through his mind. *Then Godfrey was right,* he told himself urgently, *and I have to catch them before they reach the south coast*. Once the soldiers boarded those ships bound for faraway lands, he would lose all chance of ever finding them. He was gripped by panic, sensing his enemies getting further away with every passing moment while he wasted time here chattering. 'You say your cousin John lives at Thatcham,' he said to Percy Naldrett, gripping his elbow. 'Tell me how to get there. Is it far?'

'Thirty miles due south of here,' Percy replied. 'Took me all day with a good horse. By the time a man reached there on foot they would be halfway to the coast.'

'Then I need a horse,' Will thought out loud.

'I have one for sale,' Percy said. 'But can you afford the price?'

'All I have in the world is what is in this purse,' Will said. He tipped the remaining coins out on the bar top.

Percy shook his head. 'God help you. That wouldn't pay for a clapped-out nag from the knacker's yard, let alone a fine animal like mine. Sorry, son. Looks like you are on foot, after all. But tell me, if you did catch those men—'

'I seek revenge against them for what they did in Foxwood.'

'Then I am doing you a favour by not selling you my horse,' Percy said. 'Men like that would kill you soon as look at you.' He clapped Will on the shoulder. 'Go home, son. Make your peace and live your life.'

While they had been talking, the older man in the long brown robe had finished his meal, gathered up his things and left, signalling to the innkeeper on his way out to have the young lad fetch his pony. The pair at the bar whom Will hadn't liked the look of had also departed soon afterwards, though nobody seemed to notice or care much about them. And now it was time for Will to leave too and continue his journey with all possible haste. He drained down the last of his ale and thanked the innkeeper for his hospitality. Then he gathered up his satchel, quiver and bow, and hurried out of the inn.

And it was in the yard outside that he heard the commotion, and saw with a shock what was happening.

Chapter 7

Now that the rain had cleared and the moon was again shining through the clouds, Will could plainly see the scene that was rapidly unfolding in the stable yard. The traveller in the brown robe had been waiting there for the ostler to prepare his pony for the onward journey. But he wasn't alone, because it appeared that the shifty-looking pair who had slipped away from the inn at the same moment had had a particular motive for doing so: they had secretly been keeping a watchful eye on the lone traveller with criminal intentions the whole time he had been sitting eating his dinner, waiting for their opportunity; and now they had seized this moment to accost him.

The elderly man let out a muffled cry of fright as the long-haired, bearded ruffian grabbed hold of him, pinning his frail, weak arms helplessly to his sides and clapping a big powerful hand over his mouth to stifle his protests while his squinty-eyed scrawny companion began searching the old man's robe to rob him of his purse. A long, pointed dagger blade gleamed in the moonlight. 'Where is it?' rasped a harsh voice. 'Come on, you old bastard, let's have your money!'

They were both too intent on stealing the traveller's silver to have noticed Will emerge from the inn. He froze rock-still where he stood in the shadows and watched them for a second, but that was as long as he hesitated.

At any other time in the past, Will would have unhesitatingly rushed to the aid of any vulnerable person in distress or under attack, even if it meant putting himself at serious risk. Now, seeing the two robbers brutally overpowering the defenceless elderly man at knifepoint multiplied his natural instinct to protect the innocent a thousandfold and sent an overwhelming rush of horror through his mind and body. He was instantly transported back to the moment when the soldiers had attacked Beatrice. He could see them dragging her from the barn, could hear her screams and their laughter, the roar of the flames and the whinnying of the horses. Then his horror turned to pure rage, every muscle and sinew in his body became as taut as his own bowstring under full draw, and without an instant's further thought he exploded into action.

Dropping his satchel and quiver he raced across the stable yard and cannoned with all his weight and force into the scrawny robber, sending him sprawling to the ground as though he'd been kicked by both back hooves of a carthorse. As the scrawny one scrabbled half-stunned in the dirt, his hairy companion let out a roar of outrage and wheeled away from Will, clutching his victim tightly against his chest and holding the dagger to his throat. 'I'll cut him!' he shouted.

'Let him go,' Will told him. 'Or it's you who will get hurt.' The scrawny one was trying to scramble to his feet. With barely a glance, Will swung his bow stave at him and the seasoned yew shaft caught him with a resonating crack above the bridge of his nose, knocking him senseless. He collapsed back down to the dirt and Will trampled over the top of him, advancing towards the other.

'I said let him go,' Will repeated. 'Heed my words, as there will be no third warning.'

But the bearded robber chose to ignore the first two. There was a glimmer of madness in his eyes as he retreated from Will, pulling the old man along with him and keeping the edge of the blade against his neck. He continued stumbling away backwards with his hostage until he reached the end wall of the stable building and no longer had anywhere to run. He was desperate now, cut off from any route of escape and with no option but to carry out his threat. 'I mean it! I'll kill him!'

Then the warning was fulfilled, and the robber's threatening growl became a high-pitched screech of pain as the horned end of Will's bow stave stabbed towards him faster than he could react and poked him in the left eye. The dagger dropped from his fist and his grip relaxed on the old man, and he threw up both hands to cover his injured eye, howling like the poor doomed pigs when the butcher in Foxwood put them to the slaughter.

Will reached out to grasp the old man's arm and pull him away to safety. Then closing in on the robber he battered his head twice against the stable wall, seized hold of his beard, used it to jerk his head downwards and drove an upward knee into the middle of his face. Any resistance the man might still have been able to muster was knocked completely out of him by the blow. Blood gushed bright and red from his shattered nose and damaged eye, and he collapsed to his knees, gasping and muttering incoherently.

Will picked up the fallen dagger and pressed the tip of its blade against the man's neck. In his mind he could still see the soldiers. He could still hear her screams; and then as the picture altered the vision became that of her lifeless eyes gazing up at him, her limp body in his arms, her shrouded figure being placed inside its grave. His sight became blurred with tears and all he could think of was his desire for revenge, if not against her killers at this moment, then against any malevolent wrongdoer he could get his hands on.

He could so easily have killed the robber in that moment: driven the point of the dagger through his neck, ignoring his screams and his pleas for mercy, feeling the blood welling from the wound and the life ebbing out of him. But then the fog of rage that had threatened to take control of Will's actions began to dissipate as quickly as it had risen, and he blinked like a person waking from a bad dream, withdrew the dagger and tossed it away into the bushes. 'You are not worth killing. Take your companion and get out of my sight. Don't ever come back here again.'

As the robber went limping and bleeding over to pick up his crony and half-carry, half-drag him away, Will turned towards the traveller. The old man was leaning against the wall of the inn, recovering his breath.

'Are you all right?' Will asked him. He felt quite shaken himself, not from the exertion of the fight but from having so nearly given in to a dark and dangerous side of his own inner nature he hadn't, until that moment, even known to exist. It frightened him to imagine what he might have been capable of, if his better judgement had not regained hold of him when it had.

'Thanks to you, I am,' the old man replied in a quavering voice. 'I thought they were going to kill me.'

'You're safe now,' Will told him. At that moment the young ostler reappeared, leading the pony. He seemed quite unaware of what had happened while he had been attending to his duties inside the stable.

'My name is Father Michael,' said the old man, holding out his hand. 'What is yours, my friend?'

'Where I come from people call me Will the bowman,' Will said. 'But I'm a long way from home.'

'You have the look of someone who has journeyed some distance,' said Father Michael.

'As do you, Father. You're a priest?'

'A travelling friar,' Father Michael replied. 'I too am on a journey. I set off twenty days ago on a pilgrimage to the faraway Kingdom of León.'

'I have never been there,' Will said, having not the faintest idea where it might even be. 'I've never been anywhere. This is the furthest I have ever ventured from the place where I was born.' Then a thought came to him. 'But tell me, Father – to get to this kingdom you speak of, you must be heading south through England? Towards the coast, where the great shipping ports are?'

'I believe it is necessary to do so, in order to leave these shores and venture across the sea,' the friar replied with a kindly smile. 'Then once safely landed in Normandy I plan to continue south, passing through the regions of Anjou, Poitou, our good King Richard's realms of Aquitaine and then Gascony before crossing into the Kingdom of Navarre and turning west. God willing, by the time autumn comes I plan to have reached Galletia in the Kingdom of León.'

'You know the way, then,' said Will, for whom these exotic names meant very little indeed, and held just as much interest. But the first part of the friar's long journey, the road southward through England, was one that concerned him a great deal.

'I have travelled much the same route once before, many years ago. I still remember what path to follow. Or most of it, at any rate. Age has not entirely clouded my recollection.'

'I am headed in the same direction,' Will said. 'Though not nearly as far. Will your journey happen to take you by Thatcham way?'

'Thatcham, Thatcham. Let me think.' The old man pondered a few moments. He had obviously been quite oblivious of the earlier discussion inside the inn, lost deep in his own thoughts. 'Why, I believe it lies more or less south of Faringdon, and a little to the east, the other side of the forests, hills and valleys of the North Wessex Downs. In which case, to be sure it must lie close to my itinerary, or not too distant from it. Do you have business in Thatcham? Family, perhaps?'

'I have no family,' Will replied evasively. 'Not any longer. But business, yes, of a kind. In any event that is the first point of my journey, perhaps the last though I cannot be sure. And, if you will accept my company, I hope that I might be able to travel with you at least that far.' It suddenly seemed as though this chance meeting had been a great stroke of luck, if only the friar would agree to his proposal.

'I would gladly welcome a travelling companion,' said the friar with a warm smile. 'A fellow pilgrim to talk to on the lonely road, and moreover one who is worthy and brave, bright of eye, quick of wit, polite and well spoken and doesn't wear his hair and beard long and ragged in the goatlike fashion of so many of you young men. We would need some extra provisions for the journey, of course.'

'Much of that I can provide myself,' Will said. 'I have some skill at hunting with the bow and there's always fresh quarry to be had, if you know where to look.'

'So much the better. And I'm sure we can find you a horse, something appropriate to a fellow of your size. My little mare, Llamrei, would be far too small for you.'

'That might be a problem, as I have no money for one,' Will admitted, realising that in his sudden burst of enthusiasm he'd overlooked one crucial detail. 'My own pony was taken from me, along with . . . with everything I had.' He looked down at his feet, not wanting to say more.

'No matter. There are a few silver pennies in my purse,' Father Michael replied benevolently. 'For which fact I am very much in your debt, or else I don't know how I could have continued on my journey, had those villains had their way. I will ask the innkeeper if he knows of an animal for sale. You can always pay me back later, if it pleases you.'

It soon transpired that the innkeeper did indeed know of a horse for sale, and very locally, as the tall chestnut gelding in question belonged to his brother who lived only a little way down the road and was happy to make the exchange that very same night. Better still, the vendor being short of money, the canny Father Michael was able to negotiate the asking price down to far less than Percy Naldrett would have charged Will, and with saddle and tack included in the deal.

'He is a very handsome creature,' said the friar, admiring the chestnut in the moonlit stable yard once the sale had been made and the innkeeper's brother had gone off happily with his handful of silver pennies. 'Though much too tall for a man of my meagre stature. We will name him Hengroen, as a companion to Llamrei if only for a short while.'

'I don't know how to thank you for him,' said Will, who had never owned a horse of such quality before and was extremely moved by his new friend's generosity. It made him think back to Wexby Abbey and the dear kind souls he had left behind.

'You earned him, Will, by your courage and your readiness to offer help to a stranger in need. True Christian virtue is always rewarded, in this life as in the next.

'Now,' Father Michael went on more matter-of-factly, 'it had been my intention to ride onwards a few miles tonight and make my camp somewhere along the road. But the hour being now so late and with so many thieves and cut-throats about, as it seems, I propose that we remain here within the safe confines of the inn and delay our departure until the morning. I will treat you to another pot of ale and some of the innkeeper's hot food to fill your belly. If you do not mind my saying so, you look as if you need it. Then at first light, refreshed and with a hearty breakfast under our belts, we shall resume our journey southwards together.'

Chapter 8

And that is just what they did. As the cockerel noisily welcomed the first rays of the rising sun, the innkeeper who had obligingly kept his kitchen fires lit until late the night before now provided the travellers with an early breakfast of ale, bread and cheese, the latter of which luxuries Father Michael was strictly avoiding as a voluntary penance until the evening of the Lord's Supper. Meanwhile the innkeeper's son saddled Llamrei and Hengroen, and as Will and Father Michael emerged into the grey morning light feeling fortified and ready for a long day's ride ahead, they found the horses waiting for them in the stable yard. The little mare carried Father Michael's modest pack and saddlebags. Will would be travelling with only his satchel and quiver, his water flask attached to the good leather saddle that had come with his horse and his bow strung loosely across his back.

Setting off with no further delay they continued southwards on the Faringdon road, then bypassed the small town and deviated cross country through green rolling hills and patches of forest, always watching the path of the sun to ensure they were aiming south. Father Michael talked continuously as they went, pointing out features of the landscape and educating Will on the history of the area.

'I lived near here as a boy. Do you see that tall mound of a hill there, to the west of those trees? Once there stood a fine big castle in that spot. It was built by Robert Earl of Gloucester for Empress Maud in the year forty-five, when I was around the same age you are now. It was the time of the Anarchy, you know. A very terrible period of suffering. Then the following year, as the Queen occupied the fort, King Stephen's army, who had already ravaged the castle at Radcot two years earlier, attacked and captured it. Nothing remains now but the scars of its foundations on the hillside.' The friar shook his head sadly. 'The devastation that is caused by Mankind's endless wars against his fellows is a sad thing to behold.' And Will could only agree, though he made no reply.

As they rode on, the greyness of the dawn soon burned away to a bright and warm morning. Will had already bonded to Hengroen as though they had been together all their lives. With the big strong horse under him, the sun hot on his head and an amiable companion riding at his side he felt the darkness in his heart lift a little, though the urgency of his quest burned inside him just as intensely and he was anxious to make up for lost time.

'Tell me about yourself, Will,' Father Michael said. 'Where do you come from? Do you have a family name?'

'I was born in the village of Foxwood, in the cottage that my father built. My mother died when I was little. I have lived in that same place all my life, until now. As to a family name, I have none that I know of. I have always just been William, or Will. The bowman is what they call me, on account of my skill at archery. Or,' he added modestly, 'that is what people say.'

'Are you so skilled?'

Will shrugged. 'I can loose an arrow straight enough. The Lord knows I should be able to by now. I've been shooting a bow since I was big enough to hold it. My father taught me how.'

'Will the bowman. Will Bowman,' the old man mused. 'It's a fine name. And what of your father? You said you have no family.'

'He died too,' Will replied. 'Of the fever, five winters ago.'

'I'm sorry to hear it. Then you are all alone in the world?'

Will had been growing uneasy at the line of the older man's questions, knowing where they must inevitably lead. 'I am now,' he replied quietly after a pause. 'I wasn't, before that.'

Father Michael seemed to sense the depth of his pain. 'It was not my intention to intrude on your private affairs.'

'No, it's all right.' In a low voice, Will told the story of what had happened to Beatrice and their unborn child. Father Michael remained silent as he listened. 'They are buried at Wexby Abbey,' Will finished. 'And I hope to be reunited with them soon.'

'God keep them,' the friar said, shaking his head mournfully.

'As for me,' Will said, 'I am as you see me. I set out on this journey to search for the men who did it, and to get my vengeance if I can. Nothing else matters to me. I hope to pick up their trail at Thatcham, and perhaps I will find them soon after. There, now you know everything about my life.'

'I doubt that,' said the old man. 'It seems to me there is a good deal more to this William Bowman than meets the eye.'

'Anyway, I'm tired of talking about myself,' said Will. 'What about you. Father? You said you have travelled across the sea before. I'd like to hear more about that.'

'Indeed I have, a very long time ago.'

Will rode in silence and listened as Father Michael talked about the countries he had seen, the great cities he had visited. Rome and Venice and Paris! For Will those were just remote-sounding names, meaning nothing to him except that they must be very far away, so distant that if a man were to travel too much further he might reach the ends of the earth and fall into whatever abyss lay beyond them. But he enjoyed listening to the old man talk about his experiences. It was a pleasant distraction from the sorrow and rage that constantly threatened to invade his thoughts.

Will had been hoping that a horse would allow for far better progress, and indeed they covered a good deal of ground that day. All that held them back was the rather sedate pace at which Father Michael rode his little mare, and his frequent stops when he would sit and gaze at the scenery, lost in thought with a contented half-smile on his face, as though admiring the beauty of God's creation. Which Will could appreciate up to a point, but their slowness frustrated him, and he felt he could have travelled ten miles further had he been riding alone. He had to remind himself that, had it not been for his new friend's company, he would not be riding at all.

By the end of the day, they had taken a winding beaten path that led deep through the heart of a dense forest of oak, hazel, ash and beech. As the light faded, they came to a burbling stream where they stopped and made their first camp of their journey together. Once the horses had been unsaddled and watered, Father Michael set about rolling out his blanket and filling their flasks from the stream while Will prepared the campfire in a small clearing among the trees above the riverbank. He still had some of the dried meat strips from Wexby Abbey, but was aware that his companion would refrain from touching any. Tomorrow when Easter came, Will thought, he would see about hunting some fresh game for them so that they could celebrate the end of the fast together. For the moment, out of solidarity he did as Father Michael did and contented himself with a little of the bread they had bought from the innkeeper.

'What is the reason for your journey to this Gall . . . Galletia?' he asked the old man when they had finished eating and were settling down to relax their saddle-weary muscles by the flickering light of the fire. The horses were tethered nearby, nuzzling one another in the darkness.

Father Michael explained, 'My destination is the city of Santiago de Compostela, where it is believed lie the holy remains of St James. Thereafter I plan to meet a dear old friend who is at the Cistercian Monastery of Santa Maria de Aciveiro. A more worthy and humble man of God you will never find.'

'What about the pope?' Will asked in all innocence. 'Surely he must be the worthiest of any.'

To his surprise, his companion responded with a snorting guffaw of contempt. 'The pope!' he exclaimed. 'Pray do not speak to me of popes. I'm sick of the very mention of them.'

Extremely taken aback, Will stammered, 'But as a man of the Church, I thought you would . . . I mean, is the pope not appointed by God Himself?'

Father Michael laughed. 'Is the pope appointed by God? Why certainly he is. But he is also appointed by a closed circle of greedy scheming treacherous corrupt cardinals, each secretly vying for power behind the other's back. Those are the kind of men who surround and influence His Holiness. And other than in the most exceptional of circumstances, he may very well be one of them himself.'

Will was largely ignorant about ecclesiastical matters, but he couldn't help wondering what Mother Matilda would have made of such a strong condemnation. 'Do you have something against him? The current pope, I mean? I don't know his name.'

'The creature's name is Pope Clement. Clement the third, if you really want to know. And may God forgive me for saying so, but since you ask, I must confess that I do indeed have something against him. Though it must be said, in fairness, that he is no more abjectly unworthy of the position than was his predecessor, Gregory. It was not always thus. Three years ago we mourned the passing of Pope Urban, a truly good man who was struck dead on the spot from a broken heart, upon hearing the news of the capture of the One True Cross and the capture of Jerusalem by the forces of Saladin. You know about the fall of Jerusalem?'

'Not very much,' Will admitted. 'I have heard rumours, stories, talk of great battles and many people dying. It all seems so far away, as though it belonged to another world.'

'It was a calamitous and lamentable event, to be sure. The One True Cross fell into the hands of the Turks after the Christian army carrying it into battle, led by King Guy of Jerusalem, were slaughtered almost to a man and the king himself made prisoner of Saladin. The city was taken from us shortly afterwards, along with Acre, leaving the Kingdom of Jerusalem without its capital and the city of Tyre the one and last pocket of resistance against the forces of the enemy as Saladin swept from victory to victory throughout the Holy Land. I thought I was going to drop dead of shock myself when I heard of it.'

Father Michael continued sternly, wagging his finger, 'But the Lord knows best. It is not Man's place, nor even that of a pope, to declare a bloody war of retribution that will only cost the lives of many more innocent people. Yet that is just what poor Urban's successor, the new Pope Gregory, did with his papal bull *Audita tremendi* in October of that year, calling for armies to march to the Holy Land and offering plenary indulgences for any man willing to take up the cross and join the military campaign against Saladin. As it happened, Pope Gregory did not last out the year either. But just as we were all hoping his replacement would be a worthier man, along came this upstart Clement who continues to press forward with all the worst policies of his predecessor. Sometimes I despair at the state of our Church.'

'What is a plenary indulgence?' Will asked, quite lost in all this.

'A dishonest and ungodly means of enticing men to join in this war, is what it is,' replied Father Michael. 'Those who do so enter into a fraudulent bargain with the complicity of the Church, whereby in return for their military service they are nominally forgiven for all their earthly sins past, present and future. In this world they enjoy a holy pilgrim's immunity from the powers of the law, while in the next they are excused punishment in Hell or even Purgatory. In other words, they may henceforth carry out whatever sinful and wicked acts they wish, in the name of God and with the pope's blessing.'

Will had long ago been taught to believe that a person whose sins were ultimately moderate enough to spare their soul being cast into Hell could at least expect to suffer in Purgatory for a period of time to be determined by God. The idea that the mere taking of an oath could reprieve them of any punishment at all was shocking. He immediately thought of the soldiers who had murdered his Beatrice, and his fists clenched tight. How could men like that be exonerated for their actions? 'That seems very wrong to me,' he muttered.

'It is a travesty and an abomination,' Father Michael vehemently agreed. 'And now off they go to war, granted all the freedom they could wish for and their place in Heaven guaranteed to them. Or so they think. But they are deceived, because the Almighty does not answer to the authority of a corrupt pope.'

'Then it is all a lie, just to trick them into fighting for God?'

'Absolutely so. And who knows what atrocities will be falsely permitted to be carried out in His name, just as they were nearly a hundred years ago when the Frankish soldiers first took Jerusalem and indiscriminately butchered helpless civilians by the thousand, Jew and Mahometan alike, the women and children along with the men, until it is said that the blood ran ankle-deep through the streets of that unhappy city? At the same time, they carry out their murderous campaigns against the pagan peoples of the northern lands, and in the Hispanic kingdoms to the south where the Moors have lived in relative peace for centuries alongside their Christian neighbours, using the name of our Lord to justify yet more destruction of innocent lives. This latest *expeditio crucis* of our new King Richard and those of France and the Holy Roman Empire to Outremer, as we call those lands in the east, will be no different.'

'I know nothing of these things,' Will replied. 'Neither of Outremer, nor the pagan people of the north, nor the affairs of kings and popes. I can't even imagine what a Moor looks like. All I've ever known is the meadows and woodlands, my home, my . . .' His voice trailed off. Suddenly he was back in the horror all over again, as the memories returned. He closed his eyes.

'You should keep it that way,' Father Michael advised him. 'Go back to the life you knew, and strive to rebuild what you once had. Cherish each and every day that is left to you in this world, and thank God for blessing you with the gift of a peaceful existence. So few men are able to enjoy such simple joys.'

Gazing dully into the flames, Will replied, 'I'm not feeling a lot of joy, Father. Sometimes I don't think I ever can again.'

The friar nodded benevolently, deep sadness and sympathy in his wrinkled old eyes. 'I know all too well what it is you feel.

I see such anger in you, Will, and though it is natural enough to grieve and burn for retribution, I fear it will destroy you in the end, if you allow it. Ask yourself, how will spilling more blood bring back those whom you have lost?'

Will looked at him. 'Isn't it right for a man to want to avenge his loved ones?'

'Certainly it comes easily to us weak mortals to feel that way. To a man who is reeling from a terrible wrong committed against him or those he held dear, it seems like the natural course of things to take justice into one's own hands. But the road to righteousness is never the easy one. I beseech you, don't let the Devil in by surrendering to the lust for revenge. As for the wicked men who did this awful thing, they will be judged for their actions, and punished, in time. The Lord in His wisdom shall determine their fate. Besides which,' Father Michael added gravely, 'consider that you would be one against many. A simple villager turned pilgrim, challenging professional soldiers in combat? Surely there can be no contest. Isn't it more likely that this senseless quest for vengeance would simply result in nothing other than your own death?'

'A simple villager I was,' Will said. 'That's for sure. And I might be ignorant about the world. But I know what my father taught me about the need to be true to oneself and never back down in the face of your enemies, no matter how the odds might seem to be against you. And he taught me a little about the use of weapons.'

'Your father, was he a warrior then?'

'No, he was a sheriff's man, for a time. What knowledge and skills he learned from that job, he passed on to me when I was a boy. But soon I was better than him. I—' Will was going to add more about his proficiency, how at the age of fourteen he could already shoot a running rabbit from the back of a horse, and throw a short hatchet dead true so that it would stick deep into the trunk of a tree at chest height from twenty paces away, making the most satisfying thud as the sharp steel blade embedded itself into the wood and needing a strong hand to wrench it back out. But he held back and said nothing more, because he disliked people who bragged about their exploits and wouldn't allow that vain weakness in himself either.

The friar asked, 'If your father was a sheriff's man, why did you not follow in his footsteps?'

'I said he was for a time. He left their service because he refused to cut off a man's hand for poaching a deer in the lord's forest. They beat him for it, nearly killed him. He never fully regained his health after that.'

'Then he was a noble man in the true sense of the word,' said Father Michael, 'with the integrity to be governed solely by his principles and the courage to turn away from evil. You should think about that, Will. I have already seen those same strengths in you, when you rescued me from danger and showed mercy to my attackers. For the love of God, I beseech you to abandon this course of folly.'

Will was silent for a long time, reflecting. 'I can't,' he said at last. 'You speak of my returning to the life I loved. But that life is gone now, and there is nothing to go back to, even if I could. I must keep moving forward and see this through to the end, whatever comes of it.'

'Very well. But I warn you, if you spill the blood of these men in cold, premeditated revenge, you will burn in the eternal flames of Hell for your crime, just as surely as they will for theirs. For the sixth commandment teaches us, "Thou Shalt Not Murder". It is as simple as that, my boy. And remember that the Lord in Heaven sees all.'

Chapter 9

Will said no more about it the next morning as they continued on their way. Their first day's ride had taken them more than halfway to the market town of Thatcham, where Will intended to made enquiries among the folk of the manor whether anyone might be able to tell him which way the soldiers had gone from there and how many days had since passed. With luck, he might even find them still camped in the area. Then his quest might come to an end much sooner than later. As much as it filled him with trepidation, he relished the prospect.

But there was more on Will's mind as they rode onwards, leaving the woods behind them and venturing along a narrow road that wound its snaking way roughly southwards under the warm morning sun. Father Michael's words from last night, spoken with such sincerity, had confused and perplexed him. Was it really such a mortal sin to want to bring evil men the fate they deserved? Surely to put an end to their reckless hate would save others from having to fall victim to them – and would that not be doing good, in God's eyes? How could merely standing by and allowing terrible acts to be carried out unmitigated be the right and virtuous thing to do?

I don't care, he thought to himself, and the words of the prayer he had said that first morning at Wexby Abbey returned to him, no less heartfelt than before. *I will do what I must do, with God's blessing or without it. That is His choice. If He refuses to help me and abandons me to my fate, or if He should condemn and damn me to Hell for following what my heart tells me, then He is neither a good nor a loving god and I want no part of Him.*

Needless to say, Will kept all these internal debates to himself. He spoke little, letting Hengroen's smooth and easy gait carry him along while Father Michael rode sometimes in front, sometimes at his side, doing nearly all the talking. 'Do you know what day this is, Will?' the old friar asked cheerily. 'Today is the twenty-fifth of March, and we celebrate the Resurrection of our Lord Jesus Christ, light over darkness, life over death, and the triumph of God's love for all of humanity! And what is more,' he added with a twinkle in his eye, 'it means we can enjoy a solid meal at last. I'm so hungry I could eat a horse. Present company excepted, of course.' He leaned forward in the saddle and patted Llamrei's neck reassuringly.

In his jovial mood Father Michael went on talking all morning. He seemed to be enjoying having a companion to converse with on his journey, even though that companion might sometimes be only half-listening or not at all. Will had only once before known anyone capable of such an apparently endless flow of dialogue. That had been a friend and sometime colleague of his father's whom he remembered from childhood. But while Fulke Halkin could only speak in curses and obscenities on a sadly limited range of subjects, Father Michael (when he had Will's attention) was a fascinating and eloquent conversationalist whose font of information seemed to have no bounds. The way he could quote entire lengthy passages from the Bible was astounding, as though he could see every word in front of him as he talked. Not just the Bible: he also knew the name of every tree and shrub they rode past, every bird that flew overhead, every river that the road bridged along the way, and a wealth of history of this and seemingly every other region of southern England.

'How is it that you know so much?' Will asked him.

'Because I can read,' replied Father Michael. 'It is the mark of an educated man, which I must confess to be, for what it's worth.'

'I cannot,' Will said. 'I could scarcely tell a word of one language apart from another, to look at written down. Nor spell my name in any of them.'

'If you were to forego your senseless quest and instead travel the long road to Galletia with me, you would have all the opportunity to learn your letters, and I would be delighted to teach you.'

'Teach me? To read, and to write as well?'

'Why, yes, the one does go hand in hand with the other, after all,' Father Michael chuckled. 'I am genuine in my offer. The yoke of illiteracy will shackle a man and enslave him to darkness, poverty and ignorance just as surely as any tyrannical master. One day everyone will be able to read and write, not only the clergy and the nobles. And not just in the Latin and the Greek, but in common tongues as well. How else are we to spread learning and enlightenment throughout this dark, unhappy world, if not by means of education for all?'

'Education for all,' Will murmured in wonder. Such a vision of the future sounded quite radical to him. 'I don't think I have ever met anyone like you before, Father. First you talk of a world without war and killing; now you prophecy a time in which everyone is made equal by learning. Can such things really be possible?'

'Perhaps I'm just a mad old man with too many strange ideas,' laughed Father Michael. 'Still, the offer is there, my son. I would be sorry to lose you as a companion. Come with me on my spiritual pilgrimage, open your horizons to a whole new world and gain the learning to enrich your life and prospects. An intelligent young man like you could aspire to great things one day.'

'I would love to learn,' Will said sincerely. 'But—'

'But your mind is made up and nothing can make you deviate from your course,' Father Michael said. 'I know. And I truly admire your courage and loyalty to Beatrice, bless her soul and may she rest in peace. I will say no more, in the hope that perhaps you will reconsider and accept my offer.'

As the day wore on they made their way across the rolling chalk-rich hills of the Berkshire Downs under a cloudless blue sky. Near the wooded banks of the Thames tributary the River Pang they came to the church of St Frideswide, where Father Michael stopped to pray, inviting Will to join him. Moving on, they passed villages and fields of wheat and barley where peasants laboured in the heat and were too busy to notice the passing of two riders. Some hours later they stopped again to rest the horses a while by another south-flowing tributary of the Thames, while Will set off a distance on foot and returned a little while later with a brace of rabbits and a woodpigeon for that night's camp dinner.

'We have made good time,' Father Michael told Will. 'I believe this is the River Kennet, and if I am right, then my guess is that the town of Thatcham lies just a little to the south of that large patch of forest.' He pointed down the valley to the wide expanse of green that lay across their route.

'If we can find a path through the forest we should reach the town tomorrow morning.'

'Then tomorrow morning is when I may have to leave you,' Will said.

'It saddens me to hear it,' the old man replied. 'But I understand, and when the time comes, I will wish you Godspeed and good luck.'

'And if I should learn from the townsfolk that the men I seek are still nearby, I hope you will allow me to return Hengroen to you,' Will said, affectionately stroking the horse's glossy neck. 'I'll be sorry to let him go, but I may soon have no further need of him.'

'You mean, if things go badly for you?'

Will shrugged. 'They might. Who can say? I can only do my best, and if they kill me, then let it be said that I died for a good cause.'

'I pray it doesn't come to that,' Father Michael said. 'As for the horse, he was a gift, come what may. And if you survive the encounter with these men as I wish and hope you do, then you must keep him, and don't worry about repaying me. Perhaps you will catch up with me on the road and we'll continue our journey together. I would like that very much.'

'Perhaps,' Will said. In truth he had given no thought to what the future might hold for him if he did survive his meeting with the soldiers. His sole concern was the fulfilment of his quest.

'But let us not talk of that now,' Father Michael said. 'We still have some miles to cover before nightfall. Come, let's ride on.'

By the time dusk was beginning to fall they had reached the northern border of the forest. It had seemed large and imposing even from a distance, but as they drew closer it was increasingly obvious that to attempt to ride around its edge would take them on a detour of many miles. Will was reluctant to let any delay stand between him and his objective, though the forest looked so dense and dark that the idea of riding through it seemed a daunting prospect.

'Still, even the thickest forest may be cut by many paths, whether made by man or beast,' Father Michael said. 'We can but try.'

As they ventured into the trees, Father Michael leading the way on Llamrei and Will following behind in single file, the remaining light of day diminished to a shadowy murk and the temperature dropped noticeably. The poor visibility made the difficult going even worse as they weaved through the close-packed trees, the horses stumbling over ruts and roots, while large boulders that lay strewn about the forest floor were often hidden under lichens and ferns, and fallen trunks often blocked their path. Will began to wonder if it had been a mistake not to take the long way around – but they were committed now.

The cries of birds in the dense canopy above fell silent as the murk deepened; now and then they heard the strangled cry of a vixen from somewhere deep among the forest. The pale shape of Llamrei was little more than a ghostly blur to Will as he rode along behind. He had very often hunted in Foxwood Forest at night and had never been one to fear the dark, but there was an eerie, forbidding feeling about this ancient woodland. Sometimes the trees seemed to be closing in around them, and branches raked at their clothes and their faces like hooked claws as they threaded their way through. If one stared too long into the darkness, one could become convinced that strange shapes of creatures were staring back. Had Father Michael, with all his knowledge of local lore, begun recounting stories of witches practising dark magic and evil forest spirits inhabiting the trees, it would have been difficult for Will not to believe them.

'I think this is as far as we may travel before we lose the light completely,' Father Michael said at last. They stopped to make camp in the middle of a ring of trees, great oaks with twisting roots and trunks bearded with thick growths of moss and ivy. The ground was spongy and leafy here, and rich with the earthy scent of decay. Will unsaddled and tethered up the horses where they could browse among the ferns. Both Llamrei and Hengroen seemed nervous and ready to startle at the slightest thing. Will, too, couldn't shake off the feeling of being watched by hidden presences deep among the shadows.

'We had best keep the fire going for as long as we can,' Father Michael advised. 'There may be wolves about.'

They were not the first people to have made camp in this same spot, and recently, as Will could tell from a circle of stones with charred wood and ash at its centre. It was a well-chosen place to make a campfire, and after gathering twigs and dead branches he soon had built a crackling blaze over which he arranged his cooking stands on which to spit-roast the pair of rabbits caught earlier that day. The fire was a bright and inviting sanctuary in the darkness. They settled on the soft ground and Will busied himself preparing and cooking their meal. While they waited, he shared out the last of his dried meat strips and an apple apiece, which he sliced with his knife. They ate eagerly and mostly in silence. The rabbits were lean but there was more than enough to fill their bellies.

'Oh, that was a welcome meal,' Father Michael said when they were finished. 'Thanks be to the Lord for His providence. And to you, Will for being an excellent cook.'

'The things you said today, about reading and writing,' Will said after a pause. 'They made me think that I have no idea what my name would look like, written in letters. If it is soon to be my fate to die, I would like to go to my Maker having seen it just once.'

'Put another branch on the fire to give me more light,' said Father Michael. 'Then give me a piece of wood and one of those sharp arrows of yours to use as a scribe, and I'll show you.'

Will drew out his knife and offered it to him, handle first. 'It's a fine knife,' said Father Michael. 'I wouldn't want to spoil it by my clumsy handiwork.'

'I trust you,' Will said. By the brighter firelight Father Michael carefully used the bodkin tip of the arrow to carve the letters on one side of the wooden handle. After a period of silent application, he handed it back to Will.

'So that is what my name looks like,' Will said, studying the strange, neatly carved letters with fascination. 'Thank you, Father. It will bring me good luck, I'm sure of it.'

They had eaten and talked, and now it was time to get some sleep before resuming their journey through the forest and reaching the town early tomorrow morning. But sleep could not come easily to Will. He lay awake, trying to settle his troubled mind by listening to the sounds of the forest. He couldn't stem the anxious thoughts of what tomorrow might bring, and what lay beyond if it should turn out that the soldiers had moved on. Never since his father's death had he experienced such uncertainty.

Eventually his fatigue won him over and his eyes closed. But it seemed as though only a short time had gone by when something punctured his restless dreams and he snapped suddenly awake, sitting up and blinking. It was deep in the night and the fire had died right down to a few softly glowing embers. Whatever had woken him, the horses had heard it too and were moving uneasily about at their tethers. He wondered if some wild animal might have ventured close to the camp: perhaps a boar, or more dangerously, a wolf – perhaps more than one. But as Will sat wondering he heard the snap of a twig coming from the darkness some way off.

Will knew that a prowling wolf would never tread on a twig or make the slightest noise that might alert a prey animal to its presence. Something else had made that sound. Something, or someone.

With a sudden chill of alarm, Will got to his feet. He slipped the bow out of his pack, quickly and silently strung it and drew an arrow from the quiver. Father Michael was fast asleep on the other side of the dying fire, his breathing slow and steady. Not wanting to wake him unnecessarily, Will treaded quietly over to the agitated horses. 'Shh, Hengroen,' he murmured, gently laying his palm against the gelding's neck. 'Shh, there, Llamrei.' His touch and soft voice were reassuring to the big chestnut, but the little mare was less easily placated and let out a nervous whinny.

Moments later he heard another soft snap of a twig, coming from a different direction beyond the edge of the camp, followed by the brush of a footstep through the tall ferns; and he knew then with certainty that someone was out there. More likely two of them, his instinct told him, stealthily circling at a distance. Will peered into the darkness, trying to penetrate the shadows but unable to make out either shape or movement.

'Whoever you are,' he said in a strong calm voice, soft enough so as not to waken Father Michael but clearly enough to be heard. 'I warn you not to come any closer.'

His words were met with silence. Listening intently he heard no more snapping of twigs. Nothing but the sounds of the horses and the even, steady breathing of his sleeping companion. Will remained very still, all his senses reaching out, waiting and ready for something to happen, though he had no idea what. But nothing did happen, and there were no more sounds. He waited a lengthy while longer. The horses settled, telling him that whatever danger had been lurking nearby must have passed. Eventually Will padded silently back to his side of the now-dead campfire and sat, but didn't lie down. Slowly, imperceptibly, the first grey glimmers of the dawn began to appear through the overhead tree cover.

And that, just as there was enough light filtering into the forest to see by, was when the brigands whose scouts had been circling the camp earlier now returned in greater force and launched their attack.

Chapter 10

There were five of them. It might have been they who had built the ring of stones and lit the original campfire on whose ashes Will had made his own. The scouts could have been returning to the same spot to make camp that night, only to find it was now being used by strangers. That much, Will would never know. But with certainty, he did know that these five men meant to do them no good.

They moved in quickly and without warning from different directions, appearing from behind trees and bursting through the bushes, breaking the still silence with a demented roaring and shrieking that was meant to terrify and disorientate their victims. The nearest was a powerful bald-headed giant of a man half a hand taller than Will and twice his width, wearing a shaggy fur jerkin over a chain mail hauberk, who came screaming towards him at full pelt, clutching a short-handled war axe at head height. Will raised his bow to shoot; but the simultaneous *thwack* of a crossbow bolt fired at him from behind, and thudding into the tree trunk right next to him made him jerk, his botched shot missing the giant and sailing harmlessly off into the bushes.

Will neither had time to turn to see who had fired the crossbow, nor to reload his own weapon, before the bald man closed in. The axe blade came scything towards Will in a downward blow powerful enough to cleave a man from the top of his head to the base of his neck. The big brigand was immensely strong, but Will had the advantage of greater agility and speed, and he ducked to his right out of the arc of the blade which came chopping down to bury itself at an angle in the mossy trunk of the oak tree to his left. The man tugged at the handle, but the weapon was stuck fast in the wood fibres. Seeing his moment Will plucked another arrow from his quiver and lunged it towards the man like a miniature spear, the needle tip stabbing into the soft flesh of his neck above the iron-ringed collar of his hauberk. The giant fell back with a yell, letting go of the axe handle to clutch at the wound, blood spurting from between his fingers.

Will instantly nocked the bloodied arrow to his bowstring and was about to deliver it into the man's vitals before he could draw out the long heavy dagger from his belt and come back for another attack; but then sensing a movement behind him, Will whirled about to see a second brigand rushing up, sword held high, eyes wild, mouth open in a howling battle cry. He too was wearing armour, in the form of a suit of plates riveted to a thick leather apron that hung down to his knees.

Will released his shot, and that moment was the first time he had ever killed a man. The bodkin-tipped arrow flew straight and true and punched through the man's leather apron. Passing between the plates it pierced deep into his chest with a hollow meaty *thunk* whose sound Will would remember for the rest of his life, though it was far from being the last time he'd ever hear it. The brigand tumbled backwards, dead before he could utter a cry.

The moment to reflect on what he had done would come later. Will shouted, 'Father! Danger!' The old friar was waking in a confused panic, scrabbling to his feet and staring about him, quite bewildered. The giant with the bald head was now upright again, blood streaming from the arrow hole in his neck. He tore out his dagger and flew at Will like a wounded ox, bellowing at the top of his voice. But by then Will had already fitted and drawn his next shot, and the arrow hurtled the short distance to his target and struck the giant square in the eye. At such close range the power of the longbow drove its missile straight through his head, the tip protruding from the back of his skull as his lifeless mass crashed to the forest floor.

Will barely had time to watch the man go down. Two were now dead, but he still had three more of them to account for, all rushing towards him and closing in fast. Father Michael was still standing in the same spot as though paralysed, looking to Will for direction. Will shouted, 'Run! Take shelter!'

The old man hesitated for an instant longer, then plunged into the bushes and Will lost sight of him as he had to turn to face three opponents at once. Two of them were clutching bladed weapons but the last posed a more immediate threat due to the crossbow in his hands, which he raised and aimed at Will as he ran. The heavy, stubby bolt with its large, pointed head twanged from its prod and flew towards him. At the same instant Will released a fourth arrow, this one at the crossbowman.

The two missiles passed one another in mid-air. Only one found its mark. Halting in his tracks, the crossbowman looked down in open-mouthed stupefaction at the foot and a half of ash shaft sticking from his midriff, with its white-feathered fletching at one end and Will's bodkin tip at the other, now buried deep inside his body close to his spine. The crossbow dropped from his hands; he staggered back a pace and then his knees gave way beneath him and he crumpled to the ground.

By that time the two remaining brigands were virtually on Will, and he had no chance to draw a fifth arrow from his quiver. He dodged a sword strike that cleaved the air inches from his head, and jabbed the tip of his bow towards the man to drive him back while the other swung a wicked-looking billhook at him, tearing a gash in Will's tunic sleeve. Had it sliced his arm it would have ended his chances there and then. It was more than clear to Will by now that these forest outlaws had no interest in merely holding up their victims in order to steal from them. Their strategy was to kill first and rob later, stripping whatever valuables were to be taken from the dead. And with three of their own now lying lifeless on the ground, Will knew he could expect no quarter, no mercy. It was kill, or be killed.

The two men advanced rapidly towards him. The one with the billhook said in a harsh voice, 'I'm going to cut your gizzard out, you mangy bastard.'

Forced to retreat several steps, almost tripping over the body of the second brigand, Will found the end of his bow stave snarled in a low-hanging branch. He dropped it and went to yank his hunting knife from its sheath. A knife was a poor defence against two better-armed opponents, and Will now found himself in a desperate position. Then in that instant he spied the sword that the man he'd killed had let fall, lying half-hidden among the dead leaves close by its former owner's corpse and shining dully in the dawn light that filtered through the trees. He bent down quickly, and a renewed sense of purpose flowed through him as his fingers gripped the sword by its leather-wrapped hilt.

Will had never owned a sword. He had often wondered what had happened to that belonging to his father, mysteriously vanished after his death and never seen again. Stolen by Fulke Halkin, Will had long suspected. But though it had never been his own, as a boy he had spent countless hours being instructed in its proper use. 'This here is what we call a pell,' his father had explained to his nine-year-old son, showing him the six-foot-tall heavy wooden post he had planted vertically in the ground behind the house. 'It's to teach you how to strike hard and fast with the sword. Now come on, boy, take a good grip with both hands and hit it with all your strength. Let me see those wood chips fly.' That first lesson had been followed by many more, and while Will had never become half as proficient with the blade as with the bow, by the age of fourteen his ability had outstripped his father's, to the latter's great pride.

That had all been a long time ago, however, and in the five years since his father's passing Will had not laid a hand on a sword hilt. Not until this moment. Now was when those lessons would either save his life, or fail him and end with his bloody death.

Will picked up the sword and took a two-handed grip on its hilt. The long, tapered double-edged weapon felt awkward and unfamiliar for the first few moments until he gained a sense of its heft and balance. But he would not have long to get used to it, because now his opponents both rushed towards him and the fight was on.

Retreating no longer, he took a decisive step towards the two brigands, parried a violent strike from the billhook with a clash of steel and such force that it tore the crude weapon out of the man's hand and drew a cry of pain from him. Then Will had to turn his attention towards the other, as the man's sword point came lunging at his midriff. There was no great art or finesse in the brigand's technique, but he wielded the sword with a good deal of power and speed. Will deflected the stabbing attack with a downward swing whose momentum carried his blade up and around in a slicing arc directed at his opponent's neck. The brigand met it with a rapid parry of his own and the two blades rang loudly against one another.

After that opening pass each man backed away a step, circling one another. Will's opponent was rangy and gaunt, perhaps twice his age but lean and strong. His black teeth were bared in a grimace of concentration and there was a flinty hardness in his eyes. Will could tell that he was up against a seasoned fighter if not a highly trained one, a man of far greater experience than his own. And he knew that this enemy would keep on with unbridled ferocity until one of them was dead.

They closed again, and now the blows came fast and furiously and the bright ring of steel on steel sounded through the forest, intermingled with the brigand's grunts of effort as he hacked, chopped, feinted and stabbed. He had some wily tricks up his sleeve, one of which was to swing high and then suddenly deviate to a low angled strike that, if not anticipated and deflected in time, could take off his opponent's foot at the ankle and end the fight at a stroke. Will was hard pressed to remember every lesson from his youth to stave off the onslaught.

Meantime, he had lost sight of Father Michael; and with alarm he realised that nor did he know where the other remaining brigand had gone to. He was suddenly gripped by the urgent need to end this fast; but at the same time, he must not allow himself to become distracted by his fear. Any loss of concentration would be fatal.

His opponent came at him again with redoubled fury, feinting left and slicing right. With every clash of blades Will felt the ringing vibration through the hilt into his wrists and arms. The brigand was losing patience with this upstart of half his age who thought he could best him. He, too, wanted to end this quickly, and his next idea was to bring his blade down with all his might from above, in a savage slice that would split Will's skull down the centre.

But his impatience proved to be his undoing, because as the blade came down hard and fast Will saw his chance. He met the man's sword with an angled upward block that let the descending blade slip diagonally down the length of his own and deflected it aside; then moving into the gap that had momentarily opened up, he delivered a hard pommel strike to the man's face. 'There is more than one end to a sword,' his father had taught him. It was a stunning, crushing blow, shattering both nose and cheekbone. The brigand went down, his blade still pointing upward. Will batted it aside and finished the man off with a brutal thrust that drove the sword clear through his torso and deep into the ground. The man let out a wheezing cry of pain and shock; he shuddered and his legs kicked, and then he lay still and was dead in the dirt.

Will yanked the bloody blade out of his body and looked around him. He could see no sign of Father Michael anywhere. With a cold dread gripping his heart he leaped over the brigand's corpse and pushed into the dense thicket of bushes where the friar had disappeared. And then Will saw him, standing twenty paces away through the trees, in a shaft of red light from the rising sun.

Just in time to witness the last surviving brigand plunge a dagger deep into Father Michael's belly. The old man collapsed to his knees and the brigand withdrew the dagger and cut his throat.

Will wanted to cry out, but his mouth was dry and no words would come. He burst into a run, raising the bloody sword. The brigand let the old man's body slip to the ground, turned to see Will racing towards him, and fled. A thicket of thorns blocked his way; he turned in a panic and headed back in the direction of the camp.

Will chased. The two of them tore through the bushes. The brigand was a small man and surprisingly nimble. Will tripped on a tree root, and by the time he had sprung back up to his feet the fleeing man was nearly thirty paces ahead and getting away.

But Will could not let that happen. Just beyond arm's reach was the giant's short-handled war axe, still stuck in the mossy oak trunk where he had wedged it fast before Will's arrow had claimed him. With an effort Will waggled it free. He hefted the weapon in his hand, took aim and hurled it with all his strength and skill in the direction of the escaping brigand. And again, the hours of practice from Will's earlier days now paid off. The axe spun through the air, turning end over end; then with a thud the curved forward edge of the blade struck the man midway between the shoulder blades. With the weapon buried in his back he stumbled, lost his footing and crashed headlong into a tree, fell flat and did not move again.

Will didn't bother to go to check that he was dead. Instead, his heart pounding in his throat, he ran back to the spot where Father Michael was lying face-down in the moss and leaves.

Chapter 11

'Father Michael!'

Will reached the place where he was lying and crouched beside him. With a trembling hand, terrified of what he might see, he gripped his friend by the shoulder and rolled him over onto his back. He was so slight that he seemed to weigh almost nothing. 'Father Michael!' Will repeated, and could hear the desperation in his own voice.

Father Michael was still alive and conscious, but he would not remain so for long. His face was a mask of blood, and more and more of it was gushing from the open slash across his neck. His eyes rolled from side to side and seemed to be searching blindly for Will. An awful rattling croak came from his lips. Will cradled his frail body in his arms, not caring about the blood, knowing that nobody, not even a master healer, could save him. All he could do was hold and comfort the old friar as best he could until the last ebb of life had leaked out of him and he was gone: this generous, kindly and learned man he had known for barely two days but whose death brought all his grief flooding back renewed.

The end came within a mercifully short time. Will laid him down, closed his eyes and said a faltering prayer over his body. 'Lord, he is yours now. Take care of him.'

It was a short prayer, as Will found he had little to say to a God who could once again turn his back on the faithful and allow a worthy person to die like this. The friar's vision of a world without war and killing had been a wonderful one to imagine, but the world men lived in was a very different place. One day perhaps, God would work His influence to bring peace to those who deserved it. Until then, it seemed to Will, the good people of the earth would be left deserted and alone to fend for themselves.

Will stood up. In the aftermath of combat his muscles were shaking and he felt drained and weak. He looked around him at the bodies of the dead brigands, the four scattered about nearby and the fifth lying thirty paces away with the axe sticking out of his back. The realisation of what he had done gradually began to sink in: how could it have come to this, that he, Will Bowman, who only days ago had been a simple freeman villager living a quiet and unassuming life in the place he loved, could be standing here now with the blood of the five men he had just slain on his hands? And yet here he was. A killer.

It was not murder, he told himself, refusing to feel remorse for his actions. *I was defending my friend. If only I could have saved him.*

'I'm so sorry, Father,' he murmured.

He was shaken and upset, but somewhere deep inside him he felt a kind of fierce strength at having faced such odds without backing down. Perhaps the same inner strength would serve him again, when it came to facing his next challenge, whenever that might be. It could be today, he thought, God willing. But at the same time, he understood only too well that his coming encounter with the black eagle horsemen would be a far tougher test than this, and that he must do all he could to prepare for it.

Will tentatively went over to the body of the first man he had killed, the giant. His bald head was horribly thrown back, his mouth agape and the remaining eye staring glassily with the arrow shaft protruding from the other. His fur jerkin and the iron-ringed mesh of his chain mail were spattered red. It was the chain mail Will was interested in. With a great effort, his nostrils filled with the dead man's unclean stench, he propped the heavy corpse half-upright against a tree and managed to yank the mail hauberk off him, using a handful of leaves to wipe away the blood. He stripped down to his linen undershirt, shrugged the hauberk over his own head and arms and let it slip down the length of his body. It hung to mid-thigh on him, felt hard and heavy, and the iron rings jinked like a sack of coins when he moved.

Next, Will walked over to the dead man whose sword he had taken. The empty scabbard was attached by leather straps to a thick, broad sword-belt buckled around his waist. Will removed the belt, and once he had cleaned the blood off the blade, he slipped the sword into the scabbard. The man had also been wearing a heavy leather jerkin, studded across the chest and back with iron rivets, laced at the sides and fastened at the front by four stout buckles. The sword blade had pierced through the leather, but the garment had fared better than the man inside it. Will decided to take that for himself, too, as a replacement for his old tunic. It fit him well enough, and hung down low enough to just cover the hauberk under it. He buckled his new sword belt about his waist and cinched it tight. The scabbard felt strange, hanging there at his left side, but he would soon get used to it.

The last item he plundered from the dead men was the axe that was buried in the last one's back. The crossbow, he rejected as being an inaccurate and crude contraption, in his opinion far inferior to even the worst longbow. He retrieved his own, then set about the grisly task of plucking the arrows out of the corpses, something he was very used to doing with hunted quarry. Two of the bodkin tips were damaged from impact, but he still had plenty of loose replacement arrowheads in his bag. He cleaned them and replaced them in his quiver.

Finally, he had to attend to the horses. Hengroen and Llamrei had both broken free of their tethers during the battle and run off into the forest. He found them not far away, and with a little coaxing led them back to the camp. When both were saddled again, it was time to turn to the grimmest task of all. He gathered up the body of Father Michael and carried him over to Llamrei. The mare turned her head to nuzzle at her former master, as though wondering what the matter was with him and telling him, 'Wake up!' Such a display of love and tenderness brought tears to Will's eyes. He gently laid Father Michael across Llamrei's saddle and secured him with a length of rope. The bodies of the brigands would receive no such care. The wolves and other wild things of the forest would find them soon enough, and know how best to dispose of their remains.

Will left the camp and continued on his way through the thick woods, leading the mare behind Hengroen. Shafts of morning sunlight pierced the overhead canopy here and there. Then as they emerged from the treeline, the brightness and warmth shone over them and Will gazed across the green valley beyond. Based on Father Michael's prediction he had been expecting to see the town of Thatcham there to the southern side of the forest, which he had imagined as being somewhat like a larger version of his own dear Foxwood. It now appeared, though, that the friar's bearings had been somewhat off course, because as far as Will could see across the pastures and hills and occasional smaller patches of woodland, there was no sign of the town anywhere.

'Where am I?' he wondered out loud, anxious that he might have difficulty getting back on the right road. As he scanned the horizon, he sighted a solitary greystone building nestled among some trees perhaps a half-mile distant. A church, he thought, or perhaps another priory, where surely he might find someone to direct him. He hoped also that they could take Father Michael, so that he could receive the proper burial.

'Come, Hengroen.' He rode off down the valley at what was an easy trot for the big horse, not wanting to strain little Llamrei. They made their way along a narrow track across a meadow where tall grasses and wildflowers swayed in the breeze. The sky was a perfect unbroken blue. It was an oddly fine day to be carrying the dead body of a friend to his grave. And, perhaps, later to be heading towards his own.

As Will drew closer, he saw that the grey building, larger than it had seemed from afar, resembled a small castle. A low bell tower was visible above the surrounding trees, but no steeple. Presently he drew up at the tall front gate, a great arched double door with a smaller one inset. A rope bell pull hung by the doorway like the one at Wexby. Will dismounted and tugged the rope, and heard the muted clang of the bell from somewhere within the thick stone walls. After a while, there was the grate of a bolt and the smaller inset door creaked open a few inches. Through the gap appeared an ancient face belonging to a haggard old man dressed in a long black hooded robe.

Will presented himself, and the ancient old man peered at him with the utmost suspicion before rasping at him, 'Wait there.' The door closed and was rebolted. Will waited patiently enough, and after a while longer came the sound of footsteps, followed by the thump and grind of a larger deadbolt, and the main arched doorway swung open. To Will's surprise he was faced with another man, much less ancient and also wearing a black robe, but with a long sword sheathed at his side.

'What kind of monastery is this?' Will wondered out loud.

The man pulled down his hood. His silver hair was short and bristly, and there was a jagged scar running down one side of his face. His eyes were penetrating and he wore an air of great authority.

'We are not a monastery,' he replied in a deep voice. 'This is Greenham Preceptory, a house of the Knights of the Order of St John. Many call us the Knights Hospitaller. There are no monks here, only a handful of sworn servants of God including the preceptor, two chaplains, a sergeant-at-arms and the steward, which is I. What business brings you here, and on the second day of Eastertide, when folks are attending to their prayers?' As the steward spoke, he was eyeing Will very closely, looking him up and down in a somewhat stern manner.

Will knew how rough and unkempt he must look, after days of hard travelling, his fight with the brigands and the patches of dried blood that stained his jerkin and breeches. He briefly explained that he was a pilgrim on his journey south through England, and that he had with him the body of a man of God, a friar who had been murdered on the road by outlaws.

'Please can you take care of him, as I cannot. And if you can offer a good home to his mare, her name is Llamrei and she will serve you well, as long as you treat her kindly and do not ask too much of her.'

The steward considered him for a moment, saying nothing. Then at his summons, four more black-robed men who must have been waiting close by came out to take poor Father Michael's body down from his saddle and carry him inside. The steward looked mournful and made the sign of the cross as they bore him through the doorway. 'He will be taken good care of,' he assured Will. Then he asked, 'How came you by him?'

'Our paths crossed back along the road. He had only recently set off on a pilgrimage to the Kingdom of . . . of León,' Will replied, remembering the name, 'and I was riding with him for part of the way. We were accosted in the forest.' He pointed back towards the great broad mass of green in the distance.

'That forest is crawling with cut-throats and bandits,' the steward said with barely contained disgust. 'The local authorities seem either unable or unwilling to catch them. It is a sign of the times, may the Lord stand between us and evil.'

Will might have told him that five of those bandits would no longer be a threat to anyone. But instead he said only, 'I am sorry I could not have done more to save him. He was a worthy man, and I lament him very much.'

'Can we offer you shelter, pilgrim?' the steward asked, laying a hand on Will's shoulder and ushering him inside. 'That is one of our main functions here, to bring respite and aid to weary travellers in these dark and dangerous days. A cup of wine and some cheese and meat to fortify you on your journey?'

'I would be glad of a cup of goat's milk,' said Will, who had never in his life tasted wine and was unsure of the idea. Since leaving the forest he had begun to realise how hungry and thirsty he was after the ordeal of that morning. He had heard the name of the Knights Hospitaller before, though he knew little of them and was pleasantly surprised by their open generosity.

'Follow me.' The four other men had disappeared. The steward led him through the stone corridors and stairways of the preceptory. It made Will think of the inside of Wexby Abbey, only it was somewhat more austere and dark than even that cold, ancient building. Very little light filtered through the tiny windows, little more than slots in the thick stonework through which defenders could launch arrows at a besieging force. Deeper into the interior, flaming torches affixed to the walls lit their way, giving off a dim haze of smoke that gathered like mist among the vaulted arches overhead.

The steward arrived at a low doorway, warned him to be careful of the steps, and ushered him through. Will found himself inside a large refectory hall with thick stone columns and rows of wooden bench tables at which the inhabitants would gather to eat. But the room was less than welcoming, with no fire in the hearth and the tables bare. An enormous mastiff hound looked up from where it lay gnawing a meaty bone on the bare stone floor, and fixed him with a baleful eye.

The door closed behind them, and there was the click of a lock as the steward shut them in. Then out of the shadows stepped seven more men in black robes, their faces hidden by their hoods.

That was when Will realised that he had been led into a trap. At the steward's signal the seven threw off their robes, and in the dim light he saw that under them they wore mail and long black surcoats each marked by a white cross. Before he could speak, they moved to form a circle around him and with a flash of steel they drew out their swords.

'Now,' said the steward. 'Perhaps you would care to tell us the true story of how you brought back the body of our friar brother? You are no kind of pilgrim that ever sought refuge here before. Explain yourself. Be brief. And you had better be convincing.'

Chapter 12

'I have told you the truth,' Will protested, shocked that they could disbelieve him. It had never occurred to him until now that by taking some of the brigands' items of clothing he might give himself the appearance of being one of them. 'Father Michael was my friend. He was kind and generous to me, even paid for my horse.'

'Why should he have done such a thing?' the steward asked dubiously.

'Because I saved him from a pair of robbers who accosted him at the inn he had stopped at, the night before last. I only wish I could have done the same when we were attacked in the forest.' Will searched his mind for some way to convince them. 'Look, let me show you.' He drew his knife from its belt sheath, and the circle of swords instantly all closed around him more menacingly. The steward raised his hand, understanding that Will was acting without threat. 'That is my name,' Will said, pointing out the inscription on the handle. 'You can see the wood is freshly cut. He carved it for me only last night. Had we continued journeying together he was going to teach me my letters.'

The steward took the knife from him and examined it, turning it over in his hands. 'This is no proof. You could have taken it from its real owner.'

'But I did not,' Will said. 'I am no liar, nor a thief.'

'And I am supposed to take your word for that?'

'Yes,' Will replied simply. 'Why should you not?'

The steward looked at him long and hard. 'You have a good deal to learn about the world, my young friend. Then tell me, Will Bowman, if you are indeed Will Bowman, how is it that your companion was slain, but that you are still alive and unharmed?'

'Because they are dead,' Will told him. 'All five. This sword and axe and the chain mail and jerkin, I took from their bodies.'

'You are telling me that you slew five men, by your own hand, and did not suffer a scratch yourself?'

Suddenly feeling strangely ashamed of himself, Will looked down at his feet and replied awkwardly, as though making a confession, 'I . . . It all happened so fast. Three I shot with my bow. The fourth I fought using the sword I took from one of them, as I had none of my own. The fifth, I took down as he was trying to escape. They were murderers.'

'If that is so,' the steward said, 'then by rights I should hand you over to the authorities, to stand trial. Murderers they may have been, but only a sworn servant of the crown may enforce the law by strength of arms.' He paused, and a wry smile passed over his face. 'Then again, if you are telling the truth, perhaps it is reward you deserve, rather than punishment. The only good brigand is a dead one, and travellers may now make their way a little more safely. But why did you take their weapons and armour? Do you not know that only a knight is entitled to wear a sword in such fashion?'

'I needed them,' Will replied. 'I am on a journey of my own, one that will bring me into danger.'

'And what journey is that?'

With seven swords pointed at him, Will had little choice but to tell the full truth. 'I hunt a party of mounted men at arms, hailing from the north. They wear the livery of their lord marked with a black eagle, and travelled southwards through this area within the last few days on their way to join the king's army.'

'They are bound for the Holy Land?'

Will nodded. 'But there is nothing holy about these men themselves, plundering and destroying as they go. In Thatcham the same soldiers raided the homestead of a man named Adam Foreman, husband to Arabel, cousin to Percy Naldrett of Faringdon. They cut off his head and fired his barns.'

'Hmm,' the steward said. The details of Will's account seemed to have helped to persuade him of his sincerity. 'So we have heard. And Adam Foreman was not the only victim of their cruelty, may God have mercy on them.'

'God may have mercy on whom He wishes,' Will said, feeling emboldened and the anger rising within him, 'but not I. If you know where they are now, I would be most interested to hear it.'

'What personal stake do you have in the matter?' the steward demanded. 'Are you also related to Adam Foreman?' Then, seeing the look on Will's face, he softened. 'No, do not tell me. I sense that these men have done you a great harm. You have our sympathies.' He handed back the knife, then motioned to the knights to put away their swords. They all sheathed their weapons and stepped back.

'It is not our business to act on behalf of the local authorities,' the steward went on after a pause, 'but our sacred duty as Knights of the Hospital of Saint John requires that we do whatever is in our power to protect the people of the community. When we heard what had happened, several of us rode out with the intention of driving the soldiers off. After much searching we came upon the remnants of their camp two miles to the east of the town.'

This was concerning news. 'You're saying they have moved on?' Will asked.

'Heading south towards Oakley,' volunteered another of the knights, 'by the last report we received, and riding fast. They could be as far away as Winchester by now. The road is a straight one.'

'How far is the coast from there?' Will asked, suddenly very worried that he was going to lose their trail.

'That depends,' said the steward. 'The king's ships are setting sail from different ports. There are the harbours of Plymouth and Dartmouth, off to the west. Then there is Portsea Island to the south-east of here. But I would guess from their chosen route that they will most likely be headed for Southampton. That is the closest, not much off due south of Winchester and a journey of only twelve or fifteen miles from there.'

Will had had no idea he was already so close to the coast, and he was alarmed at the thought that the black eagle soldiers were much closer still. 'Then I have not a moment to waste if I am to catch up with them. Once they get on those ships, I am lost.'

'Indeed, you had better hurry,' replied the steward. 'I have heard that the king's fleet is due to sail immediately after Easter. That could be today, tomorrow or any day now.'

Will sighed in frustration. 'If only I knew the way. I have no idea where I am.'

'I would send a troop of men to accompany and guide you, if I could spare them.' Turning to the knights the steward instructed them, 'Robert, Gerald, you will show him the road and escort him as far as Woolton Hill.' To Will he said, 'It is a straight and simple journey from there, steering clear of the forests lest you run into any more trouble. You may travel with the assurance that Father Michael will be given the proper Christian burial here at Greenham. And of course, his little pony will have a good home with us.'

'I'm much indebted to you, Sir Steward,' Will said. 'If there was some way I could repay you for your kindness, I gladly would.'

The steward laughed. 'You have at least the manners of a knight, if not as much of the appearance of one. Hugh of Leicester is my name, and you may call me Hugh. I wish you good luck on your quest, Will Bowman. Or should I perhaps call you Will *the* bowman, as befits a man capable of defending himself so ably with his weapon of choice, and carrying what appears to my eye an excellent yew stave. I was a fair archer myself once, and might have been still had not a damned Saracen put his scimitar through my shoulder and ended my shooting days forever.'

'You were in the Holy Land?' Will asked, looking keenly at him.

'Yes, I once had the honour to be stationed at the Hospitaller stronghold of Bethgibelin, protecting the pilgrim route between Jaffa and Jerusalem. It was many years ago. Perhaps I will see that country again one day, although I doubt I can be of much service in my old age. Now be on your way, my young friend, and may God protect you. Though, once your escorts have turned back, I would advise you against travelling looking so much like a brigand yourself. People may get the wrong idea.'

Will thanked Hugh once again. He was given a hank of cold roast mutton and a cup of goat's milk to gulp down quickly while the two knights allocated to ride with him as far as Woolton Hill hurried to saddle their horses. Then he leaped back onto Hengroen, and he and his escorts spurred their mounts and thundered away from the preceptory.

The knights rode like the wind on their heavy chargers, and without the slower pace of little Llamrei to hold him back, Hengroen was at last able to stretch to a powerful gallop, sure-footed and smooth. With his new allies flanking him left and right, the sun on his face and the wind in his hair, for the first time in a long while Will was able to feel if not happiness then at least a sense of fierce exhilaration that drove him on with rekindled energy and countered the sadness in his heart. There could be no more night camps from this point on, no stops except to rest and water his horse and take the minimum of sustenance for himself.

Will and the Hospitallers covered the miles to Woolton Hill in much less than an hour, from where the knights directed him onto the southerly road towards the town of Andover. He waved goodbye to them as they wheeled their horses around and galloped away in a cloud of dust. Then he was alone again, ready for anything. From Andover to Winchester was just fifteen more miles, a distance that Hengroen's long fast stride seemed to swallow up effortlessly. As evening came, Will rewarded him with an hour's rest by the banks of the River Itchen, to graze the long green grass and drink his fill of the clear burbling water.

Feeling neither hungry nor thirsty himself, Will used the pause to sit on the bank in the golden glow of the sunset and replace the heads of his arrows that had been damaged in the encounter in the forest. Then he took a few practice swings with his new sword, getting more used to its feel and honing his accuracy by slashing the seed heads off the long grasses that grew close to the water. Whoever its previous owner had stolen it from, it was a finely crafted weapon and had no doubt cost a great deal of money, far more than a simple commoner like Will could ever have afforded. Any sword, let alone one like this, could be considered a privilege to own. Its slender hilt was rather longer than that of the plain ordinary arming sword, allowing for a comfortable two-handed grip and the manipulation of its round pommel for a very fast and dextrous use of the blade, which was light and flexible and sharp as a razor.

Now Will had all the tools he needed to fight and kill the men who had destroyed his future happiness, except perhaps the skill required to succeed. And in the perhaps unlikely event that he survived the experience, what then? Try and start afresh elsewhere? Or, as everyone kept advising him to do, should he return to the ruins of his old home, to rebuild what had stood there and resume his old life as best he could? It was so painful to think about that he put it to the back of his mind and forced himself to concentrate solely on his short-term goals.

Before long, too restless to stay still, he was back in the saddle and riding hard once more. A good many miles remained between him and the south coast. He was determined to catch up with his enemies somewhere on that road, even if it meant galloping through the night.

Tomorrow, he promised himself as he rode. *Tomorrow is the day that will seal my fate, for better or worse. And I will face it, whatever comes.*

In truth, Will had little idea what lay ahead, and the choices he would have to make when he got there. Tomorrow would indeed be a milestone event that would change his life forever.

Chapter 13

That next day was the twenty-seventh of March 1190, two days after Easter, a date that would remain sharp in Will Bowman's memory for the rest of his life.

Just as Hugh, the steward of Greenham Preceptory had told him, the road from Winchester led almost due south until, very early that morning, Will found himself approaching the port town of Southampton. By this point along the road was a great deal of traffic, horses, carts and people on foot, and forced to bring Hengroen's pace down to a slow trot he joined the busy stream entering the town. Already Will could smell a strange and unfamiliar tang of salty air, and overhead wheeled white birds bigger than crows, which emitted screeching cries he had never heard before. He understood these as signs that the sea must be very close. *I am truly a long way from home,* he thought.

The road traffic came to a slow bottleneck as the travellers to the town filtered through its one land-facing entrance, the towering Bar Gate arch set into the centre of the earthworks that were Southampton's northern defences. A drawbridge was lowered over the wide moat surrounding the walls, and a great iron portcullis was raised by thick chains to let the crowds through the archway. Amazed by the sight of it all, Will paid his penny toll and was admitted inside the town.

It was by far the biggest settlement he had ever seen, and he was stunned at the sheer multitudes of people and the volume of bustle, clamour and chaos as he rode through streets and squares dominated by tall buildings all around. Markets and traders of all descriptions were plying their goods everywhere he looked, while here and there a loose pig or chicken ran amok through the crowds causing mayhem and merriment. The big white birds circled constantly overhead, bold enough to now and then come swooping down to steal the odd scrap of food from the market stalls. In one of the narrower lanes a wine merchant's wagon had lost a wheel, shedding two of its barrels which had split open and shed much of their contents in a red river down the middle of the street, prompting locals to rush to gather up as much as they could in whatever cups and pans came to hand. In other streets they might have been less eager to do so, because of the stinking piles of waste, both human and animal, that festered in the gutters and made even the stray dogs shy away.

Riding onwards, Will came upon a group of young women who were loitering on a corner and seemed to stare at him in a peculiar way while exchanging looks and giggles: a rough-looking lot with tousled hair and raggedy dresses showing much more flesh than would have been considered appropriate in Foxwood. Approaching them, he politely asked the way to the docks; and when they realised that was all he wanted from them he was met with a torrent of abuse and foul language such as he had never heard from a lady's mouth. He hurried away, soon obtained the directions he needed from the owner of a fishmonger's stall and continued through the town to the port. The salty tang in the air was much stronger now, mixed with those smells of the town that were far less pleasant.

As he came down the cobbled slope, the buildings that blocked his view fell away, and he saw the sea for the very first time. In reality all he was seeing was the tidal estuary of Southampton Water bearing away south-east towards the Solent, but nonetheless to him that glittering expanse of blue water was an incredible sight to his eyes. The port itself, a long quayside with various stone and wooden piers and jetties stretching over the lapping water, teemed with hundreds of vessels ranging from the kinds of small boats he knew well to great ships with towering masts and enormous sails flapping in the breeze. Eighteen or twenty of these imposing craft were moored fore and aft by ropes to the harbour wall and adjoining piers, and all around them was bustling activity as port workers and ship crewmen swarmed about the decks, and men, horses and supplies were loaded aboard by means of ramps and cranes. Other vessels were already fully laden with passengers and equipment, sitting low in the water as they cast off and moved slowly out of the harbour into the estuary with the last of the outgoing early tide.

But more than the ships, what drew his eye were the heaving crowds of people everywhere on the quayside, as though all of England had gathered in this one spot to embark on their voyage into the unknown. The multitudes assembled there were from all walks of life, commoner and noble alike mingling together in a chaotic mass that gave no sense of an organised force of men. Pushing through the crowds, which parted to let them pass, were the knights and men-at-arms on their tall powerful mounts and a bewildering variety of banners, some plain, others brightly coloured. As Will came closer he was attentively searching for the black eagle of the soldiers he most desperately wanted to find – but nothing resembling it or the men he clearly remembered from that day were to be seen anywhere on the quayside. They must be here somewhere, he told himself, and was gripped by sudden anxiety.

All along the harbour were warehouses and sheds serving the port, as well as a long, low tavern that was drawing a good-sized crowd of people in its own right. Will pushed through the throng, speaking constantly to Hengroen who was skittish and nervous at so much activity around him. He dismounted at the tavern, left the horse in the hands of an ostler and went inside the low-ceilinged building. The interior was packed and lively, full of noise and clamour. A few eyes turned towards the tall, road-stained traveller as he walked in with his sword on his hip, axe haft in his belt and his bow and arrows on his shoulder, but many of the drinkers already inside were large, brawny men with their weapons about them, and in general he was ignored as he elbowed his way to the bar and ordered ale to quench his thirst after the long ride.

Will's purpose in visiting the tavern wasn't to drink beer, but rather to make enquiries. After asking around a few people who only answered his questions with blank looks or shrugs of ignorance, he was directed to a corner where sat a solitary man it was thought might be able to help him. At first the man was gruff and unwilling to be disturbed from his pot of ale, but Will offered his last few pennies in return for information, and the man became more amenable to talking. He was a port official, an assistant harbour master taking a few moments from his busy duties, and proud to assert that no vessel entered or left the harbour, nor did anything happen anywhere on the dockside without his full knowledge of every detail.

'An ill-looking black bird of prey on a grey field? Aye, I seen it. Seen the men who wear it, too, riding in here all proud as if they owned the fucking place. The device of a northern lord, that black eagle is. Calls himself the Baron of Gilsland. From somewhere up Derbyshire way.'

'A baron?' Will asked, feeling a grim rage rising up. 'You know about him?'

'Can't say as I know much, but you hear things. They say he is a pitiless and bitter man, sat there alone and unloved in his crumbling castle and too sick and old to ride into battle himself, so sends his son who is good for nought but war and plunder, to seek what glory there is to be had in his stead. And an honest journey they will make of it, I don't think, by the look of 'em.' The harbour master took another deep swig of ale, raised one buttock off his seat and produced a loud fart. 'Sad days we live in, when our king would have unworthy scabs like that fight his battles for him. His father King Henry would never have allowed such a thing, God bless his memory.'

'Tell me more about this Baron of Gilsland.'

'Ain't much to tell, young feller. Except they say his good lady died out of pure misery at living with the old bastard, years back. One child they had, Sir Ranulf, who leads a party of thirty men-at-arms to fight in the Holy Land. That's all I know.'

'Then they're here,' Will said. His hands had begun to shake. 'When did they arrive?'

'Only yesterday afternoon,' said the harbour master. 'But they're here no longer. Sailed this morn with the early tide.'

'They're *gone*?' Will burst out, dumbfounded. 'You mean I missed them? Surely it can't be!'

By way of reply, the harbour master drained down the last of his ale, slammed the tankard down on the table, heaved himself up to his feet and with another belch beckoned Will to follow. He led him through the crowded room, shoving people out of his path, and outside onto the quay where he pointed a thick finger out to sea. Will stared in the direction he was indicating, narrowed his eyes and saw a small dark speck far away, approaching the mouth of the estuary and the open water beyond. Soon it would be over the horizon and gone.

Will felt his stomach sink as he stared a while longer at the disappearing ship. Then unable to speak more than a muttered word of thanks he turned away and walked off into the crowd. Outside the tavern was a stone bench. Utterly spent and demoralised he laid down his bow and slumped on the bench with his head in his hands. To have missed them by just a matter of hours after all his efforts was so devastating that he felt physically sick. What was he going to do now?

Will knew that the choices that lay before him now were few and stark. He could either give up his quest, turn around and journey home in shame and defeat. He could travel north to the lands of the Baron of Gilsland and wait for perhaps months or even years for the men he sought to return from the Holy Land, if they ever did.

Then, he reflected, there was the third option. That was to press on and do whatever it took to fulfil his promise. A promise he had made not only to himself, but to Beatrice and their child.

Will needed little time to make his decision, because he knew in his heart that he really had no choice at all. There was only one thing for it: he was going to have to board another ship bound for Outremer, the land far beyond the sea, in the hopes of eventually catching up with the men who had destroyed his world. And to do that, Will was going to have to take up the cross himself and join the king's army.

Chapter 14

Fired by his newfound sense of purpose, Will jumped up from the bench. Then scanning the crowds all around him on the quayside and swarming about the moored vessels, he spied a short, fat man dressed in the black robe of a clergyman, hesitantly crossing the gangplank to board the nearest of the ships that were being loaded for their voyage. The clergyman teetered dangerously for a moment on the ramp, almost plummeted straight down into the deadly gap between the ship's side and the harbour wall, then managed to right himself and scramble aboard.

'That is who I need,' Will said to himself, and he ran over to intercept him. The fat little clergyman turned to look as Will hopped nimbly over the side and strode towards him across the busy deck. A couple of crewmen carrying a heavy chest between them cursed at him and one said, 'Out the way, there, you clumsy bastard. Can't you see we're working?'

Ignoring them, Will implored the clergyman, 'Father, Father, I need your help. I wish to take the cross and join up for this voyage. How do I do it?'

The clergyman stared at him, clearly wondering at his appearance. 'You are not a man of knightly rank?'

'Just an ordinary villager,' Will said.

'Has your master released you from your duties in order to take the cross?'

'I am neither slave nor serf,' Will replied, 'but free to pursue the course of my own choosing.'

'Very well. And are you baptised?'

Will remembered his father telling him he had received that sacrament as an infant, at his mother's insistence. 'I am. At least I believe so.'

Some other men, voyagers already aboard the ship ahead of its departure, had overheard their conversation and were gathering round. 'What makes you think the king's army wants the likes of you?' challenged one of them, a bulky red-faced individual with half an ear missing. He had a crossbow slung from a piece of rope across his back, and a well-crafted dagger stuck through his belt that Will thought he must have won in a gambling match or perhaps stolen, as he instantly disliked the look of the man. He also very much disliked being prodded, which the man was doing with a grimy forefinger.

'I would ask you to refrain from doing that,' Will told him with a frown, 'and in reply to your question I would say that an army needs archers, and I can shoot better than many men.'

'What, with that thing?' the man said, scornfully eyeing Will's bow. But he withdrew the finger.

'You must have an ordained priest present in order to take the vow,' the fat clergyman said, eyeing the two men and looking anxious that a dispute might about to break out. 'I am only a lay ship's chaplain.'

'Then pray run and find me a priest,' Will replied.

While the group waited on deck for the clergyman to return, Will's unpleasant new acquaintance said, 'Come on, archer, let's see what you can do with that stick of yours. And I'll wager it's no match for my crossbow.'

'I do not think I need prove myself to you, or anyone,' Will replied. But the crowd were becoming worked up at the prospect of a contest. 'Go on, show us! Show us!'

'See that gull there on the water?' the crossbowman said, pointing his grubby finger at a white seabird floating on the swell perhaps seventy paces from the ship's side. 'Stick an arrow in his gob, and I'll believe you can shoot.'

'He has done me no harm and I won't kill what I cannot eat,' Will said. 'Besides, the range is barely further than arm's length away.' Then spying a bobbing object some twenty-five paces further off, he saw it was a small wooden cask that must have fallen from one of the ships being loaded. 'Can you hit a target at that distance?' he asked his challenger.

'Course I can,' the man said gruffly, though rather uncertainly.

'In that case,' Will said. 'I'll shoot against you. One arrow each. If you and your infernal device can place one of your bolts in that cask and I fail to match your shot, then you shall have my sword as a prize. But if you miss, then you owe me that dagger.'

'Infernal device is it?' the man replied indignantly. 'Right then. It's a bet. I shoot first. Watch this.' The eager spectators swarmed after him as he stumped over to the side. With elaborate care he planted the nose of his crossbow against the deck with his foot in its iron stirrup, then grasped the thick cord with both hands and heaved it up with a grunt of effort until it engaged the trigger mechanism and clicked into place. He drew a short, sturdy bolt from his boot, slid it into the flight groove in its barrel, and rested the weapon on the ship's side to take aim. The moored vessel was barely moving on the swell. 'Hey, that's cheating,' said one of the men watching. Others were already exchanging bets and counting their coins.

'He never said I could not use a support,' the crossbowman rasped. Then closing one eye and holding his breath, he waited for the distant cask to bob up on the next wave and released his shot. The crossbow loosed its bolt with a thumping twang. They all watched as the missile flew straight and true across the water, but then fell at least thirty paces short of the target and splashed into the sea. 'Hell and death!' the crossbowman spat. 'An unlucky gust of wind, that's all it was. That one doesn't count. Let me go again.'

'There weren't no gust of wind, you dog,' said another man. 'Fair's fair, Osric. The rule is one shot each and you missed yours. Now step aside and let the bowman show us what he can do.'

The disgruntled Osric slunk out of the way as Will took his place. Calm and in no hurry, he strung his bow, tested the tension of the string and then drew one of the long, white-feathered bodkin shafts from his quiver. He was less than happy about wasting a carefully made and valuable arrow, but a wager was a wager and he sensed that this Osric needed to be taught a lesson.

The cask rose and fell on the current, the last ebbs of the receding tide pulling it steadily further out along the course of the estuary. It was now at least a hundred and twenty paces away from the moored ship.

'He'll never hit that,' Osric muttered. 'It can't be done.'

'Shut your stinking hole, Osric,' someone chided him.

Silence fell across the deck and even the busy crewmen stopped what they were doing to gawk as Will planted his feet apart to brace himself against the gentle swell, and marked his target with a hunter's eye. Then he nocked his arrow, raised the bow and hefted it to full draw. With a snap of the bowstring and a judder of the yew stave, the arrow was in flight. It soared over the waves, the white fletching a glittering streak in the light of the sun. Not a man was breathing. Will nodded to himself as he followed the shot's trajectory.

With a solid woody *thunk* that they heard even at this distance, the arrow planted itself dead centre into the cask, just as the swell swallowed it from sight. The jubilant crowd cheered and slapped Will on the back, and money changed hands. 'Ordinary villager my arse!' laughed one of the happy winners. Meanwhile, Osric was slinking morosely away. 'Are you forgetting something?' Will asked him, pointing at the dagger in his belt.

'That's right, Osric,' another of the men said. 'A bet's a bet, and he won fair and square.'

Osric's face was dark as he pulled the sheathed dagger from his belt and reluctantly offered it to Will.

'I have changed my mind,' Will said. 'Keep it. I have no need of a dagger.'

Osric stood glowering at him. 'I'll remember you, boy,' he said menacingly.

Will wasn't inclined to make any reply. Osric turned and stalked away, followed by two shifty-looking companions who eyed Will with hostility as they left. At that moment, the short, fat chaplain returned aboard with a priest, a tall thin older man with none of the benevolent air of Father Michael about him. The priest was accompanied by two clerks.

'Which of you men is it that wishes to take the vow?' the priest asked, and Will stepped forward. 'That would be me, William Bowman,' he replied. 'But I don't know what to say.'

'Never mind that,' said the priest. 'Just take off your outer garment and unhitch your sword. Then go down on one knee with the sword before you, and bow your head. Give him room, there. Let us have silence, please.'

Will did as he was told, stripping down to his mail hauberk. One of the priest's clerks took his jerkin from him, fairly sagging under its weight. Then Will unbuckled his sword and knelt solemnly on the deck, clasping the sheathed weapon vertically in front of him with both hands. Its cruciform hilt gave it the appearance of a cross, and in that moment he could feel the power of the holy symbol shining over him like a strange light.

The men all backed away as the priest stood over Will. Some were grinning and nudging each other, but every man present had already been through the swearing-in ceremony he was about to undertake and understood its importance. 'Oi, mate, where'd you get that mail shirt?' called out an unruly voice, and another hissed 'Shhh!'

Next, the priest held up a smaller cross of his own, and in a grave, formal tone spoke a long stream of Latin words over his kneeling subject. 'Now repeat after me,' he said, and made Will recite phrases that to him were largely meaningless, other than a few recognisable expressions such as '*crucem Domini*' and '*amore Christi*'. As the words of the vow were being uttered, the priest's clerk had produced two strips of white cloth, a long curved needle and a bobbin of thread, and set about sewing the strips in the form of a cross to the shoulder of Will's jerkin. He had some difficulty pushing his needle through the thick, tough leather, and twice yelped as he jabbed his own finger.

'There,' said the priest at last.

Looking up, Will asked, 'That's it?'

'That's it,' said the priest. 'You are now a *crucesignatus*, one who is marked by the sign of the cross and has thereby taken his oath. You may stand.'

'Except I have no idea what oath it is I have sworn,' Will said, rising to his feet. 'Latin being foreign to my ears.'

The priest replied, 'You have taken a holy vow to follow in the footsteps of Christ, by whom you have thereby now been redeemed from the power of Hell. You have accepted that you must suffer for the name of Christ many things: wretchedness, poverty, nakedness, persecution, need, sickness, hunger, thirst, and other such troubles; for the Lord said to his disciples, "You must suffer many things for my name, and great will be your reward." Go forth confidently then, soldier of Christ, and repel the foes of the cross with a stalwart heart. A benediction has been bestowed upon your sword, that it may not fail you in this task. Know that neither death nor life can separate you from the love of God which is in Jesus Christ; and in every peril repeat the words, "Whether we live or whether we die, we are the Lord's."'

The priest's eyes glowed as he went on, 'What a glory to return in victory from such a battle! How blessed to die there as a martyr! Rejoice, brave warrior, if you live and conquer in the Lord; but glory and exult even more if you die and join Him. Life indeed is a fruitful thing and victory is glorious, but a holy death is more important than either. If they are blessed who die in the Lord, how much more are they who die *for* the Lord!'

And with that, the ceremony was at an end. Will was given back his jerkin now adorned with the white cross that he would henceforth wear as the mark of a sworn pilgrim of God. He pulled the garment on over his hauberk and buckled his sword back into place. As the priest and his clerks left the ship, Will asked the chaplain, 'What about my horse?'

'Only a knight may bring his steed aboard a king's ship,' the chaplain replied. 'And even then only at a price that you don't look as though you can afford, my young friend.'

So it was, then. With a heavy heart and a mind still spinning from the import of what he had just let himself in for, Will ran back to find the assistant harbour master still inside the tavern. The man might be crude in his ways, but he was sincere. 'As you are the only person I know here in Southampton, do you know anyone who is in need of a good horse? As for the price, I will gladly give him away for nothing to a man who will treat him well.'

'Let me see him,' said the harbour master with a smile. 'I could do with a decent mount, and I have a parcel of good grazing meadow on the edge of the town. My daughters will love tending to him.'

It was a painful wrench, letting go of such a trusty companion as Hengroen. 'I will miss you,' Will said to him, stroking his neck and pressing his forehead to his. 'But where I must go, you can't follow. If ever I return to these shores, I promise I will come and find you again, and buy you back with all the silver in my possession.'

Then Will sadly left Hengroen in the hands of his new owner and walked back towards the ship that would be his home for the foreseeable future.

Where that journey might take him, he as yet had little idea. But he was committed now to pursue his quest to the ends of the world if need be, and there was no longer any question of turning back.

Chapter 15

The loading of Will's ship took long enough for them to miss that tide, and the voyagers, with their newest addition, were obliged to wait much of the day for the next before they could finally set sail.

By now there were some twenty knightly men-at-arms aboard, belonging to the retinue of a minor lord from somewhere in Leicestershire, along with their horses and squires, as well as the sixty or so common men like Will. As with the other vessels along the quay, the carpenters had been busy adapting what was essentially a large mercantile cog into a ship of war capable of deploying infantry and cavalry troops overseas. The horses, along with their very voluminous feed stores, were housed in a covered section towards the rear that had been reworked into a form of lower deck. The knights and their squires also enjoyed the privilege of extra shelter from the elements while the lower-ranking commoners and ship's crew would have to make do with a tarpaulin awning and were mostly confined to the foremost part of the ship, before the mast. They would be sharing their cramped living space with stacks of barrels of food supplies: salted horse meat and pork and dried vegetables, along with freshwater casks and chests of weapons and other supplies.

The waiting was a difficult time for Will, as he had little to do but fret that every moment of delay only served to put yet more distance between him and the black eagle soldiers he had been so close to catching up with. There was no telling when he might do so again. Their ship had long since vanished out of sight, and he couldn't shut out of his mind the image of it sailing rapidly away over the sea, further and further beyond his helpless reach. But there was nothing for it but to try to remain patient, and bide his time while getting used to his new environment.

Will found it hard to believe that he had joined an army — not only because it was the last thing he had ever dreamed of doing, but also because there was little impression of it when he looked around him at his fellow comrades in arms. With the exception of the knights in their identical surcoats, bearing the herald of a red shield with a yellow stripe, the rest of them were a motley crew without cohesion or uniformity, related only in appearance by the sewn-on cross that each man wore on his clothing. Some, like him, were already armed for battle, while others had joined the ship quite empty-handed. It seemed to Will the oddest kind of fighting force he could have imagined.

Then at last, to the sound of shouted commands, the thump of running feet on deck, the creaking of ropes and crackle of flapping canvas, they cast off their moorings and the ship slowly peeled away from the harbour wall and pointed towards the estuary, along with several others ready to depart on the same tide. The current drew them along the stretch of Southampton Water, and now that they were freed from their moorings Will felt the unfamiliar pitch and roll of the deck under his feet and wondered what kind of mariner he would make.

As the vessel sailed down the estuary in the direction of the open sea, the shout went round for all hands to gather on deck. The knights crowded together at one side and the commoners to the other, with a general air of anticipation at whatever announcement was about to be made. Presently the ship's captain appeared, accompanied by the fat little chaplain who stood up on a small podium to address them all. In the silence on deck, broken only by the fluttering of the sail, the rush of water along their sides and the constant overhead screech of the seabirds, he unfurled a manuscript and began to read from it out loud in a strained and hesitant voice, while swaying on his feet and trying to remain upright under the movement of the ship:

'This day on the twenty-seventh of March in the year of our Lord one thousand, one hundred and ninety, here follows the proclamation of Richard, by the grace of God king of England, duke of Normandy and Aquitaine, and Count of Anjou. Know that by common counsel the following regulations have been drawn up: that whoever on board ship shall slay another is himself to be cast into the sea lashed to the dead man; that if he have slain him ashore he is to be buried in the same way. If anyone be proved by worthy witnesses to have drawn a knife for the purpose of striking another, or to have wounded another so as to draw blood, let him lose his fist; but if he strike another with his hand and draw no blood, let him be dipped three times in the sea. If anyone cast any reproach or bad word against another, or invoke God's malison on him, let him for every offence pay an ounce of silver. Let a convicted thief be shorn like a prize-fighter, after which let boiling pitch be poured on his head and a feather pillow be shaken over it so as to make him a laughing stock. Then let him be put ashore at the first land where the ship may touch.' And on it went in the same vein, listing an interminable series of further rules and statutes apparently designed to spoil any chance of fun aboard.

'Ballocks to that,' shouted a voice from the back of the crowd. 'And ballocks to King Richard.' The chaplain and ship's captain shot hostile looks at the assembly, searching for the culprit who had magically disappeared among his fellows leaving only innocent, expressionless faces all around.

Before long the procession of ships had reached the mouth of the Solent, and a south-westerly breeze filled their sails to carry them in a wide sweep around the cliffs of the land mass that Will learned from a crewman was the Isle of Wight. As they slowly crept around the island Will now had his first real view of the open sea, and the perfectly flat horizon where water and sky met in a seemingly infinite stretch from east to west. His sense of geography was somewhat hazy, but as he understood it, unless other unknown islands stood in-between, the nearest landfall to the south was the north coast of France. It might have been another world.

It soon appeared, however, that southwards was not their set course. Hugging the English shoreline the ship veered towards the sun now beginning to dip in the west. Not being called upon to perform any other tasks, Will stood in the bow and watched the sunset from its first golden inklings to the splendour of colours as the flaming orb at last sank below the waterline in a final blaze of glory. He was beginning to get accustomed to the living, vibrating feel of the ship under his feet, more pronounced now that they were on the open sea. The shallow-keeled craft was susceptible to every wave and cross-current, twitching like an anxious horse.

Behind him was the tumult of constant commands and adjustments to sail and rudder as they worked their slow and steady way west within constant sight of the land.

Come nightfall they had begun to steer a course south by west, and with the fading of the light and the emergence of the stars — an amazing multitude that lit up the heavens — Will saw his home country disappear into the ship's pale wake like a great dark shadow slipping beneath the waves. He might never see it again.

That was the moment when the question burned strongest in his mind: *have I done the right thing?* In his heart he knew he had taken the only road open to him. But that belief didn't prevent the feelings from welling up: the familiar presence of his constant grief now joined by a sense of desperate isolation. Here surrounded by a hundred or more men crammed in close proximity onto this boat with barely room to move and absolutely no privacy, he had never felt more alone.

Whether permitted or not by King Richard's charter of maritime regulations, later that night someone broke out a cask of ale and there was a good deal of drinking and merriment, dancing and flute playing. Will kept his distance, speaking to nobody. Then just a few hours afterwards the wind picked up sharply, and the joyful mood aboard turned sour as the ship pitched and tossed on the waves, lashed by a sudden violent downpour that saw almost everyone aboard racked with seasickness. This being Will's first voyage, he wasn't spared the suffering.

When eventually his stomach had no more to yield up over the ship's side, feeling miserable in body and even lower in spirits he staggered over the pitching, sloping deck to a nook among the storage barrels where he could wedge himself a little more comfortably against the movement of the ship and gain at least a little shelter from the rain, wind and salty spray of the waves crashing against the hull. He laid his precious things down beside him, curled up as best he could in his confined space, closed his eyes, and within a short time the noise and chaos around him faded away into the silence of a deep, dreamless sleep.

When he awoke in the darkness, the wind and rain had stopped and a bright moon was shining, but he immediately knew something was wrong. Reaching out his hand he found that his bow and arrow quiver, which had been lying close by, were no longer there. He pulled himself up to his feet and hunted around in case the motion of the ship had caused them to slide away from him while he slept. But no, they were gone. Someone had taken them.

I'll remember you, boy. Will remembered those words, too, and the man who had spoken them to him. The one enemy Will had made aboard this ship was the only person who could have been jealous, vindictive and conniving enough to want to steal the bow by which he'd been made to feel humiliated in front of the others. But unluckily for Osric, there weren't many places he could run and hide aboard a vessel less than eighty feet from stem to stern and twenty wide.

Most of his fellow voyagers had done as Will had, and found themselves nooks and boltholes among the cargo in which to spend the night hours. But not everyone was asleep. He found Osric sitting on a cask on a section of deck by the prow. With him were the same two shifty-looking companions from before, the three of them engaged in a moonlit game of dice. Lying on the wooden boards at Osric's feet was his crossbow — and there in plain view next to it, Will's bow and arrow quiver.

'Hey,' one of companions hissed, nudging Osric with his elbow as Will came up out of the shadows and stepped towards them. Osric looked up, startled at first but then collecting himself and grinning widely.

'The way a man accepts defeat tells much about the quality of his character,' Will said. 'Yours is nothing to be envied, but you still have a chance to redeem it.' He pointed. 'Give me back my possessions and we can forget this theft took place.'

Osric shook his head, still grinning. 'If you can't take care of your things, you don't deserve to keep them. They're mine now.'

'I offer you reconciliation,' Will said. 'But the offer is made only once. To reject it would be a mistake.' His right hand strayed to the hilt of his sword and rested on the pommel. His eyes were fixed on Osric, but he was watching the other two also.

Nobody spoke for a long moment. All that could be heard was the wind in the sail above them, the constant roar of the sea and the creaking of the ship's timbers. Then the three men all rose to their feet. One wore a short broadsword, Osric the long dagger that Will had let him keep, and the third a wicked spiked maul thrust through his belt. They stood shoulder to shoulder facing him with ugly expressions on their faces.

The last thing Will wanted was to become embroiled in a fight with these men, but he could not relinquish that bow. If a fight was necessary to reclaim what was his, then so be it.

'You heard the chaplain read out the king's articles of law,' he said to them. 'But if any of you draws his weapon I fear you'll lose more than just the hand that held it.'

'Not if you're bleeding out like a stuck pig on this deck,' said Osric. 'I think you had best turn around and walk away, scum. There's three of us and you're all alone.'

'Not quite alone,' said another voice from the shadows.

Chapter 16

The sudden and unexpected arrival of reinforcements came as an even greater surprise to Will than to Osric and his companions. From under the shadow of the sail to one side of the mast stepped a figure; then a second from the other side. As they emerged into the moonlight, Will recognised their faces. They had been among the crowd watching the shooting competition that morning, and then later when all hands had been gathered on deck. He had paid them little notice at the time. The first was a fair-haired man perhaps ten or a dozen years his senior, handsome in features and slender of build, dressed in a hooded cape that looked silvery in the moonlight. The second was considerably taller, not much above Will's height but as massive as a bear on two legs, with huge fists balled at his sides and a furious glint in his eye. A white line of spittle along his lips gave him the look of a rabid madman.

'Don't you go getting involved in this, you hear?' Osric warned the newcomers. 'It ain't your fight.'

Osric's words fell on deaf ears. Will's helpers stepped closer to stand either side of him, the fair man to his right and the bear to his left. The contest was now equal, three against three, but Osric's companions looked as frightened as if they were facing fifty.

'Give him back his bow,' the fair-haired man said. He spoke in a low, assured tone and with a particular accent, lilting and oddly melodious, that Will didn't recognise. 'Or all three of you will be food for the fishes before you can say "Hail Mary".'

Osric's friends might have been afraid, but Osric himself was not quite so easily deterred. He snarled and lunged forward, his fist closing around his dagger hilt. Before Will's sword was half drawn from its scabbard in response, the bear moved with startling speed for one so large and Osric's advance was halted as if he had run headlong into an oak tree. A fist that could have enclosed his neck in its grip slammed into the middle of his face and sent him sprawling on his back.

Now the fair-haired man came forward drawing a long, curved sword from under his cape and stood over Osric with its tip against his throat. 'The matter is settled,' he said in the same tone, quiet but deadly. 'You will apologise for your actions and swear never to repeat them.'

'I-I beg pardon,' Osric stuttered pitifully, gulping hard as he stared up the curved length of the blade and the steely expression of the man holding it ready to plunge through his neck. 'Don't kill me.' Blood leaked from his broken nose. His two companions had edged away as far as they could without falling into the sea.

'Do you find his response satisfactory?' the fair-haired man asked Will.

'I'm satisfied,' Will replied. 'But if he ever comes near me again he will regret it.'

'I think he understands that,' the fair-haired man replied. 'Do you not, Osric?'

Will picked up his bow and quiver. The fair-haired man withdrew and sheathed his sword and the bear retreated a step, still with raised fists and a ferocious snarl on his face. The conflict was over, resolved as quickly as it had begun. Will and his new allies left Osric to bleed on the deck, and returned abaft the mast to Will's place among the barrels. All around were sleeping men, a soft chorus of snores in the darkness. Nobody else seemed to have noticed the incident.

The fair-haired man was chuckling with amusement, while his large companion seemed to be taking longer to calm himself. 'Thank you for your help,' Will said. 'But why should you have taken my part in the argument, when I am a stranger to you?'

'I watched you shoot against him,' said the fair-haired man, adjusting his sword as he made himself comfortable on the deck. 'And I cannot abide a bad loser. A thief, even less. Nor can I tolerate any form of injustice or unfairness against my fellow man, especially one worthy of greater respect. I'm sure you could have beaten those weaklings on your own, but we felt obliged to step in, nonetheless.'

'Well, I am grateful,' Will said. 'Will is my name.' He leaned across extending his hand, and they shook. He offered the same to the bear, but the big man shied away and lowered his eyes.

'I know who you are, bowman,' said the fair-haired man. 'I was also present when you took your oath. I am Gabriel, Gabriel O'Carolan. And my friend here goes by the name of Samson. Pray excuse him; he is simple in his ways, uncomfortable in social company, and does not speak much to strangers.'

'Forgive me for saying so, but I find that you yourself have a strange manner of speaking, unlike any I have heard before.'

Gabriel laughed. 'Then you must never have met another man from my country, because we all talk this way. I come from the west of Ireland, near a place called Baile Chláir.'

'No, I have not been there,' Will said. 'I did not know men spoke differently there. You are even further from home than I, Gabriel.'

Gabriel laughed again. He had a winning kind of charm that Will was quickly taking to. 'That I am, and more so by the hour. It is a long and sad story with which I won't bore you.'

'Tell it to me. How did you come to be here, on this ship?'

'Very well, if it pleases you to hear it, then what else have we to do on such a pleasant balmy night?'

Gabriel related how he had left his home many years earlier. 'I was born a bastard, you see. My mother, in her shame at having a child so young and out of wedlock, died when I was but three days old. Her brother promised her on her deathbed that he would raise the infant as one of his own sons until he was old enough to make his own way in life. And so I was brought up by my uncle Cormac, whose lands you could not easily ride across in three days even on the swiftest horse. He was an honourable man, treated me well and educated me in many things. But true to his word, when I turned fifteen years of age he sent me from his house with nothing but a bag of silver and the clothes on my back. I crossed over the sea for England to seek my fortune, but ended up in Wales where I lived for many a year. Being skilled in music and chess, which my uncle had taught me, I made my living as a minstrel and a player of games. Sometimes I earned extra money showing men the finer points of swordplay, as my uncle was a fine hand with the blade and also instructed me in that discipline from a young age.'

'What is chess?' Will asked him.

'Don't you know? Then I'll teach you, should you wish. It is a most engaging pastime, and we will be on this ship for some time together, with little else to do.'

'I would like that. But please go on with your story.'

'It was in the Welsh county of Carmarthenshire that I had the blessing to meet my beloved. Eryl was her name. Ah, such beauty as was almost painful to behold,' Gabriel reminisced sadly. 'Her hair was as golden as the sunrise over Lough Corrib, her eyes bluer than a spring morning sky. The music of her voice . . . but it grieves my heart to say more.' He heaved a sigh.

The only problem with his and Eryl's romantic liaison, Gabriel explained, was that she was married to another, though he was a cruel and jealous husband and she had no love for him, instead returning Gabriel's affections with equal passion. Before long, however, their affair had been suspected and Gabriel had to run for his life.

'So that is what brought you here?' Will asked.

'Not then,' Gabriel told him. 'I could not stay far from my beloved. Our plan was that she would escape from him and we would be together. But then, the situation became more complicated. Her husband was found dead, with his throat cut to the bone, and it was generally believed that it was I who had murdered him, in order to claim his wife as my own.'

'But you were innocent of the crime?' Will supposed.

Gabriel made the sign of the cross over his chest. 'I am entirely without sin, I assure you. Or in that regard, at any rate, since I have never killed a man in my life. Eryl had once told me that her husband was heavily in debt to an even worse rogue than himself, and it is he who was certainly the true murderer. But I could scarcely remain there to protest my innocence, now could I? For if they had caught me, they would instantly have put a rope around my neck. Hunted like an animal by men on horseback with packs of hounds, I was forced to flee further afield and hide deep in the Forest of Glyn Cothi, a place so dark and wild that few have set foot there since the time of the Romans.'

'How did you manage to get away?' Will asked, engrossed by his tale.

'Good fortune smiled upon me,' replied Gabriel. 'As it so happened that around this same time the royal envoy, Giraldus Cambriensis or Gerald of Wales as he is known, was journeying around the area recruiting men to take up the cross and join King Henry's expedition to the Holy Land. It was near Whitland Abbey that I heard him talk, just months after Jerusalem had fallen to the forces of Saladin. The envoy was charged not only with enlisting the wealthy and the nobility to his mission but also the commoners, the lowliest villains and cut-throats among them, who flocked to the gatherings of men wishing to join up with the army and thereby receive the pope's forgiveness for all sins and the pardoning of crimes, past and present. For my own part I had little desire to journey to the Holy Land, but considered such a fate preferable to a rope's end. I had only to take the vow, and from that moment I was safe. My accusers could no longer touch a hair on my head.'

'I cannot say I blame you for making that choice,' Will said.

'This was two years ago,' Gabriel went on. 'Since that time much has happened, what with King Henry's death, may God rest his soul, and his throne passing to his son. They say Richard was among the very first to take up the cross upon hearing of the fall of Jerusalem, while he was still only Count of Poitou, and has been mustering his forces and making his plans all this long while. As for me, alas, never again did I see my beloved

Eryl, whose family took her away to where I could never find her. I wandered for a time, trying to forget my woes; then as word reached Wales that the king's fleet would at last be ready to sail this Easter I joined a band of fellow pilgrims marching east into England, then southwards for the coast. It was a hard and dangerous road, and only a few of us made it as far as Southampton. Those remaining were separated and the others joined different ships. Finding myself alone once more, I soon became acquainted with Samson here. Though that is not his true name.'

Gabriel looked fondly at Samson. They could speak openly about him, because while they had been talking the big man had nodded off to sleep with his chin on his chest, snoring softly.

'I don't think I have ever seen anyone punched so hard as Osric was tonight,' Will said.

'He has the most tremendous strength,' Gabriel replied. 'More than he realises. And to look at him would be enough to make most men quake in their shoes. He is actually liable to foam at the mouth when incensed, as you might have observed. Do not be fooled by his terrifying appearance, however, for a gentler soul you could not hope to find anywhere in this world. He has the mind of a child and the temperament of a lamb, unless crossed, which I would advise to no man. I have known him only two days, but I have great affection and trust in him. Shall I tell you how we met?'

'Please do.'

'It was back there at the docks, shortly after I arrived in Southampton. I was weary from my journey and searching for my travelling companions, from whom I had been separated amid all the confusion and the crowd. Then what should I spy there on the busy quayside but the most exquisite creature, a vision from Heaven, wafting by as though in some dream?'

'A woman?' Will asked.

'To call her a mere woman would be to do her no justice. For those few moments that I had sight of this angelic apparition I was transfixed, transported, wondering who she could be, thinking perhaps she was there to bid farewell to her loved one boarding his ship, yet wishing she was alone so that I might find some way to speak to her. My eyes were still fixed upon her when I stepped blindly off the edge of the harbour wall.'

Gabriel chuckled at the memory of his own foolishness. 'I very nearly dropped straight into the water, where I should certainly have been drowned or crushed by the hull of the moored ship next to me. I was hanging there by my fingernails, quite helpless and ready to drop like an apple from a bough, when a pair of powerful hands reached down, grasped me by the wrists and pulled me up to safety as though I had weighed as little as a babe in arms. "You have saved my life," said I, thanking him. "What is your name?" He would not reveal it to me at first, until after much insistence I was able to glean that he had been christened Simon but had an aversion to the name. "Then in honour of your prodigious strength," I told him, "I will call you Samson instead."' Gabriel looked at Will, realising that the biblical reference was lost on him. 'Samson, from the Book of Judges, the mighty Israelite warrior who demolished the pagan temple of the Philistines? Never mind.'

'I know some parts of the Bible,' Will said. 'But only what I remember hearing others repeat to me. Do you read and write?'

'My uncle taught me,' Gabriel said, somewhat dismissively. 'Anyhow, he likes his new name very much, and has been following me around like a very large hairy dog ever since. I would not be without his companionship, for all his childlike ways.'

'Why did you not board ship sooner, if you have been here for two days?' Will asked, and Gabriel smiled.

'I was hoping to see the apparition again, but in vain. Perhaps fate intended that I should delay, so that I could find another interesting new acquaintance. Now, Will the bowman, I have told you my entire story; pray tell me yours.'

Will was reluctant to begin with, but he felt that Gabriel was someone he could trust, as he had trusted Father Michael. The older man became very serious as the account unfolded, listening attentively with a growing frown. At last, he said, 'What little I understand of grief and heartbreak is as nothing compared to that which you have suffered. The burden that has been placed on you would be too great for most men to bear. What is there I can say that could bring solace to your heart?'

'Nothing,' Will replied. 'But it does me good to talk to a friend. I am glad to have met you, Gabriel. And Samson too. Tell me, though. What kind of sword is that, with a blade so curved?' He pointed at the weapon in its scabbard on Gabriel's belt. 'All the swords I have seen were straight in form.'

'It is a falchion,' Gabriel replied, touching the hilt. 'My uncle gave it to me. I treasure it much. A curved edge cuts better and more cleanly than a straight one. On the matter of arms, I have been admiring your bow. Did you make it yourself?'

'I did,' Will replied, picking it up to let Gabriel see it more closely.

'It reminds me of those in Ireland, crafted with such care and expertise. The Welsh archers I have met carve theirs out of the dwarf elm trees of the forest and often leave them in a crude and unpolished state with the bark still on. You could not shoot far with them, but they are strong and powerful enough to inflict terrible wounds in a close fight.'

'You can shoot a bow?'

Gabriel smiled. 'With unmatched accuracy. That is, on condition that the target is as large as a barn and no more than two steps away. No, I find that my talents, such as they are, lie in other directions.'

They talked until the light of dawn crept into the sky, when the sunrise lured the pair closer to the stern to watch the fiery colours spread along the horizon in their wake. By now the ship was back to life, activity and noise all around them once more. Samson slept peacefully on, undisturbed by all the bustle. There was no sign of Osric and his cronies, wisely keeping as far from Will and his friends as space allowed.

'I've never been able to see such a distance,' Will said, gazing at the perfectly still, calm and seemingly infinite expanse of sea to every direction, utterly empty but for the scattered fleet of their companion ships to their front and rear. 'Not even on the clearest of clear days standing on the top of Foxwood Hill do you get such a view.'

'If you could see right across the water,' replied Gabriel pointing over the ship's larboard bow, towards the south, 'I expect you would be looking at King Richard's Duchy of Normandy, over which he rules along with the lands of Aquitaine, Gascony, Poitou, Brittany and Anjou.'

'I don't know much about France,' Will admitted. 'But that sounds as if he must reign over all of it.'

'A great deal of it,' Gabriel agreed. 'Indeed, a greater portion than is ruled over by Philip Augustus, its nominal king, who has little love for Richard. Still, I hear that the two kings are reconciled to travel together to the Holy Land. They depart from the port of Marseille, in the far south of France.'

'How are we to join them?' Will asked. 'Will we land on the northern shores and march overland?' He was thinking again of the Baron of Gilsland's men, and his far better chances of catching up with them by land than by sea. If that opportunity arose, then at the first chance he got he would desert, somehow procure a horse – though he doubted he could ever find another like Hengroen – and ride like thunder day and night to make up his lost ground.

'No,' replied Gabriel. 'As I understand it, we will be sailing the long way round. The sunrise at our stern means we are currently bearing west, with the great sea by which men journey to my homeland on our right. This course will carry us around the northern coast of France, after which we bear down towards the Kingdoms of Navarre, Castille and León. Having skirted those lands we continue southwards, touching at the Portuguese port of Lisbon for supplies. From there we will proceed for many leagues until we are able to bear east once again, hurrying as fast as ever we can around the treacherous dominions of the Moorish Almohads until we reach safer waters off the Kingdom of Aragon, and thence to the southern shores of France and our meeting point with the rest of the fleet. The voyage will take three months, perhaps longer.'

Three months! Will could barely conceive of such a journey. Already he was beginning to understand that this world he lived in was a far larger place than he had imagined it to be. And somewhere out there among the infinite expanse of blue were the men he hunted, now further away than ever.

Chapter 17

The weeks passed. The daily rhythms of life at sea, its habitual customs and numerous activities – the bustle of the crew as they attended to their duties, the necessary cleaning chores and cooking and animal husbandry, the smoke from the galley, the slaughter of the livestock and allocation of fresh meat to a hundred hungry mouths while their supplies lasted, the creaking of ropes and timbers and the flap of canvas, the constant movement of the deck underfoot, the ever-changing weather now sunny and now grey and drizzling, the sea sometimes as smooth as a millpond and sometimes treacherously choppy, the twice-daily gatherings on deck when the ship's chaplain would lead them in fervent prayer – all became so instilled in Will and his shipmates that it was sometimes easy to imagine that this little wooden world of theirs was all that existed.

Being essentially passengers with little in the way of regular duties to perform, the non-crewmen all had to find ways to bide their time and stave off what could have been a maddening degree of boredom – or in Will's personal case a state of mounting frustration that might have broken his spirit entirely if not for the companionship of his new friends, especially

Gabriel. The two of them spent many an hour sheltering from rain or sun in what became their regular spot under the canvas awning, with Samson invariably close by.

Despite coming from very different backgrounds, they discovered they had much in common, such as their shared love of nature and growing things, an appreciation of beauty and the simple things in life. Most of their time, however, was occupied with the study of the game of chess, entirely new to Will but at which Gabriel was an expert. He would unroll his sheet of leather patterned with dyed squares of black and white and pour out the carved ivory and rosewood men from a draw-string pouch, and he and Will would face each other cross-legged on the deck, often engrossed in the complexities of their game from sunrise to sunset. Gabriel had been playing from a young age and had long since honed his skills to the point where he could reliably defeat almost all comers, often making a pretty penny in wagers.

By contrast, as a rank beginner Will had to puzzle long and hard over the most elementary rudiments before his understanding began to take shape. He was a keen learner, however, and once he had grasped the essentials he quickly developed as a player. As the weeks flew by, he came to appreciate more and more the subtleties of tactics and planning, the beauty of a well-thought-out strategy, the infinite range of possibilities, patterns and combinations that the board afforded and the game's often brutal reflection of real-life combat when irresistible superior force battered the enemy into inevitable submission. The better he got at it, the more rigorously his mentor was able to test him, and the level of their play rapidly rose. Having at first lost game after game, in time Will learned to put up enough of a resistance to score the occasional draw; and on the last day of April, he astounded Gabriel by deploying his forces in a surprise assault on the latter's king and announcing 'check mate'.

'A decisive endgame that was,' Gabriel said with a smile. 'Congratulations, brother. In only a short while you have become quite a dangerous opponent.'

'I had a good teacher,' Will replied.

During their voyage, Will was also becoming acquainted with several of his other shipmates. Often the men would gather in groups and share blood-curdling stories about the nature of the enemy they would be facing in battle when they eventually reached the Holy Land. The chaplain liked to involve himself in these discussions, doing all he could to stir up their zeal. He talked at length about the terrible acts perpetrated by Saladin and his Saracen forces against the holy city of Jerusalem: the pillaging and desecration of churches, sacred relics vandalised, bells silenced and crosses broken off. As for its innocent inhabitants, he intoned gravely, 'the beast Saladin ordered some fifteen thousand of them into slavery: families torn apart, wives made to watch the pitiless slaughter of their husbands; droves of children marched off in chains never to be seen again, amid the pitiful howls of lamentation of their mothers. How many virtuous Christian women were taken as concubines, stripped of their modesty and profaned; how many young virgins forced to yield themselves and nuns dishonourably used by dozens of these savage heathens upon the very altar of Christ, while their devilish comrades stood slavering in line awaiting their turn to give vent to their passions!'

The chaplain's dramatic accounts of rape and violence, which grew more graphic and scabrous with every retelling, never failed to draw the desired angry mutterings from his audience. Muted growls of 'fucking godless bastards' and 'we'll serve 'em out when we find 'em, my lads, don't you worry about that' were the usual response. Will could see the vengeful gleam in their eyes and understood all too well their desire for retribution; but he also knew that Saracens and heathens were not alone in bringing hurt and death to helpless women and children. He listened, allowed his pain to simmer inside him and said nothing.

By far the most exalted figure on the ship was Lord Colvin, the commander of the troop of knightly men-at-arms who considered themselves much superior to the commoners aboard. The knights and their lord kept largely to their own company, eating together and seldom deigning to speak to their subordinates. The latter were nominally commanded by a man named Howard of Gloucester, a sometime sergeant of King Henry's infantry whose previous military experience had earned him his position of leadership. He spent most of his time playing dice and drinking with the ship's captain, and was often seen stumbling about the deck in a drunken stupor.

'A more tightly-led band of fighting men I never saw,' Gabriel dryly observed. 'The Saracens would be shaking in their shoes if only they knew what was coming their way.'

The Saracens might in fact have been more afraid of Roderick Short, short as indeed he was. A butcher by trade who had taken up the cross more out of pious enthusiasm than some of his other shipmates, he daily sharpened his meat hacker to a shaving edge in anticipation of chopping to pieces his first infidel. When it came to the killing of animals, though, he was much less bloodthirsty: having strongly objected to what he regarded as the inhumane slaughter methods employed by the crew, he soon took over this duty and became the ship's butcher.

Then there was Arnold the Idiot, who had earned his name for obvious enough reasons: a harmless soul possessed of perhaps three or four words of vocabulary as well as a chronic stutter that combined to make him a rather hopeless conversationalist. Among the sharper-witted pilgrims aboard was Bartholomew Root from Lincolnshire, a former sheriff's man like Will's father, whose air of authority encouraged many of the men to regard him as a more capable leader figure than the ale-addled Howard. That admiration was not shared by all, however. 'There is something about that man I do not trust,' Gabriel confided in Will over one of their chess games. 'Time will tell, soon enough.'

For the moment, time was all they had, and plenty of it. As Gabriel had predicted, over the weeks the ship and its fleet companions cruised steadily south-westwards in a strung-out squadron around the coastline of France, sometimes in view of land, sometimes further out to sea. By the time Will had won his first chess game against his friend they had left the waters of the English Channel far behind them. Their last sighting of land before cutting down through the Bay of Biscay was the very north-western tip of the Brittany coast, where the crew bought a haul of fresh sea bass, mackerel and shrimp from a friendly local fishing boat. For three days afterwards the deck was rich with the aroma of fried fish and all hands were well fed and contented.

Such happiness was not to last. For now, they were truly out in the open sea, and out in the Bay of Biscay off the west coast of King Richard's French domains was where they could expect to encounter some of the fiercest weather of the Atlantic Ocean. The more seasoned mariners aboard had warned that their course would lead them into troubled waters, knowing from their own bitter experience that the Bay's reputation for unseasonal sudden squalls, violent gales and abnormally high waves was well earned. Two of the crew had personally been aboard a merchant cog vessel that had foundered in a terrible storm only a little to the south of here, narrowly escaping with their lives while many of their shipmates had been less lucky.

It wasn't long before the crewmen's stark predictions were proved accurate. Out of a flat blue calm on what had been a perfect balmy day, the first Atlantic storm hit them from the north-west. For two solid days and nights the ship struggled through an unending onslaught of heavy rain and screaming wind, never for a moment out of danger of being broached to and sunk by one of the enormous waves that loomed above them as tall as a church steeple and burst with stunning power against their sides, rocking the fragile vessel onto its beam ends and threatening again and again to capsize them entirely. The crew were forced to change course and sail directly into the wind; and now horses whinnied in panic and men clung desperately on to whatever solid purchase they could find as the ship's prow rose almost vertical into each oncoming mountain of water and then crashed down into every trough, white water swamping the deck up to their waists.

The first casualty was a cage full of live poultry, swept overboard and engulfed in the foam. The other, occurring late on the second night when the storm was peaking at its most intense, was Arnold the Idiot. The poor simple soul had been trying to make his way aft when a powerful gust of wind blew the vessel sideways and almost laid her down flat, followed only moments later by a freakish white-crested wave that struck her amidships and carried away everything in its path. Will, Gabriel and Samson had been crouched down low among the cargo barrels, soaked to the bone and barely holding on, when they heard the cry of their terrified shipmate being washed over the side. Arnold was swallowed up into the deep and never seen again.

When calm was restored the following morning, they discovered that the storm had carried them right around the north-west corner of the Iberian coast. By a miracle none of the other ships had been lost, and it was under a clear blue sky once again that the little fleet made their new southerly course with the Kingdom of León in sight to the east. 'Not far inland from that shoreline is Santiago de Compostela,' Gabriel said to Will. 'Where you told me your friend Father Michael had intended to travel.'

'If only he could have been here with us,' Will murmured sadly, shaking his head. Thinking about the friar only made Will reflect on his other losses, and he fell silent for the rest of that day.

On and on they carried southwards for the next two weeks, the routines on board having quickly returned to normal in the wake of the storm. The coastline of Portugal slipped slowly by to their left, often clearly visible. The demise of their shipmate Arnold, however saddening, was frankly not considered a major loss to the general order of things. But just as it seemed that some kind of peace had been restored to their daily lives, worse was to come.

It was on the afternoon of May third, the day of the Lord's Ascension, after a sultry morning with barely a breath of wind to bend the sail, that the captain and crew clustered along the ship's starboard rail to peer with growing concern at the great black and purple bar of cloud gathered on the western horizon. 'It will be a worse one than the first,' warned the oldest and most grizzled of the mariners. 'I'll be damned to Hell if it ain't.'

'Don't you know you are already damned to Hell, Joe Cook?' said another man named Tobias Smith, and some of the pilgrims laughed, but without much conviction.

As the ominous storm clouds drew closer and darker throughout the afternoon, the captain (in one of his more lucid moments of sobriety) ordered the sail taken down and the crewmen duly carried out his command, grunting in unison as they strained at the rope to lower the heavy spar down the length of the mast to the deck, where it was hurriedly furled up and made secure.

'What do you think?' Will asked Gabriel, who had described his experience of being caught and nearly wrecked in a black squall during his sea crossing from Ireland.

'I think that for once the captain is in his right mind,' Gabriel replied, his eyes fixed on the horizon. 'We cannot be far off the port of Lisbon where we were to put in for supplies, but I doubt very much we shall make it in time. We had best get ready for a nasty blow.'

When the promised blow came that same afternoon, it came with shocking speed. By now the captains of their companion vessels had followed their example and lowered sail in advance of this new, and likely far worse, storm. The men stood on deck and watched in trepidation as the line of black cloud, now virtually covering the entire western sky, raced towards them covering ten sea-miles in only a matter of moments.

'Find a rope to cling to,' Gabriel advised Will. 'Find anything you can that will not carry away, and for the love of Christ do not let go.' He tugged at Samson's sleeve, and the big man bent so that Gabriel could offer the same advice into his ear.

'Be not afraid, men!' shouted the chaplain over the rising howl of the wind. 'If the men of this ship keep themselves from evil deeds and do penance for past offences the Lord will grant them a prosperous voyage and direct their steps in His paths!'

THE PILGRIM'S REVENGE

In so saying, the chaplain seemed to have forgotten that his flock already had been granted all the plenary indulgences they would ever need to keep them from the gates of Hell. Regardless, the sea was paying no attention to the clergyman's words, because no sooner had he finished speaking than the extreme force of the squall was directly upon them.

Chapter 18

The storm front hit the ship with a blast of sound and turmoil that instantly reduced visibility to nil and engulfed all aboard in chaos. Even the panic-stricken shouts of the chaplain as he was almost torn from his place by the mast – and would have been flung overboard if not for several strong hands that quickly grabbed whatever parts of him they could and pulled him back from the edge – were drowned out in the enormous roaring and howling of the gale. Within the space of a few racing heartbeats the deck of the ship was awash and sloping like a steeply pitched roof as the force of the wind rolled them over at such an angle that the spar and sail, had they still been raised, would have been dragging them down into the water. Items of loose cargo were rolling and crashing about, bowling over any man unlucky enough to be in their path. With a frantic neighing, one of the knights' horses, crazed with terror, smashed its way out of its stall, lost its footing on the slippery deck and crushed its owner and two of the crew as they struggled to gain control of the poor animal.

Through packets of solid flying water that lashed over the side, Will caught sight of Gabriel, the hulking shape of

Samson and several others clinging on for dear life. The canvas awning over them offered nothing in the way of shelter, flapping wildly from the four ropes holding it at the corners; then with a rending sound it was split in two by the power of the wind and fluttered loose from its anchor points, the tattered remains flying away with the ropes that had held them. If the sail had not already been taken down, cautiously furled and made secure, there was no doubt it would have suffered the same fate, lost and gone forever.

Will had experienced storms by land, some of them severe enough to bring down trees and strip every shred of thatch from a roof, but nothing remotely of such a magnitude of raging fury. Blinded by salt spray and almost completely deafened by the blast, he momentarily caught fragments of someone's shouted warning *here com . . . another . . .* before the ship was struck yet again by a seemingly even greater wave than before, and he felt himself violently flung against a solid wooden bulwark. A jolt of pain flashed through the length of his spine, but there was no time to assess the extent of any injury as the irresistible weight of the water pummelled and crushed him flat. He felt himself sliding down the deck that was suddenly tilting at an extreme angle under him. More thundering torrents of water crashed over his body, and for a few instants he could neither breathe nor see and thought he was going to drown. Then his searching foot found a purchase on something solid and he was able to push himself up against the near-overwhelming pressure of the water.

In the next moment, just as he had been convinced the ship was about to tip right over, the deck righted itself and he managed to crawl back to what remained of his sheltering place. A big hand gripped his arm and helped him the last part of the way; he looked up blinking and saw the familiar broad hairy face spit into a grin. Samson alone appeared to be heartily enjoying the thrill of the storm.

But presently even Samson's spirits had to be dampened as the raging gale continued unabated for hour after hour. When night came at last, it was almost indistinguishable from the darkness of the day. The ship struggled on, tossed directionless and helpless like a piece of driftwood on the waves. With nothing to do except hang on tight and pray for survival, crew and passengers alike huddled together sodden and miserable wherever they could find a safe bolthole. The most extreme violence of the storm might now have passed, but at any moment they might still broach to and be sunk by an unlucky wave.

Meanwhile other dangers were gathering to threaten them. The land mass that had been little more than a distant blur on their eastern horizon when the storm had struck could now be seen looming up larger and darker in the sporadic intervals where anything could be seen at all; and at this point there was a real and fast-growing risk of the ship being carried right up against it. Will, the fledgling mariner, was about to learn that of all the horrors of the sea, that which filled the experienced ocean-going sailor with the greatest dread was the peril of a lee shore, where wind or tide or both combined could drive a vessel onto reef, rock and cliff and there hold her trapped until she was pummelled to pieces and every man aboard perished.

That unthinkable nightmare might soon become a reality. As the wind tore a hole in the storm clouds surrounding them, they saw to their horror that the gap of water between them and the dark land had narrowed by another half mile since the last reckoning and was continuing to diminish at an alarming rate. The captain was nowhere to be seen, and some men thought (perhaps not without satisfaction) that he must have been washed overboard in the first, worst moments of the squall. In his absence they looked to Howard of Gloucester or Bartholomew Root for leadership – but the former was too busy retching up his guts in the bow and the latter had turned ghostly pale and seemed to be paralysed by terror. It was one of the ordinary crewmen, old Joe Cook, who took charge and ordered for the oars to be broken out. These had never yet been needed on the voyage and were kept lashed down on deck, only to be used to row the ship out of the deadest of dead calms – or, in an emergency like the one that occupied them now, to propel the vessel against the adverse tide and current that would soon otherwise destroy her. In a flurry of activity, the oars were cut loose and deployed over the bows, held in place by a system of rope loops and thole pins mounted to an outrigger beam, twelve to a side and each one requiring three men to work it. Will, Gabriel and Samson all ran to take their part in saving the ship from disaster.

And so it was the combined strength of seventy-two men that battled and strained all through that interminable night and all through the next terrible morning to steer shy of the ever-encroaching cliffs, now so close as to tower above them and blot out the eastern sky. Several times every man aboard held his breath and gritted his teeth as they all felt the ship's hull beneath them grind and scrape over the unseen, submerged reefs that stretched in bars away from the shoreline. One severe impact could be enough to tear out their bottom; then all hope and probably every life aboard would be lost.

But for all their exhausting labour, despite which for every foot gained against the power of the sea they were forced back another two, the ship was inexorably drawn nearer and nearer to the foot of the cliff, drifting towards it broadside-on. When

Will felt the tip of his oar hit hard against solid rock, he knew the battle was all but lost, unless they acted immediately.

'Shove!' he shouted at the top of his voice, and he, Gabriel and Samson heaved their oar clear of the water to try to fend off the approaching wall of the cliff face. They were joined by Tobias Smith, whose strong hands helped to keep their oar steady. 'Shove as hard as you can!' Soon the other men were following their example, and the lee side of the ship bristled with raised oars to act as buffers between them and disaster. The rowers on the other side shipped their own and dragged them across the deck to reinforce their comrades' efforts. Time and time again as the ship drifted too close and the long, thick wooden poles hit against the rocks, the juddering impact threatened to tear them from the steadily weakening grips of the exhausted men.

But as desperate and grim as they were, they were if not winning the fight then for the moment at least staving off impending doom. The ship dragged and scraped its wearisome way hour after hour along the rocky coastline avoiding more collisions than anyone aboard could count. Not until mid-morning did the wind finally change direction and the turning tide begin to help them draw further from the cliffs, bringing a sense of relief so powerful that some of the men bowed their heads and wept, or clasped their hands in prayerful thanks to God. It was only then that the captain reappeared, more inebriated than ever having been drinking ale in the lower deck with Lord Colvin.

Now at long last the order could be given to raise sail once more, and amid grunts and groans of extreme fatigue the crew tugged on ropes and the broad single spar was painfully hoisted up the length of the mast. With a weary cheer, they saw the sail fill and felt the forward lurch as the ship steered towards safety.

'Heaven be praised!' the chaplain exclaimed, spreading his arms in joy.

'I am not sure Heaven had much to do with it,' Gabriel muttered.

But whether God had had a hand in their salvation or not, the sense of jubilation was short-lived. Only minutes later, with a terrible grinding crunch the ship struck full onto a jagged reef lurking just below the surface. At their former pace, crawling against the tide, they might have survived the impact – but now with the easterly wind strongly behind them they were moving so much faster that the damage to their underside was very cruel indeed. For a few instants the ship remained stuck on the unseen rocks, waves crashing against her stern; then with an ominous groaning and cracking of timbers she dislodged herself and sailed onward.

It was hard to say which fate might have been worse: to be grounded fast on the reef or to take their chances trying to escape when all could see she was fatally wounded below the waterline. The sea gushed in, white and foaming, through the great rends in the hull. Suddenly the scores of men who had earlier exhausted themselves at the oars were set to bailing, using every empty cask, bucket, pot and cup they could find, while the crew were up to their knees in churning water doing everything possible to fother the holes with rope and spare canvas.

Their efforts paid off, but it was only a temporary reprieve and everyone aboard knew it. As the ship limped on parallel to the shoreline mile after mile and at a safe distance, the water level was rising steadily in the hull and they were settling lower in the water, beginning to list badly to one side. Below deck the horses were up to their bellies in it, and had to be brought up to the main deck as the water rose still further – though they were doomed in any case, should the ship go down.

Now the battle against the elements entered its final and most desperate phase. Anything heavy had to be flung overboard in an attempt to lighten the vessel by all means possible, including all their freshwater supply, much of the food provisions and the horse that had been obliged to be killed after its legs were broken in the storm. The bodies of the knight and two crewmen crushed under the fallen animal splashed unceremoniously into the water moments later.

'Things ain't looking good, boys,' Tobias Smith said ominously. 'I hope you can swim.'

But just as hope was fading, a cry went up and weary heads turned to see the break in the cliffs and the indented cove beyond, with a long, curved sandy beach sloping up to distant dunes and trees beyond. For a shallow-bottomed ship that could float in close to shore, it was the perfect landfall short of finding an actual port. Suddenly salvation was at hand, and the men's strength was redoubled as they heaved at the oars again to row her in against the outgoing tide. At last, the bows came sliding up onto the fine wet sand and she was safely aground.

A raggedy cheer of relief filled the ship. Their landing had not come a moment too soon. Vast volumes of seawater spilled from the gash in the hull onto the beach. And now began the laborious process of disembarking and unloading all the surviving horses, livestock and cargo, since it was clear that the ship in her present condition would go no further and they would need to make camp in this place until whatever necessary arrangements could be made to repair the damaged hull. The delay would also allow the wounded to be tended to: two men with badly sprained ankles from being knocked down by rolling barrels on deck, one severe hernia, a suspected broken arm and several other debilitating injuries from the storm.

Will clambered over the side, jumped down to the firm wet sand and stood for the first time in his life on a foreign shore. After all these weeks at sea he was no longer accustomed to solid ground, and he felt strangely unbalanced as though he still had a rocking deck under his feet. He staggered and had to lean against the grounded ship for support. 'Oh, oh! What's wrong with me?'

'Only that you will need to recover your land legs,' said Gabriel, jumping down beside him. 'Do not worry, it's perfectly normal and lasts only a short time, a day at most.'

'I have a feeling we'll be here longer than that,' Will replied, eyeing the terrible holes that the reef had torn into the ship's side. 'Wherever here is,' he added, with a glance inland at the rising dunes and the trees beyond. Now that the storm had completely cleared, the sun was scorching fiercely down from a pale blue sky. The stretch of beach on which they had landed was quite deserted. More disconcertingly, so was the sea behind them. From one end of the western horizon to the other, there was no sign whatsoever of their companion ships.

'All sunk to the bottom,' growled Samson, who had jumped down to join them on the shore. 'And every one of them poor bastards drownded.' It was rare to hear him utter so many words together.

'Perhaps,' Gabriel agreed, nodding. 'Or perhaps our fleet may simply have been scattered in the storm. I suspect we have been blown a great distance southward.'

'What land do you suppose we find ourselves in, Gabriel?' Will asked.

'I am no expert navigator,' his friend replied, 'but I would not be surprised if we had bypassed the port of Lisbon.

That could put us somewhere along the southern shores of Portugal, unless I am mistaken. As to where the nearest town or city may be found, from which we might hope to obtain supplies and materials to continue our voyage, your guess is as good as mine.'

'Portugal,' Will said quietly, mostly to himself. The name felt unreal to him, like a place in a dream, inhabited by God only knew what manner of strange beings. 'What kind of folk live here?' he asked. 'Are they Christians? Are they friendly? Are they hostile?'

'That I cannot tell you either,' Gabriel said. 'But I think we are soon about to find out.' He pointed.

Will turned. And there far up the stretch of sand, lined up along the dunes, he saw the crowd of people who had gathered to meet the foreign sailors grounded on their shore.

Chapter 19

If some of the sailors had feared they were about to be met with fierce attack by the unknown inhabitants of this land, their concerns were soon allayed. For the small mixed crowd of local folk that came down the beach to greet them had no weapons and showed no sign of hostility, but rather were filled with excitement and wonder at the sight of the beached vessel. Children clung to their mothers' skirts and pointed, calling out shrilly in their own language. At the head of the crowd was a tall, long-bearded man who wore the unmistakable vestment of a priest. As he came closer it was clear from his expression that he was in a state of great agitation mingled with sheer delight at the unexpected arrival of a Christian ship.

The chaplain, who until then had been staying well in the background, went to meet the priest accompanied by Lord Colvin and Howard of Gloucester. Several others followed in their wake, Will included. He had not seen a woman or a child since leaving England, and though his own family were never out of his thoughts the sight brought a pang to his heart.

The chaplain and his fellow churchman very soon fell into conversing in Latin, the only tongue common to them.

'Can you understand what they're saying?' Will whispered to Gabriel, standing at his shoulder, and his friend translated phrase by phrase as the two clerics talked. The local priest, who introduced himself as Padre Xavier Malagrida, confirmed to them that they had indeed landed on Portuguese shores, the nearest large settlement being the coastal city of Silves. These people with him, he explained, motioning to the crowd, were from the village where someone had spotted the approaching ship and run to tell him, as he happened by chance to have been tending to a sick man there.

But it was the city of Silves that Padre Malagrida appeared mainly eager to talk about, being the cause of his agitation – and it soon transpired why. It was the furthest outpost of Christian possessions in these parts, he told the chaplain, having been snatched from the hands of pagan infidels only the previous year, thanks to the help of other warrior pilgrims like themselves who had stopped en route to Outremer to repel the Moorish enemy forces then occupying their beloved city.

Now, the priest went on, speaking in a flurry and gesticulating back up the beach as he talked, they had only just received the terrifying news that the same Moorish army of the Almohad Sultanate, under the Emperor of Morocco, had returned to wreak its revenge and reclaim Silves from Christian hands, and were at this very moment gathering their troops, building their fearsome siege engines out of archery range of the city walls and preparing their dreaded onslaught. Word had spread like wildfire around the whole region, as it was widely feared that once the Moors had overrun Silves and massacred or enslaved every man, woman and child within its walls, as they surely would, the same appalling fate would next be suffered by the surrounding villages. They had known it happen many times before. Their land had been ravaged by these heathens for generations.

'I believe he is asking for our help,' Gabriel said to Will.

King Sancho had already refused the Emperor's demand to surrender Silves, Padre Malagrida said, the terms being too egregious. Now the city stood alone, cut off, and desperate for assistance. To make matters worse, this unusually warm summer had dried up all the rivers and left them struggling to find enough water for the people, let alone to withstand a long siege. But the Lord Almighty in his beneficence had seen fit to send them another ship full of great warriors to deliver them from evil! Would they rally to the cause of their fellow children of God?

Perhaps not, it soon appeared. As the chaplain related Padre Malagrida's account back to them, both Lord Colvin and his co-commander Howard of Gloucester were reluctant to commit their aid. Bartholomew Root, who until lately had held much influence among the men, seemed oddly reticent.

'This is not our fight,' insisted Lord Colvin. 'Our duty is to our mission alone, and King Richard, not Sancho.' His knights remained silent and expressionless in the background, unable to go against the judgement of their master.

Will was under no such constraint, however, and without waiting for anyone's permission to do so he stepped forward to speak. 'But we are stranded here unable to move and meanwhile these people need help. How can we turn our backs on them?'

Howard of Gloucester turned to stare coldly at him. 'Since when did a commoner dictate orders to the army?'

'And since when did the army refuse to prevent innocent people from being murdered in their homes by an enemy bent on destroying them down to the last man, woman and child?' Will countered. He was being dangerously insubordinate towards a commander who could have him severely punished for speaking so boldly, but he was unable to stay quiet. It was almost as though another voice were speaking from inside him.

'Remember your station and keep your tongue behind your lips, peasant,' Lord Colvin warned him sternly, 'unless you would like to have it cut out. What would you know of such matters?'

More of the men had gathered behind, and Will could sense from the tension in the air that many among them shared his desire to help the folk of Silves and would deeply resent the commanders for disallowing it. He glared at Colvin and replied in a clear voice, 'I know that a man of courage and integrity would not hesitate to do what is right.' There was a grumble of assent from the others. Colvin and Gloucester exchanged anxious glances. The last thing either commander could afford to risk was an open mutiny.

Emboldened, Will turned to the chaplain. 'Father, please tell Padre Malagrida that I will go to the city and offer what help I can.'

'And I,' echoed Gabriel, stepping forward. Samson did the same, saying nothing but looking at the commanders as though he could gladly twist their heads from their shoulders with his bare hands. More men followed their example, including Tobias Smith whose bravery had helped them survive the storm at sea.

The ship's captain was dubious. 'We cannot leave the vessel unguarded, to be pillaged and stripped for firewood and our precious food stores reduced to nothing. Damaged as she is, there may yet be hope of saving her.'

As the chaplain translated the captain's objections for Padre Malagrida, the priest replied in Latin, in turn translated back to the men: 'I make no promises, but I am confident that if you help to deliver our city, Bishop Nicholas will surely agree to provide you with a new ship, or repair the one you came in. Please, in the Lord's name, I beg you. The Moorish army could be gathering at the gates of Silves by nightfall.'

After some discussion, during which the commanders seemed increasingly unwilling to challenge the rising spirit among the men, Lord Colvin reluctantly agreed to go to the aid of their Portuguese brethren. It was decided to leave six of his knights and twenty common men on shore (along with Howard of Gloucester who seemed especially anxious to remain behind) to guard the vessel and her stores while the rest travelled inland to Silves.

They set off within the hour, Lord Colvin leading his troop on horseback together with Padre Malagrida and the chaplain, who was needed to act as interpreter. Behind him rode the rest of the mounted knights, while Will and the rest of the commoners followed at a rapid pace carrying all the arms and fresh water they could. Samson possessing no weapon other than his bare hands, Will had made him a gift of the short-handled axe he had taken from the forest brigands. The big man thanked him with a hug and a smile of pure joy, clutching his new acquisition like a child with its first toy.

The three friends marched close to the head of the column, behind the riders. Will was glad that Osric and his cronies were right at the rear, where he didn't have to be close to them. Meanwhile, Bartholomew Root had lost most or all of the authority he had carried among the men, and was somewhere in the middle, subdued and brooding. 'That man is no kind of leader,' Gabriel said to Will. 'Much as I suspected.'

It was a long, dusty and sweltering trek to the city some fifteen miles inland. Will had experienced many hot summers in England, but the heat in this utterly alien part of the world was of another order. The sun's glare was blinding and beat relentlessly down, bleaching the colour from the sky as they trudged on hour after painful hour, only the urgency of the task ahead stopping them from pausing to rest in what little shade they might hope to find. The ground was iron-hard underfoot and much of the vegetation around them was burnt yellow and brittle. 'Drink,' Samson said, offering Will the heavy leather water flask he carried.

'No,' Will replied. 'Others may be thirstier than I am.'

The infernal heat subsided as evening finally, mercifully drew closer – but for Will and his comrades the relief was tinged with the growing apprehension of what awaited them, and the wondering at how many would live to resume their journey. Gabriel had fallen into a thoughtful silence as they walked through the arid landscape, and Will was left to dwell on the moral questions that came up in his mind now that the initial eagerness had passed. He was marching to war for the very first time; men would die. And though he was already tainted with men's blood, those he was soon to confront were perfect strangers who had done him no harm, and against whom he had no quarrel save that they fought under the banner of his king's enemy. What was that to him? It was not for a king, nor out of loyalty to any banner, cause or patriotic fervour that he had left behind the world he had known. By all rights he should not be here at all. And yet the thought of the helpless city dwellers being persecuted, put to the sword or led off in chains, was an unbearable alternative.

The dusk was falling and the first stars were out by the time the marching column at last caught sight of the high walls of the fortified city, a dull orange glow emanating from within. In the hills beyond Silves they could see the innumerable bright specks, like a cloud of fireflies or the starlight reflected on the moving ocean, that they realised were the countless burning torches of the approaching Moorish forces.

Padre Malagrida had been right. By full dark the enemy would be at the walls and ready to mount their first assault. Silhouetted against the evening sky were the shapes of the siege towers and giant ballistas the army were slowly rolling towards the city, a sight that Will could not have imagined in his strangest dreams.

'There must be thousands of them,' said one of the men marching behind Will. 'And not a hundred of us. How can we make any difference?'

'You wait till the buggers get a taste of my hacker,' growled Roderick Short. 'They'll look different enough after that, mark my words.'

'Another hour, and we might have been too late,' Will observed as he watched the movement of the lights, still distant but approaching steadily step by step every minute. 'Once that army surrounds the walls there will be no way in or out of the city for any living man.'

'It seems we are about to engage in our first battle,' said Gabriel with a smile. 'A little sooner than expected. I pray you brought enough arrows, my friend.'

Padre Malagrida broke away from the troop and rode ahead to alert the city authorities that he had come with unexpected reinforcements. Minutes later the great high gates opened, and from them hurried a procession of the city leaders, along with Bishop Nicholas of Silves who welcomed the newcomers with boundless thanks and tears of joy and gratitude. Even those to whom Latin was as incomprehensible as the Portuguese tongue were left with no doubt of his sincerity.

Then they were inside the walled city, and the massive gates closed behind them with a portentous resonating thud that to a superstitious mind might have sounded like the sealing shut of a tomb. 'That's that, lads,' Tobias Smith said with a dry laugh. 'Caught like rats in a trap.'

Beyond the great gateway the city was a warren of narrow cobbled streets and clustered buildings, lit by flickering torches whose glow shone up to the towering battlements above them. Most of the women and children were already cowering in their homes or had run to hide elsewhere. The streets were teeming with soldiers of the city guard along with any able-bodied man of fighting age, which ranged from the much too young to the much too old. Quaking, terrified youngsters clad in oversized helms and chain mail hauberks that draped down to their feet, clutching weapons they could barely lift; bent ancient, wizened men who should have been in their beds, pressed into service against an enemy they could not hope to stand up to.

Out of the throng came a tall, swarthy soldier in plate mail: the commander of the city guard, Diego Pérez. His black hair was turning silver at the edges and he was missing an eye from an old combat injury that had scarred one side of his face, a hardened veteran of never-ending wars who spoke neither Latin nor English, and was too grim and tense ahead of the coming assault to say anything much at all. With his one steely eye he scrutinised Lord Colvin's men-at-arms and seemed little impressed; then he just as dispassionately surveyed the rest of the Christian reinforcements supposedly come to save the city. 'Hmm,' was his only comment. Then spying Will's bow and quiver he seemed to take an interest in him, and immediately motioned to him to follow as he turned away and hurried up a flight of stone steps.

'Go n-éirí leat,' Gabriel called after him as Will went to follow. 'As we say in Ireland.'

'I'll see you again soon,' Will replied.

'In this life or the next, brother. God be with you.'

The steps led to the east-facing section of the city battlements, where perhaps thirty more archers had already been posted at intervals along the rampart. Will could not understand a word of the few terse instructions Pérez fired at him, but his sense of pressing urgency was clear enough. Will formed the impression that the man saw him as a seasoned fighter and was placing him in command of the archers, even though most of them were visibly twice his age or more.

He felt like protesting, 'You have the wrong impression of me, sir. I have no more been in battle than those children down there.' But he held back his admission, swallowed hard and quietly vowed that he would step up to the task and not let them down. To his relief his archers appeared to have plentiful arrow supplies, each man issued with three sheaves of twenty-five apiece, placed point downwards ready for use in a wooden barrel at his feet. The shafts were not as true or as well balanced as those he carried in his quiver, but as munitions of war they would serve their purpose well enough. Of curiosity to him, aside from the conventional arrows issued to the archers, were the noticeably different hundred or so that had been fitted with special tips expertly fashioned out of strands of iron twisted together to form a pointed bulb-like cage, each stuffed with a wick of wool or hemp that had been soaked in tallow. These were a new kind of projectile for Will, but he knew what they were: incendiary arrows that would burst alight when touched to a burning torch and remain lit in flight to carry the devastating weapon of fire to the enemy. Such innovations could elevate the common archer to become the most dangerous man on the battlefield.

Adopting as leaderly a look as he could, he walked along the rank of archers and used a crude form of sign language to get each one in turn to show him how well they could draw their bow. With a few corrections of stance and position here and there, their training was as complete as time would allow. Because indeed time was running short. All the while the Moorish army was steadily coming closer, the front ranks barely two hundred paces from the foot of the walls. The entire moonlit valley below teemed with men and horses and the equipment of war, a sight to chill the blood. The enemy's strange black armour was unlike any Will had ever seen. The flames of their torches glittered off steel weapons and helmets and a thousand upheld lances resembled a newly sprung forest.

The atmosphere was almost unbearably tense in the long, painfully slow lead-up to battle. Within the city there was scarcely a man present who did not wish for it to begin soon, just to end the lingering suspense. Will had drunk his fill of water from the butts on the battlement but his mouth remained as dry as a stale breadcrust. There was a tremor in his hands. He gazed at his fingers and clenched his fists tight, and the shaking diminished but didn't disappear.

'I am here,' he said to himself, gathering his courage. 'I will do my best. And if I die tonight, then I died trying to do the right thing. Beatrice would have understood.'

Then the attack began.

Chapter 20

When it came, it was like the long, oppressive gathering of storm clouds that suddenly gives vent to the irrepressible violence of the heavens. To the resounding clash of weapons on shields, the sounding of trumpets, the rolling of drums and the unified shriek of their war cry that echoed up to the top of the battlements, the large Moorish army all at once unleashed the full force of its hellish fury upon the city.

Will had never even heard of the fearsome devices of war that the enemy had brought to the attack, still less seen them in action until this moment. Now he was about to witness the terrifying power of the infernal giant machines that were arrayed in a line at the rear of the massed infantry. At a shouted command and with a terrible groaning of timbers and twanging of ropes under massive tension the first of the great trebuchets released its throwing arm and the flaming missile it carried was launched high and far, a fireball streaking through the air towards the walls. Will watched its trajectory with cold dread, and saw that it was going to fall short; moments later the missile crashed to the ground a spear-throw shy of the foot of the walls, smashing a crater in the earth and shooting flames and debris harmlessly against the city's fortifications.

But Will understood that this first attempt had been only a ranging shot —and sure enough, when after a breathless lull during which the enemy rolled the machines a little closer to their target the second missile was launched, its curving flight carried it straight and true and struck the city walls with a force that made the battlements quake under his feet. Then another, and another; and another again, raining destruction on the defenders. The teams of Moorish soldiers operating the trebuchets worked with frenzied speed to crank the monstrous machines into readiness for the next shot, while others ran back and forth collecting the incendiary projectiles piled high in ox-drawn wagons. What fiendish kind of combustible substance the missiles had been steeped in to make them burn so powerfully, Will could only guess. Those that had landed short or bounced off the walls lay still blazing, setting fire to the desiccated, sun-parched grass and shrubbery and creating a wide blackened circle where each had fallen.

How could anyone withstand such a bombardment, he wondered, staring in awe from the battlements as yet another flaming missile came streaking towards them. Yet withstand it they must. This time the shot struck high against the walls, smashing away stone blocks and rubble. Splinters of flying masonry stung Will's cheek and he flinched, put his fingers to his face and saw they were red.

The sight of his own blood was what tore him from the almost dreamlike state in which he had watched the opening of the attack unfold. His hands were no longer shaking and he felt strangely calm, yet intensely alive, as though his senses were suddenly twice as acute. The cries of alarm from within the city and the enemy's shouts of jubilation told him that that last shot must have breached part of the wall. Now came a pause in the bombardment, and Will realised that was because the enemy were about to mount the second wave of their assault. Down below their close-packed infantry ranks, swarming like the nest of ants he had once disturbed as a child, were already bringing up great long ladders with which to scale the battlements. Meanwhile, the tall, wheeled siege towers were being slowly, inexorably rolled forward into position.

'Archers, to the shooting line!' Will commanded. His voice was loud and strong, but quite composed. 'Nock your arrows!' Though his men couldn't understand his words they imitated his actions as he fitted a shaft to his own bow. 'Wait! Hold your fire until they come at us and make every shot count!'

Then as with howling battle cries the enemy rushed towards the foot of the walls, Will shouted 'Loose arrows!' The volley hurtled down from the battlements as thick as rain. Some stuck harmlessly in the ground below, but in such a dense melee of men it was inevitable that most found their mark. Will saw his own arrow strike a Moorish soldier in the gap between helmet and breast armour, and the man stumble and go down, followed by twenty more of his comrades. The archers reloaded and again the bowstrings were twanging all along the rampart, to deadly effect as another two dozen of the enemy were skewered and fell, to be trampled underfoot by the wave of men rushing at the walls. Now the siege ladders were being planted at their foot, with hundreds of strong eager hands reaching out to push them upright. Instantly a black mass of bodies was swarming up each ladder, shields and lances and other weaponry slung over their backs and their daggers clenched in their teeth as they clambered up the rungs.

Will and his archers leaned out from the battlement and refocused their fire straight downwards. All along the wall the uppermost climbers went tumbling down with shafts jutting from their bodies, giving way to the men below them who swiftly met the same fate. But they were so many, and coming so fast, that Will knew the battlement defences were insufficient to ward off the onslaught for much longer. All the while the siege towers were rolling closer and closer, each one pushed by scores of men and loaded with many more waiting to come swarming over the walls the instant they were close enough. Once that moment came, the defenders on the battlements would be rapidly overwhelmed.

Meanwhile, the hordes on the ground below were massing around the breach in the wall, through which they were pouring only to be met with fierce resistance from the Christian warriors inside. The clash of weapons, the cries of battle and the screams of the dying filled the city. Will badly wanted to run down there and help his friends, but he couldn't leave his post up here on the wall. And yet, how could he hope to hold back the tide that threatened to come spilling over the ramparts at any moment? For a few instants he was lost in helpless indecision, his heart thudding in his throat.

Then something came to him, a memory from long ago and, it seemed, from another world. The sight of the still-burning trebuchet missiles at the foot of the wall suddenly reminded him of the time in Foxwood when a carelessly dropped lantern during a rainless summer spell had caused the total destruction by fire of Harold Cotterel's barn, despite all the villagers' attempts to douse it with water from the river. Transported back to the present moment, Will gazed at the advancing siege towers and the idea was suddenly sharp in his mind.

'Keep firing! Hold your ground!' he shouted at his archers as he ran along the wall to where the barrel stood containing their supply of incendiary-tipped arrows, untouched until now. He plucked one out, nocked it to his bowstring and bathed its iron head in the flame from one of the torches that illuminated the battlements. It burst eagerly alight, the tallow-impregnated woollen wick spluttering and fizzling brightly. Without hesitation he leaned far out from the wall and sent the burning arrow flying vertically downwards, not at one of the countless living targets massed on the ground but at the ground itself, the tall sun-dried grass and shrubbery at the base of the nearest advancing siege tower. The arrow stuck in the dirt right by one of the great wooden wheels. Its fierce flame almost instantly caught hold of the parched vegetation and within moments a curtain of fire was leaping up around the foot of the tower. The men heaving at the wheels jumped back, and the tower stopped advancing.

'More! More!' Will shouted, pointing at the barrel of fire arrows and grabbing another for himself. The archers rushed to copy his example, and soon the flames were rising up higher and higher around the siege tower. The lashed-together timbers from which it was built were themselves as dry as the grass, and quickly caught light as burning arrow after arrow thudded into them. The light breeze blowing from the east was enough to fan the flames into an angry blaze. Very quickly the ropes and leather straps holding the tower together were burned away and the entire construction fell apart and toppled to the ground, spreading fire everywhere. Men were buried by the debris or fell burning and screaming from the collapsing edifice, only to be cut down by more arrows.

That first tower was followed by another, which stopped in its tracks and was soon likewise consumed by flames, its occupants leaping out to their deaths. As his archers rained fire down on the enemy, Will considered the range from the battlement to the wagons containing the flammable munitions for the trebuchets. It was a long, long shot indeed, perhaps twice as far as he had ever launched an arrow before. But if he angled his bow high enough and coaxed from it all the power it could deliver, it might reach.

The supply of fire arrows was diminishing fast. He quickly nocked and drew, pulling the string all the way back behind his right ear and calculating the upward angle necessary to carry his shot such a distance. The flaming arrow tip flickered yellow against the darkness, its curling plume of smoke stinging his eyes; then with a twang and a whoosh it was away. It arced high up into the night sky and began its graceful curved descent, a faraway pinpoint of light like a falling star. As it dropped to earth it seemed to vanish for a few instants and Will's heart sank, thinking he had missed his mark; but then the archers cheered wildly as a bright fireball suddenly shot up from one of the munitions wagons, lighting up the night. The wagon was engulfed by fire along with several soldiers too slow to get away. Flames spread rapidly all around, quickly lighting the ropes of a nearby trebuchet and the missile that had already been loaded onto its throwing arm. With a sudden crack the giant weapon released its heavy projectile, which flew straight up into the air and landed in the midst of the soldiers, crushing many of them.

It was a moment that felt as though victory was theirs. But with the archers' attentions momentarily directed away from the ladders, the throngs of men clambering up them had now almost reached the top. The first one to come leaping over the rampart, screaming his foreign battle cry with his blade raised triumphantly in the air, was stopped dead by Will's burning arrow that punched through his breast armour and into his heart. Behind him came hundreds more, flooding over the top and surging along the battlements, their manic shrieks and howls filling the air. The archers valiantly stood their ground and arrow after arrow thudded into the oncoming mass of bodies. Will saw one of his men cut down by an enemy scimitar. Then another, and another, and soon the top of the wall was overrun as he had feared would happen.

Suddenly the defenders on the battlement were no longer alone. Will heard Samson's throaty roar behind him, and turned to see the big man racing towards the enemy with incredible speed, hurling himself into their midst like a human battering ram, eyes flashing with lunatic rage and foaming at the mouth as he swung wildly with his new axe at any that came within his reach. Many more fell back, retreating from his berserker rage. Then Gabriel's sword was sweeping left and right, taking them down like a scythe harvesting the spring wheat. Two of them tried to attack him from the rear, but Samson grabbed them and drove their heads together with frightful force before flinging their limp bodies off the battlement. With only two arrows left in his quiver Will planted the first deep into the chest of a brave but foolish Moor who was rushing towards Samson with a raised dagger. The second thudded through the armour of another man who had been aiming a crossbow at him. The man clutched at his chest and somersaulted off the wall into the city streets below, landing dead on the paving stones in the middle of the battle raging around him.

Will now cast aside his bow and drew his own sword, and joined Gabriel and Samson in repelling the attackers in close-quarter battle. This was the time when the fighting became fiercest, a concentrated, relentless and bloody few minutes when there was no time for anything but to swing, chop, block, parry, duck and hack with all the energy in one's body. The ramparts were littered with the dead and their severed limbs, and blood ran in streams. Samson used the enemy corpses as missiles to fling down on their comrades coming up the ladders; then seizing the top of one of the ladders themselves in his huge fists and bellowing like an enraged bull he heaved it away from the wall and it toppled backwards, thirty men falling to the ground far below.

Will drove two soldiers back along the battlement and ran one of them through. Hearing Gabriel's shout of 'Will! At your back!' he spun around barely in time to dodge the descending blow of a long, broad scimitar that, had it landed, would have split him from shoulder to belly. The great sword was in the hands of an enormous man, larger even than Samson, who had already hewn down several of Will's archers and was now coming for their leader. His dark eyes blazed from behind the nose bar of his helmet and his teeth were bared. Shouting a curse or threat in his own language he raised the scimitar again and charged at Will.

Will blocked the strike, responded with a wild thrust that was savagely knocked aside, then was once more on the defensive as the powerful Moor lunged and stabbed. As competent a swordsman as Will was, he realised with a chill that he was no match for this opponent. In two more passes the hilt of his weapon was torn out of his hands and the sword fell to the ground with a clatter. Will backed away, stumbled and fell. The big Moor stood over him, grinning behind his helmet, and raised his scimitar to strike the head off the infidel. But as the sword lingered at the apex of its swing, fire glinting along its length, the man's grin fell away and he let out a sharp grunt. His knees buckled under him and he crashed heavily to the ground. Behind him stood Gabriel, withdrawing the bloody point of his own sword from the gaping wound in the Moor's back.

'It seems we may have to offer you some tuition in the use of the blade,' Gabriel said with a smile, extending his left hand. Will grasped it and got to his feet, gasping. He bent and retrieved his fallen sword. At that same moment, the shout went up from down below. 'They run! They are falling back!'

Will, Gabriel and Samson, along with the remaining archers and a handful of other defenders who had come up to the battlement, hurried to the edge and peered over the ramparts, to see to their amazement that it was true: the Moorish army was retreating in disarray from the city walls leaving countless dead and dying in their wake.

'We did it,' Samson muttered softly with tears of sadness in his eyes, the raging bull of battle now once more as docile as a calf.

As they descended the steps from the battlement they found a scene of utter carnage in the city streets. Rubble and bodies were piled higher than a tall man where the wall had been breached and the enemy hordes had come flooding through, meeting the fury of the Christian forces in vicious hand-to-hand fighting. But now it was over, and the battle was won. Through the slaughterhouse of the streets came Bishop Nicholas, weeping tears of grief and joy in equal measure. One by one, Will and his friends were reunited with the survivors of the battle: Tobias Smith, bloodied but still on his feet; Roderick Short, still brandishing his hacker which had cut through a great deal of flesh that night; and Will was even pleased to see Osric and his cronies alive and breathing. Not all had been so fortunate. Diego Pérez had been severely wounded, slashed so deep across the left shoulder that his arm was barely still attached, though his joy at their victory enabled him to smile through the pain.

'But I am very sorry to say . . .' the chaplain announced with a mournful look; and by way of finishing his sentence led them to a corner of the adjoining street and pointed. The dead body that lay there, bloody and torn, would have been unrecognisable if not for the tattered knightly surcoat with its familiar crest. Lord Colvin's surviving men-at-arms stood around him, heads bowed in sorrow.

For all their losses, however, the enemy had paid a far heavier price. Over a thousand Moorish soldiers lay dead among the streets, at the foot of the walls and on the battlements. Their general had fled in confusion, having grievously underestimated the strength of the Christian resistance.

'They will be back,' the bishop said. 'But not for some time. Silves is saved! God's blessing be upon you.'

The rest of that night was spent replenishing their weary bodies with food, water and rest and tending to the wounded. Just after dawn, a rider appeared at the city gates bearing the unexpected news that more English vessels had landed on the shore, and that a host of warriors would soon be coming to join them.

'Well, Will,' Gabriel said. 'Our first battle is over. I am certain it won't be the last.'

The English pilgrims remained at Silves for four more days, but that time was not spent idly. While a team of carpenters headed for the beach to set about fulfilling Bishop Nicholas's promise to repair their vessel, none but the seriously injured was spared the grim labour of gathering up the broken and pierced bodies of the enemy dead. They were piled ten deep in a pit that took eighty men an entire day to dig, doused in olive oil and burnt to a cinder lest their rotting remains contaminate the soil and the water. Those who had given their lives in defence of Silves were honoured with a Christian burial. Many of the women tore out their hair in their grief, and gouged their faces with their nails until the blood ran down their clothes.

The following day the scorched battlefield was cleared of the wreckage of the destroyed siege towers. The machines of war left abandoned by the retreating army were broken up for firewood. Fallen weapons were gathered by the hundred. Arrows that had been stuck in the ground or plucked from the dead were either cannibalised for parts or cleaned and put away for reuse.

It was during this period of intense activity that Will tasted his first drink of wine, from the large quantities gifted to them by the grateful merchants of the city. He had found himself gripped by a state of deep melancholy in the wake of the battle, and on the second evening, with so many of his painful emotions returning to haunt him, he was tempted to consume far too much of the rich red liquid in the hope that it would dull his grief. This it did, but it also made him miserably ill.

Then in the early morning of the fifth day, with a favourable tide and a fresh westerly wind at their heels, the reunited ships sailed on from the Portuguese coast en route for the Mediterranean shores of southern France and their rendezvous with King Richard's main battle fleet. For Will's comrades, the voyage would only be over when they set foot in the Holy Land. Will himself had another final destination in mind, the one he would reach sooner or later when he came face to face once more with the Baron of Gilsland's son Sir Ranulf and the black eagle soldiers.

That time was coming.

Chapter 21
August 1190

They had been scorched and baked under the merciless sun; pummelled by punishing rain and screaming winds that threatened to rip sail from mast; been tossed upon the towering waves and stood for interminable days becalmed on a flat blue millpond surrounded by a circle of their own filth a quarter-mile wide. Navigating through the perilous straits between Cádiz and the Moroccan coast with the ever-watchful Moorish enemy on both sides, they had suffered both bombardment from the land and attack on the water. Yet more difficulty had come their way as they sailed further eastwards into the Alboran Sea, a stretch infested with Berber pirates whose fast, light and highly mobile galleys ruthlessly plied their trade upon whatever foreign merchant shipping fell into their hands, stealing their cargo and massacring or enslaving every man aboard. Only by sailing in close formation and remaining constantly vigilant had the small pilgrim fleet managed to ward off the threat. Fire being one of the sailor's most feared enemies at sea, the supply of incendiary arrows Will had brought from Silves provided a most effective means of destroying any pirate vessel that dared venture within bow-shot range, as one bold corsair captain had discovered to the cost of his own life and that of his entire crew.

Only when they reached the benign waters off Valencia and Catalunya, provinces ruled under the Christian Crown of Aragon, was the danger behind them for now. At the friendly Port of Barcelona they put in to hurriedly replenish their badly depleted water and food supplies, before setting sail once again for the Gulf of Lions and the southern coast of France.

And so it was that, after all these long and arduous months at sea, fraught by so many perils and delays, on Wednesday the twenty-second day of August the English ships at last coasted into the crystal blue waters of the Port of Marseille. The ancient city, which according to Gabriel – with his often surprising and inexhaustible supply of facts – had been founded by the Greeks six hundred years before the birth of Christ, stood protected by the three hills of Saint Laurent, les Moulins and les Carmes, as well as the natural defensive barrier of the islands of Pomègues and Ratonneau. On the day of their arrival the sun was shining so brightly that the walled city seemed to gleam with a dazzling light of its own, so that Will, standing at the ship's side as they slowly sailed into the harbour, had to shield his eyes against the glare of the white stone buildings.

All throughout the long leg of their voyage from Silves the fleet had sighted not a single other Christian ship – let alone that carrying the black eagle knights – nor any other vessel small or large save for the many fishing boats that worked the coastlines and the pirate galleys that hunted in deeper waters. Now suddenly they were met with the sight of countless sea-going craft of all kinds and sizes, teeming around the old port, a thick forest of masts pointing into the clear blue sky.

There was a great deal of anticipation aboard, as many eagerly awaited to clap eyes on the king's magnificent main battle fleet. It was said that the ships numbered more than a hundred, including fourteen busses of vast size and speed, their hulls laden with huge quantities of cargo. The king's own esnecca was a long and stately galley ship bristling with warriors and arms, unsurprisingly reputed to be the largest and most glorious vessel of all. But what stirred the imagination of the men even more was the speculation over the king's enormous treasure, whose inestimable value was understood to be divided equally among the ships so that if one part was endangered the rest would be saved. King Richard had stripped his kingdom bare and forced the church to yield up a great portion of its wealth to fill the casks of silver and gold coin that would fund the expedition to the Holy Land. Imagine the honour, said some of the men, if their own ship were chosen to carry a portion of the treasure!

Will kept out of their excited conversations, preferring to occupy his hours in a hard-fought game of chess with Gabriel, or alone with his own thoughts. His moods were often bitterly gloomy these days, and talk of kings and treasure meant nothing to him. But in any case, the expectations of his shipmates were soon to be disappointed, as upon entering the port there was no sign of the huge battle fleet.

'We are too late,' Gabriel said to Will. 'They must already have sailed.' Hours later, when they had finally docked and disembarked and were standing on the thronging quayside, twice as busy and crowded and noisy as that of Southampton, Gabriel was proved right. A harbour master who spoke a little disjointed English informed the dismayed captains that the great battle fleet had remained in port for three weeks, so cramming every corner of the harbour that there was barely room for the smallest fishing boat to dock, before embarking on the seventh day of August, bound he believed for Sicily. And what a noble sight it had been, he told them, glowing as he described the fantastic spectacle of the long procession of warships setting sail with the galleys of the king's party at their head, those alone carrying six hundred and fifty knights and one thousand, three hundred of their squires with their horses, food provisions for eight months and wine enough to last half that time. In their wake followed the fourteen cargo busses, the largest of which had three rudders, thirteen anchors, two masts, and was laden with forty war horses together with their riders and forty extra footmen with all the weaponry and equipment needed for the campaign, as well as vast stores of supplies and provisions. The harbour master proudly listed these figures at some length, not omitting of course to mention the nearly six thousand gold marks that the king had paid to Genoese merchants for the hire of the fleet.

To the men of the English vessels – with a few exceptions – the news came as a cruel blow, although after their delays in getting this far it could not have been entirely unexpected that the king would have set off without waiting for their small additional contingent to catch up. Had news reached him of the successful intervention in the siege of Silves? Did he even expect the ships to have survived the voyage the long way around, while he and his troops marched overland through his French possessions? Nobody could say.

In their disappointment it was agreed that they must waste as little time as possible in setting sail in pursuit of the rest of the fleet. While the vessels were being made ready in time to catch the evening tide, Will and Gabriel left their weapons and scant other belongings in the safekeeping of Samson, made their way up from the harbour into the district of Le Panier and spent their few hours of freedom exploring its climbing serpentine streets and squares lined with venerable old buildings and colourful houses. Everywhere were flowers and verdant gardens, market stalls crammed with countless exotic varieties of fresh fish, fruit and vegetables, street musicians performing, the solemn sounds of plainchant echoing from within the cool confines of the churches. Now and then as they wound their way up through the town they caught a glimpse of the blue sea and the hive of activity that was the harbour below. The sunshine was warm, the sky cloudless and perfect.

'Paradise must be very like this,' Gabriel mused as they wandered. 'Think what kind of a contented life a man could have in such a place. I could happily abandon this voyage and remain here forever. What say you, brother?'

'I say that I would not be free to make that choice, even if I wished to,' Will replied. 'My destiny must take me where it may.'

'I was forgetting myself,' Gabriel said apologetically. 'And I would be there to help you, by all the means in my power.'

'I know you would,' Will told him. 'But I must face my troubles alone, or not at all.'

His mind was now fixed on the distant island of Sicily, to where the English fleet would soon set sail in the hopes of rejoining the main expedition. With all his heart he wanted the Baron of Gilsland's men to be there waiting for him. If they had no idea of the force of vengeance that was coming their way, they would very soon learn of it. What happened next would rest in God's hands, or perhaps the Devil's. Either was the same to Will.

As the day cooled and the evening tide approached, the two returned to the port and reboarded their ship. Amid all the usual stamping of feet, hauling on ropes and shouted commands the squadron cast off one by one from their moorings and steered out of the port towards the open sea, spurred on by a lively breeze from the west. As the land behind them sank and the sun dipped, the horizon was like a vast bowl of fire in their wake.

A blood-red sunset gave way to the darkest night. Will slept fitfully, surrounded by the snores and grunts of his fellow pilgrims and the slap and rush of the waves against the ship's side. Morning found the squadron on a south-easterly course out of the Gulf of Lions, the wind still in the west, a choppy sea breaking over their bows and the lightening clouds scudding overhead. Will was by now so thoroughly used to the rhythms and routines of life aboard that the days ahead slipped by with remarkable ease. He and Gabriel spent their many hours playing their beloved game of chess, at which the pair were now almost evenly matched in skill with Will winning as many bouts as he lost. Other times, Gabriel would reminisce about his home in Ireland and his travels through Wales, people he had known along the way and adventures he had encountered. Many of the stories Will had heard before, but he found it comforting to sit listening to his friend's retelling of them. For reasons of his own, he was less willing to talk about his old life in Foxwood. Gabriel sensed his unease and never pressed him.

And so the voyage continued its course, day after uneventful day, week after week. The wind being so often slack, progress was slow going. Apart from the occasional sighting of land it was easy to slip into the now-familiar sense that they and their companion vessels were completely alone in the world.

Will awoke one morning to the sight of two large islands between which they were crossing, and learned from a crewman that these were the islands of Sardinia, to their right, and Corsica on the left. From those straits they bore southwards for several more days, their diminishing food supplies relieved when they came upon a huge school of anchovies that came aboard by their wriggling thousands in net after net, and whose aroma was soon wafting deliciously across the deck as the silvery little fish were grilled over charcoal fire baskets.

'I believe we must by now be nearly approaching the *Regnum Siciliae*, the kingdom of Sicily,' Gabriel mused one evening as the two friends sat locked in a very deadly and equal game, with Samson as usual sitting nearby in his own trance-like state, as peaceful as a kitten by the dim glow of their candle.

'Is it a very great kingdom, then?' asked Will, who had no idea of what to expect of the place itself. 'As large as England? And what are the people like?'

'As an island it cannot be half the size of my homeland of Ireland,' Gabriel replied. 'But it has fine big cities and castles, to be sure, as well as great wealth and many subjects living under the rule of its king. It was our Norman brethren, once the same marauding pagans who ravaged my country but then turned towards God, who seized it back from the Saracen or Moorish emirs many, many years ago. As I understand it, they did so at the behest of the Holy Roman Emperor in Constantinople and also the dukes of Lombardy, who then gave the land to the pope. Though I may mislead you in the details, as my knowledge is far from exact. In any case theirs is a Christian kingdom of sorts, though we call them Greeks or Griffons.'

'I wish I knew half as much as you about the world,' Will said glumly, reaching out to move one of his knights to attack Gabriel's king.

'It appears you know a good deal *more* than half what I do, when it comes to chess,' Gabriel replied as his now suddenly losing position became sadly evident. 'That was a brilliantly devious move, brother.'

Their conversation was interrupted by a shout from the larboard bow. 'Are we under attack? Is the boat in danger?' Gabriel asked as men hurried past to see whatever it was that had caused the alarm. They jumped up from their place and joined the crowd lined up along the larboard rail, followed by a sleepy Samson rubbing his eyes.

'God in Heaven, what is that?' Gabriel murmured as he spotted the amazing, *amazing*, sight their shipmates were pointing and marvelling at. Will was as transfixed as anyone else by the surreal, nightmarish vision. For there, far off in the middle of the dark sea, miles between the ship and the eastern horizon, stood a solitary mountain of fire. Its truncated conical mass was silhouetted against the sky and lit by the flames and burning rivers that spewed from its flattened summit, their reflection shimmering red and yellow over the sea for miles around.

Many of the first-voyagers were frightened by the spectacle, whispers passing up and down the ship that this must be some evil omen or a harbinger of their destruction. But the more experienced crewmen acquainted with these waters knew better. 'That be the island of Stromboli,' explained old Joe Cook. 'The mountain is often aflame as if the very fires of Hell was bursting up from the depths. There is another like it some leagues to the south-west, which they call Vulcano. Sometimes you may see them both shooting up at once, one on each side like. That is how you know you are close on the north shores of Sicily.'

'Then I was right,' Gabriel noted with satisfaction. 'In which case, Will, tomorrow you will behold that kingdom with your own eyes.'

Sure enough, come the dawn they were sailing through the dangerous strait of Messina that separated the eastern tip of Sicily, the Punta del Faro, from the western tip of Calabria, the Punta Pezzo. It was in those waters that another strange and mysterious sight greeted them – not a burning mountain this time, but the apparently inexplicable appearance of what looked like a castle floating on the waves.

The apparition was too distant to make out clearly, but again many of the men nonetheless took it as an accursed sign and became anxious. Gabriel, perhaps keen to make up for his ignorance of last night, was dismissive of their foolish superstition and attempted to offer a more rational explanation. 'I take it to be a phenomenon of light and temperature,' he told them, 'though its precise nature is still unknown to our understanding, and certainly to mine. But you should not be afraid, my friends.' Few of the men seemed much reassured.

It was the morning of the nineteenth day of September in the year of our Lord 1190 when the pilgrim ships now eventually came to their current destination, the Port of Messina. Under the flat glare of the already hot sun the walled, fortified city lay sprawled along a flat coastline with verdant forests and hazy mountains rising up in the distance. In the foreground, the port itself was crammed with countless vessels of all shapes and sizes, among them anchored the vast, mighty force of warships whose hundreds of flags and pennants fluttered in the breeze. It was a sight to make a man hold his breath in awe.

'And here we are,' Will murmured to himself. At long last, after their late arrival at Marseille had separated them from the main fleet and all the months at sea before that, they were reunited with the entirety of the English expedition to Outremer. Whatever that might represent to his shipmates, for Will personally it could mean only one thing: that the killers he had pursued all this way must surely be here, suddenly closer to his grasp than they had ever been since that day in March when they had sailed out of Southampton Water.

And now that he had finally caught up with his quarry, the time of reckoning for which he had been preparing himself for so long, the fateful confrontation whose prospect had dominated his thoughts by day and haunted his nightly dreams, might very soon be upon him.

Chapter 22

Will and his shipmates were presently to learn that the grand fleet had already been in port for several days. King Richard's ship was not among them, however. Soon after their departure from Marseille their monarch had parted company, leaving them to sail through the straits between Corsica and Sardinia while he took his royal galley and a small escort of vessels around the coast of Genoa and thence on a cruise down the Italian coast, stopping at Pisa, Naples, Salerno and then Mileto in Calabria. The appearance of His Highness at Messina was eagerly anticipated any day now.

But as the newly arrived pilgrims could see from the flags on many of the docked warships in Messina's great port, another exalted royal presence had preceded Richard's: namely that of King Philip of France, accompanied by an army of his own. He too had sailed from Marseille, reaching Messina on the sixteenth of September, en route to the Holy Land. It seemed to many as though the two kings were not entirely in a hurry to get there, despite beleaguered Christian troops having already been laying siege to the city of Acre for over a year and being badly in need of reinforcements.

With so many great ships already in the overcrowded port, it took some time before the stragglers could find docking space, several having to opt for anchoring outside the harbour and unloading by boat, an extremely difficult and dangerous undertaking when it came to taking off the horses. Will's ship was among the more fortunate ones that were able to dock within the port. As they were getting ready to disembark, the chaplain prepared them for what they could expect to find here.

'You should be aware,' he warned them gravely, 'that the city of Messina abounds in every pleasant and essential thing, but its people are cruel and of the very worst sort, save of course for the heathen infidel Saracens. A wicked bunch these are, commonly known as Griffons. Many are in fact the offspring of Saracen fathers, and you may expect them to be absolutely opposed and hostile towards our people. I counsel you to be extremely cautious and never venture alone among them.'

According to such wisdom, it was the insolence of its godless citizens that had prompted the army to avoid entering the city and instead set up its camp before its walls. And what a camp it was, a sprawling city in its own right, comprising its many thousands of men – and not a few women and even children who had travelled with the expedition, all receiving their plenary indulgences for doing so – in countless tents and pavilions spread over a vast area of open ground.

Already the Christian pilgrims had made themselves at home here at their temporary base. Campfires and braziers were burning, a good deal of commerce seemed to be going on, and things appeared somewhat less chaotic than might have been expected given the sudden arrival of such an enormous foreign landing force. Stockades and stables had been built to contain the many hundreds of horses the army had brought with them; and further from the encampment was the necessary pit that had been dug out to serve as a latrine. The French forces, including a number of their noblemen in splendid gold-embroidered tents, were mainly grouped within their own large compound from which they were flying their banners, though from the mixture of languages being spoken among the English part of the camp it was clear there was a good deal of intermingling going on. The French king himself, it was thought, was not inclined to live in camp and had taken fine lodgings inside the city.

Will, Gabriel and Samson, along with Roderick Short, Tobias Smith and old Joe Cook, weaved their way through the noise, smoke and bustle of the makeshift streets of the camp in search of a place to make their own. Finding a large square tent that was only slightly threadbare and situated in an area not too polluted by campfire smoke and general litter, they agreed it would suit them well enough. The only problem was the group of pilgrims who had already laid claim to it, and were currently engaged in a game of dice, laughing and joking among themselves in a strange guttural language Will had not heard before. 'They are Welshmen,' Gabriel explained sotto voce. 'From their accent and dialect I would guess they are of the folk of the Teifi valley, from Llanfihangel-ar-Arth or thereabouts.'

'In that case,' growled Roderick Short, jerking his thumb, 'they can sling their hook. Fucking Welsh.'

Will was about to object to what seemed to him like a rather unfair demand, but before he could express his thoughts on the matter Samson had stalked up to the dice players and stood over them looking like a shaggy and rabid dog of bear-like proportions and with such an intimidating glint in his bulging eyes that they quickly gathered up their possessions and fled.

'That's how you get things done,' Roderick Short chuckled. 'Nice one, mate.'

And with that, the shipmates moved into their vacated accommodation, unpacked their belongings, stored their weapons and set about exploring their new surroundings. Will was already on the lookout for any banner or emblem bearing the black eagle of the Baron of Gilsland, but in a camp so vast as this he had to accept it would take a good deal of searching. He was tired and hungry; his quest could wait until he was fed and sufficiently rested to face the men he sought. Even a fight to the death wasn't a prospect he was prepared to face on an empty stomach. Within a short walk of their tent they discovered an enterprising vendor selling fish and crabs caught that morning along the beach and grilled on the flat of a shovel. Buying up as much of the man's wares as they could carry, they took their feast back to the tent and ate greedily until they were sated and full.

That evening, as the others entertained themselves with a cask of ale Gabriel had won in a very short-fought chess match against a Yorkshireman three tents away, Will quietly picked up his sword, slipped away unnoticed and wandered at length among the flickering fires searching for the black eagle. He found nothing. But at first light on the morning of the twentieth he was back, scouring the busy encampment from top to bottom, drinking in all of its sights except for the one he most wanted to see.

It was on this exploration that he discovered an area, at the well-protected heart of the English compound, reserved for many of the expedition's more illustrious travellers: the bishops and lords and their various knightly entourages. 'No commoners allowed beyond this point,' barked a guard, one of a pair who blocked his entrance with crossed pikes. Will immediately began to suspect this was where the Baron's son and his men might be camped. Forced to double back, rather than return empty-handed straight to his tent, he made his way along the city wall to the main gates and ventured inside for the first time, thinking there might be some vague chance of spotting one or more of Sir Ranulf of Gilsland's men wandering among the streets.

The chaplain had been right about Messina: it was indeed a fine and very beautiful city, especially to a man like Will who had had so little experience of anything more sophisticated than a rustic village. The streets were broader and the buildings richer and grander than those of Silves, while they almost matched those of Marseille for charm and elegance. But he soon discovered that the chaplain's warnings about the people of the city, and more specifically about their attitude towards the foreign pilgrims camped outside their walls, were just as accurate. As he wandered the streets intent only on his own business it was hard to ignore the antagonism of the townsfolk who instantly identified him as an enemy invader. An old woman tried to poke a finger in his eye and a group of children flung dung at him, thankfully poor in their aim. 'Stinking dog' was one of the gentler insults that were hurled at him, before he finally decided to venture no further into the city and turned back towards camp.

The next day passed in the same manner. Several times Will set out to wander about the camp, alert and ready for anything, only to return from each sortie feeling demoralised and low. The following day, the twenty-second of September, looked to follow the same dismal course, and he could feel the pent-up energy inside him beginning to gnaw at his soul and fray his nerves.

Early that afternoon, a podium was erected within the camp and horns were blown to summon a crowd to listen as a royal official in brightly coloured robes, struggling to make himself heard, read out an edict of proclamation governing the conduct of the army while living in camp.

'Here we go,' muttered Joe Cook standing behind Will's shoulder as they gathered to listen. 'Spoiling what little fun as a man might hope to have around here.' The old man's guess was right, and as the rules were announced one after the other in a harsh monotone, Will quickly found his attention wandering so that he only caught snatches here and there:

'. . . *Let no one in the whole army play at any game for a stake, saving only knights and clerks, who, however, are not to lose more than twenty solidi in a single day. The kings, however, may play at their good pleasure; and in the royal lodgings the kings' servants may play for twenty solidi if the king chooses. If any sergeants, mariners or common men are found playing by themselves they shall be beaten naked through the army for three days unless they will pay a fine to be agreed accordingly.*

'. . . *If, after starting on the journey any pilgrim has borrowed from another man he shall pay the debt; but so long as he is on the pilgrimage he shall not be liable for a debt contracted before starting.*

'. . . *If any man, saving only knights and clerks, shall neglect his duties or desert his lord on the pilgrimage, such transgression will be subject to excommunication and punishment in accordance with the will of his king.*'

The decree droned on for several more edicts of a threatening nature against any form of transgression against royal authority, before progressing to some lesser points that some of the men found baffling, even absurdly amusing.

'*Moreover, it is decreed that no merchant may buy bread or flour in the army to sell it again, unless some stranger has brought the flour and the seller has made it into bread. But it is utterly forbidden to buy any light bread, neither may it be bought within the town. No one is to buy any lifeless carcass for the purpose of selling it again, nor any live animal, unless he have killed it in the army. No one is to raise the price of his wine after he has once had it cried. No one is to make bread except at penny cost. And let all merchants know that the whole strait of Messina and its nearby islands is within the banlieue of the city, and that within that region one English penny shall equate in all mercantile transactions to four Anjou pennies. And it is to be understood that all of the aforesaid decrees are promulgated with the consent of the kings of France, of England and of Sicily.'*

'What the fuck are they going on about?' grumbled Roderick Short.

'Beats me,' said another man in the crowd.

But whatever specific and sometimes odd regulations the royal authorities might wish to impose, it seemed to Will that the camped army was subject to a generally lax schedule of rules, with little sense of organisation and no attention whatsoever paid towards activities of a military nature, such as drilling or training. Passing the French compound that mid-afternoon he did catch sight of some of their finely clad knights engaged in some spirited horsemanship practice, jumping over trestles while swinging swords at hanging targets. It was a stirring spectacle and it made him reflect on something Gabriel had told him some time ago on their sea voyage.

'Your offer to teach me some of your skills with the blade,' he said to his friend back at the tent. 'Does it still stand?'

'Of course it does,' Gabriel replied, looking at him with some concern. 'At any time, brother. You need only ask.'

Will was about to answer when they heard the thundering of drums and the hooting of war trumpets coming loudly from the direction of the port. Running out of the tent they saw others emerging from theirs, gathering in crowds and joining the throng that were hurrying that way.

'What's happening?' Will asked one man as he rushed by.

'The king!' the man replied, in a state of high excitement. 'King Richard has arrived!'

Chapter 23

The king had indeed arrived, and that day of the twenty-second of September was one that would not soon be forgotten. Amid great fanfare and pomp, his majestic galley ship and its escort came sailing into the port of Messina with a host of smaller vessels that had sailed out to meet them, their standards and pennants fluttering triumphantly in the warm wind blowing from the sea. Their prows were all painted differently in blues and golds and crimson, and rows of glittering shields hung on their bows. The king's ship was by far the largest and most ornate, its prow high above the water and the towering poop deck at the rear resembling a sea-going fortress. It was a sight intended to inspire awe and wonder; and that it did for the crowds of pilgrims, both common and knightly, and the hordes of people from the city who had flocked to the port to witness his coming.

Will and Gabriel pushed their way through the crowd and stood near the edge of the dock. The harbour was buzzing with anticipation of the moment when the king would appear. Then there he was, to a blast of trumpets and a clamour of voices, the tall manly figure clad in shining chain mail and his snow-white tabard marked with the crimson cross of Christ, the crown on his head gleaming in the sunshine and his shoulder-length red-golden hair catching the breeze. He paused for a moment on the prow of his ship, as if deliberately putting himself on show for all to see; then as the galley came up alongside the harbour wall he sprang down in a long-legged leap and was immediately joined by the knights and royal guards of his entourage.

'So that is the king of England,' Will said to Gabriel above the noise of the crowd. Even he found it hard not to be impressed by the sight.

'Aye,' Gabriel replied. 'The man himself, in all his grandeur, and set to outshine Philip of France in every way he can. For technically, our king is Philip's vassal for his lands in France, though you would never think it to look at him. And he knows it, too. The man you see, you expect him to be.'

'The French king does not come to meet him?'

'Seemingly not,' Gabriel replied with a knowing smile. 'I am not sure how much love there is between the two. Let us hope their rivalry, if that is what it is, never comes to open disagreement or we are all in trouble.'

Many of the onlookers who had flocked from the city were visibly stunned by the impact of King Richard's appearance. Everyone had heard of his reputation, but here the reality in front of them seemed even greater. Surely here was a man worthy of respect and unquestioning loyalty, whose magnificence and authority set him higher than any other ruler. The show continued as the king, surrounded on all sides by his joyful welcomers, mounted the splendid grey-dappled war horse that had been led down the loading ramp from the ship, tossing its head and clattering its hooves, and reined the frisky animal in tightly as he pranced past the crowd. A host of knights in their silvery mail and red-crossed tabards like his own followed in procession as he made his way from the port and by the walls of Messina towards the royal tent already erected at the centre of the English camp.

But not everyone from the city was quite as taken by the glory of the moment. Some in the crowd looked at him with hostility, and there were a few resentful murmurings that made Will wonder just how peaceful a time the army would have of it if they remained in Messina for very long.

The king's very first action after his arrival might have been thought to encourage such resentment, because shortly after he was settled on shore, even before his ships had finished being unloaded, his carpenters set to work building a gallows near his tent. The message was clear to all: that anyone who might in any way provoke the displeasure of the mighty monarch would swiftly suffer the consequences. And not just his own subjects, either – for as everyone soon became aware, word having spread rapidly around the camp and into the city, King Richard was in a mood of great fury concerning his personal family matters with Tancred, the present ruler of Sicily.

'But why? What has this Tancred done to him?' asked Will that evening, as he and his fellows sat by the crackly, smoky driftwood fire outside their tent. Samson had eaten too much grilled crab and had now fallen sound asleep, snoring softly into his beard. Both Tobias Smith and Roderick Short were drunk on wine, the latter beyond the point of unconsciousness and apparently dead; and old Joe Cook was unable to answer Will's question. As usual, it was Gabriel who came up with the explanation.

'I can only tell you what little I have heard. I had it from a squire of one of the knights serving an English lord who is close to the king and privy to such information. You see, the king's sister Joan was formerly the queen of this land, having been married to King William II of Sicily. But he died last November, the marriage having been childless. It seems that by rights the crown should have gone to William's aunt Constance, whom he had declared as his heir. But it was seized instead by her illegitimate nephew Tancred, who they say is an ill-looking villain more resembling a monkey than a man.'

'The Monkey King, that's what they call the little bastard,' said Tobias Smith in a slurred voice.

'Has he a tail like a monkey?' asked Joe Cook, apparently quite sincere.

'I am sure that he must, and keeps it curled up and hidden beneath his royal gown,' Gabriel replied. 'Anyhow, having earlier sworn fealty to the future queen, Tancred now broke his word, rebelled against her and usurped the crown for himself, taking the island by force and placing Joan under house arrest. As I understand it, she has been his prisoner ever since, confined to the summer palace of Ziza in Palermo.'

'The sister of our king?' Will said. 'Made prisoner?'

'It gets worse,' Gabriel replied. 'Not only that, but Tancred stole from her the lands that had been given her by her husband, the late King William. And to further compound the insult, he also seized the fortune that had been the dowry our king's family paid to William at the time of their marriage: according to the talkative young squire who told me all this, perhaps too talkative for his own good, the treasure includes a golden table twelve feet long, a hundred fine galley ships, sixty thousand seams of corn, another sixty thousand of barley, twenty-four golden cups and twenty-four golden plates.'

'And King Richard wants it back?' Will guessed.

'Certainly he does, every penny repaid with interest. As well, needless to say, as the safe return of his sister. He also requires that Tancred should honour the financial commitment made by William towards this expedition of ours to the Holy Land.'

'You think Tancred will agree to those demands?'

'Not a chance,' interjected Tobias Smith, smacking his lips after another swig of wine. 'You can't trust that goddamned little monkey as far as Samson here could toss him, tail and all. And there'll be Hell to pay over it, mark my words there will.'

Gabriel gave a dark smile. 'I tend to agree with Tobias. Our good King Richard is not a man to be trifled with. He will expect results, and expect them quickly. And if Tancred should prove foolish enough to goad him any more than he has done already . . . well, I wouldn't be at all surprised if our stay here should turn out more eventful than we might have wished.'

*

It was uncertain at first whether Gabriel's dire prediction would be proven true. One thing he was right about, though, was that King Richard wasted little time in setting matters into motion. On the twenty-fifth of September he dispatched his royal envoys to Palermo to make his formal demand to Tancred for the release of his sister and, most importantly of all, the immediate and complete restitution of her dowry.

To begin with, it appeared that the Sicilian king was prepared to cooperate with the request. Within two days Joan had been freed from house arrest. Tancred graciously placed her aboard a galley ship that carried her from Palermo to Messina, where she was safely received into her brother's hands. But no sooner had the galley arrived than did the difficulties between the English and the Sicilians enter a new, much worsened, phase. For all Tancred had sent Joan back with was her bed gear, along with a curt note addressed to Richard, in which he flatly refused to pay back so much as a single coin of the dowry or to return an inch of the lands he considered to be legitimately his own.

Tancred's letter was a slap in the face that drove Richard into a boiling rage. The English king immediately donned his armour, mustered two hundred of his mounted troops and led them by sea across the Straits of Messina to the mainland region of Calabria, where within a matter of hours he had captured the fortified town of Bagnara with a view to establishing a heavily guarded base. On the first day of October he had his sister Joan taken there, to be kept safe under the protection of a large cohort while he returned to Messina, ready to deal with the upstart Tancred.

By this time the king was in such a dangerously angry state of mind that even his closest aides had become terrified of him. Advised against allowing a state of full-blown war against Tancred to develop, he raged at them: 'How do you imagine you will ever overpower the Turks and Arabs and restore the kingdom of Christ if you show your cowardice before these effeminate Griffons? Do you wish to be the subject of mockery by children and old women back home? I will first take Messina, then by God I will remove this ugly little wretch of a usurper from the land he has stolen.'

While all this was happening, the tension that Will himself along with many others had sensed was building between the foreign pilgrims and the folk of Messina was intensifying at a rapid pace. Rumours abounded of the locals conspiring to send raiding parties to invade the camp in the dead of night, cut the people's throats as they lay sleeping and steal their goods. Some believed the hostilities were exacerbated by reported instances of certain members of the pilgrim camp having been seen conversing with – and in some cases perhaps making improper approaches to, which may or may not have been reciprocated – the wives and daughters of Messina.

And as though the state of affairs were not already precarious enough, the presence of a large army camped directly outside their walls was causing a serious additional strain on supplies and inevitable food price increases within the city, which the traders and merchants imposed not only on the foreigners but upon their own people as well, much to their resentment. Then on the second day of October, an incident took place that would play a decisive part in what was to come. It had begun when an English pilgrim wandering alone in the streets of Messina against the better advice of his peers tried to buy a loaf of bread from a woman vendor. The transaction had quickly turned ugly when she demanded an inflated price for the goods; and when he refused to pay so much, she rounded on him shrieking out a stream of abuse, threatening to attack him and pull out his hair. The commotion attracted the attention of a crowd of local men who grabbed the pilgrim, beat him mercilessly and left him virtually trampled to death.

Hearing of the potentially dangerous episode and wishing to avert violent reprisals from his own camp, Richard tried to restore peace by assuring both sides that it would, and could, not happen again. But the further damage caused to the relations between the people of Messina and the foreigners had left its mark. In such volatile circumstances, with so many antagonisms rising on both sides, it would not be long before the pot boiled over – and it happened the very next day, on the morning of October third.

To a candid observer it might sometimes have appeared that King Richard of England did not always adhere to his own logical train of thought. Less than twenty-four hours earlier he had been so deeply concerned with maintaining the peace that he had subdued his own people's angry response to one of their fellow pilgrims being almost fatally assaulted. Now, in an inexplicable change of heart, he threw all such diplomatic cautions to the wind by declaring that the Greek monastery of St Saviour's, close to the city, was to be commandeered by the army, the monks forcibly driven out, and the holy buildings used to warehouse excess stores from the ships of the fleet.

Will had awoken long before dawn that morning and gone down to the shore to walk awhile, be alone and wash himself in a small freshwater tributary that fed into the sea. His spirits were very low after days of fruitless searching, restless nights that allowed little sleep, and the exhausting mental strain of being so constantly in readiness for the confrontation with his enemies. Night and day he prayed it would come soon, but the waiting was wearing him down. They were so close, and yet sometimes they had never felt so far out of his reach. In his fitful dreams he saw himself storming into their camp to find and challenge them, only to be met with wave after wave of opposition; and then to discover that they were not even there at all.

'Your mind is elsewhere these days,' Gabriel observed as they played a game late that morning, one in which Will was making one ill-advised move after another and recklessly losing pieces. Gabriel could easily have crushed his opponent but was making as many allowances as he could for him. 'I would ask what it is that burdens your heart, if I didn't already know. You look tired, brother.'

Will sighed, shrugged and was about to make another desultory move towards losing the game entirely when Tobias Smith burst into the tent and interrupted their play. 'Look alive there, boys, we have work to do. The king needs men to help shift stores over to the monastery, and we are recruited to the task.'

Will was initially glad of the distraction as he and Gabriel hurried out of the camp with Tobias Smith and Samson and joined the party of men charged with the arduous task of loading large quantities of mainly dried and salted food provisions in casks and barrels from the docked ships onto wagons and transporting them up a long, steep hill to where St Saviour's stood overlooking the city. But when they got there, they found a scene of bitter uproar as a group of knights were expelling the last of the monks and their attendants from the holy place where many of them had dwelled all their lives. 'We have nowhere to go,' one of the monks tried to reason with the commander of the knights. 'Have mercy, I implore you!'

'Shut up and move along there,' the commander replied harshly. 'King's orders.' Then another very ancient monk, a wizened white-bearded man who looked at least seventy or eighty and was physically frail, hobbling with the aid of a crutch, stumbled and fell as a soldier urged him to move faster. The soldier drew his sword and stood over him shouting, 'Up, up on your feet, you old cripple, or I'll put you out of your misery with this.'

Already brimming with frustration, before Will even knew what he was doing he had put down the load he was carrying and taken a determined step towards the soldier with his hand on his own sword hilt. He would have unsheathed his blade and committed himself to an action from which there would have been no return, if Gabriel and Samson had not quickly intervened and held him back.

'Don't be a fool, William,' Gabriel said in a low voice close to his ear, gripping his arm. Fortunately, the soldiers had not noticed. Samson hurried forward, gave the knight a look that instantly persuaded him to back off and put away his sword, and gently helped the old monk back up on his feet. Others came up to take care of him and thank Samson for his good deed, and the incident passed over without any more drama.

But Will and his friends weren't alone in their objections to the brutality of the king's men. A growing crowd of the residents of Messina had climbed the hill from the city and gathered close to the monastery. Some were primarily concerned with helping the evicted monks and other residents, but many others had come with lances, axes and other weapons and looked quite prepared to use them. Will couldn't understand the undercurrent of mutterings that ran through the crowd, but their angry expressions spoke for themselves and the sentiment was clear: quite apart from the sacrilege being inflicted on the poor monks, if the English king could take it upon himself to seize the monastery like this, what was to stop him from seizing the whole island if he so desired? Rebellion was in the air and the situation clearly capable of descending into bloodshed at the slightest provocation.

'This is bad,' Gabriel confided in Will. 'Tomorrow we shall be in a state of open war with these people, you'll see.'

Chapter 24

It was surprising, in fact, that trouble did not erupt even sooner than it did. The night passed peaceably enough, but early the following morning were heard cries and violent commotion coming from the city gates. Reports soon spread through the camp that another quarrel had taken place and, this time, finally degenerated into serious fighting with several pilgrims having been slain in the streets.

King Richard's response to this latest outrage was swift and decisive. The Griffons had gone too far this time, he declared, and the only way to settle matters was to attack and seize Messina by force. Some might have guessed what his closest advisors already knew: that this had been his intention all along.

'But how can he?' Will asked as the news reached him and his friends. 'I thought the French king was living in the city.'

'You think Richard gives a damn for that little Frankish fart Philip and his poxy army?' laughed Roderick Short. 'Come on, boys, looks like we're in for some action at last. I'd rather be chopping Saracens, but Griffons will do me fine for now.'

For the second time in just a few days King Richard donned his armour, strapped on his sword and rode out on his charger at the head of his troops. He seemed eager, even joyful. This was a man raised from his earliest boyhood to be a consummate warrior, skilled in every aspect of combat and never more in his element than when he was in the thick of bloody battle. The people of Messina were just as quick to declare a state of war against the foreigners. The gates were closed, and from behind the walls came the sound of drums and trumpets and every bell within the city ringing to call the population to arms.

While the hostilities were mounting there was no sign of Philip of France becoming involved. Confusion reigned in the French camp, with everyone wondering what position, if any, they were supposed to take in the conflict. Envoys were sent looking for their lord king, who was taking refuge in his palatial lodgings and refused to come out. Among the English camp some said the Frenchman was torn between his unwillingness to displease the Sicilian merchants or so-called Lombards and the need to honour his accord with Richard. Others were convinced that Philip was at that very moment negotiating a treacherous deal with the authorities of Messina, who would agree to surrender the city to his sole control if he agreed to take up arms against the English on their behalf. Others again simply disregarded him as being a weakling and a coward. Nothing was going to stand in their way, least of all the fucking French.

As the English pilgrim army was being mustered it was in fact the Griffons who opened the attack. A group of their mounted soldiers launched a sortie against the camp, happening by chance to target the lodging of Hugh le Brun, a count of one of Richard's domains of Poitou. Their assault was quickly headed off by a contingent of Richard's elite cavalry, fewer than twenty knights but a formidable sight as they charged them with lances lowered, the thunder of the heavy war horses making the ground tremble. The terrified Griffons fell into retreat and headed for a small gate in the city wall, but not all made it back to safety as Richard's horsemen rode them down and left many lying pierced and trampled in the dirt.

Now battle broke out in earnest, and as the English forces massed in front of the walls and advanced on the gates the fifty thousand Griffons within the city began to resist with all their might. The defenders lined the ramparts, flinging down rocks or whatever heavy objects came to hand, their archers and crossbowmen firing salvo after salvo into the teeming ranks below. In the first wave of fighting, the Griffons inflicted numerous casualties on the attacking army. Men were crushed and broken by missiles from the walls, skewered by arrows and crossbow bolts that pierced shields and chain mail. Word quickly spread that three of Richard's best knights had fallen: Peter Tirepreie, Matthew de Sauley and Ralph de Roverei. Remaining utterly cool and composed under fire, Richard marshalled the cavalry for a fresh attack.

While all this was going on, Will and his friends were deployed to the general assault on the walls. Will had been directed by a sergeant-at-arms to join the division of archers raining return fire up at the battlement defences. He did as he was told, not out of loyalty to the king, certainly without any enmity towards the Sicilian people, only because he feared for the safety of his friends as long as the deadly hail of arrows kept coming down on them. He drew and loosed; drew and loosed; and with every shot he saw his arrow strike its mark and the man go tumbling to his death, if the strike had not already killed him outright.

While the archers kept down the resistance from above, Richard himself was where he belonged, in the thick of the fiercest part of the assault. Having failed to cut the hinges of the main gates, he led his cavalry to the crest of a hill to one side of the city and charged down towards a secondary gateway that he suspected to be less strongly defended. Sure enough, the charge succeeded in smashing through the postern gate and entering the city, quickly scattering the few Griffons who had been posted to those lesser defences and hacking and trampling their way along the inside of the wall to open the main gates from within. Now ten thousand of the king's soldiers flooded into Messina with screaming battle cries and in a short time had completely overwhelmed the Griffons inside.

In the confusion and sheer mass of bodies Will had long since lost sight of Gabriel, Samson or anyone else he knew; and with no longer anything to shoot at on the now-abandoned ramparts he slung his bow across his back, drew his sword and joined the great press of roaring, yelling men streaming in through the main gates. What he found inside was a slaughterhouse no less sickening than the scenes he had witnessed at Silves months earlier. The fighting men of Messina and the city guard were putting up some resistance, though it was sporadic and hopelessly ineffective against the mass of Richard's soldiers rampaging through the streets putting everyone they could catch to the sword. From behind the houses and buildings he could hear the clash of steel, the screams of fear and the raging shouts as the invaders pushed deeper into the city, killing as they went, storming dwellings and terrorising the townsfolk into a blind panic. People were leaping from their roofs to escape being hacked to death, or kneeling in the streets begging for mercy that more often than not they didn't receive.

Will's mind was spinning at the horror of what was unfolding all around him. So much so, that when he caught a glimpse of the emblem on a tall shield among the melee, he thought at first that he must have been dreaming.

Stunned to a standstill, he remained frozen for several instants in the midst of all the noise and fury around him as though none of it were really happening. What he had just seen brought a welter of memories and emotions tumbling through his mind. It was the same black eagle imprinted forever on his memory, with its three-forked tail feathers pointing down like spikes and that cruel hooked beak. Now the soldier who bore the emblem on his shield was gone again, vanished around a corner of the winding, cobbled street; and for a few moments longer Will could not be certain that he hadn't imagined it.

His reverie was broken as a Sicilian guardsman suddenly came at him from nowhere and lunged at him with a pike. Reacting by sheer instinct Will knocked the pike shaft aside with the flat of his sword and then cut the man down before he could stab at him a second time. He couldn't shut the image of the black eagle out of his mind's eye, and he knew for sure now that he hadn't dreamed it. It was not some vision of his fevered imagination, conjured up to haunt him after all these months spent consumed by his desire for revenge.

He jumped over the fallen body of the guardsman and gave chase, pressing his way through the fight, the ring of weapons and the shouts of men in his ears. The black eagle soldier had been no more than forty or fifty paces from where he had been standing. Will rounded the corner of the street at a fast run. And now in a momentary gap in the heaving press of men up ahead, there he was once again.

This time Will got a better look at him. Any of Ranulf of Gilsland's men-at-arms could have been carrying a shield with the familiar black eagle emblazoned across its front; the odds were against its bearer being one of the particular individuals he sought. But now Will's heart gave a lurch and his blood turned icy in his veins, because behind the nose bar of his helmet that ugly, weathered face was one Will had seen before and would never be able to forget. He was one of the pair of men who had dragged his Beatrice from the barn, the one whose dagger she had managed to jerk from its scabbard in a futile attempt to defend herself before they had snatched her life away.

Will suddenly found it difficult to breathe. His pulse was thudding like the drums of war that had heralded the attack on the city. His hands were shaking and his legs were unsteady beneath him. *No*, he told himself, *you cannot let your emotions get the better of you now.*

He ran towards the press of soldiers, eyes fixed on the one he wanted. A pocket of city defenders had appeared from a side street and were putting up a last-ditch though spirited resistance, counter-attacking the pilgrims with spears and maces. As he raced towards his quarry, Will found himself encircled by a group of Messina's guardsmen, coming at him from all sides with raised weapons and hostile cries, and his attention was diverted as he battled ferociously to ward them off. The first two were hewn down by his sword; the third he managed to gain just enough distance from to lay down his blade, snatch his bow from his shoulder, nock the last arrow in his quiver and loose it lightning-fast into the man's chest, the bodkin head punching deeply through his coat of mail. The fourth and fifth fell back and ran for their lives, dropping their weapons. Will let them go. Breathing hard and filled with the wild energy of the fight he stooped to pick up his sword, then turned to resume his chase.

And with a shock he came directly face to face with his enemy.

For a few moments they stood there eyeing one another. The sounds of battle seemed suddenly to have faded into the background of Will's awareness, as though the two of them were completely alone in an empty city. The surcoat that the soldier wore over his mail armour was grimy and spattered red, but under the stains the black eagle was as clearly visible as the matching emblem on his shield. His sword was drawn and dripping with the blood of those he had slain. He had lost his helmet in the fray and a fresh gash across one stubbly cheek was bleeding down his neck. But he otherwise appeared unhurt, and fully alert. Seeing him up close for the first time, Will guessed that the man was perhaps sixteen or seventeen years his senior. Old enough to have accrued plenty of experience in the art of war. Young enough to still be a powerful and dangerous opponent. His eyes were hooded and startlingly pale, devoid of feeling. Their gaze flicked down to Will's shoulder where the white cross sewn onto his leather jerkin designated him as a *crucesignatus* and therefore an ally. And yet, as the man went on staring curiously at him, a frown of doubt came over his face, growing into one of recognition that was anything but friendly.

'Wait a minute,' said the man. 'I know you.' His speech was of the northern parts of England, like some of the voices Will had heard among his fellow sea voyagers.

The tremor had quite gone from Will's hands and his legs felt strongly planted under him. His heart, which before had been pounding so hard and fast, now hardly seemed to be beating at all.

'We have met before,' Will replied in a steady voice. 'In a place called Foxwood. Do you remember that day? I do. And now one of us is going to die.'

Chapter 25

Will's quiver was empty after his encounter with the city guards, and in any case he was standing so close to his enemy that there would have been neither time nor space between them to use his bow. He let the weapon slip from his hand and fall to the cobbles.

'That village,' the soldier said, still staring at Will. 'That's where I saw you. That wench. I remember her, too.'

'She was my wife,' Will said. 'And the mother of the child I will never see, nor hold, nor raise as my own and watch growing up.'

The soldier smiled. 'How touching. So you've come here to kill me now, have you?'

'Or to die seeking my revenge,' Will replied. 'God will decide.'

'No,' the soldier said. 'That's for me to decide.'

Will had thought he was prepared for the speed and ferocity of the man's attack, but nonetheless it was going to take every bit of skill and courage he possessed to have any chance of withstanding this vicious onslaught. Their swords clashed high, then low as the soldier's flashing blade came down to cut at Will's middle, which Will narrowly avoided by ducking out of its path. His enemy's lines of attack were well practised and he fought with speed and fluidity, moving his body around his sword with deft footwork as he transitioned from guard to guard, strike to strike. In a matter of moments, Will found himself on the defensive and forced to retreat.

But even as he was fighting for his life, he was fast learning to anticipate the soldier's sword moves. The man favoured a two-handed downward cut from a raised position, chopping diagonally from the shoulder, but in so doing again and again he betrayed his intentions and three times in succession Will was able to parry each blow, his enemy's blade bouncing off its course with a jarring ring of metal on metal. Then when the soldier broke his pattern by slipping in what was meant to be a feint followed by a wily cut to his opponent's centre, Will was able to anticipate that too. Suddenly he was no longer so much on the defensive, and able to launch cutting strikes of his own that his enemy had to react quickly to block.

Just as it seemed the contest might begin to equalise, in dodging a swing that slashed through empty air inches from his throat Will's heel caught against a raised cobblestone and he stumbled, thrown off balance. As he had learned to his cost playing chess against Gabriel, a skilled and clever opponent was always quick to exploit any weakness, however small. Seeing his opportunity the soldier lunged his blade hard and fast into the opening left by Will's dropped guard, and it was only by a violent twist of his body that Will was able to prevent it from slicing deep into his mid-section, a blow that would surely have been fatal.

He couldn't save himself entirely, however. The soldier's sword might have missed its intended target but on the follow-through its sharp tip cut a slash in the left sleeve of Will's leather jerkin. His hauberk underneath protected him from being too badly cut, but the pain of the injury shot through his left arm and left him gasping for an instant.

Now the soldier pressed his advantage, grinning widely in triumph as he came charging forward with his shield raised to slam into Will's face. Its flat upper edge caught him below the cheekbone in a savage blow that sent him staggering backwards and seeing stars.

You are going to lose, he thought to himself. He swayed on his feet, stunned, bracing himself for what was about to come. He could almost feel the agonising shearing of his flesh as the tip of the enemy's weapon pushed into his guts, and then the rest of the broad double-edged blade following on to pierce him through and through. The fight seemed as good as over. He had tried, but he was not strong enough to win. Will Bowman was now facing a brutal and bloody death at the hands of a more powerful enemy.

It was at that moment, when luck and hope seemed to have both completely deserted him, that he saw a vision of Beatrice's face in his mind, as clear and vivid as though she were standing in front of him. Her fair hair was blowing lightly in the wind and she was smiling, the light of the sunshine twinkling in her eyes. He blinked. Was she really there? Was he already dead, and going to join her?

Then the vision dissipated like smoke and through it came Will's enemy, charging at him once again to repeat his effective shield slam and this time follow up the blow with a low stab that would run Will through the middle. This time, Will was ready for him. In an explosive surge of strength, he raised his sword up high and then brought the edge of the blade down with enormous power to strike the upper edge of the soldier's shield. He had intended only to deflect it away from crashing into his face a second time, but the sheer force of his strike cleaved the shield completely in half down the middle and took off three of the fingers holding it. The two split pieces of the shield fell to the cobblestones.

The soldier staggered back, blood pouring from his hand, his eyes wide in shock and surprise. Will advanced purposefully on him. A year ago, he would have felt nothing but empathy for his fellow man. But the black eagles had shown no mercy to Beatrice that day, and neither mercy nor quarter would be given now. There were many things Will wanted to say to his stricken enemy. Instead, he raised his sword, and in a single horizontal swing he struck his head off his shoulders.

Then his enemy lay dead at his feet, and the fight was done. Will stood over him, breathing hard. His heart felt cold and empty. Blood ran down his wounded arm and dripped from his fingertips to merge with the red pool spreading among the cobbles. Will stared for a moment at the black eagle emblem he had been visualising in his mind all these months. Then he used the dead man's surcoat to wipe the blood off his blade and slipped the sword back into its scabbard. It would not be needed again today.

Suddenly back in the present, Will turned and looked around him. All about the city the clash of steel and the cries of the oppressed were falling silent. The battle for Messina was over. It would later be said that King Richard had taken the city in less time than it would take for a priest to sing Matins.

Will walked out of the open gates and surveyed the desolation of the battlefield before him. Men and horses lay dead on the ground. Survivors of the battle moved among the piles of corpses, searching anxiously for their comrades. Fallen weapons lay strewn everywhere, and arrows were planted in the dirt like a field of reeds. With a deep pervasive melancholy descending on him like a cloak of mist, he began looking for Gabriel, Samson and his other friends. He found them a while later among a larger assembly of pilgrims gathered at the foot of the walls, battle-stained and weary but mercifully unscathed.

'You are hurt,' Gabriel said with concern, looking at his bloody hand.

'I found one of them,' was all Will needed to reply, Gabriel being the only one of the group who understood his meaning. 'He will not hurt anyone again. Now I just have three more to go.'

'Three more what?' Samson asked innocently.

'Three more of what need not concern you,' Gabriel told him in the kindest way, and that was good enough for Samson. Filled with delight at seeing Will safe and sound, the gentle giant opened his big arms wide and clasped Will in a bear hug that threatened to crack his ribs. Even Roderick Short looked happy that none of their little band had been hurt in the battle.

Soon afterwards, the looting began. Following the king's decree that the remaining residents of Messina be spared but their material wealth forfeit, whatever gold and silver the occupying army could lay their hands on was fair game. By sundown a vast fortune in coin and treasure would be plundered from the city and removed by the cartload, the majority to be poured into King Richard's coffers while the rest went directly into the pockets of the looters. Many a pilgrim enriched himself many times more in that one day than he could have earned by honest means in his whole life, if he lived to be a very old man indeed. Their number included several Englishmen of Will's acquaintance, such as the ignoble Osric and his cronies who snatched up all the booty and shiny trinkets they could carry and then began disputing between themselves with daggers drawn over who got what.

While Messina was being systematically stripped of its wealth, by order of the king every Sicilian ship and galley in the harbour was burned to the waterline in order to prevent any of the city folk from escaping. Meanwhile, Tancred the Monkey King was still holding out, hiding in his palace in Palermo and refusing to agree to terms. This reportedly enraged Richard so intensely that he began ordering the taking of hostages among the nobility of Messina, holding them to ransom while threatening dire consequences if Tancred continued to resist his demands.

'Will he send the army to Palermo and overthrow Tancred himself, do you think?' Will asked Gabriel as the latter attended to his wounded arm that evening in the tent. They were alone and free to talk openly, as the others were taking part in the riotous celebrations they could hear outside. The king had requisitioned much of the stocks of Messina's wine merchants for the entertainment of the troops, and they were enjoying his royal generosity to the full.

'I doubt it,' Gabriel replied after a pause for thought, his face half-lit by the soft glow of their guttering tallow candle. 'It seems to me that his accord with Philip has already been stretched far enough, without breaking whatever bounds of diplomacy may exist between France and Sicily and risking tipping our two nations into a state of war at a time when we must remain allied against our greater mutual enemy in the east. It is a delicate situation, and though our ruler may not possess the most delicate touch at times even he must surely respect certain political constraints.'

'You talk as though the whole thing were like one big game of chess to you,' Will said to his friend with a weary smile. His wound was hurting him a good deal and he felt utterly drained.

'Because that is just what it is,' Gabriel replied, gently winding the bandage around Will's arm before the candle burned out and they lost what little light they had inside the tent. 'But enough of the ambitions of our great King Richard. I would rather hear about my friend Will, and what he plans to do once he has achieved his own. You have come a step closer today, though I wish you could have done so at less cost to your hide. I do not much like the look of that gash. The blade went deep and I am no surgeon. The wound may become poisoned over the coming days.'

'Pah,' Will said, dismissing it.

Gabriel hesitated. 'William, these men you seek—'

'What of them?' Will replied, a little sharply, anticipating words of advice that he might not welcome.

Looking kindly at his friend, Gabriel said, 'After all the dangers we have faced along the way, how can you be sure that the rest are even still alive? I have to ask: is it not possible that fate may have already intervened on your behalf? That you are just chasing ghosts?'

Will looked back at him, and shook his head. 'No. They're alive. Don't ask me how I know. But I know. I can feel it. I can feel *them*.'

'Very well. And supposing you are right, and your pursuit is successful. Once you have got them all, your quest is fulfilled. Have you given any thought to what happens then?'

Will was silent for a few moments. 'I can't bring myself to care about what happens afterwards,' he said quietly.

'Perhaps that will change,' Gabriel replied.

'Or perhaps I'll be lying in a grave of my own.'

*

The three golden lions against a crimson background that was the royal banner of King Richard now fluttered triumphantly over the city of Messina, alongside his war flag bearing a white dragon. Not everyone within the occupying armies was so pleased with the display, however. In the immediate aftermath of the taking of the city a bitter quarrel broke out between the two kings Richard and Philip regarding who should take credit for the victory: this despite the fact that the French monarch had steadfastly withheld his involvement at the time. In the spirit of conciliation, and bowing to Philip's nominally superior rank, Richard agreed to allow the French banners to be raised alongside his own. This was still not enough to satisfy Philip, who now raised objections to the quantity of booty taken from the city and demanded his share.

Incensed by the quarrel, Richard immediately set his army to work on constructing a large wooden fort on a hill overlooking the city walls. The structure was so designed from prefabricated sections that it could be erected quickly, then dismantled and transported for use elsewhere. Nonetheless, it took a large number of men many hours to build, and Will and Gabriel were among those drafted in to provide their labour. Again, Samson's enormous strength was put to good use, as he carried loads of timber over his massive shoulders that would normally have taken an ox to transport. Richard called his fort 'Mategriffon' which as Gabriel explained to Will could loosely be translated 'Griffon-killer' or 'destroy the Greeks'. With the local populace freshly reeling from the violent plunder of their city, that choice of name did little to assuage their fears that Richard's hostilities against them were set to go much further. 'He will slaughter us all,' was the general consensus of the people.

But their concerns were soon eased when, just three days after the conquest of Messina, the ruler of Sicily was persuaded to give in to Richard's demands and agreed to pay twenty thousand ounces of gold by way of recompensing Queen Joan's dowry. Perhaps to rub Philip's nose in his munificence, Richard offered to share this fortune equally with his fellow monarch. Whether or not his display of generosity was enough to placate the French, it earned Richard a good deal of glory and approval from his own side. Bringing with him an escort of his most noble princes he met in person with Tancred the Monkey King at the city of Catania, midway between Messina and Palermo, and the two kings made a great show of mutual regard and affection as they exchanged splendid gifts and feasted together as though allies. It was remarkable, some observed, what magnanimity and goodwill could be brought about by the application of just the right amount of brute force and bloodshed.

For Will, these lofty goings-on were of no consequence whatsoever. Whenever he could find a spare moment from his duties he was either scouring the camp from end to end for the remaining three black eagle soldiers, or taking Gabriel up on his offer of sword instruction. Their lessons took place on a lonely stretch of the beach, away from prying eyes. Using wooden substitutes to save their blades they went through every conceivable exercise in offensive and defensive skills, tactics and footwork. For every move Will already knew, his friend was able to show him three or four variants which were drilled and repeated again and again. He was a strict and exacting teacher, even more than he had been with chess. 'I could have cut off both your arms in the time you took to react. Let us try again, a little quicker this time if you please.' Or when he grew impatient with his pupil, 'God's teeth, William. This is a fight, not a child's game.'

The rest of the time, thankfully, Gabriel was his usual affable self, willing to please and utterly loyal to his friend. It was on the fifth day after the sack of Messina, while the teams of labourers were putting the finishing touches to the fort of Mategriffon, that he shared with Will some new information that he had obtained from his contact, the same loquacious knight's squire who had previously told them of the political machinations of the Sicilian court.

'Brother, I think you need to hear this,' Gabriel said in a breathless rush, having been searching for him all over the construction site. 'It would appear that after the uprising of the Griffons, being anxious about a further revolt, the king decided to double the guard on the Lady Joan. To that end he has deployed numerous extra men across the water to the fortified town of Bagnara. My informant is quite certain that Sir Ranulf, the son of the Baron of Gilsland, was among them, along with his retinue of knights.'

'In Calabria?' Will said, startled by the news. The relentless hammering of carpenters' mallets all around them seemed to have disappeared in an instant. 'Can his information be trusted? How can he be sure?'

'Because he saw them riding out of the camp and heading towards the harbour with the rest of the guard reinforcements, to board a galley for the passage north across the Strait of Messina. According to him this took place early on the morning after the city was taken. They have not returned.'

'All these last days I was looking for them, and they weren't even here,' Will muttered.

'What will you do?'

Will reflected in silence for a moment. Then he shrugged resignedly and replied, 'I can do nothing. What hope have I of reaching them there, in a secure fortress protected by a hundred professional men-at-arms? All I can do is wait here for their return, and take my chances then.'

Will was lying, though, because in the instant he had heard this revelation he had made up his mind to go to Bagnara with all possible speed. He knew he must keep his decision to himself: if he told them the truth about his intentions his friends would only try to insist on coming with him. To cause them to be put in danger was a burden of responsibility he could not accept. Moreover, the royal decree on the severe punishments meted out for desertion had been clear. Will would run the risk of being caught and hanged from King Richard's gallows, gladly and without a moment's hesitation, but it was a risk he must run alone.

Tonight, he told himself. *Tonight I will slip away and go hunting for them, any way I can.*

Chapter 26

A military encampment the size of a town, an ocean of clustered tents and makeshift shelters and huts of various kinds housing thousands upon thousands of men could never be said to be entirely dormant. There was always some activity taking place, even in the dead of night when the more nocturnal of its residents would be awake and sitting by their fires now that the evenings were becoming colder, drinking wine, indulging in games of dice, or else in illicit activities of a different nature involving the loose women of Messina – for whom a large contingent of ruttish strangers camped just outside the walls, many of them recently enriched with more gold and silver coin than perhaps was good for them, offered bountiful opportunities for trade.

For all these reasons, as well as the fact that both Gabriel O'Carolan and Roderick Short were extremely light sleepers – unlike Samson who was difficult to rouse at the best of times – it was something of a challenge for Will to sneak out of the tent that night. Even just the *jink* of his chain mail or the rattle of loose shafts in his arrow quiver as he quietly, carefully pulled on his outer garments and gathered up his weapons could so easily have betrayed him – but many was the time he had called upon his hunter's skill to creep up on an unsuspecting wild creature in the forest, barely breathing and mindful of the least twig snapping underfoot, and for a large man he was capable of moving with great stealth and lightness of foot.

Managing to sneak away without disturbing any of his companions he threaded a convoluted path between the tents, staying well away from campfires and watchful eyes, his soft footsteps unheard over the sounds of snoring men. Some without tents slept in the open, huddled under blankets or whatever coverings they could find, and once he almost trod on a slumbering shape in the darkness. The man stirred, spluttered and mumbled something incomprehensible as Will stepped over him and moved on. Twice more he had to lie low and remain very still when a patrol came by, as sneak raids and incursions by the resentful Griffons of Messina were an ever-present concern and armed guards regularly circulated on watches throughout the night. But again, the skill of a silent hunter served him well, and they took no more notice of him than they would have a patch of shadow.

At last he reached the camp's eastern perimeter where the heavy equipment, food and water stores, smithies and animal stockades were located. Will paced by the horse corrals, murmuring reassuringly to the creatures as they sensed his presence and milled nervously about, snorting and blowing. Many were of the smaller, hardy variety used as pack animals, others the palfreys and coursers belonging to the regular men-at-arms; while the finer mounts, the large powerful destriers belonging to the wealthiest and most important knights, were kept away from the rest of the herd, within a purpose-built stable building. Like the king's fort of Mategriffon, it had been transported in pieces aboard ship.

If I am to take a horse, Will thought, then I want a steed that is fast and sure-footed, strong and reliable and able to carry me a long distance. What he truly needed was a beast resembling as much as possible the worthy Hengroen he had been compelled to leave behind in England. He still missed that horse. And to find one of such quality, the place to look was inside that stable building.

During the daytime the stockade was busy with grooms, farriers and stable hands coming and going to attend to their various duties, but by night the only guard was a young fellow posted on watch by the stables. He was barely more than a boy, and he lay snoring on the ground beside the empty wine flagon whose contents had lulled him to sleep. Will slipped quietly by him. As his eyes grew used to the darkness of the stable block, he saw the long, narrow building was divided into stalls each containing a single animal along with its feed and its tack.

He moved from stall to stall, whispering, 'There, boy, do not be afraid,' and 'Shh; I will not hurt you.' Some of the horses shied away at his approach. But there in the fourth stall stood a tall, magnificent white charger that did not shy away, but loped closer to the half-doorway to press his velvet-soft muzzle into Will's proffered hand and snuffle curiously at his hair and face.

'You really are a fine beast,' Will whispered to him, reaching up to stroke his massive neck and long, thick mane. 'Your owner must be a person of great wealth and importance. But I'm sure he would forgive my borrowing you for a day or two, if he understood my need. Will you carry me where I must go?'

He had heard tell that some of these big highly bred creatures, especially the stallions, could bite or lash out dangerously when a stranger entered their stall. But this one remained perfectly placid as Will stepped in and set about saddling him. The saddle itself was like none he had ever ridden on, with a strangely high pommel and back that he supposed was designed to provide greater rider support in battle. It was the same kind that the black eagle riders had been astride that day. With his bow and quiver slung over his back and his sword at his side Will mounted the horse and said to him, 'Now run like the wind.'

The horse needed almost no urging. The gentlest kick unleashed a surge of power and energy that well surpassed Hengroen, and Will had to duck his head quickly for the low doorway as they went thundering out of the stable. The sudden flurry of activity woke the guard out of his drunken stupor, and he jumped up waving his arms and shouting 'Stop! Stop!', but had to leap aside to avoid being trampled. Will rode for the camp gate, where the two sentries manning the wooden barricade had become alerted by the shouts of the stable guard and came rushing to block Will's way with their lances crossed. But this was a horse bred and trained for war and he was not about to be deterred by such a paltry obstacle. The sentries dropped their weapons and flung themselves out of his path in panic. Then Will had to hang on tight as the destrier gathered his power and cleared the barricade in a tremendous leap, barely even slowing down.

Now Will's mount was truly able to show what he could do as they galloped away into the night with astonishing speed. Clinging on to the reins with the cool night wind tearing at his hair, Will glanced back over his shoulder and saw the burning torches of the camp guards as they rushed to open the barrier and give chase; but by the time they managed to organise a party of riders, Will would already be a mile beyond their reach.

He had some idea which way to go, Calabria lying off Sicily's north-east shores. Leaving the city behind them they streaked across the hills that edged the coastline. The horse seemed almost to be relishing the chance to demonstrate his limitless energy, but presently, fully certain they were not being chased, Will reined him in and they settled down to a smooth, long-striding canter. The terrain was rocky and arid, tall hills rising up to blot out the stars to his left, the darkly shimmering sweep of the ocean stretching away to his right. This was the Strait of Messina that Will would somehow have to cross in order to reach the mainland.

As first light began to creep above the eastern horizon they came to a tiny white-stone coastal village on a sandy cove, where Will stopped to rest the horse and try as best he could to ask directions of the local people. They were simple fishing folks who were up with the dawn and gathering on the beach to prepare their nets and small boats ahead of a long day's work. At first, they were somewhat intimidated by the sight of him with his weapons and the big war horse, but after several attempts and doing all he could to show he was no threat, by pointing across the water and repeating the name Bagnara – as best he could pronounce it – he was able to make them understand that he needed transport over the Strait for himself and his horse.

'I can pay,' he told them, showing the few silver pennies he had left in his purse. It was no great wealth, and pitiful compared to the little fortunes pillaged from Messina by many of his comrades, but the fishermen eyed the money and seemed to think that it was payment enough to warrant doing whatever they could to help him. To carry a single passenger across the water could present no problem; but the horse was clearly another matter, far too large and heavy for their little boats.

After a lengthy huddled conference among themselves, with a great deal of gesticulating and rapid talk that meant nothing to him whatsoever, they signalled for him to wait here and all promptly hurried back to the village, leaving him alone and somewhat baffled.

A short distance away he found a parched area of ground with enough greenstuff for the horse to nibble at. It was only now that Will noticed how ornate his saddle was, richly decorated and inlaid with gold and silver. His owner must be a very wealthy knight indeed, Will thought as he sat by the horse and watched the beauty of the sunrise. If today was the day he finally caught up with the men he sought, he might never see another. As that prospect now grew closer again, he felt a fluttering in his stomach and his heart beat quickly.

Some time later the fishermen returned, this time bringing a new man with them who was obviously a personage of importance, though Will had no idea why until by means of sign language and mimed gestures they made him understand that this man was able to offer him passage across the water to the mainland. His boat was moored on the far side of the cove, and for a price he was willing to act as ferryman. Payment up front was clearly a requisite part of the bargain, so Will emptied his purse into the man's cupped hands. He had few qualms about parting with the last of his money. There was a good chance he might never need it again.

An hour later they were afloat. Will had been doubtful about loading the horse aboard, but need not have worried as the worthy animal showed no fear of the makeshift wooden ramp from the jetty on which they embarked. The boat was ancient and much in need of repair, though still serviceable enough, and compared to the cramped ship on which Will had spent so much time it even felt comparatively roomy. As the sun rose the morning was turning out warm and pleasant, and the sea was vivid blue and as flat as a pond under an unclouded sky.

Live or die, it was a good day to meet one's fate.

*

The crossing was short and uneventful, and before the sun had reached its midday zenith he was back on solid ground. If anything, the terrain here in the mainland region of Calabria was even wilder and more rugged than the Sicilian landscape now familiar to him, little but desiccated scrub and rocky scree. The sun was hot and the wind warm and dry as he rode inland. His wounded arm ached and last night's exertions had caused it to start bleeding through its bandage again – though with so much else on his mind he barely felt the pain. Reason told him that King Richard's choice of a fortified garrison in which to hold his sister safe must be somewhere close to the coast, for the guarding force to have travelled directly there by galley ship. Going by that logic he hugged the shoreline, keeping always in sight of that fine stretch of flat azure-blue sea to the north with the mountains to his right, in the south.

It was along that stretch of coast that he arrived at another fishing village, perched up on the cliff above the sea and dominated by an ancient castle. At first, he thought he must have found his destination, and the blood once more quickened in his veins as he pictured his enemies close by. Then, sighting a laden pack mule and its owner making their slow way along the dusty coastal road towards the village, he stopped to make enquiries of the extremely wizened nut-brown old man leading the animal. When Will pointed up at the cliff-top castle and asked 'Bagnara?' the man shook his head and told him a quite different name that after a few repetitions Will understood was 'Scylla'. Communication was difficult, but he was finally able to glean that Bagnara was some way further up the coast, perhaps no more than two hours' ride on a good horse. Will thanked the old man, wishing he had something more than words to offer by way of gratitude, and rode on at a gallop.

If the white destrier was weary after covering such a distance, he made no show of it — and feeling so close at last to his goal Will pressed him on at a fast pace, pausing only once to water at a stream. The scenery grew steadily more rugged as they progressed northwards, tall mountains to the south with thickly forested foothills and barely any sign of habitation save for a ruined old church on whose half-demolished bell tower Will spied three large black birds roosting. He halted the horse to look up at them, shielding his eyes against the sun with the flat of his hand. They were bigger than the common ravens he had known back in England, and though he could not tell whether they were eagles the sight gave him an uneasy chill as if he beheld some evilly significant omen. 'Let us ride on,' he said to the horse. 'This place has an ill-favoured feeling about it.'

On and on up the winding coastal route, endlessly hacking up sharp rubble-strewn slopes and down into deep troughs and valleys where the ground had crumbled away and the horse's hooves scrabbled for grip and caused small rock slides. Here and there the terrain grew more verdant with the edge of the forest almost reaching the cliffs, while in other places it was as arid and bare of vegetation as a stone quarry. All of it was heavy going, and their progress became slower and slower.

Just as Will was beginning to despair of ever reaching his goal, thinking that perhaps the old man with the mule had misinformed him, his mount scrambled up a steep, shaley piece of track and there it came into view at last: the town of Bagnara with its walled fortifications high atop the cliff, the sun-sparkled blue sea horizon stretching infinitely in the background.

'I have found you,' Will said.

Chapter 27

Only then did Will pause to consider how a lone rider was ever to gain access to the town. Now that its residents had been expelled and the place entirely taken over by the soldiers of the English king, with its tall, arched stone gateway, battlements and corner turrets it must be as heavily guarded and impenetrable as any military castle. And though Will was recognisably one of their fellow *crucesignati* by the now rather travel-worn but still intact cloth cross sewn to the shoulder of his jerkin, it seemed doubtful whether he could simply ride up to the gate and be welcomed inside by the men of the garrison. To make matters worse, he reminded himself, he was also technically a deserter from the Messina camp and could expect to be treated as such, even before he made known his hostile intentions towards three of their people.

Will dismounted and led the horse to a cluster of tall rocks from where he could observe the town unseen. The gates were shut and he could see no sentries manning the battlement, but he could not afford for his presence to be detected. *How?* he asked himself over and over. *How am I going to get inside?*

He had been reflecting on his dilemma for a while when the rattle and creak of wooden wheels on the stony ground caught his ear, and he peered out from between the rocks to see a large high-sided wagon approaching along a track leading down from the forested hillside. Hauled by a pair of slow-moving oxen it was carrying a load of straw, firewood and barrelled provisions that Will guessed were being supplied to the garrison from some other small town or village further inland. As he watched, the wagon reached the foot of the hill and turned up the track towards Bagnara's towering main gateway.

He was quick to make his decision, knowing that this might well be his best chance to get inside. 'Wait for me,' he said to the horse. 'But if I do not return, you have to make your way back to your master as best you can.' The stallion gazed at him with big eyes shining with intelligence, as though he understood Will's words.

It was now or never. Will patted the horse farewell and then broke away from the cover of the rocks at a fast sprint, clutching his sword scabbard so as not to trip on it as he ran. Neither of the two men driving the ox-drawn wagon noticed him chase them along the track. It lumbered along at such a sluggish pace that he quickly caught up with it, and jumped up onto the open tailgate to burrow his way into the loose prickly straw. Now all he could do was stay hidden aboard the rocking, lurching wagon and hope that nobody had spotted him from the walls – or else his infiltration attempt might be over before it had even begun.

It seemed to take an eternity to reach the town gates. Presently Will heard the sounds of activity and voices as guards emerged from inside to meet the supply wagon. A pause while they halted; and for a few tense moments he was convinced the sentries must suspect the presence of a stowaway aboard and were about to thrust their spear-points deep into the straw to either pierce him through or flush him out. To his relief, instead he heard the sound of laughter and soon the wagon rolled on again. There was an echoing thud as the gates of Bagnara swung shut behind them.

He had made it inside. With that he was a giant step closer to achieving his goal. Peeking cautiously out through the straw he gazed around him. The town appeared much less grand than Messina, with streets of sand and dirt and disorder everywhere. Knights in their white surcoats and more commonly dressed foot soldiers and men-at-arms milled about singly or in groups. He worried that the wagon-drivers might start unloading their goods and find him. To his relief, instead they rolled into a stable yard where the oxen were unhitched and the men wandered off. Seeing his opportunity Will crawled out from his hiding place and slipped away unnoticed, picking bits of straw from his hair and mouth.

On his journey from Messina he'd wildly imagined himself entering the town to immediately find his enemies standing there waiting to fight him, as though his appearance had been expected. Now that he was here, the reality would be somewhat different. Some of the common pilgrim warriors among the garrison guard were attired not dissimilarly to him, in mail hauberks and haubergeons and plain tunics or doublets of various mismatched non-uniform kinds, with their stitched-on cruciform insignia and a variety of weapons worn about their persons. That would allow him to mingle among them while remaining as inconspicuous as possible, and discreetly search the streets just as he had searched the camp at Messina – only this time he stood a far better chance of finding what he was looking for. He was ready for that. The flutterings in his stomach and racing heartbeat he had felt earlier were entirely gone.

Such had been his plan, at any rate – but suddenly all was changed. He had not walked three hundred paces through those narrow, labyrinthine streets when the door of a building directly in front of him swung abruptly open, and from its low archway appeared not three, but five men all wearing long white tabards bearing the emblem of the black eagle of the Baron of Gilsland.

Will halted in mid-step and stood staring at them as though they had appeared from a dream. Except that this was no dream. This was the same vision that had haunted his every moment, waking or asleep, these last months. Of the five, two were strangers but the faces of the other three brought back a rush of vivid recollections and feelings that were nearly overwhelming. One of the three he recognised was disfigured by a facial injury that had not healed well. The livid, raised purple scar ran from the left corner of his mouth to what had been his left ear before Will's arrow had torn most of it away, leaving little more than a tattered pink nub.

The men saw him looking at them from across the street and the conversation between them died abruptly away. The first one to have emerged from the doorway was a man Will had not seen before. By his manner and bearing he gave the impression of being their leader. 'What are you looking at, soldier?' he barked at Will.

'At three bloody murderers who are doomed to Hell,' Will replied. 'I have come to send them there sooner.'

They laughed in amazement. 'Says who?' demanded the one with the scar. His lips were twisted into a permanent sneer by his disfigurement and he talked with a kind of wet sucking lisp.

'Says the man who gave you that,' Will told him, pointing. 'The same man who cut down your filthy comrade in Messina, not five days ago. Now the three of you go to join him.' As he spoke, he unslung the bow from over his shoulder, drew an arrow from his quiver and had the weapon at full draw before any of them could make a move.

'I am Sir Ranulf of Gilsland,' said their leader in an outraged tone. 'By what authority do you dare to threaten me and my esquires? Do you not know the penalty?'

'Neither you nor anyone could do me greater harm than has already been done,' Will answered. 'But I have no personal quarrel against you, Sir Ranulf. Step aside and I promise you will be spared.'

And now here the moment had come at last when he had Beatrice's killers in his sights. The three were all equally guilty and it was no matter to Will which one died first; he pointed the tip of his arrow towards the one with the scar. The bow was utterly rock-steady in his grip, his aim true and unflinching. The iron-hard tension of the drawn string pressed into his right fingertips as he prepared to release his deadly shot.

But he was unable to do it. Not like this.

'Draw your sword,' he said to his scarred enemy. 'Let it not be said that I killed a man who had nothing in his hand.'

'No?' laughed the soldier. 'And what if I choose to leave my sword in its scabbard? Then we could be here a long time, waiting for you to pluck up your courage to shoot.'

'Who is this impudent idiot?' Sir Ranulf asked them.

'I never saw him before,' replied one of the others. He was the second of the pair who had dragged Beatrice from the barn.

'Well, whoever the devil he is, what are you waiting for? Go over there and kill him.'

'My lord, he is pointing a longbow at us,' said another, not of the three.

'He'll probably miss. Or at worst he'll only get one of you. Kill him, I say. Split his guts open and we'll hang his carcass from the gates as a warning to any other hedge-born peasant who thinks he can threaten violence against a lord's men-at-arms.'

Will's mouth was dry. He was a heartbeat away from loosing his arrow.

And he should have done so. Because in the next instant something very hard and heavy struck him over the back of the head. Too late, even as his misfired shaft shattered against the building wall, as the bow dropped from his hand and he felt himself pitching forwards with his vision bursting into a million spangling white stars, he realised that another of their comrades had come creeping up from behind with a mace. That was his last conscious thought before the darkness rushed up to engulf him.

*

When he awoke it was with a searing flash of pain in his wrists, arms and shoulders and the realisation that he couldn't move. Such light as filtered inside the bare, stone-walled room came from the open doorway, making him blink. Managing to crane his neck painfully upwards and focusing his blurred vision he saw that the rope binding his hands together was lashed to a thick wooden beam overhead. He didn't know how long he had been hanging here, but it was long enough for his captors to have laid into him with fists and cudgels. Blood ran down his face and neck and dripped from his hair. He could feel his lips were split and one eye was swollen almost closed.

The six figures stood around in a half circle as he hung helplessly in front of them. 'So you would send my loyal men to Hell, would you, peasant scum?' said the mocking voice of Sir Ranulf of Gilsland. 'Bold words, coming from a fellow who will shortly be on his way there himself. What more have you to say for yourself?'

Will hung his head and made no reply. His battered face hurt too much to speak.

'I remember him now,' lisped a different voice, that of the man whose face had been ruined by Will's arrow that day. 'Thought he was dead. Tough bugger, aren't you?'

'And clearly quite tenacious,' Sir Ranulf chuckled. 'To think that he followed us all the way here from England, taking his oath so that he could join the army.' He plucked disdainfully at the cloth cross sewn to Will's jerkin, now red with blood. 'He would even risk having his neck stretched as a deserter to abscond from his post and come looking for us in this godforsaken desert. Truly remarkable. One might almost be inclined to reward such fighting spirit, if he weren't so dangerous.'

'Don't look so dangerous now, do he?' said another of Beatrice's killers.

Sir Ranulf stepped closer to Will and pushed his face towards his, so that their noses were almost touching. Will could smell his rancid breath. 'The only reason you are still alive, you whoreson wretch, is that I want to hear the truth of what happened to my esquire Thomas Cawburn. I believed him to have been slain by a treacherous Griffon, but you say differently. Do you wish to recant your story? Or do you claim responsibility for his death?'

'I told you,' Will managed to croak through the pain. 'I killed him. And I will kill the rest of them.'

'Then that makes you a murderer as well as a deserter,' Sir Ranulf replied, stepping back. 'To say nothing of the madness of a man who believes he can escape such a predicament. And now you have made your confession, I intend to exercise my power to have you executed as such. I look forward to the spectacle.'

'Let me do it, my lord,' the scarred one said eagerly. 'In settlement for what he did to my face.'

Sir Ranulf nodded. 'That seems only just. You will settle your score soon enough, John Scrope. You, Henry Godard' – this to another of the men – 'run and find a stout block on which we may cut off his head in the proper fashion. And you' – to a third – 'despatch a messenger to the king to tell him we have caught a deserter and criminal, and are dealing with the matter appropriately. John Scrope, I will leave it to you to choose the means by which to perform the execution. One of the men may lend you a good stout axe for the purpose, if you find it answers better.'

John Scrope's hideous face crinkled into a grin of satisfaction, and he wiped away a sliver of drool from the corner of his damaged lip. 'Thank 'ee kindly, my lord, but I would just as soon do it with this.' He wrapped his fingers around the hilt of his arming sword and began to draw the blade from its scabbard.

'Not *now*, you imbecile,' snapped his master. 'Do I not make myself clear? Are you incapable of grasping the simplest instruction? I have wasted enough time on this murdering vermin for one day. And besides,' he added with a knowing leer, 'I have a most willing young wench waiting for me in my quarters and risk losing my enthusiasm if I tarry here any longer. Let him remain hanging where he is until morning, and then we shall cut him down and have our entertainment.

Nothing like a good swift execution before breakfast, would you not say?'

'Yes, my lord,' the men mumbled in reply, deeply disappointed.

And so they left him, the closed door shutting out the light as they departed. He heard their voices fade away as they walked off. Then he was alone, gently swinging on the end of his rope. Another time he would have struggled madly to free himself, but he was too hurt and demoralised to even shake away the flies that buzzed around his head, drawn by the smell of congealing blood.

I have failed, he thought to himself, and the hot salt tears ran down his swollen cheeks and dripped from his nose, his chin. Tomorrow he would die at the hands of his enemies, not in combat but ignominiously like a common criminal, his quest only partly fulfilled. Beatrice and their child would never be properly avenged. And though he longed to be reunited with his lost loved ones in Heaven, he didn't know how he could face them in the knowledge that he had ultimately proved too weak to fulfil his promise.

Don't trouble yourself with such thoughts, said Beatrice's voice in his mind. *You did not have to prove yourself to me, nor try to win my everlasting love. It is yours and yours alone, Will. It always was.*

Left there hanging, every muscle and sinew and joint in his wrists, arms and shoulders strained until the agony filled his body; and then, as merciful unconsciousness carried him off, gradually died away to nothing. The flies stopped buzzing after night fell, and the sounds of the garrison dwindled into silence punctuated only by the periodical changing of the guard. In his dreams he was with her again, running hand in hand through a field of tall golden grass that seemed to stretch forever. The glow of the warm sunshine filled him with light.

Then his dream was ended abruptly. His good eye blinked open, the other swollen completely shut, and in his waking confusion the light he could see was the chink around the edges of the door as the sun rose over the battlements. The burning pain in his arms and shoulders came flooding back. Moments later he heard the tramp of heavy footsteps outside, followed by the clatter of the lock and the groan of hinges. The early morning sunlight dazzled him as the door swung open.

John Scrope, his fellow man-at-arms Henry Godard and the third man whose name Will didn't yet know came striding in through the doorway. 'Hope you had a restful night, my sweet prince,' Scrope joked mockingly in his wet lisp as he drew out a knife and reached up to slice the rope holding Will to the beam. 'You won't be getting another. And now we're going to have some fun. Ain't we, lads?'

'Almost as much fun as we had with his pretty little wife,' laughed Henry Godard. 'That was a good day, that was,' he said for Will's benefit. 'Rodney here' – pointing at their other companion – 'he wanted to go first but the bitch put up such a fight that he stuck her with his dagger instead. Right in her belly, like skewering a fucking piglet. "Rodney Hake, you wicked bastard," I says to him, "could you not have waited for us to take our turns?" But he's like that, is our Rodney. Ain't you, Rodney?'

'Damn you all to Hell,' was all Will could mutter. As the rope was severed he dropped from the beam like a sack of grain, his legs folded under him and he sprawled to the floor. His captors aimed several vicious kicks to his face and ribs before they seized him roughly by his still-tethered wrists and dragged him across the floor and out of the doorway into the harsh light. Will was too groggy to resist them. He looked around him with his one open eye and saw that the building in which they had imprisoned him was to one side of a small square. At its centre had been set down a plain wooden block, aged and cracked.

Some soldiers, most of them bearing the crest of the black eagle but a few others belonging to different lords, had gathered around the square to watch the execution. They looked on impassively as Will was dragged across the dirt ground and dumped in front of the wooden block. Now up stepped Sir Ranulf of Gilsland. His contented smile might have been from his night with the wench, or perhaps it was due to the pleasure of seeing a man decapitated on his orders.

Sir Ranulf walked over to where Will lay and gazed down at him. 'I have not asked your name, peasant, as I do not give a damn who you are. You are charged with the crimes of desertion and murder, for which the sentence is death. I wish I could say that you die a Christian martyr, having taken your vow. But only God can make that judgement. If you are sorry for your sins, it would be wise to repent.'

'I am sorry,' Will said quietly. 'Sorry that I didn't kill you all. But you will be burning in hellfire before long.'

'Pathetic,' spat Sir Ranulf. He nodded to his man John Scrope. 'All right. Now get on with it. We haven't got all day.'

Henry Godard and his crony Rodney Hake grabbed Will, looped a rope noose over his head and laid him roughly across the block with the back of his neck exposed and held steady by the noose. Two other men pinned his legs down, though he made no attempt to struggle. Then Scrope, his distorted features twisted even more horribly into a beaming smile, slowly drew his sword and stepped over to the block. Bending down so he could speak close to Will's ear he lisped, 'Forget what they say about it being quick. This'll hurt like a bugger. And I'm going to make it last as long as I can.'

He raised the sword.

Chapter 28

For a man who had lived under the constant shadow of death for as long as Will Bowman had, the moment itself held little fear. He consigned himself into the hands of God and waited for the blade to fall.

It never did. For in that same instant a loud command sounded from across the square, echoing off the buildings and breaking the anticipatory silence of the spectators. 'Stay that sword! That man is not to be executed!'

The shout had come from the leader of three horsemen who now rode into the square. Their mounts were lathered in foam after a long, hard run and their fine gold-embroidered blue and crimson robes were dusty from the road. It was clear to all that the riders were men of high authority: certainly high enough for Sir Ranulf to quickly, though most reluctantly, signal to his man-at-arms John Scrope to withhold his killing strike.

'On whose orders is he not?' Sir Ranulf demanded indignantly, his cheeks flushed red.

'On the orders of King Richard,' the rider replied, reining in his horse as it wheeled and tossed its head. 'The prisoner is to be taken back to Messina to face judgement before his Highness personally.'

'That's absurd,' Sir Ranulf exploded, unable to restrain the outburst. 'A common criminal? A deserter?'

'And a thief,' said the rider. 'One who broke into the camp stables and stole one of the king's horses. We came across the animal outside your town walls a few moments ago, proof that he is the same man. Now hand him over to us.'

'I will not,' shouted Sir Ranulf, as furious with himself for having sent word to the king of the deserter's capture as he was with these officious envoys who now wanted to deprive him of his prize. 'He's mine.'

'Then regrettably I will have to inform his Majesty that you and your men disobeyed his direct order,' the royal envoy replied coolly. 'In such a case you, too, would be required to come back with us to Messina to answer before him. Is that what you wish, Sir Knight?'

Sir Ranulf hesitated, turning an ever darker shade of red as the envoy's calm threat and its very deadly implications sank in. 'Very well.' He turned and motioned to his men, who were staring ashen-faced at the envoys. 'Release him.'

Will was dragged away from the execution block and forced to stand, unsteady on his feet, as the party of heavily armed king's soldiers who had accompanied the envoys to Bagnara now rode into the square and took command of the scene. They had with them two riderless horses, one of them the white stallion Will had thought he would never see again, and the other a plain brown palfrey.

Two soldiers dismounted and clapped Will into a pair of heavy iron cuffs joined by a chain that was just long enough for him to ride, then half-marched, half-carried him to the palfrey and heaved him into the saddle. 'Until our next meeting,' he called defiantly to Sir Ranulf and his men.

'I doubt that, son,' one of the king's soldiers said quietly, and not entirely without sympathy. 'I wouldn't be in your shoes for all King Solomon's gold.'

Within the hour they were en route back down the coast to meet with the galley ship that was to deliver them back to Messina. What fate awaited him there Will could only guess – but its outcome was unlikely to be much more favourable than the one from which he had just narrowly escaped. One form of execution was much like another, unless they inflicted on him the far greater cruelty of impalement or burning at the stake.

Once they had him loaded aboard the vessel, Will was put in leg irons and chained up in a dark space below the main deck. There seemed little point in protesting his innocence or pointing out to the soldiers that he had not known it was the king's horse he was taking. Would that knowledge have changed his actions? Probably not, he reflected. And in any case, better to be executed by the king than suffer the humiliation at the hands of his hated enemies. Though he still faced certain death, he felt a tingle of triumph at having defied them.

The return voyage was over all too soon, and presently they were sailing back into the familiar port of Messina. He had expected to be put back on the brown palfrey and led up the hillside across from the city walls to the fort of Mategriffon to face the king's wrath. Instead, they marched him at lancepoint in his clinking chains from the harbour into the city itself. He kept turning to gaze across at the distant camp, in the vain hope of catching a last glimpse of any of his friends, however fleeting. 'Keep moving,' his escorts commanded him, prodding him in the back with their lances.

Townsfolk gathered to stare, point and sometimes laugh as he was led to an ancient, forbidding stone building in the heart of the oldest part of the city. Flanked by armed guards its doorway was a massive, riveted iron gate, and the windows set into its thick walls were so heavily barred that a snake could barely have slipped through them.

'Am I not to see the king?' Will asked the soldiers.

'Not before you have cooled your heels in here for a while,' one replied. 'And God help you, if half of what they say about this rat-infested hole is true. Let's go.'

The old prison of Messina was as dark as night inside, so dank and airless that the burning torches that offered the only source of light smoked and guttered and cast long flickering shadows over the craggy stonework. The stench that made Will gasp was of vermin, decay and human waste, and it grew more overpowering and sickening the deeper they led him into the bowels of the building. The soldiers handed him over to their Griffon counterparts, who spoke no English and barked harsh commands as they prodded and shoved him through one barred iron door after another, and then down a worn spiral staircase to the dungeon that was to be his home for the present moment.

In the murky firelight the last iron door grated open on its rusty hinges; a rough hand pushed Will through it and he staggered and fell to his knees on the stone floor thick with years, decades, centuries of dust and filth. Then the dungeon door crashed shut with a resounding clang, and the guards turned and left him there, taking their flickering torches with them and plunging him into total darkness. One of them made some joke in their language and another laughed.

Those were to be the last human voices Will Bowman would hear for a long time.

*

Time, time, time. He could never have guessed that the thing itself could constitute a torture in its own right. Down here where night and day were perpetually intermingled, there was no telling how fast or slowly it passed by. Time just *was*, unable to be measured or gauged by any kind of predictable daily routine. Now and then, at apparently irregular intervals, his jailer — a mentally deficient slave who seemed to be both deaf and mute and whom Will named Griswold after Barnabas Griswold, the poor unfortunate village simpleton of Foxwood who had been dropped on his head as an infant — brought him a jug of what tasted like sewer water and a bowl of appalling, inedible food that made him gag in disgust. It often contained living maggots he could feel squirming in his mouth as he forced himself to gulp it down. There was no form of latrine, not even a bucket that could be taken away and emptied. Will made use of the furthest corner of his cell, which was exactly seven and a half paces away from the side where he spent much of the time sleeping on a mat of filthy straw.

Time did have one valuable use, and that was to allow his wounds to slowly recover. The swelling around his eye gradually diminished until it felt normal to the touch. When Griswold came with his dull flickering torch, the only light that ever shone inside the cell, by closing his good eye Will was able to test that the sight of the other hadn't been permanently impaired. While his eye was improving, the sword cut wound he had suffered to his arm healed bit by bit as well, having mercifully never turned bad. Once the severe bruising and muscle strains in the rest of his body had eased away to nothing, he was able to perform exercises on the cell floor to help keep himself physically strong. During these times he would push himself to the limits, until he could take no more and collapsed back into his makeshift bed, covered in sweat.

When he wasn't sleeping or exercising he would lie there awake for extended periods, staring into the darkness and listening to the rats scuttle about, his only living company. Occasionally they would break out into vicious fights, when their shrill screams would fill the cell. Sometimes those fights would be to the death, and he would find himself tormented by the desire to grope around in the dark for the corpses while they were still fresh and warm, rip them open with his hands and teeth and devour the raw flesh. He never once gave in to that temptation, knowing that if he ever did, it would open the door to madness and spell the beginning of the end for him. But at the same time, he also knew that he risked slowly starving to death.

Why had the king not yet sent for him? The thought of even the most terrible punishment at his hands seemed like a blessed release compared to the long torment of the darkness. Often the anguished thought came to Will's mind that he had been forgotten about. Or, rather than choosing to winter here in Sicily, had the urgency of his expedition to the Holy Land already led the king to continue on his way, along with Will's friends as well as his enemies, leaving him here to rot?

How long had he been here already, he wondered: a considerable length of time, of that he was certain. The days and nights, merged into one, grew steadily colder as the autumn slowly moved towards winter. He would lie there shivering in the blackness, with nothing to cover himself, his only means of keeping warm being to punish his depleted body with more rigorous exercise. Try as he might to train himself to savour the maggoty slop he had to eat – never mind learn to love it – the best he could manage was to get it down without gagging.

It was a cruel, crushing, soul-consuming rhythm of life, if it could even be called living. His one consolation was that he had not led Gabriel, Samson or any of his other friends into trouble along with him. He spoke to them sometimes, wishing them well wherever they may be; and he often talked to Beatrice, long tender imaginings of the life they could still be sharing together, they and their child, if things had not happened the way they had. Beatrice's face was clear in his mind in those moments and he sometimes thought he could hear her voice. As faint and distant as it might be, he believed she was out there somewhere and could hear him. One day they would be together again.

At other times Will spoke to God, though that seemed to him very much a one-sided conversation as the Heavenly Father never once replied to his oft-repeated pleas of *Lord, why am I here? Why do you turn your back on me? Is this your punishment for having gone against your wishes? What would you have had me do instead?*

Silence. Perhaps the Lord failed to appreciate being questioned so directly.

'Then if you will not answer me,' Will would tell Him, 'then I must already be damned. And if I am, then I ask no forgiveness for what I would have done to those men, and what I still mean to do if I ever get out of this place alive.'

If he ever did. That prospect seemed less and less likely. As time and time and yet more time went by, Will began keeping a tally of the visits he received from his deaf-mute jailer and the number of dishes of unspeakable food the man brought him. Using a piece of loose stone chipping he had managed to prise out of the wall, after each of these deeply ungenial visits he would make another mark in the corner of his cell near where he slept, and often he would count them by feel, groping with his fingers in the darkness. If he had been in the habit of doing so from the start, he told himself, it would have given him a far clearer sense of how long he had been here. Then again, perhaps it was better not to know – and when the grim tally equated to the number of the fingers on Will's two hands ten times repeated, he gave up the practice for fear that it would drive him insane.

What good will it do me to count the days to my death? he asked himself. *For it is clear now that I will remain in this place until the rats have picked the flesh from my bones. Nobody will ever come for me.*

And so he went on, and on, alone in the dark, somehow finding the strength within himself to endure. Around the time he gave up counting his days the icy temperatures of winter sank to their lowest ebb. Then, imperceptibly, as the world outside grew warmer, the tormenting cold began to ease.

One day as he lay staring at the darkness, he heard the usual footsteps outside his cell door, the scrape of the lock and the grinding creak of the hinges, saw the burning torch cast its dull glow against the rough-hewn stones of the doorway. 'Just leave it there, Griswold,' he muttered, knowing of course that the man could not have understood him even if he could hear.

But this time the dark silhouetted figure behind the torchlight was not Griswold. To Will's stunned surprise a gruff voice replied, 'Come with us. King wants to see you.'

Chapter 29

It was the first English voice Will had heard in all this time, and the sound of it was profoundly strange to his ears. So the army hadn't travelled onwards after all – they were still here in Sicily, and King Richard too! That meant the same must be true of Gabriel, and Samson, and his other friends he had been certain must have long since departed these shores. As a second and a third of the king's soldiers appeared in the doorway and stepped inside the cell to escort him out, Will asked them, 'What month is it? What year?'

'Today is Saturday the thirtieth of March, in the year one thousand one hundred and ninety-one,' the first soldier replied. 'God's holy trousers, what a stench there is in here. It's a wonder you could survive so long in a place like this, lad.' Will recognised him as the sympathetic soldier who had been among those who had brought him from Bagnara.

'The end of March,' Will murmured, shaking his head in dismay. The light of their three torches was dazzlingly bright for him and made his eyes water. With a shock he realised that the first anniversary of Beatrice's death had been and gone without his knowledge. 'Then I have been here for . . . for five months. What has been happening all this time? Are Sir Ranulf of Gilsland's men back in camp?'

'Quiet,' said another of the men. 'Conserve your energy for meeting the king. He had best be cleaned up first,' he added. 'Lord, what a stink.'

'For what it's worth,' said the third, chuckling. 'They're only going to stretch his dirty thieving neck, after all.'

After months of living in almost complete darkness the bright early spring sunshine seared him painfully as the soldiers marched him from the prison to a waiting hay cart. He was weak and disorientated and had to be lifted aboard the cart. The kindly soldier climbed into the back to guard him lest he try to run, an unlikely possibility clad as he was in heavy leg irons and barely even able to walk from hunger. Another clambered into the driving seat and the third mounted a horse. With a creak and a rumble of wooden wheels over the cobbles, the cart rolled away from the prison.

'Where are we going?' Will asked, still somewhat dazed and confused.

'To Mategriffon,' said his guard; and in an undertone, 'A busy day it is there today. The king has got visitors. Just this morning a galley ship arrived from Naples bringing Queen Eleanor and Princess Berengaria, the daughter of the King of Navarre, whom he is to wed.'

Such a welter of information after all these months of total solitude was making Will's mind reel. 'Who is Queen Eleanor?' he asked weakly, slumped against the side of the cart. It wasn't that he cared particularly – but for a man who had been incarcerated for so long it felt wonderfully good to converse with a fellow human being.

'Why, Eleanor Duchess of Aquitaine, the king's mother, of course,' the soldier replied, doffing his helmet out of respect for the venerable lady. 'And a right state of affairs it has been these last few days and longer,' he went on, 'what with his sister back here in Messina and us all running about on double shifts of guard duties day and night in case them fucking Griffons get up to more of their nonsense, like the trouble we had at Christmastime.'

'I must have missed it,' Will muttered.

'Meanwhile that ill-mannered Frenchie fopdoodle Philip decides on the very same day as our good King Richard's royal guests arrive to set sail with all his fleet for the port of Acre, leaving the camp in a bloody mess as you could scarcely imagine and who do you suppose has to clean it all up? And as though we didn't have enough to attend to already, now the king has sent for the abbot of the Cistercian monastery at Corazzo and all his entourage. Joachim is the fellow's name, and a queer old sort he is too. They say he has visions of St John the Evangelist and can foretell the future, and so the king wanted to hear his prophecies and good omens. All yesterday and today until the queen arrived they have been nattering away twenty to the dozen, God help us.'

'A right rotten dreary winter we have had in this place,' the soldier driving the cart commented over his shoulder. 'The hole bored off of you one moment and run off your legs the next. Still, a good hanging will cheer us up no end.'

*

Much had changed about the fort of Mategriffon since Will had been present at its construction the previous year. As his escorts delivered the bound prisoner a royal secretary took a single look at him, sniffed the air and said disdainfully, 'So this is the thief the king wishes to see? Very well. Yet he cannot be brought before his Majesty in such an offensive state of filth. Let him be stripped, his garments burned or boiled, his beard shaved and his person thoroughly scrubbed and clad in whatever suitable robe comes to hand. You have one hour.'

The order was duly carried out by a group of attendants who plunged their naked charge into an iron cauldron of hot water and mercilessly set about him with stiff brushes until his skin was as clean and pink as a baby's, rubbed him down with scented oils and wrapped him in a linen gown. It was a far more presentable and sweeter-smelling Will Bowman who found himself being led by royal guardsmen into the great wooden hall of Mategriffon and made to kneel humbly before his monarch.

King Richard sat on an ornate wooden throne, illuminated by a shaft of sunlight that shone down from the great windows above him. His robe was richly embroidered with gold thread and he wore a bear's fur pelisse around his broad shoulders. To his right a gigantic hairy hound lay gnawing on a meaty bone, and to his left a hooded falcon was perched on a stand. Also present, as well as a whole assembly of servants, were the two female visitors Will had learned of earlier. Eleanor, the former queen of England and present duchess of Aquitaine, stood at his left shoulder. She was a remarkably upright lady of a certain age, her features sharp and animated, with bright pale blue eyes that seemed to watch everything and miss nothing. The black-haired princess bride-to-be, Berengaria, was extremely young and pretty and as delicate as a songbird, seated on a velvet chair of crimson and gold on the king's right side. Such elegance and finery were a jaw-dropping sight to Will, who in his amazement had almost forgotten the grim reason he was here.

The third visitor to the royal fort was an old, old man with a long white beard and robed in black, sitting on a stool at the foot of the king's throne. All eyes had been on him until the moment Will was marched into the hall.

'What is this?' King Richard asked curtly, displeased at the interruption.

'The deserter who stole your horse, Sire,' said the head guardsman. 'You asked to see him.'

'Yes, yes,' the king replied with an irritable gesture and barely a glance at the kneeling prisoner. 'Let it wait for a moment. Can't you see we are busy? Abbot Joachim, pray continue.'

The white-bearded old man spoke in Latin, with an interpreter translating for the benefit of those among the attentive audience who were less well educated than the king. Carrying on where he had left off, he said, 'The Lord is to grant you a magnificent victory over His enemies and will raise your name above that of any other prince upon the Earth. By your courage and infinite mercy you will be immortalised as the greatest leader who ever lived.'

If such words had been intended to please King Richard, they appeared to be having their desired effect. By contrast, Will observed that Queen Eleanor was listening with a raised eyebrow and a wry smile, clearly taking the abbot's flattering comments with a pinch of salt. Noticing this too, Richard turned to her and asked, 'Why, Mother, what amuses you? Do you not find us brave?'

'Oh, my Lord is certainly unmatched in his knightly prowess and the noble art of warfare, of that there is no doubt.' She was smiling graciously but there was a needling edge to her voice that was not lost on her son.

'And merciful?' Richard said indignantly. 'Are we not the very essence of forgiveness and compassion? Did we not for instance show infinite benevolence towards that little homunculus the Monkey King Tancred, despite his intolerable actions against us and our kin? Did we not treat him honourably after he returned Joan's dowry, agree the most generous diplomatic terms and even make him a present of the great Excalibur, the sword of Arthur?'

'It was a handsome gift indeed,' said the queen, with a chuckle. The old lady seemed to be enjoying teasing her son and was plainly quite expert at getting under his skin. Nor did she appear to feel the least bit constrained by the presence of the others in the room. 'But Richard, you know full well that you only gave him that sword because you plan to marry one of his daughters to your three-year-old nephew, Arthur, heir to the Plantagenet crown. When the boy reaches marriageable age, he is to be knighted by King Tancred with that same sword, and receive it as his own. Arthur and Excalibur reunited, the ancient legend reborn. That is what I find amusing, my son. Your little schemes are quite transparent, you know.'

'Oh, do be quiet, Mother,' said the king, beginning to fume. 'Please go on, Abbot. You were saying . . .?'

They seemed to have all forgotten Will, kneeling there with the guards standing behind him. Will was watching Richard with such intensity that the king must have sensed it, because before the wise old seer could continue, he turned and pointed. 'Tell that man to stop looking at us in that impudent manner. How dare he defy his king?'

'Keep your eyes to the floor, wretch,' said the head guardsman, kicking Will harshly in the ribs. But it was too late, as now the king's attention had been diverted from listening to prophecies of his greatness and he addressed Will directly, leaning forwards in his throne to glower down at him. 'So you're the reptile who stole one of our best horses and used it to desert his duties, eh? As well as being a murderer who slew one of the men-at-arms of the Baron of . . . Baron of . . .'

'The Baron of Gilsland, Sire,' the guardsman said.

'Or whomever,' Richard went on angrily. 'Did you suppose you would get away with it, eh? Go on, let us hear what lame excuses you have to offer for your misdeeds, before we order you to be taken away and executed. We would gladly do so with our own hand this very minute, if ladies were not present. Speak!'

'No impudence was intended, my liege,' Will said humbly. 'And I am sorry about the horse. I chose him for his quality but did not know he was yours, or I would have taken another in his place. I hope he has been returned to you safe and well. As for the man I killed, I can only say in my defence that it was he who struck the first blow.'

The king raised his eyebrows in disbelief. 'Struck the first blow? You lie. Witnesses have sworn they saw you accost him.'

It might have been highly improper and unusual for a commoner of Will's lowly status to address his king so directly; but then again, it was no less highly unusual to be asked. Despite his weakened state Will looked the king in the eye and replied, 'I mean, Sire, that he struck the first blow when he was among the men who murdered my dear wife Beatrice, and in so doing took away the life of our unborn child.'

Hearing this, Princess Berengaria gasped in horror and cupped her tiny slender hand over her mouth. Queen Eleanor frowned and asked Will, 'But how could this have happened? Surely you mistake?'

'There is no mistake, my lady,' Will said to her. 'It was in England, before Easter of last year. That is the reason I took the cross and journeyed over the sea, in the hope of finding the men who committed the crime.'

'So you dared presume to take the law into your own hands, did you?' the king raged. 'Meting out justice as though you were God Himself? Or a king?'

'And not a merciful king,' said Queen Eleanor, turning towards her son with a twinkle in her pale blue eyes. 'Certainly most unlike the exalted being who sits before us now, immortally renowned for his compassion and kind-heartedness.'

Richard looked uncomfortably at his mother, thrown by her words and suspicious that there was some ploy at work. 'I . . . yes, that's right. Well, man? What have you to say to that?'

'Only that I am guilty as charged,' Will replied, 'and must face whatever justice my king sees fit.'

'Oh but my Lord,' Berengaria burst out, speaking for the first time, which she did with a strong accent. 'You cannot execute this young man for honouring his poor wife and . . . and their dear sweet *child*!' Tears misted her eyes and she blinked them away with her long dark lashes. 'How could those men have done such a wicked and terrible thing? I can't hear any more! I will not!'

Richard glanced at his distraught future wife, and then again at his mother, who was fixing him with a very hard and stern expression. For a few moments he seemed quite lost for words – then collecting himself he cleared his throat and said in a kingly manner, 'Well, soldier, it's fortunate for you that you find us in a generous mood, soon to be wed and celebrating a successful campaign in which one can only assume you played your own part with courage and valour prior to this, ah, incident, and will continue to do so as we proceed onwards to Acre and Jerusalem.'

'My sword is yours, Sire,' Will replied, bowing his head. 'And my bow. Or they were, until they were taken by Sir Ranulf and his men. Now I have none.'

'We will have the items sent for at once,' Richard said magnanimously with another glance at his mother, who was now smiling and nodding her approval. The princess dabbed her tears with a look of devotion and gratitude towards her betrothed.

The king went on, 'And you, soldier, are to return to the camp and resume your duties. But,' he warned, raising a finger, 'there is to be no more killing of our Christian knights, do you hear? Some may be less than angels, granted. However, we need all the fighting men we can get, and so you can save your bellicose impulses for the Saracens, when we reach Outremer. God knows we will find a great many of them there, and they will be waiting for us. Now, we will have a word with this Sir Ranulf whose men you claim have sinned against you and yours, and by God we will have his solemn assurance that nothing of that sort is to happen again. Believe me, he will understand, and agree to keep the peace henceforth. You are to do the same. Is that understood?'

Will made no reply.

'Does he not need some new clothes, after being locked up in that nasty prison all this time?' Berengaria asked. 'And he looks so pitifully thin and hungry.'

'Let it not be said that we do not treat our men as though they were our own flesh and blood,' declared King Richard. 'Certainly this man shall be fed, like a fighting cock. And guards, you are to provide him with the finest suit of wedge-riveted mail you can find for a fellow of his size, along with decent breeches, a pair of stout boots and anything else he requires in order to serve well in our army. Now let that be an end to the matter. Take him to the kitchens and give him all the good red meat and wine his belly can hold.'

Dismissing Will and the guards with a wave of his hand the king turned to one of his royal servants hovering attentively nearby. 'Anselm, muster up four of our Templar knights and have them bring us Sir Ranulf of Gilsland.'

Chapter 30

Much later that day, well nourished and feeling somewhat restored in body if not in mind, Will made his way back down the hillside from Mategriffon to the pilgrim camp. He was clad in his new armour and suit of clothing: a padded gambeson under his mail and a sleeved red leather tunic over it to replace the shabby old one he had taken from the brigand. Baggy new breeches were tucked into his boots. Even his linen underclothes were being worn for the very first time. His sword was back in its familiar position at his left side, now hanging from a freshly oiled and gleaming new leather belt; while his refilled arrow quiver dangled from its shoulder strap and he carried his trusty old bow like a staff in his right hand. Under his left arm was the shining iron helm he had been given to wear, its previous owner having been one of the knights who fell during the assault on Messina the previous autumn.

And nor did the king's startling display of generosity end there, because Will was accompanied by no fewer than four servants from the fort, two of them carrying a whole roast hog between them and the other pair struggling under the weight of a full wine cask bearing the royal seal. Heads turned and people came out of their tents to gawk as Will led the unlikely procession through the camp. But theirs was nothing, *nothing* compared to Gabriel O'Carolan's utter open-mouthed wide-eyed astonishment at the unexpected return of his friend.

'What, what is this?' Gabriel managed to say when he had found his voice again. 'Am I deceived by some waking dream?'

'Why, do you not recognise me?' Will asked with a smile. He was still very weak after his long incarceration, but the sight of his friend buoyed his spirits.

'Barely. How long has it been? I had all but given up hope, William. At first, after you had left us the way you did, we all thought you must be dead. Later there was talk of an English pilgrim incarcerated in the city prison. And now here you are, looking as though you had been made a knight of the king, and not only that but laden with this splendid feast. How can it be true?'

'You wouldn't believe me if I told you.'

'After this, I might be able to believe almost anything. It does my heart much good to see you again.' They shook hands and then embraced warmly. A sudden commotion shook the tent as though a young bull had been set loose inside, and a moment later the giant form of Samson came bursting out with a garbled cry of joy. Will found himself enveloped in another of those rib-splintering hugs that squeezed the breath out of him.

As the four servants departed, all Will's other friends and a few more besides crowded all around him, patting him on the back, welcoming him home, marvelling at his safe return, and clearly careful not to ask indiscreet questions about the circumstances of his imprisonment. Will supposed he had Gabriel to thank for that.

Roderick Short was much taken with the shiny new suit of mail. 'Wedge riveted,' he exclaimed, examining it closely.

'A man would be hard pressed to get his sword point through that. It must be worth a fortune. Where did you get it?'

'The king gave it me.'

'Ballocks, he never did!'

'And what about the rest of us?' asked Tobias Smith, feigning indignation. 'Do we not get one too?'

'You'll just have to go and ask him yourself,' Will said.

As evening fell, they assembled around their crackling fire of driftwood and feasted on roast pork to the envy of all their surrounding campmates. The bung was drawn from the cask and the wine flowed freely into whatever drinking vessels came to hand. 'This must be the finest wine I have ever tasted,' Gabriel said.

'Better than what they give you in the prison of Messina,' Will replied. 'That's for sure.' Though his heart was heavy, the company of his friends did much to lift his mood, and he was able to smile and laugh freely with them, something he had never thought he would do again. It was the rarest of moments, to feel that it was good to be alive. At first, he resisted their insistent requests to tell them all that had happened, but the clamour was such that he had to relent.

'You did not steal the king's horse!' Joe Cook burst out, shocked and delighted in equal measure.

'I did, too,' Will said.

Roderick Short gave a loud belch. 'Cheeky sod.'

'How was I to know who he belonged to?'

'Our friend is an excellent judge of horse-flesh,' observed Gabriel.

'Go on with the story, Will,' urged Tobias Smith.

Will passed over the details of his encounter with his enemies in Bagnara and his close brush with execution, and he likewise preferred not to dwell too much on the horrors of his captivity. Moving on, he related his meeting with King Richard and the intervention of Lady Eleanor that had more than likely saved him from the gallows.

'So you have met the great Eleanor of Aquitaine,' Gabriel said. 'A most remarkable woman. In her day she has been queen of both France and England, though in the latter role she spent many years imprisoned by her husband King Henry and was not released until his death and the ascension of King Richard. And in her younger days she took up the cross and journeyed to Outremer with the pilgrim army of King Louis the Younger. She must be nearly seventy, though once a great beauty they say.'

'She is beautiful still,' Will replied. 'And as wise as she is fair. As for Princess Berengaria, she is the loveliest and sweetest creature I ever saw, but for one. It's she we have to thank for this food and wine.'

'And the king himself?' Gabriel asked, with real interest. 'Pray tell us what you made of him. For how many of us will ever be as close to him as you were?'

'He likes to hear great things about himself,' Will replied, after a moment's consideration. 'He is full of pride that way, and he will think nothing of using his terrible power, even if it means sending an innocent man to his death. Men are right to be afraid of him. And yet, in that short time I was in his presence I saw a side of him that was neither tyrannical nor harsh. He could have ordered me killed with a stroke of his hand but instead he treated me kindly. He not only spared my life, but even personally saw to it that I got my weapons back.'

'My, we do have friends in the highest of places,' laughed Roderick Short.

'And the lowest ones, an' all,' old Joe Cook added, digging an elbow into Roderick's fleshy ribs. 'Here, Samson mate, pour us some more of that wine.'

'We could get used to such fine living,' said Tobias. 'Better keep in with Will here, lads. You never know what good things may come of it. Perhaps we shall all become knights, with castles and lands and pockets full of gold.'

Will smiled, though a heavy sadness was descending on him again like a curtain of thick fog. 'Enough talk about me. What has been happening here in camp all this long while?'

'Ask Gabe,' Roderick Short said knowingly. 'He's been busier than the rest of us. If you know what I mean.' He raised an eyebrow and stuck out his tongue.

'Gabriel?'

'Forgive our friend's crass ignorance,' Gabriel said, shooting a look at Roderick. 'He lacks the finesse to understand.'

'Understand what?' Will asked.

'The vagaries of the human heart,' Gabriel replied, and a grin quickly spread all over his face as though he could barely contain his joy. 'Mine has been entirely captured. How else can I describe it? I am smitten, consumed, rendered helpless as a babe by the purest, sweetest love a man could ever know or even dream of. I have been bursting to tell you about her.'

'In love?' Will asked. 'With a woman of Messina?'

'And don't we all know it,' Tobias Smith said, rolling his eyes.

Gabriel ignored him. 'She is the younger daughter of the city's most eminent wine merchant. Her name is Maria.'

'Which half the camp has a Sicilian girlfriend called Maria,' snorted Roderick. 'Whether they have paid for her services or not,' he added in a very quiet undertone.

'But none half so fair as mine,' Gabriel said with a sigh. 'Such perfection of beauty, such heavenly poise! Eyes that flash like diamonds, hair as black as the night, and a neck like a swan. I have asked her father for her hand. Oh, if she could be mine, how it would gladden my soul!'

'I am extremely happy for you,' Will said. 'Only . . .'

'Only what?' Gabriel asked a little sharply, looking at him.

'I meant, after all the trouble you had over Eryl.'

'Who is Eryl?' Samson asked, blinking.

'Never mind,' Will told him. He was unwilling to get any more deeply involved in the discussion, seeing that Gabriel clearly took the matter quite seriously. 'And now, my friends, if you'll excuse me, I think I have eaten and drunk enough. After being stuck in that cell all these months I feel like stretching my legs.'

'I will walk with you, brother,' Gabriel said. 'If you don't mind the company.'

The two headed away from the tents and walked without speaking down the shoreline to a lonely, quiet section of beach out of sight of the campfires and the dark city walls. The moon was full and bright and the tide was coming in, gently lapping up the sand a little further with each wave, swirling and foaming around the rocks and sending up little packets of spray. The two friends stood quietly and gazed out to sea a while; then breaking the silence between them Will said, 'I'm sorry for what I said, Gabriel. I really am happy for you. I meant no offence.'

'None taken, brother. But that isn't what I wanted to talk to you about.'

'No?'

'No. You should have let me come with you. Swear to me, William, that you will never sneak off like that again, or go getting yourself into situations where your friends cannot be of any help to you.'

'Gabriel—' Will began.

Gabriel held up his hand. 'I know. There are things you prefer not to talk about. That is your nature, sure, and I respect it greatly. But all the same, speaking as your friend and, I would like to think, your very closest friend, I cannot help but infer from the noticeable gaps in your story that during this long absence you have faced worse dangers than prison and the wrath of King Richard. The rest of the men you have been seeking – you found them, didn't you?'

Will nodded. 'I found them, yes. But it no longer matters.'

Gabriel looked at him curiously. 'I do not get your meaning. In what way does it no longer matter?'

'My quest is at an end. I am to make peace with them.'

'Explain. Says who, are you to make peace with them?

'Says the king,' Will replied. 'And how can I refuse? He is my king.'

'As he is to all of us. But you did not come here to serve his wishes alone.'

'Yet I am here,' Will said. 'So I must serve him, regardless. I made no specific promise to him, except to pledge my loyalty. Does my Christian duty not require me to honour the mercy and generosity that he showed me today? Is that not as good as an oath, one I make to myself?'

Gabriel was silent as they walked on another stretch, the incoming surf sizzling over the moonlit sand and washing away their footprints as soon as they were made. 'Perhaps it is better that way,' he said quietly.

'Whether better or not, Gabriel, it's over. I have to learn to accept that fact. I will not speak of it again, and ask you to do the same.'

'As you wish, William,' Gabriel said. But his tone of voice betrayed the pain he felt in his own heart.

Chapter 31

With the passing of late March into early April now came the time for departures, as the army's winter sojourn in Sicily finally reached its end. The first to set sail was Queen Eleanor, whose long voyage back to England would take her via Salerno and then Rome where she planned on meeting the new pope, Celestine III, his predecessor Pope Clement having recently died.

After seeing off his mother and placing his fiancée in the care of his sister Joan, King Richard spent the next eight days busily preparing to embark on the next leg of their journey. While the fleet was being stocked and victualled, he set a large work party comprising hundreds of men to the task of dismantling Mategriffon and carrying it piece by piece down to the harbour to be loaded aboard the royal galleys. In the meantime, the king was deep in discussions with his senior military advisers, including a committee of Knights Templar and Hospitaller, to whom he intended to entrust the control of Sicily lest the untrustworthy Monkey King get up to any more of his tricks.

For Will these were such hectic days that he barely had a moment to reflect on his choices or what might now lie ahead. In the meantime, his friend Gabriel had his own preoccupations.

Unhappily, his passionate love affair with the beautiful Maria had proved ill-fated: her father, the prominent Messina wine merchant whose business had been badly hit by the sack of the city and the subsequent forcible handing over of his stock to the conquering troops, had staunchly proscribed the least notion of marriage between his beloved daughter and one of the enemy. For her part, Maria was unwilling to become disowned by her family over the liaison – and so the romance had come to a swift and sad end, Gabriel's idyllic vision of bringing his beautiful bride with him to the Holy Land now in ashes. For the last several days he had been inconsolably stricken with a broken heart – though Will privately suspected that his friend's heart was in fact rather more robust than he liked to pretend, and he would soon get over it. Everyone had their foibles.

On the sunny and clear morning of the tenth day of April, with a favourable tide and wind, the voyagers said a last goodbye to the locals they had befriended (Maria and her family were not among them). Some eight thousand or more pilgrim soldiers and sailors boarded their ships, raised their sails and plied their oars and cast off their moorings, and in wave after wave began heading out of the port of Messina. It was said that the city would never again see the likes of such a massive war fleet. At the head of the first line sailed the enormous buss carrying the two female passengers, the island's former queen and 'the girl from Navarre' Berengaria, as well as a large portion of the king's treasure. The second line followed with thirteen vessels, the third fourteen, the fourth twenty, the fifth thirty, the sixth forty, the seventh sixty; and bringing up the rear was the king himself with his personal squadron of heavily armed galley ships.

It was aboard one of these galleys that Will, Gabriel and Samson had embarked among many other men of the expedition force. The esnecca was quite unlike the cog-like vessel that had brought them here from England: for one thing it was vastly larger, with two great tall masts and two superimposed decks allowing for one row of oars above the other. Such a might of man-powered propulsion gave them the advantage of being able to move swiftly through the water, against the wind or in a dead calm where other sailing vessels would be left helpless. At her stern end was the raised fortress-like poop deck where Will, as an archer, would be stationed in the event of a naval engagement to help rain arrows down at the opposing forces. The front of the ship was a weapon in its own right, equipped with a huge wooden beam called a spur that in a closely fought battle could be used as a ram to smash through enemy hulls and hole them fatally below the waterline.

An immensely powerful vessel she was, but being so long, slender and shallow-bottomed she was more at home navigating rivers or coastal waters than embarking on long crossings of the open sea, where her design made her and her fellow galleys vulnerable to the sometimes extreme violence of the elements. And so it happened that, having set out under a clear blue sky with the sea as flat and smooth as could be wished, the following morning of Maundy Thursday, the eleventh of April 1191, brought them rolling dark clouds and a fast-rising wind that whipped the sea into a storm whose power grew and grew throughout the day. Visibility soon dropped to the point where Will and his shipmates could no longer make out their companion vessels, not even the king's own flagship galley that carried a great burning candle lantern at her maintop as a guide to the others. By mid-afternoon they were completely separated from the fleet, alone in the grips of the tempest with all sense of their bearings or direction lost.

Hour after hour it went on, more violent even than the storm that had battered Will's ship off Portugal. The hardiest of sailors was terrified by the crash of the waves against the hull and the tortured groaning of the timbers that at times gave the nightmare impression that the ship was about to tear apart and send them all to their watery graves. Since the helm was powerless against the seething force of the sea there was no question of steering, and as beyond human aid as they were they could only trust God to get them through. Even with their sails lowered and securely lashed to the deck the uncontrollable roll of the vessel was so extreme that they were in almost constant danger of capsizing, now to one side and now to the other. All Will and his companions could do was to cling on to whatever solid purchase they could find and pray that the ship did not tip right over onto her beam end.

It was at one of those heart-stopping moments that over the shriek of the gale Will heard Gabriel's shout, 'There it goes!' and looked up from the sloping deck to see the foremast above him giving way under the immense leverage of their angle of lean. It came down with a rending crackle of splintering timber, like a tree falling in the forest after being struck by lightning. The weight of the stricken mast could easily have dragged them right over, acting like an anchor to pull them to the bottom – instead, by pure chance it tore loose entirely and was instantly engulfed by the waves, the ropes that had held it in place snapped like so many strands of a spider's web. Somehow, magically, the ship righted herself and they braced themselves for the next monstrous wave.

But even the wildest, most insane fury of the elements could not go on forever, and by late evening the wind began to drop and the angry sea at last diminished to a moderate swell. Men were able to stand upright again and emerge from whatever minimal shelter they had been able to find. The deck was strewn with wreckage and loose cargo, the vomit of the seasick and the blood of the injured washed clean away by the tons of water that had come aboard and drained from the scuppers.

'It's a miracle,' someone cried out, and murmurings of agreement passed around the ship that only Divine intervention could have enabled them to survive such a storm. Whether indeed God had listened to their pleas or whether by natural causes, as the wind died away entirely and the clouds rolled back to reveal a perfectly clear, starry sky, once again they could see the masthead beacon of the king's flagship less than a mile to the west and they knew they had not survived alone.

One by one throughout the rest of the night, the scores of other vessels reappeared from the darkness and gathered around the stationary mother ship like chicks nestling close to a hen, some of them badly damaged and limping over the sea, one or two totally dismasted and having to be towed. Many hours went by before the fleet was reassembled, but with the morning mist it was hard to tell whether all had come through the tempest. That was a question that would remain unanswered for some time.

In the aftermath of the storm came a return of favourable sea conditions that continued through Easter Sunday. For four more days they struggled on until their lookouts sighted the island of Crete in the distance, with its tall mountains and the peak called the Camel that sailors familiar with these waters knew marked the exact midpoint between Messina and Acre. The next day after that, the wind picked up once again to fill the sails of those ships that still had them, and they wafted majestically over the waves all that day and all of the night, until at dawn the following morning they reached the island of Rhodes. There was still no sign of their missing ships, and nor was any port to be found there with deep water right up to the land. The fleet anchored and stood offshore, in the hopes that the vessels scattered by the tempest would find them there.

Day in, day out for nearly all the remainder of that month they waited under the unseasonably warm sun. During that time a few stragglers managed to find them, reducing the number of missing ships from twenty-five. Those vessels that had suffered damage in the storm now had a chance to refit using whatever materials they could procure. A replacement for the lost foremast from Will's galley was transported across from one of the great cargo busses laden with spare parts, and hoisted into place by means of an ingenious system of ropes and pulleys. Even so it took the brute strength of sixty men to raise and then gently lower the mast into position; one slip and the massive wooden post, seventy feet tall, would have plunged right through the deck and the ship's bottom and sunk them.

Their exhausting task done, the men went back to sitting idly around, drinking, gambling and fretting. Now and then small boats plied back and forth to the shore. The once noble great coastal city of Rhodes was now largely ruined and a mere faint shadow of its grander days, but some residents remained, mostly monks and some fishing folks, from whom the pilgrims bought essential foodstuffs and the copious quantities of fresh water required for so many thirsty men and horses. But as time passed and no more stragglers appeared, their spirits sank deep and their worst fears began to grow on them. The official tally still confirmed that sixteen ships of the fleet were unaccounted for and, it had to be presumed, were likely to have been destroyed in the tempest.

And of those sixteen, one was the buss that had been carrying the king's sister and Princess Berengaria.

Chapter 32

'Aha, I believe I have you now.' Gabriel was reaching for his castle to make the winning move when their game was interrupted by a sudden commotion on deck. 'Is something happening?' he said, looking round.

The event that jolted the galley's crew and passengers from their long period of inactivity was the arrival of a boat messenger from the flagship, informing them of the king's decision to despatch four vessels, including theirs, to search for the missing ships. No sooner had the messenger disappeared back over the side than everything was in an uproar of organised chaos, sails being hoisted, the fore and aft anchors hurriedly brought up, the pounding of feet on deck as the oarsmen rushed to their stations. Within a short time they and their three companion vessels were pulling fast away across the sparkling blue waters.

There was no telling in what directions the lost ships might have been blown off course, and so from the shores of Rhodes the search party split up and went their separate ways: one doubling south-westwards back towards Crete, the second north-west aiming for Naxos and the many other scattered islands of the Aegean; the third bore southwards into the

Levantine Sea towards the very hostile Arab strongholds of Alexandria and Damietta — God help any Christian ship that landed there — and finally the fourth, Will's ship, pointed east for the Cilician Sea where lay the island of Cyprus.

For five frantic days they held their steady course over the open sea with never a sight of land or ship. When the wind failed them they manned their oars with almost manic zeal, one shift taking over from the next when they were too exhausted to row another stroke. Will's palms were raw and bleeding after just three hours of heavy, heavy work. Many of the men wore bloody rags wrapped around their hands. The sun beat down cruelly and water threatened to run short.

'I am not sure we can abide much more of this,' Gabriel confided to Will as they slouched on deck, parched with thirst and utterly spent after a long session at the oars. Then on the fifth day many prayers were answered when the merciless sky was blotted with rainclouds. When the unbelievably heavy deluge finally lashed down on them they covered the deck with whatever receptacles they could find to catch the water, and with their barrels replenished man and horse were able to drink their fill.

It was early the following morning when the lookout's cry alerted them to a distant ship due east, hull-down on the horizon. 'God send that it be one of ours,' murmured Gabriel from where he and Will stood in the bows, shielding their eyes against the low sun. As the hours passed and the distance between them and the unidentified ship gradually closed, they could see it was a large cargo vessel, twin-masted, flying a pennant whose colours and emblem were hard to make out at this distance with the sun's glare. Beyond it rose the land mass that the experienced sailors aboard declared to be the island of Cyprus.

Soon their hearts lifted as the conviction grew that the strange ship was in fact the buss carrying King Richard's sister and bride-to-be. It was an astounding distance to have been blown off course, and an even greater stroke of good fortune to have found them – but here they were indeed, tacking back and forth off the coast of the island as though searching for a place to land. In another hour the galley was alongside them, and the crews greeted one another with cheers and laughter. The galley lowered a skiff to carry its captain across. Will was one of those who volunteered to row it, and not long afterwards they were tethered to the side of the huge buss and clambering aboard.

'You are a sight for sore eyes and no mistake,' said the captain of the buss as he received them on deck. 'I would offer you a drink, but we are down to short rations of water and must preserve every drop.'

'We have plenty to spare you. The royal passengers?'

'Safe and as well as can be expected,' the buss captain replied. 'I wish I could say the same about those other poor devils.'

The poor devils in question, he explained, were those unfortunate souls whose ships had been blown off course along with theirs and not been so lucky. Several vessels had been dashed to pieces on the island's rocky coast, and despite all the efforts of those valiant sailors who rowed out from the buss to rescue them, many had drowned. A number of valued servants of the king were among the dead, including his vice-chancellor Roger Malus Catulus.

Worse news was to follow. The buss captain told them that even as the few half-drowned survivors from the wrecks were being washed up on shore, soldiers of the island had appeared and taken them captive, dragging them away up the beach at the point of their spears. Soon more islanders had gathered on the beach, looting whatever they could find from the foundered ships as well as stripping the possessions of the dead. 'Then they sent out an envoy aboard a boat,' he explained, 'to tell us that their ruler, his Excellency Isaac Comnenus emperor of Cyprus, forbade our landing in his harbour of Limassol.'

'He did, did he?' replied the galley captain, outraged. 'And the prisoners they took?'

'Held hostage in his dungeons. If they have not murdered them yet, the filthy animals. They are Griffons, no better than those in Messina.'

The galley captain turned to Will and the others of his crew. 'We must hurry back to the fleet and tell the king.'

'Should the Lady Joan and Princess Berengaria not come with us, for their safety?' Will ventured to ask. 'The sooner we get them away from here, the better.' The buss captain would not hear of it, however. The royal passengers were his responsibility and he was not about to hand them over to anyone. And so, as fast as they could row, Will and his crewmates raced back to the galley to convey the news.

The next days passed in a blur. No more storms hampered their progress, and they thanked God for the strong westerly breeze that carried them at such a pace all the way back to Rhodes, where they found the other three ships of the search party had already returned empty-handed. King Richard, having been sick with worry all this time, embraced his galley captain when told about the success of their hunt and that his sister and fiancée were alive and in good health. But on hearing what the emperor Isaac had dared do to his men and ships he exploded with a rage beyond anything even his closest aides had seen before.

'Follow me and we will take vengeance for the wrongs which this perfidious emperor has done to God and to us in unjustly keeping our pilgrims in chains!'

*

It was the sixth of May when a group of Cypriot soldiers who had been sent down to the shore from the imperial palace of Limassol to hunt for more valuable shipwreck booty noticed a sail on the horizon. Then two, then three; and they watched in horror as a vast war fleet came into view, seeming to cover the entire sea and heading straight for their island. In a panic they ran to alert the emperor.

'Them Griffons is in for it now,' Samson said happily as their galley neared the shore, with the massed fleet all around them and the royal flagship leading the pack at a pressing pace.

'It is Messina all over again,' Gabriel replied in a doubtful tone. 'At this rate, the war in the Holy Land will be over before we ever get there.'

'I wish it were over already,' Will said. 'And that there could be an end to all war, so men could live in peace.'

'That may be a little too much to hope for, brother.'

Rather than launch an immediate all-out assault on Limassol, King Richard took a more diplomatic approach, for the time being at least. With the enormous battle fleet lying at anchor outside the harbour, messengers were dispatched ashore, demanding the immediate and unconditional release of the prisoners and the return of all goods looted from the wrecked ships. It wasn't long before the messengers returned to report the emperor's haughty reply: a flat rebuttal of their demands. The king responded by sending a second envoy to Isaac's palace, this time begging him for the love of God – and for his own good – to comply.

The men of the fleet watched intently as the second envoy was rowed back from shore to the flagship. 'It will be another refusal,' Will muttered to himself.

'And there will be no prizes awarded for guessing what comes next,' Gabriel observed. '"For he who, when asked for simple right says 'No', yields all things to an armed foe".'

Gabriel's poetic prediction was unsurprisingly accurate, and Emperor Isaac in his palace must have anticipated as much, too. Presently a horde of Cypriot troops flooded out of the city gates and lined the shore from end to end, making clear their ruler's intentions if the foreign invaders dared attack. The emperor set his numerous army to work obstructing the beach with as many barricades and obstacles as they could set up, piles of old timber and doors, windows and any kind of junk they could bring out in a hurry from the city. A pair of ancient galley ships, half-foundered and rotting at their moorings, had been towed across the port entrance to block the way to the invaders, while three more galleys bristling with men and weapons had rowed out and patrolled the shore. The emperor himself had come out to join his forces massing on the beach, clad in full armour and parading up and down on horseback with his knights under their fluttering imperial banners. It was an impressive showing, and aboard Will's ship could be heard some anxious mutterings that this Griffon army was too large and powerful to defeat.

By this stage conflict was inevitable. As the fleet approached the shore, weapons were sharpened, armour donned, mounts tacked up and devout prayers made to God. From the flagship came the order that the initial assault be made against the harbour, and skiffs were lowered so bristling with crossbowmen that they rode dangerously low in the water. Will and his fellow archers would join the land assault that was to follow.

As they watched with bated breath, several of the skiffs made their attempt on the blocked harbour while the rest rowed straight for the Cypriot galleys and were met with a determined resistance from the archers posted on their high forecastles. Soon arrows and crossbow bolts were flying thick between the opposing sides, and though the pilgrims were very exposed in their fragile craft their superior skill quickly began to tell. Dozens, scores, of the enemy fell into the sea, pierced through and turning the water red. Many jumped into the waves to escape the rain of missiles, and either drowned or were shot as they tried to swim to safety. To the gleeful cheering of the fleet, the attackers quickly boarded the galleys and captured them along with their surviving men.

Now the land assault was mobilised, as the king's galley was first to ground on the wet shaley sand and hundred after hundred pilgrim warriors splashed down into the surf, followed by horses and squires, and gathered on the beach in massed battle formation. Will was among them, having said goodbye to his friends and wished them luck and Godspeed as he hurried off to join the ranks of archers.

The beach was seething from end to end with the sheer mass of the advancing invasion force. Somewhere among that vast crowd of men, Will knew, were Sir Ranulf and his black eagles. With a great effort he wrestled those thoughts to the back of his mind, swallowed his rage and forced himself to focus on the present moment. He and his fellow archers were deployed to the front line, to soften up the enemy ranks for the advance of the infantry troops and the cavalry at their rear. King Richard in all his finery and with his drawn sword gleaming under the sun marched up the beach, turned with his back to the enemy and addressed his men in a strong, clear voice that echoed over the shore:

'Loyal soldiers, do not fear. It behoves us to fight manfully to free God's people from destruction, knowing that we must win or die. But we have confidence in the Lord that He will give us victory over this treacherous so-called emperor and his people!'

And here we go, Will thought to himself. His heart began to thump faster. All up and down the line the four hundred archers and crossbowmen drew their first arrows and bolts, fitted them to their weapons and stood ready, waiting for the order. They did not have to wait long. From behind the enemy barricades flew a spear, so poorly thrown that it sailed only a few dozen yards and planted itself upright in the sand a long way from the English front rank. It was an entirely futile gesture, but it was provocation enough. There were some scattered laughs and derisive calls from among the pilgrim troops; and then came the fierce cry 'Archers! Loose!' and the air was filled with the simultaneous massed twang of bowstrings, the crack of crossbows and the whooshing hum of hundreds of missiles hurtling across the sands and showering down like rain on the enemy.

The first salvo inflicted huge damage on the Griffons' forces, and their fallen bodies lay heaped one on the other and staining the sand with blood. Immediately afterwards came the command to loose a second wave, then a third. Will plucked arrow after arrow from his quiver, marked his targets and fired with deadly accuracy. His arrows found their way between the gaps in the barricade, punched through armour, perforated chests, throats, bellies. Blood spurted in the sunlight and the cries of the dying could be heard over the repeated thudding impacts of metal into meat.

From the start, it seemed destined to be a rout. Isaac's soldiers were no match for the onslaught they faced. Even after the first archery salvo they were already breaking ranks, many of them throwing down their weapons and running for their lives. With a wild roaring and howling of battle cries the pilgrim infantry and cavalry pursued them up the beach, and hundreds were brutally slaughtered before they ever reached the dunes, hundreds more taken prisoner.

'Forward, men!' Richard shouted, leaping astride his horse – the same excellent animal, Will noticed with a pang, that had borne him to Bagnara five months earlier. The king rode off at a thundering gallop as the whole of the army moved up the beach towards the city, to finish what they had come here to do. Seeing his forces collapsing into total disarray, the emperor and his retinue spurred their mounts and fled, with King Richard in pursuit and loudly challenging Isaac to stop and face him, so that the outcome of the battle could be decided by single combat. Nobody could have doubted the king's willingness to stand and fight him man to man. That was certainly what the emperor was most afraid of.

The outcome was already determined, however. The routed Griffons were beaten back further and further towards the city until their bodies were thick on the ground and the crowds of captives rounded up like sheep. Isaac and his people having managed to escape up a path that led into the hills, King Richard returned to join his troops and led the advance on Limassol.

On entering the wide-open gates head they expected to be met with at least some resistance – but in the event they encountered none at all. To Will's amazement the city seemed entirely abandoned, and indeed it was. The people, down to the last woman and child, had fled in such a hurry that they had left everything behind: including, to the victors' delight as they riotously plundered every house and invaded the deserted halls of the imperial palace itself, an abundance of food, oil, wine, treasure and other spoils of war there for the taking.

'Too goddamned easy,' complained a disappointed Roderick Short, when by chance Will stumbled upon him near the palace some hours later, his tunic bulging with booty, clutching a torn-off leg of roast fowl in one fist and swilling wine from a golden goblet with the other. Will hated the senseless looting and wished that the king would make it stop — but it had been the rule of war since time immemorial that to the victor belonged the spoils. At least, he reminded himself, with all the womenfolk run to the hills there could be none of that other, infinitely worse, kind of plunder going on. That he could not have been able to stand.

Roderick Short certainly wasn't alone in believing that the conquest of Limassol, and indeed of the whole island, had been a virtually uncontested knock-down victory and a sure sign that God held them in his favour. That was the consensus among the thousands of men who spent the rest of that day and night revelling in their heroic achievement, so that the whole city resonated with raucous celebration.

Though as Roderick himself had unintentionally suggested, and as Will felt in his heart, perhaps the taking of the city really had been just a little *too* easy. He suspected that his fellows were being premature in their triumph, and that the battle for Cyprus wasn't over yet.

The next day would tell if his suspicions were right.

Chapter 33

The following morning, May seventh, the first rumours began to spread that Emperor Isaac and the remnants of his fighting men were hiding in the surrounding countryside and planning a counter-attack. The pilgrims bided their time all that long, sweltering and dusty day in anticipation of trouble, but nothing happened. Will, Gabriel and their group made use of an abandoned house within the city, whose vanished occupants had left them a plentiful larder of dried meats and sausages, along with enough wine to satisfy the most unquenchable thirst.

Meanwhile, King Richard had set up his headquarters in the imperial palace, where his sister Joan and Princess Berengaria were also now housed under heavy protective guard. Needless to say, the king had no intention of letting Isaac Comnenus re-form his scattered forces or have any chance of retaking the city. Cautioned by one of his advisers to beware of engaging with an unknown quantity of the enemy on their home ground he replied, 'Lord clerk, it is best for your profession to stick to your scriptures, leave the fighting to us and concentrate on keeping yourself out of the thick of it.' As the sun dipped over the mountains he personally led one of several night-raiding parties consisting of small, well-armed and highly mobile squads into the hills and forests to seek out the pockets of resistance. The fifty or so knights the king chose for this purpose belonged to a tightly knit circle of warriors who kept very much to themselves within camp, barely spoke to anyone outside of their group and exuded an air of steely-eyed gravity and menace.

'Templars,' Tobias Smith muttered. 'Little better than assassins, they are; slit your gizzard soon as look at you. A bloody night they will make of it.'

'It's said that they are answerable to none but the pope,' added Roderick Short. 'Not even the king can command them.'

'I have heard that there are Hospitallers among them too,' Gabriel said. 'Although it seems the two orders have often been bitter rivals, to the extent that their initiates can barely pass one another in the street without drawing their swords.'

'I happened on some Knights Hospitaller during my travels through England,' Will recalled. It seemed so long ago now. 'Their leader was generous towards me, helped to direct me on my journey and even offered an escort of knights for part of the way.'

'That is a damn sight more kindness than they'll show to them Griffons,' laughed old Joe Cook. 'I wouldn't trade places with the poor buggers, not for all the bounty in the world.'

Sure enough, by the time the raiding parties returned shortly after dawn, such plans as Isaac might have had to recapture his city had been brutally thwarted. The Templars and Hospitallers had left very few survivors among the Griffons they had surprised in their tents in the forest that night. The unsuspecting Cypriots were slaughtered en masse, and by first light the gruesome killing ground was littered with their dismembered bodies, piled helmets and bloodied mail shirts, broken spears and shattered shields. The only disappointment was that Isaac himself had again escaped – though narrowly, after an encounter with the king himself who had reportedly flung him down from his horse with his own lance. By accursed bad luck the deposed emperor had managed to flee in the chaos, seeing that he was likely to be the only survivor and vanishing into the mountains. The knights hunted for him for two miles in the wilderness, to no avail. As compensation the victors plundered his tent and came away with a fantastical booty of arms, silks, gold and silver plate and all manner of other finery, not to mention the quantities of food and wine, horses, cows and oxen, sheep and goats and poultry, that had accompanied the emperor's troops. There was so much plunder to be had that they eventually became bored with it and came back to the city carrying whatever they could bring, leaving the rest. With these trophies and the certainty that the city was theirs to keep, Richard rode triumphantly back into Limassol to spend the next three days feasting and relaxing in peace and security.

On the fourth day three mysterious approaching ships were sighted out to sea, and soon afterwards the new conquerors of Cyprus received an unexpected visitor. Guy de Lusignan, a forty-year-old Frankish knight who by virtue of a lucky marriage had for a time reigned as king of Jerusalem before being routed by Saladin's forces at the Horns of Hattin in July 1187. The deposed monarch had become discredited in some circles for having not only foolishly led the great army of Jerusalem to a humiliating, devastating defeat and lost nearly the whole of his kingdom in the process, but having additionally contrived to relinquish one of

Christendom's most revered holy relics, the piece of the One True Cross that the Franks had carried into battle fully expecting it to give them victory. Released from captivity on the promise he would leave Outremer forever, though honourably treated by his captors, Guy had immediately gone back on his word, gathered whatever vassals would still follow him and laid siege to the walls of Acre. He had been battling the fortified city ever since.

Taking a break from his military endeavours, he had now sailed the three hundred miles across to Cyprus to pay his respects to the English king who would soon join his army in their struggle in the Holy Land. He was accompanied by a contingent of lords and knights who likewise wanted to pledge their allegiance to the king.

The emperor's former residence now became the scene for a great deal of lavish banqueting, whose uproar could be heard from the house where Will and his friends were living. The joyful celebrations were a precursor to the regal pomp and ceremony of the following day, May twelfth the feast of St Pancras, when Richard of England and Princess Berengaria were married and his bride crowned queen consort. It was a solemn affair attended by senior luminaries of the Church including the archbishop of Bordeaux and the bishops of Evreux and Bayonne, along with many other distinguished magnates and nobles. Once the formalities were concluded, even the most staunchly pious churchmen were happy to fill the cup and partake of the festive atmosphere.

'Not for the likes of us to be invited among the great and the good, my boys,' said Roderick Short as they bided their time sitting around their humble abode with very little to do but consume the spoils of war. 'We shall just eat, drink and be merry where we are.'

Be merry. Perhaps the others could — and he wished his comrades joy with all his heart — but that was something Will himself was unable to share in. He found no pleasure in food or wine, and spent much time brooding alone. He understood the reason why. The hunger for revenge, that raging impulse that he had all but allowed to take over his entire being, had been his sole motivation, the one thing that gave his life meaning and purpose. Without it he felt hollow and empty, as though the inner man had died leaving only a flimsy outer shell that walked and talked and superficially resembled its former living self, but was no longer Will Bowman.

In his heart he knew the truth: that by vowing to lay down his quest he had made a promise he could not keep, not even if he had made it to the king himself. No, come what may, he must see this through. Nothing, no man, not God Himself, could stand in his way. For honour. For valour. For Beatrice. For the sake of his own soul.

'I will finish it,' he murmured aloud. Nobody heard him, though only Gabriel would have understood.

Soon, gladly, he would have far less time for personal reflection. Almost the moment the festivities had ended, the king returned to business and pressed on with consolidating his conquest of all of Cyprus. His first concern was to continue pursuing the errant Isaac Comnenus wherever he might try to escape, until he was captured or forced to surrender. There were still any number of castles, abbeys and other places scattered about the island in which he could be hiding, all the while plotting with those who remained loyal and wished to see their emperor restored to power. The matter needed to be resolved quickly, as Richard was under intense political pressure from Guy de Lusignan and the other nobles to sail onwards to Outremer. Some believed that the king was wasting time and resources on a useless exercise, needlessly persecuting fellow Christians here on Cyprus when he should be engaging the far more important enemy in the Holy Land. It was thought that Philip of France would not fully commit himself to the ongoing siege of Acre until the English forces arrived there. Yet despite all, Richard was determined not to leave Cyprus without first ensuring that Isaac's reign was permanently ended.

Splitting his galley fleet into two large squadrons, the king placed one of his knights, Robert de Turnham, in command of the first while he himself would lead the second, with the intention of surrounding the island on both sides, neutralising whatever naval opposition they might meet and taking down one coastal fortification at a time. Meanwhile Guy de Lusignan would take charge of the rest of the army and march them overland up the middle, capturing towns and castles in search of Isaac. One of their major objectives would be the city of Famagusta, some seventy miles away on the eastern coast of the island, where many suspected the emperor could have gone to ground.

Such a massive body of men, horses and ancillary personnel required to be organised into many separate units of foot soldiers and cavalry each with its own divisional officers. It so happened that Will, Gabriel, Samson and the others of their familiar group now found themselves again under the command of the same Howard of Gloucester who had led them on the first leg of their voyage from England. His division now comprised several hundred mainly infantry troops, with a strong contingent of crossbowmen and a few archers, those proficient with the longbow being always in the minority. Heavily laden with supplies and guided by local scouts the marching column made its way up the length of the island, keeping on the move for many hot, dusty hours each day, making camp by night.

The country was largely wild and untamed, the mountains rugged and impassable but for winding goat tracks and the boulder-strewn ravines carved out over eons by ancient rivers, the forests dense and filled with all manner of things that crawled and slithered, giant spiders and venomous reptiles. The wild goats whose paths the army often followed roamed the hills in large numbers and were given the name *agrino* by the native scouts. Despite their extreme shyness of humans and the supreme agility over rocky ground that made them a difficult quarry Will would now and then break away from the column to stalk in pursuit of the nomadic herds, sometimes taking a few of the more nimble-footed of the crossbowmen with him, and his capabilities as a tracker and hunter provided a steady supply of meat for the troop.

'You show natural leadership, Bowman,' Howard of Gloucester told him, after summoning him to his tent one night. The commander seemed capable of longer periods of sobriety these days than he had aboard ship. 'For that reason, I have decided to put you in charge of a unit. You will have twenty archers under you and be responsible for their deployment in battle.' Will was reluctant to accept the promotion and almost requested his commander's permission to refuse, but after a moment's hesitation he kept his mouth shut.

Onwards they marched. Every town they came to, it appeared that word of the army's approach had spread far in advance of their arrival and the inhabitants had fled, leaving each place deserted in turn. Several more days' weary progress under the burning sun later, they finally reached the coastal city of Famagusta. They were joined there by the larger forces of Guy de Lusignan and King Richard, the latter having landed on shore after a successful campaign up the eastern side of the island. But once more they were disappointed of the promised encounter with Isaac's fighters, as this city too had been evacuated.

After a brief stay in Famagusta the combined army turned back inland towards the city of Nicosia, where thanks to fresh intelligence provided by their scouts it was anticipated that Cypriot imperial forces were likely to be lurking in wait. The troops approached Nicosia in ready battle formation, with the king and his knights for once taking the rearguard. Will moved his twenty-strong unit into the front line where they would be of the most use in case the intelligence reports proved true. But would they?

Nothing seemed to stir behind the city walls as the pilgrims edged cautiously closer, and the rugged rocky landscape and the tall escarpments to each side of them appeared empty and still. To the private relief of many of the men, Will included, it seemed at first as though they were to be cheated yet again of an engagement.

Then, just as the pilgrims were at their most exposed on the open ground in front of the city walls, a shouted command echoed from behind the rocks and suddenly a hail of missiles rained down on them. In the next instant a thousand or more of Isaac's soldiers came swarming out to attack, and hurled themselves screaming towards the pilgrim front line.

Chapter 34

'Stand fast!' Will shouted to his archers, sending an arrow into the oncoming horde. The man standing immediately to his right let out a cry as a crossbow bolt thudded through his chain mail and deep into his shoulder. Will immediately spotted the Griffon who had released the shot and dispatched him with one of his own, but it was too late for his fallen archer. Looking down, Will could see not only the bright red blood pouring from his wound but a dribble of sticky black substance that confused him until he understood with a shock what it was. The Cypriots were firing poisoned arrows, so that even the slightest of wounds could bring about the most agonising slow death.

Spurred on by fear and anger against an enemy that could stoop to such low tactics, Will fought back with unbridled energy. He released shot after shot until his quiver was empty, then threw down his bow and drew his sword and charged into the melee. Now in the heart of the close-quarter battle the violence reached a new pitch. Men were howling like wild animals, weapons were clashing, blood was flying, limbs hacked, terrible wounds given and received. To both sides

King Richard's cavalry were cutting a ground-shaking swathe of destruction through the enemy lines. The Griffons wavered for a few moments, seemed to regain their impetus and came on again, but then began to fall back once more in the face of the pilgrims' savagely determined resistance. Before Will knew what was happening, the enemy battle line was crumbling into a retreat. The cavalry tore into them as they fled, spearheaded by the king on his charger slashing left and right.

By the time the fight was over, more than seven hundred Griffons lay dead in front of the city walls and three hundred more were taken prisoner. The pilgrims flooded into Nicosia, whose nobles immediately offered their surrender. Will was afraid that Richard would order the entire city put to the sword; but as it became clear that the citizens were keen to reject the rule of their emperor and pay homage to their new lord, the king graciously accepted their fealty. As a gesture of their compliance, he ordered every man have his beard shaved off, while Isaac's imperial banners were torn down and the golden lions and white dragon of England were hoisted high over the city in their place.

After Nicosia, one by one the castles fell: Cerine, Paphos and Deudeamur all quickly surrendered to the pilgrim army. The fortress of Cherinas, considered impregnable, caved in to a ferocious siege from land and sea within three days. When the pilgrims looted it, they found the emperor's beloved daughter hiding in a secret chamber filled with caskets of gold and silver coins. The terrified young girl, little more than a child, threw herself at the soldiers' feet begging for mercy. Once it became apparent who she was, she was quickly seized as a valuable hostage.

Such ruthless actions were sure to drive Isaac deeper and deeper into a state of unhinged fury. As they moved on to their next conquests, rumour reached them of the emperor's violent grief at the news of his daughter's capture, not to mention the loss of the vast great treasures the army had also discovered hidden at Cherinas. Isaac's growing desperation inevitably resulted in the use of increasingly cruel and insidious methods by the Cypriot forces. Using spies and scouts to covertly tail the army by day, they began launching daring night raids into the enemy camp. Deep in the early hours their soldiers would creep up in silence, target a tent near the periphery and surprise its sleeping occupants, who would be bound and gagged and carried stealthily away to be tortured or beaten to death. As a tactic designed to instil terror into hearts and minds, it worked very well indeed. Anxious talk spread all around the army — some men held the nocturnal abductions to be more the handiwork of demonic spirits than enemy soldiers — and others, like Will, were unsure whether even to believe it was true.

Then one night he, Gabriel, Samson and the others were jolted awake by a stifled scream that had come from a nearby tent. Earlier that same evening they had shared their campfire roast goat with their neighbours; now as they grabbed their weapons and ran to the scene, they found the men gone and their tousled blankets spattered with blood. The bodies were found in a thicket at dawn the next morning. Their eyes had been put out, noses cut off and hands and feet severed. It was obvious enough from the agonised expressions frozen on their faces that the mutilation had been done while they were still alive.

For all the malicious and spiteful harms he could inflict on his enemies, however, the deposed emperor must have known that it was futile to go on resisting. And perhaps it was a genuine love for his young daughter that finally broke his spirit, out of fear that her captors might harm her. On the last day of May, the Wednesday after the feast of St Augustine, he emerged from the fortified abbey of Cape St Andrew on the far eastern tip of the island, where he had been hiding all along. Dressed in humble robes he travelled with the last few of his faithful servants to King Richard's base at Nicosia. There he delivered himself up to the king's mercy, begging and pleading on his knees, gladly relinquishing his claim over his domains in return for his life and that of his poor helpless daughter. He asked only that he not be humiliated by being put in iron fetters and manacles unbefitting his station. He could not bear to be seen that way by his people.

'Why, my dear Isaac,' the king assured him, speaking as though to an equal, 'of course we would never dream of treating a lord of your eminence in such an ill manner!' To show his humanity and kindness towards his vanquished enemy he reunited Isaac with his beloved daughter. Then as father and child sat weeping in each other's arms, Richard quietly sent for his chamberlain and instructed him to have a set of silver and gold chains, cuffs and leg irons made for the occasion, in which the hapless Isaac soon found himself bound. What the emperor had wished for, the emperor had been duly granted. He was then dragged away to spend much of the rest of his life in prison, while his daughter was placed in the care of Queen Berengaria to be educated in the customs of the west.

Within just fifteen days, Richard's army had almost completely conquered the whole of Cyprus, stuffed his treasury coffers with its riches and added a precious strategic asset to the domains of England. *Almost* conquered, because despite Isaac's now total defeat there remained a few scattered minor strongholds still loyal to him, and the king was adamant that these must be cleared up before he could in good conscience leave the island. Under continuing pressure from Guy de Lusignan and those other nobles who were most anxious to return to Outremer, he began making preparations for the voyage. Meanwhile, he formed his plans for the final sweep of Isaac's last holdouts.

While these events had been unfolding, Will and his unit were camped in the thickly wooded high country some miles north of the ancient city of Karpasia. The several hundred men under Howard of Gloucester had been posted to that barren and almost completely deserted region to ensure the surrender of the few small towns and villages not yet claimed. It had been a dismal and pointless exercise: many of these peasant communities, scratching a bare living from the rocky soil, were completely unaware that the conquest of the island had been going on at all. Then, on the hot and hazy morning of the third day of June, as the pilgrims were getting ready to strike camp, a messenger unexpectedly appeared searching for William the Bowman.

'I am he,' Will said.

'Commander wants to see you.'

Wondering what this could be about, Will followed the messenger back across camp to the commander's tent. Howard of Gloucester greeted him warmly, only mildly inebriated as it was still early in the day, and got straight to the point. 'William, you have done well for yourself on this campaign. For that reason you have been chosen for a special duty.'

'What duty?' Will asked.

'Word has come to me that emperor Isaac is defeated and in prison, and that we are to rejoin the rest of the army and embark for Outremer within the next three days. However, the king is anxious that all possibility of a Griffon rebellion is to be eradicated before we leave. To that end he has ordered that small combat units be formed to flush out and destroy these pockets of insurrection. Moreover,' the commander went on, 'it happens that we have received reports from our scouts of a small but well-entrenched stronghold that remains in place half a day's ride to the north-east of here, within a certain ruined fortress in the mountains. The Griffon rebels there are to be killed or captured, whichever is most expedient. I am entrusting this mission to you and a group of volunteers under your command.'

'What about the Templars and Hospitallers who carried out the night raids at Limassol?' Will asked, taken aback and somewhat perplexed. 'Would they not be better suited to such a task?'

The commander shook his head. 'They are too far away from here, and too busily occupied with garrisoning the various cities and castles the king has captured across the island. It is his intention to leave Cyprus in their care when we leave. Instead, this mission falls to common soldiers chosen for their skill at arms and ability to move quickly and lightly over rough terrain. You have already proved your worth in that domain.'

'How many of these so-called rebels are hiding in this stronghold?'

'According to our sources,' Howard of Gloucester replied, 'no more than twenty and probably fewer. They are quite cut off and may not even be aware that their emperor is defeated.'

'Surely, for such a small number it is hardly worth risking the lives of our people?'

'Those are the orders of the king. It is not for me to question them, and even less so for you. You are to select a team of five suitable men. Each will receive five silver pennies for his trouble, payable on successful completion of the mission. If he is killed, the payment is reduced to three pennies for his kin back home.'

Will looked at him. 'You would pit six men against twenty?'

'I should say that will be ample, as they are only Griffons,' Howard of Gloucester replied carelessly. 'In any case, those are all the horses we can spare. A local scout will ride with you, acting as a guide. He knows the location of the ruined fortress well. Now, I believe that is all. Get your men together. You leave at once.'

*

'Ballocks to that,' spat Roderick Short when Will told them the news. 'They could send a squad of Templars up there to take care of business, but why risk the necks of their precious bleeding knights when they can foist the job on the likes of us commoners? We ain't worth a pound of pig dung to them.'

'There is no obligation on you to come with me,' Will said.

Roderick laughed. 'No, mate. But for five silver pennies I will follow you into the red jaws of Hell itself, and woe betide the Devil if he gets in my way.' He grasped the handle of his cleaver, jerked the weapon from his belt and brandished it in a manner that would have sent the Evil One scurrying for cover.

'Gabriel?'

'I am surprised you should even ask, brother. It goes without saying that you can depend on me. I am with you every step of the way.'

'And me,' Samson said, puffing out his great barrel of a chest.

'Me too,' Tobias Smith told them.

Old Joe Cook had overheard their conversation and came rushing over. 'Now boys, you wouldn't leave out your pal Joe, would you?'

'This is a job for strong young blokes,' Roderick sneered at him. Then added, sucking in his belly, 'Well, youngish, any road. Not a broken-down old whoreson pox-ridden crock of a sodomite like you.'

'You want broken down?' Joe Cook fired back, raising his gnarly fists. 'I'll give it to you, you pot-bellied bastard.'

Samson stepped in between them, placed a giant hand on each of their shoulders and prised them apart before they could do injury to one another.

'It appears you have recruited your complement of five, William,' said Gabriel, laughing. 'That didn't take much persuading.'

Will nodded, though he was far from happy with the whole thing. 'It seems I have.'

'Then let's go and kill us some Griffons,' said Tobias Smith.

Chapter 35

The half dozen mounts provided by their commander were little better than pack mules, dull, unresponsive, stunted creatures fitted with rope bridles and worn old saddles. As for their escort, he was a morose and apparently nameless Cypriot with a rounded stump for a right hand, shifty eyes that avoided contact with anyone else's and an ugly burn scar on his forehead that denoted he had once been branded as a runaway slave. He spoke only his own language, and that in a drooling mumble. But he seemed dependable enough as a guide, and after they had departed from the camp late that morning, laden with weapons, water and provisions for the journey, he plodded ahead of them on his swaybacked nag hour after hour, leading them deeper and higher into the mountains along rutted boulder-strewn tracks and through sparse, parched forest that thinned out as they climbed. The fortress ruins they sought were still a long way off and a good deal higher up. Higher up still, the sun slowly traversed the pale sky, its intense glare washing the colour from the landscape.

'This is bloody torture, this is,' groaned the saddle-sore Roderick, standing up in his stirrups to rub some circulation into his numb backside. 'My poor arse feels like it's been beaten with clubs.'

'It'll soon be getting my boot up it and all, if you don't stop your whining,' warned Tobias riding behind him. Samson guffawed, but he too was suffering from the long trek. As was his unfortunate horse, which was struggling to bear the weight and so undersized that its rider was barely any taller in the saddle than if he had been walking along beside it.

A little further ahead, Gabriel and Will were riding abreast following the guide. 'This country is a far cry indeed from the homelands you and I left behind,' Gabriel observed, scanning the rocky, scrubby terrain around them. 'How trees and shrubs manage to grow in such a desert waste is beyond comprehension. It is so dry and barren as to make a man pray for rain. There seems barely enough moisture in the soil to sustain a single blade of grass; and yet the people of this island are nonetheless somehow able to raise crops and livestock, and presumably have been doing so since the days that our Lord Jesu walked in Galilee, or longer.'

He fell silent for a while, with the faraway look in his eyes that he often had when he reminisced about the green hills and valleys of his dear Ireland. 'Shall we ever return to our native soil, I wonder? I should be happy to see Connacht again one day, revisit the haunts of my youth, gaze across the sparkling waters of Lough Corrib and the holy islands there. My country is a veritable Eden, compared to this godforsaken benighted backward unchristian place. And I thought Wales was bad,' he added by way of a parenthesis.

'I sometimes dream of my home in England,' Will said. 'And everything that I held dear still untouched and perfect, as though nothing had changed and I had never gone away. Then I wake up and it is lost to me all over again. The pain and sorrow would be too much to bear, if I ever went back.'

'Never say never, my friend,' Gabriel counselled him. 'Not even the wisest among us can tell what the future holds. And time changes all things.'

'Not all,' Will replied. 'Some things, not even the Almighty could change. All men can do is try to make them right, so that we can at least live with the memory.'

They plodded onwards and upwards as the afternoon passed slowly by. Emerging beyond the treeline now, their winding track steepened and narrowed as they gradually approached the plateau. Their destination was still a long way above them, and their guide showed no sign of stopping. Now and then, Will leaned back in his saddle to gaze towards the distant summit, trying to spot any sign of life or anyone who might be watching their approach from the high ground. All he saw was a gliding shape circling far above them on broad tawny wings, much larger than the buzzards and falcons he had been used to seeing in England.

'That bird up there,' he said, pointing. 'Would he be an eagle?'

'I would say a vulture,' Gabriel replied, looking up and shielding his eyes from glare of the lowering sun. 'He is no noble bird of prey, but an ill-omened scavenger of carrion and dead men's bones. Though there can be little for him to eat up here, apart from snakes and lizards. Whoever chose this place as a safe haven is indeed cut off from the rest of humanity. It would be the clever scout of the world who could ever learn of Isaac's rebels taking refuge in such a remote spot.'

'Ours is not to reason why,' Will replied dourly. 'Just to carry out our murder mission and collect our five pieces of silver in return for the lives we took. In aid of what exactly, who can say? Just to obey the king's orders.'

Gabriel shook his head. 'The more I reflect on it, the more it puzzles me why such a task would be allocated to us. The commander's explanation does not quite ring true.'

'All I know is that I don't like it one bit,' Will said.

'No. Nor do I.'

The afternoon had waned and evening was beginning to fall as the hand signals of their guide indicated that their long ride was nearly over. A steep path led along a narrow ridge rising up to the plateau, where just the very top of the fortress tower could be made out above the broad rocky ledge on which it was perched. The companions had decided at the outset that they should wait for the cover of darkness before making their final approach to the ruins, to have the best chance of catching the enemy unawares.

Coming to a cluster of large tumbled rocks, the remnants of a long-ago avalanche that screened them from view of the top, the six riders and their guide dismounted and tethered their horses to bide their time waiting for nightfall. The animals were thirsty after the long day's ride in the heat, and drank eagerly from the waterskins they had carried with them. The men unpacked their food provisions – strips of dried *agrino* meat and some local flatbreads and cheese – and sat among the rocks eating and saying little, each of them alone with his own thoughts. The guide appeared strangely nervous, unable to sit still and continually glancing up in the direction of the plateau even though there was no possibility of their being seen from above.

'What's wrong with him?' Roderick Short said irritably. 'Not like anyone's asking him to risk his bloody neck, are they?'

'If he wants to leave us, let him go,' Will answered. 'He has served his purpose. We'll be able to retrace our way back easily enough.' He gestured to the guide. 'Go. Go.' The man had been paid in advance for his services, and on being released he hurriedly clambered onto his nag and set off at a pace back down the track.

As evening came, so came with it ominous thunder clouds that rolled across the sky on the rising wind to blot out the moon and stars. The atmosphere grew sultry, heralding what promised to be a severe storm. 'I think your prayer for rain is soon to be answered,' Will told Gabriel. 'Let's move on before the weather breaks. Leave the horses. We continue on foot from here.'

They gathered up their things, checked weapons and tightened sword belts, then set off in single file up the track with Will leading, Gabriel and Samson behind him, Tobias Smith, old Joe Cook and finally Roderick Short bringing up the rear. The clouds were steadily thickening above, the darkness deepening and the air more and more heavily charged with the threat of the coming storm. A long growling rumble of thunder sounded in the west, moving towards them with the wind. They padded forward with increasing stealth as they came nearer the top of the track, careful to make no sound. Now at last, the ruins became visible as they stepped up onto the plateau.

'I see the glow of a fire,' Will whispered, pointing. And sure enough, it seemed as though their information had been accurate. Someone was sheltering inside the old fortress, or what little remained of it. The faint yellow-orange light flickering from somewhere deep within showed that only the part-crumbled tower and a few sections of wall were still standing, most of the roof having collapsed long ago. As he watched, looking for signs of movement inside the building, Will felt the first fat, warm raindrop spatter against his brow.

He turned to the others. Samson's shaggy great hulk seemed even more massive and forbidding outlined against the darkness, like some wild creature or a demon conjured from the depths of the night. Roderick Short was breathing heavily with anticipation. Gabriel stood as still as a statue, eyes gleaming, poised and ready as a wolf on the hunt.

Will's heart was beating fast. 'Spread yourselves out,' he whispered. 'We'll surround the walls. At my signal, we close in and surprise them from all sides at once.'

But it was they who were about to get the surprise.

No sooner had Will spoken, than out from behind the dark ruins stepped a figure carrying a burning torch. By the light of the flame they could see he was wearing a long cloak, its hood pulled up and obscuring his face in shadow. Before Will or any of his companions could react the figure was followed by another, then several more, until a procession of twelve figures in all had emerged into view. They formed a line with the first man at its centre, shoulder to shoulder, their torches raised high so that their light merged into one and glowed like a halo around them. Holding their line they came forward ten paces and stopped, with the fortress ruins behind them. The man at the centre approached three more paces.

The hooded men remained silent, while Will and his friends were too taken aback to speak. If these were renegade Griffons, Will thought, they had the strangest way of defending their stronghold by coming out into the open like this. From behind the ruins he heard the whinny of a horse tethered there out of sight in the darkness. The torch flames flickered in the mountain wind. Another heavy raindrop splashed Will's face and ran down his cheek like a tear. The deluge was about to begin at any moment.

Then the man who had stepped out in front of the line reached up to tug at the drawstring of his cloak and let it fall away. The torchlight glimmered off his chain mail hauberk. His features were lit in the flickering yellow-orange torchlight and the motif on his white surcoat stood out clear and sharp. It was the shape of a black eagle with a hooked beak and three long tail feathers pointing down like spikes.

And in that moment the realisation came flooding into Will's mind that he had let himself and his friends be led straight into a trap. His heart gave a jolt and his whole body seemed to tingle. Not with dread, not even with apprehension. It was a feeling he knew well, the thrill of a long, arduous hunt finally come to its conclusion.

'Remember me, do you?' the figure called out over the sound of the wind.

'Yours is not a face I would forget in a hurry, Ranulf of Gilsland,' Will called back. 'Nor yours, John Scrope, Henry Godard and Rodney Hake. Are you too ashamed to show them?'

Without a word, all eleven men in the line behind their master threw off their cloaks too. Just as Will had known, Beatrice's three remaining killers were among them. They were smiling, if the hideous contorted leer on John Scrope's scarred face could be called a smile. Their other eight companions were clad in the same livery of their Baron of Gilsland.

Will nodded grimly to himself as full understanding sank in. It was clear now why his commander had offered to spare only a half dozen horses for this mission. That had been part of the arrangement, so that his enemies could be assured of outnumbering their opponents two to one. And when he and his friends never returned, their comrades back at camp would assume they had fallen prey to the renegade Griffons. It had been a neat plan.

'So tell me, my lord,' he called out. 'What reward did you offer to Howard of Gloucester to betray us?'

Sir Ranulf laughed. 'Oh, he came cheap enough. I would have paid him far more, for the pleasure of meeting you again.'

Will bowed his head. 'I'm honoured that you should value it so highly. I too have been looking forward to this moment.'

'Would anybody tell me what the fuck is going on?' Roderick Short muttered. Gabriel signalled to him to hush.

'We have both had to wait a long time,' said Sir Ranulf. 'But here we are at last. You have been a thorn in my shoe long enough, William the Bowman. First you injure one of my men-at-arms and slay another. Then you not only cheat me out of my satisfaction but you somehow contrive to go bleating to the king, causing me to have to humiliate myself to beg and plead for his charity. *Me*, the son of a noble lord, the future Baron of Gilsland, denounced and made to look like a fool by a miserable common piece of filth! And all over some silly bitch of a peasant girl?' His voice had risen to a furious shout.

'She was all I ever loved or will love again,' Will said. 'You knew that your men were raiding homes and killing innocent people. And you let them take her from me.'

'Bah. If he serve me well, of what consequence is it to me what a man does for his amusement? I do not give a damn for your woman, and may she rot in Hell. As for you, peasant, you are going to pay the price for all the trouble you have caused me.'

'I have not quite finished yet,' Will said. 'God help me, you'll never inherit your father's title, because neither you nor your three men will leave this place alive. As for the rest, I have no grievance against them. They can walk away now and go in peace.'

'We cannot do that,' said one of the other eight.

In that instant the first lightning flash split the dark sky above them, arcing in multiple forks over the mountainside and followed almost instantly by a reverberating crash of thunder that seemed to shake the ground under them. Now the heavens opened and the sudden violent deluge came down at last, rain filling the air thick enough to make a man gasp for breath, spattering the rocks, bouncing off the ground. The warm rivulets trickled through Will's hair and poured from his nose and chin. Blinking the water from his eyes he replied, 'So be it. Then you will have to die with the rest.'

'We will soon see who does the dying here tonight.' Sir Ranulf gripped the hilt of his sword and ripped it from its scabbard, the blade slashing at the rain. Simultaneously the other eleven black eagles drew their weapons in a chorus of ringing steel.

'Well, we came here looking for a fight,' said Roderick Short, yanking out his cleaver. 'Looks like we're getting one.'

Beside him, Gabriel silently unsheathed his sword. Tobias Smith and old Joe Cook already had theirs at the ready, and Samson his precious axe.

Twelve professional knights and men-at-arms against half as many simple pilgrim warriors. Will and his friends had gained more than their share of combat experience in the battles they had come through in the last few months. But with the odds so stacked against them, this could be their last. Turning to his friends Will told them earnestly, 'This is my fight. I would not have you die for me.'

Gabriel smiled. 'I should be happy to die as your friend, Will Bowman. God be with us.'

'And to the Devil with them bastards,' yelled Roderick Short.

At their lord's command the black eagle soldiers tossed their burning torches in a heap on the ground. The combined flames leaped high, blazing wood impregnated with oils defying the pouring rain. By the time the fire had burnt out, blood would have been spilled and this would be over.

Will turned back towards his enemies. He took a deep breath. He had long been preparing for this moment and he felt quite calm.

This was no time for archery. He laid down his bow and quiver and drew his sword. Raised its cruciform hilt to his brow and uttered a silent prayer.

Then for the last time, come what may, he stepped towards the black eagles of Gilsland.

Chapter 36

William went striding through the flames and made straight for Beatrice's killers. It was of no concern which one of the three he killed first. They all must die.

But in order to reach them he must get past their lord Sir Ranulf, standing three paces in front. Thinking that Will was coming for him the baron's son lashed out with his sword, a horizontal cut that might have separated a man's head from his shoulders if it had not been delivered so impetuously and given Will ample time to duck out of its way. The long blade swished over him, glittering in the firelight. As its momentum carried it on by, Will straightened and drove the pommel of his own sword hard into Sir Ranulf's face, sending him staggering back with a howl of pain.

First blood had been spilled. Much more was to follow. As their lord and master stumbled away, John Scrope and his friends instantly closed in on Will, three blades coming for him at once. He met John Scrope's sword, arrested its downward chopping swing with a powerful upward block, then lunged quickly to the right to parry the second blade that came swinging his way, that of Henry Godard. No quarter was to be given and none was expected. These were the heaviest and most uncompromising of blows intended to sever limbs, hack through leather and armour, flesh and bone and send men straight to Hell. Steel contacted steel with such a resonant impact that Godard's bound wire sword hilt was torn from his grip and the weapon spun away and went clattering to the ground. Will saw it fall, swiped it aside with a deft kick, and it slid hilt-first over the stony ground into the heap of flaming torches.

Now Rodney Hake's sword was flashing through the rain-filled air towards Will, but it never reached its target. Suddenly there was Gabriel at Will's side to step in and skilfully parry the strike, following up with a furious counterattack that drove Hake into retreat. In the space of a few heartbeats the night had dissolved into a wild confusion of the shouts of men and the ringing clash of metal against metal. Will was too occupied with John Scrope and the others to pay much attention to the tumult happening behind him as the rest of his friends came charging in to close with the black eagles.

Roaring like a mad bull, eyes popping and flecks of foam appearing at the corners of his mouth Samson brought his axe down with devastating force on the head of one of them, cleaving through the crown of his helmet and the skull inside. The man was dead on his feet before he had crumpled to the ground; by then the axe blade was humming through the air on the end of its short oaken shaft to chop deep into the chest of the next soldier too slow to leap out of its path. Meanwhile old Joe Cook, Tobias Smith and Roderick Short were battling with demonic fury, striking left and right as the enemy flocked around them.

To the other side of the leaping flames from where Will faced John Scrope, Gabriel was still locked strike for strike in his deadly combat with Rodney Hake. Meanwhile the third of the killers Henry Godard fell on his knees and scrambled frantically towards the fire to retrieve the sword that had been knocked from his hand. He found the hilt and gripped it tight, then let out a tortured wail as the red-hot bound wire handle seared the flesh of his right palm and fingers. Will stepped over to strike him dead where he knelt, but he was intercepted by John Scrope.

Faster than Will could dodge its incoming attack, Scrope's blade caught him across the chest. The power of the blow knocked him off balance and he fell with a grunt of pain – but the wedge-riveted suit of mail that King Richard had given him could resist the edge of all but the sharpest blade and it served its blessed purpose now, saving him from a mortal wound. Seeing his enemy down, Scrope moved rapidly in to strike him again and finish him before he could get up. At the very last instant Will managed to roll out of the way of the blow, and the blade struck sparks against the rocks. Will sprang to his feet and circled away.

'You were lucky the first time,' John Scrope snarled at him. 'This time you die.'

'Not alone,' Will said.

With his burnt right hand tucked underneath his other arm Henry Godard rushed over to snatch up the fallen sword of the soldier whose skull Samson had crushed. He came stumbling back, weapon raised left-handed, to join Scrope's attack on their enemy. As the pair closed in on him together Will retreated, ducked, parried, struck and retreated again, barely able to keep up with the speed of two flashing blades coming at him at once. But the pain of his injury had slightly dulled Godard's reflexes and he was less effective fighting left-handed; as he swung wide, he momentarily exposed his torso, leaving open a line of attack for Will who instantly lunged forward, gripping the hilt of his sword with both hands, and drove it into his chest with such force that the tip of the blade sheared through the mail links and deep inside him.

Henry Godard looked down in open-mouthed astonishment at the double-edged steel buried in his body. His arms hung limply at his sides and the sword dropped from his left hand. For a moment no longer than a heartbeat but which seemed to Will much more drawn out, Godard stood there impaled on Will's blade, the rain dripping from his hair and beard. Then Will tore out the bloody steel, and Beatrice's killer slumped dead to the ground.

At almost the same instant there was a cry from the far side of the burning torchlight. Will glanced through the rain, flames and smoke to catch a glimpse of Rodney Hake's sword hand flying through the air. A hand no longer attached to his right arm, because it had been sliced clean off by a stroke of Gabriel's curved blade. Its fingers were still wrapped around the hilt of the weapon as it sailed away into the darkness. Without an instant's hesitation Gabriel mercilessly finished him with a stab that pierced through one side of his neck and out of the other. Rodney Hake collapsed face-down at Gabriel's feet, the rain pounding his back and washing the blood into the ground.

It was a moment Will would never forget, but he had little time to register it at present before John Scrope was on him again, attacking with redoubled fury as he saw his black eagle comrades fall. Will successfully blocked Scrope's next raging blow but the second glanced off his blade at such an angle and with enough momentum for its tip to bite through the right sleeve of his hauberk and slice the flesh underneath from elbow to wrist. Will felt the pain lance through his arm and he staggered, almost dropping his sword. Gabriel had seen him wounded and was rushing across to help, but his way was blocked by two more of the soldiers and he again had his hands full as they assailed him at once.

Was the tide of the fight suddenly turning in the black eagles' favour? Sir Ranulf had recovered from Will's pommel strike, and with blood leaking from his split lip he hovered uncertainly in the shadows away from the burning torches. Their fire was beginning to diminish though the battle went on raging violently all around. Yells of anger, grunts of pain and effort; a crunch as Samson's axe split open another helmeted head. Through the chaos Will saw old Joe Cook fall, and Roderick Short come leaping in hacking and chopping furiously at the soldier who had felled him. Samson was beset by three at once, jabbing at him with swords and daggers. The big man seemed about to be overwhelmed – but then Tobias Smith was there at his side, driving them back. Another black eagle went sprawling to the wet ground, pierced through the middle.

John Scrope smiled at the blood of Will's wound. Spying Henry Godard's fallen sword on the ground near his feet, he stooped and snatched it up. Now Will was battling for his life as his enemy surged in to finish him off, one strike after another windmilling towards him, seeming to come from all angles. By the flicker of the dying fire, Scrope's scarred face was a mask of hate, teeth bared, more animal than human. Will blocked one powerful ringing strike, then the next. A smashing impact against the crossguard of his sword, and his hand was numbed by the blow and lost its grip on the hilt. The weapon dropped to the ground.

'You're mine now, Bowman!' Armed with two swords where his opponent had none, Scrope crossed his blades one over the other and pressed forward intent on scissoring off his head. Will retreated, stumbled, fell backwards. His groping hand found a heavy, jagged rock on the ground beside him and he flung it with all his might at Scrope's face, knocking off his helmet. Scrope dropped a sword and clapped his hand to his left eye. Blood poured from between his fingers. 'Oh God! I'm blinded!'

The delay gave Will just enough time to scramble back up to his feet. Screaming in pure loathing, his one eye staring wide, John Scrope stabbed at Will with his remaining weapon. Will caught his wrist and yanked the man hard towards him while simultaneously dodging to one side and letting the blade come darting past. While Scrope was off balance he drove a knee upward and caught him hard under the chin, snapping his jaw shut and nearly causing him to bite off his tongue. Scrope dropped to his knees but was just as quickly back on his feet, hurt but by no means defeated. He swung his sword viciously, and this time the blade cut a long slit in Will's breeches and gashed his thigh deep. Will barely felt the pain. He closed with his enemy, reached out and grasped his blade near the hilt, where the edges were blunter. They struggled back and forth for a few instants, wrestling for control of the weapon. Scrope tried to lever Will's fingers off the blade, and then to bite them off with his teeth. Will kicked him again, felt Scrope's knee cave in the wrong way and heard the crunch of breaking bone. With a sharp cry Scrope let go of the sword, but his other hand managed to gain a grip on the collar of Will's jerkin, and as he fell back he pulled Will on top of him.

The fight became savage, the death struggle of two wild beasts. Will smashed his forehead into Scrope's face and felt the man's broken teeth gouge the flesh of his brow. Scrope gasped and his grip on Will's collar weakened: only for an instant, but that instant was long enough. Will staggered upright, still clutching the sword by the thick of its blade. Grasping it with both hands he drove the point downwards with all the strength he could muster. The razor-sharp tip sheared through Scrope's hauberk, just a few inches deep before the mail rings tightened around the blade and stopped it from penetrating any further.

Scrope was howling, blood streaming from his open mouth, his shattered teeth gnashing like a rabid dog's. Will leaned on the sword hilt, using all his weight to drive it in deeper. Inch by inch it sank downwards through Scrope's pierced breastbone and into his heart. Then deeper still, all the way through his body until it was buried more than halfway to the hilt and the point had nailed him fast to the ground. Blood bubbled in torrents from the terrible wound. Scrope's undamaged eye fluttered open and shut a few times. He tried to grasp at Will's hands and face. His tongue protruded from his bloody mouth. Then he let out a ghastly rattling wheeze, his head rolled back, and the last of Beatrice's killers was no more.

Will was still leaning on the sword when he felt a hand on his shoulder and looked up, like a man awakening from a dream, to see Gabriel's face. At the same moment he realised that the rain had stopped and the wind had blown away the thunderclouds to reveal the bright moon and stars.

'He's dead, William,' Gabriel said. 'They are all dead.'

All but one.

'Where is Sir Ranulf?' Will asked.

They looked around. 'There!' Gabriel pointed. In the moonlight they could see the running figure making its way back towards the fortress. One of the horses let out a whinny as the fleeing baron's son grasped it by the bridle and untethered its reins. A cocked and loaded crossbow hung from the saddle; Sir Ranulf wrenched the weapon free and discharged it at his enemies, the bolt humming past Will and striking Tobias Smith behind him. Sir Ranulf leaped into the saddle and spurred the neighing horse away at a mad gallop across the plateau.

Will and the others ran to Tobias, but the bolt was embedded up to its fletchings in his chest and he had only a few breaths left in him. Will had feared the worst for old Joe Cook, too, but now he saw to his relief that he was only injured and propped against a rock. The others were mostly unhurt, except for a few cuts and abrasions. Samson's forehead was gashed open and Roderick Short had blood on his neck, but they cared only for their fallen friend Tobias and gathered around him as he breathed his last.

Sir Ranulf of Gilsland was getting away.

'Shoot him, William!' Gabriel urged.

Will stepped over to where he had left his bow and quiver. By now the clouds had rolled fully away, and in the aftermath of the storm the entire plateau was bathed in the diaphanous light of the heavens. The fleeing rider was clearly visible, though only a small dark shape in the distance. There must be some other path that led down the mountain, along which he and his men had climbed up to the plateau. In only a few more moments he would be gone. Will's wounded arm was on fire. Ignoring the pain he selected an arrow from his quiver, nocked it to the string, marked his target and drew.

But no, it could not be done. He lowered the bow and let the tension off the string.

'What are you doing?' Gabriel burst out.

'I will not shoot a fleeing man with his back to me,' Will replied.

'We can't let the bastard escape, Will!' Roderick Short called out from where he knelt by Tobias. His voice was full of grief and desperation.

What did a man like Sir Ranulf, the pampered son of a noble, himself destined to become the rich and powerful Baron of Gilsland, care about the loss of a few men-at-arms? Common men could be replaced, unlike a lord. All that truly mattered to him was his own survival, and he must have been filled with glee at this moment. Perhaps that was why, exulting in his triumph at having got away, he wheeled his horse around at the far side of the plateau to hurl a last expression of defiance at his enemies. Rearing his horse up onto its hind legs he raised his arm and made an obscene gesture. They could hear his laughter and shouts of abuse on the wind.

That was the last mistake Sir Ranulf would ever make. Because now he was no longer fleeing with his back to Will Bowman.

Remember the hare, Will thought. He had thought he was safe, too.

He raised the bow again. Drew the string back past his cheek, calculated the distance, adjusted for height, and released his shot with a juddering twang. The arrow whooshed up into the air, a silvery dart flashing through the moonlight almost too quick for the eye to follow. He followed the line of its steep upward arc, watched the curving trajectory reach its zenith and begin to drop. Range was good. He had judged the wind just right. He held his breath. Two heartbeats. Three.

On Will's count of four, the faraway figure suddenly seemed to stiffen. His arm fell. The horse wheeled and pranced as though it sensed something had happened to its rider – and its instinct was right.

Slowly, Sir Ranulf of Gilsland leaned further sideways in the saddle. Then like a sack of grain he fell from the back of the horse and lay still, the shaft of the arrow sticking straight up in the moonlight.

Epilogue
June 6th, 1191

The battle fleet was gathered at different points along the eastern and southern shores of Cyprus, ready at long last to embark for Outremer, the city of Acre and King Richard's holy war. Among the many thousands of pilgrim soldiers who had been stationed all over the island and now made their way towards the coast for the final leg of their journey were the five companions, originally six, travelling south on horseback from the mountains.

They had buried their friend Tobias Smith the day before, in a remote spot among the hills where his grave would lie undisturbed, marked by a simple headstone with his initials inscribed on it. From there they rode through forests and across the plains to a place called Stavrovouni, where a monastery stood high upon a hill overlooking the distant coast. The good monks provided them with food and water for themselves and their weary horses, as well as herbal salves and poultices to treat their wounds. It had been late in the afternoon by then, and the companions accepted kindly old

Abbot Vasilios's offer of shelter for the night before they joined their ship in the morning.

In the last golden light before sunset, Will and Gabriel left their friends resting in the coolness of the monastery and walked out across the hillside. From the very top the spectacular view extended beyond the island's southern shores and right over the shimmering blue sea to the far-off eastern Mediterranean coast and the forested mountains of Lebanon and Syria on the extreme horizon.

'There lies the Holy Land,' Gabriel said, pointing. 'And the sacred Kingdom of Jerusalem that it is our Christian mission to protect and deliver from the hands of the Saracen.' He turned to Will and smiled. 'But it is over for you now, is it not? Your path need not lead you to the same destination as ours. Perhaps not back to England; but there are many places in this world not ravaged by war and suffering, where a free man can settle and find peace. Though it would grieve me bitterly to say farewell, maybe the time has come for us to part ways.'

Will gazed eastwards across the sea and listened to his friend's words. 'You're right,' he replied after a silence. 'What I set out to do is done, and my future is my own to decide. I could choose to go anywhere from here, and live out my days in some quiet spot, serving no duty except to myself. But would I ever find peace, in my heart?'

'I believe you would, sooner or later. Does not eternal peace await every one of us in the end, God willing?'

'I won't know until my day of judgement what fate He has in store for me,' Will said firmly. 'But until that day comes, I do know what I must do.'

'Indeed?'

Will nodded. 'Not for God, nor for the king, nor for loyalty to my country or creed. But for those who have become my bonded comrades, the nearest thing I have left to blood kin, to family. How could I abandon them, after all we have been through together?'

'And so many more adventures to come, no doubt,' Gabriel replied with a broad grin he couldn't prevent from spreading all over his face. 'I am very happy to hear you say so. Then it seems we need not say our goodbyes just yet, William Bowman. You will sail with the rest of us to Outremer? Share in our hardships and joys, in victory or defeat or whatever fortunes may come our way, standing together as brothers in arms?'

'What would you do without me?' Will asked. A twinkle appeared in Gabriel's eyes and he reached out to place his hand on his friend's shoulder.

And so it was decided. The pilgrim's quest for revenge was at an end. But his real journey had only just begun.

Historical Note

Flash back to sometime in the mid-to-late 1980s, and a much younger version of the author is in the rooms of The Eminent Professor, suffering through the dreaded weekly one-to-one tutorial. I am wearing my commoner's gown and feeling distinctly nervous, while The Eminent Professor sits perched, oddly birdlike, behind his cluttered desk, framed in the dusty light from the ivy-clad gothic arch of the window through which can be seen the lawns and trees of the college meadows, the river beyond. It is springtime, the sun is shining bright and there are many places I'd rather be than sitting here in this austere room, dissecting some thrown-together essay I'd written about a French medieval author whose name is lost to me now.

But then The Eminent Professor says something I will never forget. He says, 'Remember this, Scott. We can never fully understand the medieval mind.'

While this statement makes a deep impression on me at the time, decades of further study and reading are to pass before I fully grasp its truth. These people were in so many ways utterly different from us: their philosophical outlook, their political and religious values, their social mores, their lifestyles and customs, are often so far removed from our own today that it can be hard to place ourselves in their shoes. Among other things their code of warfare seems exceptionally harsh and brutal to us now, and it's challenging to imagine that such ways were entirely the norm. And yes, they were deeply devout too (though perhaps it doesn't hurt to remind ourselves that it was from these beliefs that we inherited much of the moral framework of today's secular age). As best as I can understand it myself, I've tried to paint as authentic a picture as possible of the world in which Will Bowman lived.

But how much have we really changed? Our medieval ancestors were human beings just like us, with all the same frailties and contradictions, quirks and faults, hopes and dreams. They loved like us, experienced pain and anguish like us, felt every bit of the same joys and woes as us. In that respect, we are still the same people they were.

One thing that *has* changed a great deal is language, and the terminology by which we describe the events of the past. It might seem odd that a novel set against the events of what we nowadays call 'the Third Crusade' makes no mention of the words 'crusade' or 'crusader'. In fact, these labels only came into use centuries afterwards, and so to use them here would have been anachronistic. Those who took part in the quasi-religious, quasi-military expeditions to reclaim the Holy Land for Christendom were engaged in what they regarded as a form of pilgrimage – albeit an armed one – and that's what they called themselves: pilgrims. It has been argued, I think with some justification, that the ubiquitous terms 'crusade' and 'crusader', with their connotations of an aggressively expansionist colonising enterprise, tend to project a potentially misleading view of this episode of history especially when taken in a modern context. True, terrible atrocities were committed; but they were committed by all sides, and not just in the wars of conquest for the Holy Land. Such was the nature of those often tough and brutal times.

But let's not get ahead of ourselves, as our story has yet to reach its destination. I hope you enjoyed *The Pilgrim's Revenge* and will stick around to join Will Bowman and company as they land on the shores of Outremer, ready for their next adventure in *The Knight's Pledge*.

Scott Mariani

Acknowledgments

It's that old trope again about no man being an island and nobody ever writing a book alone, etc. We've all heard it before, but it's true. And never more true than when an author is embarking on a whole new series quite unlike anything he's done previously, and finds himself blessed with the excellent sort of editorial and production team that has made the writing of *The Pilgrim's Revenge* such a smooth and pleasurable ride. Many special thanks are due to Phoebe Morgan and Jake Carr at Hodder & Stoughton, along with the many hidden figures I'm unable to name personally but who have all played their part in bringing this book into your hands. Likewise to Oliver Malcolm, whose support has meant a lot to me over the years. Last but not least, I'm much indebted to the historian Matthew Lewis, medieval specialist, host of the brilliant Gone Medieval podcast and a prolific author in his own right, who was a great help in keeping me straight on the historical facts of the story. Any errors, omissions or occasional liberties are, needless to say, mine and mine alone.